THE RISE AND FALL OF THE BARNES BROTHERS

Parts 1-3

NIKKI BROWN

Copyright © 2020 by Nikki Brown

All rights reserved.

No part of this book may be reproduced in any form or by any electronic or mechanical means, including information storage and retrieval systems, without written permission from the author, except for the use of brief quotations in a book review.

Chapter One
KAYSON

"How many times you gone count that shit, Kayson?" my brother Omari said with a blunt hanging from the corner of his mouth.

"As many times as it takes to make sure this shit right, nigga." I glared at him.

"If yo' paranoid ass would just use the money counter you wouldn't have to go through this shit."

"I don't trust that shit and you know it."

He shook his head and focused his attention on the last of his blunt. I was sitting in the trap on Beaties Ford that me and my brothers ran. We were slowly but surely making a name for ourselves in the drug game. We started out as corner boys in our Uncle Ray's organization and now we ran the house on Beaties Ford. This shit was just the beginning and we knew it. Patience was everything, so we made the best of everything.

It was me and my brothers Jaako, Omari, and that ignorant ass Denari that made up our little crew. We didn't do too many friends because the one thing that Uncle Ray taught us was that friends can turn to enemies real quick, especially if money was involved. Uncle Ray made sure that we worked for everything we had because he didn't want people to think that we were just handed shit because they wouldn't respect us. Me, I didn't give a shit about what people thought but I understood where he was coming from.

Even though we didn't come out of the same pussy, blood couldn't make us any closer. I loved my brothers and would give my life for them. With that being said, me and Denari didn't get along for shit. I just didn't have patience for his nonsense. The rest of them niggas liked to baby his ass because of what he witnessed as a kid, but hell we all went through some shit, which is why we ended up with Ma, so that didn't work for me. I treated him just like I treated the rest of them muthafuckas.

Hell, my ass was born a fucking crack baby, my mother was on that shit bad and the fact that she was pregnant with me didn't change shit about how she lived her life. When I was born, they tested my blood and found so much shit they took me right away and I was grateful because I was placed in the hands of a fucking angel.

Ann Barnes worked at the neonatal unit at the Children's Levine Hospital inside of CMC Main, where I was housed for the first four months of my life. My egg donor was 33 weeks when she went into labor with me. I was only three pounds when I came into this world. Ann cared for me from the moment I took my first breath and when she found out that I was a ward of the state she fought for me. She used to tell me all the time that me being her son was fate.

Mama wasn't able to have kids on her own. She was attacked when she was a teenager and the man did some horrible shit to her. She was infertile after that. So, she found happiness in helping others which is why she became a nurse and adopted four bad ass boys. We would forever be grateful for her love.

"Nigga, yo' ass don't trust shit." Jaako said laughing.

"Do you blame me?"

He didn't say anything because we had been through some shit in our day. All of us were fucked up in some form or fashion, but we were making it and that's all that mattered.

I flung my dreads out of my face and looked in Jaako's direction. "Where in the hell is yo' brother?" I asked referring to Denari. His ass was never anywhere to be found when it was time to handle business, but let someone say party or club and his ass was on the way.

"Nigga, that's yo' brother." Jaako said snatching the blunt out of Omari's hand.

"Y'all chill; you know how that nigga do so I don't even know why y'all keep talking about it."

Omari was frustrated with some of the shit that Denari did because he and Denari had the same genetic makeup; they were blood brothers, so he in a sense felt responsible for him. He felt like Denari's fuck ups were his fuck ups, but that was far from the truth. Denari did whatever the fuck he thought that he could get away with and expected everyone to be okay with it. They accommodated him; me on the other hand would get in his muthafucking ass. Denari was the youngest out of all of us and he played that part so well, but we all had to grow up at some point.

"Yeah, O, but that shit is not a fucking excuse, we gotta get this shit straight so we can show Unc that we good."

"I know man, but—"

"No buts O, you need to talk to his ass before I do." I warned and he nodded his head. He knew I gave no shits when it came to the business. It was a time for work and a time for play, and right now we needed to work our asses off, so all this shit could be ours.

"Fuck," Jaako yelled out and looked at his watch.

"Fuck wrong with you?" I asked.

"I was supposed to meet Krista for lunch and I fucking forgot. I'm never gonna hear the end of this shit." He shook his head.

"She bout to beat yo' ass nigga." Omari laughed.

"Fuck you, O."

"You betta be saving all yo' fucking energy for Krista." Omari laughed and I laughed with him. "You know what happened last time you forgot to meet her for lunch." Omari was referencing the time that she showed up on the corner showing her ass thinking that Jaako was with some bitch, when he really was out making money for them.

"Man, shut the fuck up, I don't have time for this shit." he said already frustrated. "I gotta roll man."

"Aight, hell I'm the only person around here doing shit anyway." I said and knocked Omari's feet off the table. "Hell, I'm bout done anyway, then I'm headed to go and help Jenacia move her shit out of that bitch nigga's house."

They both looked at me like I was crazy. Jenacia and I were best friends, we tried the dating thing before and the shit backfired like a muthafucka. She was ready for something that I wasn't but instead of telling her that, I hurt her. She didn't talk to me for years and I hated that shit. Deep down I knew I loved Jenacia, I would do anything for her and eventually I planned on making her Mrs. Barnes. I just hoped that she would wait around on a nigga.

"You may as well marry that girl." Jaako said shaking his head.

"I will but you know what happened last time." He smirked because it was his got damn fault she caught me anyway. "So, when I get my shit together you already know what it is."

"If she ain't skipped off in the sun with another muthafucka." Omari chuckled.

"And we all know what would happen if she did." I tilted my head.

When Jenacia finally started talking to my ass again, I

explained to her that I wasn't ready to settle down and I was just trying to get my shit together. She told me that she understood and that until I did we would just remain friends, friends that didn't fuck. I was cool with that because I understood that sex complicated things. I just made her promise that when the time was right that no matter who we were with that it would be us.

"Man, let me go Krista's ass is blowing my shit up." Jaako shook his head and headed out the house. I looked on the monitor to make sure that crazy bitch wasn't outside ready to show her ass. She was known to act a fool so I needed to make sure that wasn't the case. We didn't need the attention.

"Hello." Omari answered his phone and listened to the other person on the other line. He looked at me and I could already tell that it was some bullshit and I could bet my life it had to do with Denari's ignorant ass. "What the fuck, D?" Omari listened intently trying his best not to look me in the eyes. I wasn't even about to get upset, he could deal with that shit on his own. "Aight man, I'm on my way got damn."

He hung up the phone and started collecting his shit to leave. I didn't even bother to ask what the fuck was up, because I was sure that it was something dumb as hell. He walked to the door and turned around. I held up my hand and shook my head because I didn't want to know, he nodded his head and headed out the door to fix whatever the fuck Denari had done.

"I don't have time for the shit Roger." I could hear Jenacia yell as I pulled up in my truck so I could help her move her shit. "I just wanna get my shit and go. You didn't give two shits about me when you were lying with the city whore."

I told her ass not to fucking move in with this clown, "but he's good to me," was her favorite line, not once did she say she loved him and I was happy about that. She had just found out that he had twin girls on the way by the hoe of the Ford, better known as Beaties Ford Road. Now here she was moving her shit out of his place.

"You just trying to be laid up with that nigga that's all that is, this is just an excuse to be with his ass. You never loved me, you saving yo' self for a nigga who don't give two shits about you," he pointed to my decked-out Silverado and I jumped out of it and ran right up on that nigga.

"I've stayed out of y'all shit even though I knew you wasn't nothing but a bitch from the beginning." My chest heaved up and down. I wanted to rock his shit so bad I could fucking taste it, but I didn't need the fucking attention. "I ain't got shit to do with what you got going on so don't bring me in it. You fucked up nigga and that's on you. What I got with Jenacia is none of your fucking concern. If I ever hear about you even attempting to mention my name again you gone wish ya mama would've swallowed your ass. Now Jen go get your shit and let's go before I bury this bitch."

I stood right in front of his bitch ass while Jenacia got all her shit and filled up her car and started putting shit in my truck. And just like I thought he didn't address her again. He just stood there chewing on his bottom lip like that shit meant anything to me. He knew like I knew that he wasn't gone do shit but stand there like the fuck he was doing.

"Kayson." Jenacia grabbed my arm and attempted to pull me away, but I didn't move. "Kayson enough, I'm good let's go, my mom is waiting for me."

"You're not going to your moms; I got room in my crib. You can just stay there." I said more to piss him off. I didn't know how the fuck that shit was gonna work, but the offer was out there.

"Kayson, we can talk about that later, let's just go."

I looked at her and she was pleading with her eyes for me not to do anything crazy. Too bad, I was pissed off. I took a step back and hit that muthafucka with the haymaker of a lifetime. Sent his ass swirling to the ground like a fucking clown.

"Stay the fuck away from her and I mean that shit, now try me."

I walked away and got in my truck. I watched as that nigga mugged the hell out of Jenacia's car as she backed up when his eyes met mine his bitch ass turned away. He knew better.

I followed Jenacia and I realized that she was headed to her mother's house. I knew she hated her mother with a passion and I didn't blame her. The bitch was money hungry something serious. She would do anything for a buck and she used Jenacia every chance she got.

Jenacia was an up and coming photographer and she had

already made a damn good name for herself. She was trying to open her own studio, but for right now she did freelance work for different websites and the local magazine, "The Word."

When we pulled up I hopped out of my truck and headed over to where she was. I looked at her with the meanest look and she knew that I was pissed because she refused to look me directly in the eye.

"Kayson, don't, okay?"

"No, you don't." I pointed at her. "What the fuck did I tell you to do?"

"That would just complicate things with your women."

"Shut the hell up, you know well as anybody I don't bring hoes back to my house so don't even go there." I shook my head because she was thinking of another excuse as I was shutting this one down. "You hate your mom and she just wants you here so you can pay all her got damn bills. Come to the house you can have the spare room and save up your money and get your own shit if you want to."

"If I want to?"

"Yeah, you might wanna make this shit permanent, I don't know." I smirked and shrugged my shoulders.

She looked down at her shoes and then back up at me. While she was thinking about it I was admiring her beauty. Jenacia was average height about 5'5", short compared to my 6'3" frame. She drew me in with her sexy ass gray eyes and those pouty lips that she kept shining. Her real hair was beautiful and swept past her shoulders but she insisted on wearing that bundle shit. Hell, she could be bald headed and still be beautiful to me. I could see her booty poking from the back, I didn't know how her little self could carry that much ass, but I didn't mind it.

I licked my lips and had to focus my attention somewhere else because my other head was making some decisions that my big head may not be able to deal with. She smacked her lips and I looked her way and she was staring at my semi erect dick.

"Really Kayson? That's why this wouldn't work." She pointed at my dick.

"Shut up. You know how I feel about you and you knew I was coming, why you out here in those little ass shorts if you didn't want me to look?" she rolled her eyes. "I thought so, come on."

She rolled her eyes again and then walked off in the direction of her car. I watched as her ass fought to stay in them shorts. I licked my lips and hopped in my truck. This shit was about to be hard as hell. I needed to call one of my freaks. I was gone need some pussy, and bad.

Chapter Two
OMARI

I was headed to go and get my brother from jail. I was so tired of him fucking up; I always felt the need to make his shit right because I was the one that knew the shit he went through as a kid. They knew what happened but they weren't there, they don't know how that shit affected us. Denari dealt with his shit in different ways then I did. I just closed myself off and didn't give a fuck.

I mean fuck, our dad made us watch as he raped and killed our moms. I still see her face when I sleep. Hell, I can't get that shit out my head for nothing. Shit I remember that shit like it was yesterday.

It was the last day of school and I was so excited to be out for the summer. We had just moved to Charlotte with our mom. She left our dad because he used to beat her ass daily. Originally from Key West, Florida, trying to adapt to Carolina's ways was difficult. Things were so different but I liked it, mainly because I was away from that monster that went half on creating me.

My dad was always puffed up on coke and if mom would pay the bills before he got his stash he would flip out and beat her ass. He never hit us but he never missed a chance to tell us how much he hated us and wish we were never born. I guess when he had kids that cut into his get high money.

One day, he came home high and my mom had taken us to McDonald's to get dinner instead of cooking. She was sick and it was a Saturday, so we just grabbed happy meals. He got home and beat her so bad that we had to call the ambulance. When she got to the hospital she found out that she was pregnant and he had killed the baby. They arrested him and we fled.

When we got here the woman that helped us leave got Mama a good job with the county and got us an affordable apartment. We were happy for once, Mama was happy. Until he found us.

Me and Denari had just got off the bus and we ran to the apartment. We were so happy because Mama's car was home. She was usually at work but today she was at home. Running into the house, I ran right into the man that I hated the most. My father.

"So y'all little niggas just let ya mama put me in jail huh?" he asked and I said nothing. Denari was only six and I was nine, but I was wise beyond my years, I had to be.

"Dad, what are you doing here?"

"Oh, you don't wanna see your old man?" he smirked.

"Reggie please." Mama cried and the way he looked at her sent chills down my spine. I could feel that this wasn't going to go good.

"Denari, go to Ms. Jenna house." I told my brother but then my dad took a gun out of his waist band pointed it at us.

"Sit the fuck down," he yelled. "Both of you."

We both ran over and jumped on the couch. Mama had tears running down her face and she just kept mouthing the words I'm sorry and I love you. It was like she knew it was her end.

"Just please don't hurt my boys." She cried.

"Shut the fuck up Cheryl, you should of thought about that before you took my kids and ran all the way here." he pointed the gun at her head and Denari started to cry. "Cry baby ass, shut the hell up before you be going the same place ya mama going."

I grabbed Denari's head and buried it under my arm so that his cries would be muffled. I said a small prayer that one of our nosy neighbors would hear the commotion and call the police. My dad laid the gun down and walked over to where Mama was sitting and took her by her feet and drug her to the floor and started punching her.

She tried to fight back but the more she did, the more he hit her until after a while she just stopped. Tears were falling freely from my eyes and I didn't know what to do, what could I do. My dad started tearing all my mom's clothes off, she was still fighting and I will always admire her for that. Once he had her all the way undressed, he looked at me and my brother.

"Look here." he yelled and we looked his way. "This is what you do to a bitch that don't listen to you."

He put his hands around her throat and raped my mother right in front of us. He was laughing and grunting like he was putting on a show. He will never know what he did to us that day.

"Look at me baby, look into my eyes." My mother said through bruised lips. "It's gonna be okay. Denari baby..." Denari's attention was on what my father was doing and I hated that. I tried to turn his head but he wouldn't budge. "Take care of your brother."

"Mama." I cried as she reached up and clawed his eyes. He screamed and rolled off her cursing her like she wasn't nothing. She grabbed me and my brother off the couch and moved us to the door and opened it and pushed us out. Right as we got out the door and turned around to make sure she was behind us, he shot her in the back of the head. "MAMA!" I screamed and he looked around and took off out of the apartment. "SOMEBODY HELP MY MAMA." I screamed with all my might.

"Mommy wake up, wake up Mommy." Denari cried as we watched the blood seep from her head. That sight would forever be etched into my mind.

Someone called the police and the ambulance but there was no use because she was gone and I would never hear her call me by my whole name when I was in trouble, or hear her tell me she loves me. He took that from me and I promised my mama in that hallway that I would make sure that he paid for what he had done.

He was apprehended while trying to get to the highway, back to Florida. We were put into the system, they tried to get family to take us in from Florida but no one would respond. No one even came to claim my mother's body. The lady that helped us came down and helped bury her and she had a friend in Charlotte that helped boys like us.

The day we met Ann Barnes was a day that changed our life. She was an angel and she became our new mom. I missed Mama but I felt the love that Ann showed and I would forever be grateful.

I wiped the lone tear that had made its way down my face and pulled into the police station. I hated this fucking place, shit made me itch like I was allergic or something. I walked in and talked to the lady at the desk. She let me know that his bail was five g's.

There was no telling what the fuck Denari did but like I said I understood why he acted the way he acted because I was there. I just wished he wasn't so selfish in his actions.

"My nigga." He said walking out about an hour later. "Good looking out, bruh." He tried to dap me up but I looked at his hands and walked away. I wasn't with that shit today.

"Nigga I want my five g's back and today, muthafucka."

"Man, I got you." He said following behind me. "You tell them what was up?"

"I tried to tell Kayson but he didn't even want to hear it."

"Damn I ain't wanna hear his shit." Denari put his hands on his head. "He pissed huh?"

"Yep."

"Hell, what's new." He said and sat back in the seat. I wanted to snap on his ass but honestly, it wasn't any use, Denari was who he was. "Don't be mad."

"D man, you doing shit all wrong, we on the come up my nigga we don't need this shit."

"I know man but it wasn't my fault."

"Nigga it's never your fault, fuck you mean?"

Denari didn't take responsibility for anything that he did, shit was never his fault and he thought the world owed him something. It was time for him to grow up, I couldn't keep doing this. Although I knew what he was dealing with, I also knew there was a better way to deal with it.

"Man, for real I was riding and chilling, Jizzy called and said come scoop. We rolled over to the liquor house off Sugar Creek. I bought a pint of that white jug and we were on the way back to the block to drink and shit. Cops pulled me over and searched my shit."

"Cops just don't pull you over D tell the whole fucking story."

"Nigga said I ran a stop sign but I didn't do no shit like that," He smirked.

"With everything you just told me please explain how none of that is your fault."

He didn't say nothing and I knew he wouldn't. I just shook my head and dropped his ass off at his crib. I wasn't about to go there with him, I didn't have the fucking energy. Who knew the saying "I Am My Brother's Keeper," was so much got damn work.

Chapter Three
JAAKO

"Fuck Jaako." Krista moaned as I skillfully explored her center.

Krista was flexible as shit and right now her ass was in that human pretzel shit and I had full access to her sopping wet pussy. The way my dick was glistening brought a huge smile on my face. When I got here she was pissed the fuck off, she wanted more time from me and I understood that, but I was a young nigga on the come up. I didn't really have time for the wining and dining and I thought that Krista understood that, at least she said she did.

"Make me cum baby." She moaned and that shit was a turn on.

We argued a lot but the one thing that always worked for us was our action in the bedroom. I knew that it wasn't enough but it worked for now. My biggest fear was being alone and I hated that about myself. I've been that way since my parents died.

"Shit Krista." I was about to nut and I wanted to make sure that she got hers too so I placed my thumb on her clit and pressed as I hit her with long deep strokes. I needed to remind her that there was nothing to fight about.

"Yes, baby yes. God I love this." She screamed.

"Well paint my dick with ya love."

"Yes yes yes." Her eyes rolled in the back of her head and her pussy muscles clamped around my dick and in minutes I could see our mixed juices covering my dick.

Both of us were panting and trying to catch our breath. I loved fucking Krista and I cared a lot about her, but I can honestly say that I wasn't in love with her and she wasn't in love with me. I could tell because she kept trying to make me into this nigga that she wanted me to be. Most of the time I obliged just to keep the peace and those other times turned into horrible arguments.

Krista released her legs from behind her head and I eased myself out of her. We hadn't used condoms since the day we made shit official, she was on birth control because I wasn't ready for kids. I wanted to be married and raise a family. I didn't want a baby mama and honestly, I didn't see a future with Krista. She was just my right now girl.

"Why are you staring off like you crazy?" Krista asked with a sour look on her face.

"Thinking about some shit."

"Do you have to cuss so much?" she complained.

"Krista, that's how I talk." I let out a deep sigh.

"Yeah but you could work on that I mean it's not like I hadn't asked you to do that before."

"Well maybe I'm good with me."

She didn't say anything she just got up and went to the bathroom. I heard the shower start and normally I would go in there with her, but I didn't feel like hearing her tell me what I needed to do.

Krista wanted to be the man of the relationship. She wanted to run things and make all the decisions and for the most part I let her so I guess I could say this shit was my fault. I could have put her in her place a long time ago, but I was a laid-back ass nigga. I really didn't care but as of late shit that she was doing was starting to piss me off.

I just hated to be alone. When I was younger my mom or my dad was always around. They showered me with so much love that I didn't know what to do. I was spoiled as hell. My dad was that nigga to know around these streets, and he made sure that me and mama was good. We were something like street royalty. One night while we were sleep someone broke into my house and killed my mom and my dad, had I not went into the "safe place" my dad built in the floor of my room they probably would have killed me too.

After my parents were killed, I was sent to live with my grandma and she wanted nothing to do with me. She hated the fact that my mom chose my dad and she hated me because I was a product of that. She use to beat me for no reason, she wouldn't feed me or buy me clothes. I got really sick once and she wouldn't even take me to the doctor. I passed out at school and had to be rushed to the Children's Levine Hospital at CMC where I met my angel, Ann Barnes. The state took me away from my grandmother and I was placed with Ms. Ann. I was 12 then and the last to be placed into her home. The day I met that woman changed my life.

"Dang you could have at least joined me in the shower." Krista said with an attitude.

"Damn Krista can you do something other than complain please." I gave her a nasty look and then headed to the bathroom and locked the door. I needed a few minutes. We argued like this all the time so I should have been used to it but the shit was starting to get on my got damn nerves.

I could hear my phone ringing in the room and I could have sworn I heard Krista say hello but I knew that she wouldn't do no shit like that. We had too much respect for each other to do that. So I continued my shower and I thought I heard my phone again but I wasn't sure so I finished my shower.

I got out and I dried off. I walked into the room and my phone wasn't where I put it. I looked at Krista like she sprouted two heads because I knew she didn't touch my got damn phone. Usually I was real chill and tried not to flip too much but I was big on respect.

"Did my phone ring?" she didn't answer. "You can't fucking hear."

"Jaako, language." She continued to file her nails like she didn't hear me. I walked over and snatched the file out of her hand and threw it on the ground. "What do you think you're doing?"

"Did my fucking phone ring?" I said through gritted teeth.

"Yes!"

"I know you didn't answer it." I tilted my head because she knew better.

"Why can't I answer your phone Jaako? I've never understood that," she questioned me.

"Because you don't pay the got damn bill and I don't fuck with your shit that's why." I snatched my phone and looked to see who called and I saw that it was Yameka, our lawyer and the woman that I was going to marry one day. "What did you say to Yameka?" She didn't answer and I slammed my hand on the wall next to where she was sitting on the bed.

"Calm down Jaako, is there something I should know about Miss Yameka? You sure are getting uptight about what I said to her."

I shook my head because she just didn't get it and honestly, I was tired of trying to explain it to her. Instead of sitting here arguing with her I got dressed. I didn't want to call Yameka because there is no telling what the fuck Krista said so I was just going to pop up on her at her job.

"Where are you going? I thought we were gonna go out and chill?" she asked with a confused look on her face. I laughed sarcastically and continued to get dressed. "So, you don't hear me now?"

"Krista I need to get the fuck away from you before I say something I don't mean." I gave her a look that let her know I wasn't playing right now. She rolled her eyes and mumbled some shit under her breath; I laughed and headed out the door to go and holla at my future.

"I'm here to see Ms. Tate." I said to the receptionist who was busy staring me down to hear anything that I was saying. I was easy on the eyes and I knew it and it was times like this that I used it to my advantage.

"Do you have an appointment Mr. Barnes?" She already knew who I was because of the streets and I made sure I came to see Yameka at least twice a week, more if she was being nice which wasn't very often.

"No but I'm sure if you buzz her she will tell you that I can come back." I stared her in the eyes and licked my lips and that was all that it took. She buzzed back and just like I thought Yameka told me to come back. I winked at the receptionist and headed back.

When I entered, Yameka hit her intercom that connected her to the receptionist. "Lisa next time Mr. Barnes comes in without an appointment, don't let him sweet talk you into buzzing me." Lisa giggled and so did Yameka. "Yes, he's fine but that's his damn problem."

"Yes ma'am. It's five; do you need anything else from me?"

"Nah baby girl, she's in good hands." I answered for her.

Lisa giggled. "Okay I'll see you tomorrow."

"See you tomorrow Lisa." Yameka said with a smirk on her face.

"Yeah, see you tomorrow." I said right before Yameka hit the button.

Yameka was a lawyer and a damn good one at that. She had been defending us for a while now and I've been feeling her ever since. I even tapped it a few times but she let me know that that's all that it would ever be. That was her mouth though; I knew I was wearing her down.

She sat on the other side of the desk with her long chocolate legs crossed. Her skin glistened under the light in her office. The way her thighs were playing peek-a-boo from under that skirt had my shit on brick.

"Down boy, I got shit to do." She smiled.

"I'll be quick." I smirked.

"You don't know what quick is," she licked her lips. "And according to your little girlfriend, you should be well satisfied." It was her turn to smirk.

Just that quick, my got damn dick went limp as hell. I didn't even wanna know what the fuck was said. The look on her beautiful oval face and the sarcasm pouring from her doe shaped eyes, let me know that the conversation was nothing good.

"Well if you stop playing games with a nigga then I wouldn't even have to worry about her, now would I?"

"You're not ready for me Jaako." She purred. "I'm not her, I don't play those games. I'm 32 years old and I ain't with the shit." She looked me right in the eye. "Plus, you know my job comes first. I wouldn't have time for you."

"Hell, my job comes first and I wouldn't have time for you either, but I think we could make it work."

"Shit's good how it is. Why fix what's not broken?"

"Because shit getting real for a nigga." I pointed to my chest and I wasn't bullshitting, I was really starting to feel something for her but I knew that she wasn't trying to hear that shit. That's why I stayed with Krista.

"Well according to your girlfriend, I am to stay away from you unless it has to do with business." She uncrossed her legs and I caught a glimpse of that pussy because her ass never had panties on. "She said that no one could handle you like she could, is that true Jaako?" Yameka hiked up her skirt a little.

"What the fuck you doing?" I rubbed my hands down my face and tried to control myself because I knew I had just fucked Krista, I wasn't trying to be no nasty nigga but she was testing me.

She laughed. "Just horrible." She pulled her skirt down and stood up. "I've got a meeting with a client in an hour so you, my dear, gotta go."

She walked around the desk and escorted me to the door. When I got to the door I turned around and looked her in the eyes. My stare was so intense that she had to look away.

"You know I'm serious, right?"

"Bye Jaako."

"You can say bye Jaako all you want but your ass was made for me and that's where you're gonna be so get ready." I smirked and left out the door. I looked back to catch her looking at me with a faraway look in her eyes. I knew right then that she was thinking about what I said. Now I just needed to make sure that I made the right moves from here on out.

Chapter Four
JENACIA

I knew that I was making a huge mistake moving in with Kayson but me and mom's relationship was so strained and I knew I would be miserable there. Kayson offered me my own room instead of my mom's couch and he promised that he would give me my space and even offered to make his basement a dark room for me. I turned him down though because I didn't want him to think this was permanent. As soon as I was in a position to get my own I was gonna do just that. Never would I depend on another man, I will never end up like I am now. That shit with Roger taught me the lesson of a life time.

It was no secret that I was head over heels in love with Kayson; I had been since we dated six years ago. I just knew that he was gonna be the man for me. That was until I walked in on him digging out the next bitch. I tried to get over it but

I couldn't. I was so broken by his actions that I shunned him out of my life for years. I couldn't bear to be around him knowing that I couldn't be with him. He was man enough to admit that he wasn't ready to settle down after everything went down; he said that I was the only one to have his heart but I needed more, I wanted all of him.

Once I got to the place in my life that I could be around him again, we decided that we would just be friends until the time was right. He made me promise that I would drop who ever I was dating at the time when we were ready. I never gave him an answer to that promise but his arrogant ass took my silence as a yes. Honestly, there wasn't a man walking this earth that could replace the hold that Kayson Barnes had put on my heart.

"Aye girl." Kayson said from behind me.

"Heyyyyyy" my words trailed off when I turned around and saw the sight before me. He was standing there with his freshly twisted dreads in a manly ponytail sitting on top of his head. The water dripped down his perfectly toned chest and made its way to the towel that was positioned low enough to see that sexy ass V that led to his special place.

"Up here." He said causing me to focus on his handsome face. His light skin brought out the light brown color in his eyes and those lips, God how I missed what he could do with those things. "I mean I could give you everything you thinking about Jen, just say the word." He licked his lips and it took me back to the slip up we had last year. I shook the thoughts out of my head before I made a mistake that I would end up regretting, like the one he never knew about.

"Shut your mouth," I smiled and turned my attention back to the clothes that I was folding on the couch. "Why you walking around like that anyway? Did you forget that you had a roommate now or what?"

"Shit I put on a towel, be grateful." He smirked that sexy ass smirk and walked to the kitchen. "Why you ain't cook nothing?"

"I did." I laughed. "I ate it." He slammed the refrigerator door and walked back into the living room where I was.

"I know yo' ass didn't cook and not fix me nothing? What the fuck Jenacia?" I could tell that his greedy ass was pissed because his nose was flaring and I thought the shit was funny but he didn't.

"Check the microwave, you big baby." I rolled my eyes and he damn near ran to the kitchen to check the microwave. He pulled out the plate and turned to smile at me. He turned on the microwave and heated up his food.

"I could get used to this shit." He said as he sat down at the bar that separated the living room from the kitchen. He took a huge bite of the eggs. "Damn girl this shit good."

"What, your hoes don't feed you?"

"I don't fuck with them hoes long enough for them to be staying over to cook and shit," he looked over his shoulder. "This food good as hell." He said ignoring what I said.

"Thanks I guess." I said trying not to look in that direction and stare at his half naked body. Hearing all his moaning and grunting over there with that food had my ass a little jealous. I was about to say something but my phone rang. *Saved by the fucking bell.* "Hello?"

"Hey, how are you?"

"Julius?"

"In the flesh," he said and I smiled. "Well not technically, not yet anyways."

"Oh yeah?"

"Yeah, let's do dinner, I'm in town for a few days and I would love to see you."

"That sounds like a plan, where and what time?"

"Ruth's Chris?"

"You know that's my favorite."

"Eight sound good?"

"Sounds perfect."

"Okay see you then beautiful."

'Okay Julius, take care."

I hung up the phone and met the coldest set of eyes I think I had ever saw on Kayson. The way he was grilling me you would have thought that I was cheating on him or something. I wanted to ask what his problem was but before I could say anything he got up from the bar and threw his plate in the sink and walked to his room and slammed the door. I had to laugh at his temper tantrum, Kayson was always the kind of man that wanted to have his way and if he didn't this is what he did.

Julius is a male model that I shoot from time to time when he's in town. He would always flirt with me but hell I thought he was gay. I never took his advances serious because of who he was. Being in this industry you kinda pick up the signs and I could be wrong but I doubt it and if he did like women he dealt with men too. I just liked his company and he always paid for dinner.

I finished up my laundry and headed up to the shower. A little payback was in order so when I was done with my shower, I went to Kayson's room in nothing but my towel on and knocked on the door.

"What?"

"Kayson stop acting like a baby." He didn't say anything so I opened the door and walked in the room, he donned a pair of red boxers. "Why are you acting like that?"

"Why are you walking around like that Jen?" He completely ignored my question.

"What's good for the goose is good from the gander." I raised an eyebrow and shrugged my shoulder.

"Yeah well I'll throw ya ass on this bed and rape your ass and then what?" I laughed and he just looked at me with no signs of humor present. "Keep standing there and I'll show you better than I can tell you. Plus, I don't think your little boyfriend will like the fact that you around here getting that ass tore out the frame before y'all date."

"It's not a date, he's my client. I shoot him from time to time."

"Client my ass."

"Kayson who I do and don't see is not your concern. I mean you showed me that last night, right?" I was confused on why he was acting like this, seeing as though I met one of his hoes last night. "Didn't your little hoe pick you up from here last night? Did I say anything? It was disrespectful as fuck, but I kept that shit to myself because this is your house and we are not together. So as much as that shit bothered me, I swallowed that shit and kept it moving." I said with more attitude than I wanted to portray. I mean she did just pick him up, it just sucks that even after six years I still feel as strong about him now as I did then.

"You're right, I just didn't feel like driving my car and I had been drinking and shit but it was disrespectful as fuck and it won't happen again."

I don't know why I was making a big deal out of it but seeing that big booty bitch at the door made me feel a way. I really had to get my shit together if I was gonna be here. I had to get used to seeing him with other women. That's just how our situation was.

"You don't have to explain anything to me, I'm just a guest for the time being." I said and turned to leave.

"Don't do that." Kayson said and ran up and grabbed my arm to stop me. "I'm sorry, you're right I asked you to be here. I will respect you and your privacy, but you know how I feel about you so don't expect me not to be upset about you being with other niggas. This shit ain't new; I've always been like this when it came to you."

And he was right, he was the same way with Roger and any other boyfriend I had, but who was he to be upset. I was forced to be around countless women. When it came to him, this double standard shit was a bitch. Every now and then I get in my feelings about our situation, especially when he starts this shit.

I laughed angrily, I was trying to get this under control but comments like that took me to another place. "You don't have the right to be mad, you did this." I pointed back and forth between the two of us. "I wanted this and you fucked it up." I felt the tears coming and I didn't want to do that. I fought so hard to keep them hidden from everyone even myself but like I said I still loved that man more than I cared to admit.

"Jenacia, don't—"

"Don't please, I'm okay I just need to adjust and get my mind right. I tend to have these little melt downs about you every now and then but I'll be okay." I smiled and snatched away from his grasp.

Living here was gonna be harder than I thought. I hated my mother so much but I might have to buckle down and make my way over there. Kayson was tearing away at walls that I worked so hard to build up and I wasn't feeling that at all. I walked to my room with him still calling for me to come back. I shut and locked the door so that I could get some rest and get my head right before dinner with Julius tonight.

"So tell me, how's my favorite photographer?" Julius said as he stuffed his mouth full of steak and focused on me. I was still in my feelings about the little spat I had with Kayson earlier. I was trying to shake it and focus on Julius, but it just wasn't happening. "Where are you Jenacia?"

"I'm sorry Julius, me and a friend had a fight today and it's bothering me a little. It's not fair to you." I said and laid my fork down. "Just give me a second."

I got up and walked into the bathroom, went up to the sink and put some water on my face. I looked in the mirror, "Girl get your shit together, Kayson ain't about to stop being who he is for you. Things aren't gonna change, it's time to move on."

I stood there for a few more minutes and walked out to enjoy the rest of the night without Kayson on my mind.

Chapter Five
DENARI

Uncle Ray been calling my ass ever since I got arrested. I've been dodging his ass because I didn't wanna hear his fucking mouth. I already know what the fuck he was gone say, the same thing I been hearing from my fucking brothers. What can I say, shit happens and just because I didn't move like them muthafuckas didn't mean I wasn't on the same playing field. I just marched to the beat of my own got damn drum.

I'm so surprised that I hadn't heard from Kayson, normally he was the first one to get in my ass and I really couldn't ignore him, he would pop up on my ass. Hell, I called him this morning and got his voicemail. That wasn't like Kayson but the last time we got into it, he told me that he was tired of babying me and that I was gone have to find my own way and I guess he meant it.

They just didn't understand me that's all. With everything I went through as a kid, I can't help but be fucked up. I mean damn, I did watch my old man kill my mom right in front of me. Shit that would make anybody crazy. The only person that understood me was Omari because he was there. I loved all my brothers but Omari was blood so at the end of the day he was the only opinion I cared about.

Bang! Bang! Bang!. Someone banging on my door pulled me from my thoughts. I didn't know who the hell it could be because all my brothers had keys and they didn't believe in knocking. I got up, grabbed my nine, and went to answer the door. When I opened it, I quickly regretted it.

"So, I see you are ignoring my calls nephew." My uncle Ray said as he walked in and sat down without an invitation. I started to close the door and get ready for his speech. "Nah, you may as well leave that open your brothers will be in here any minute."

"Is there something I should know?" I asked feeling a little bum rushed with everyone piling in my little ass apartment.

"Is there something I should know?" My uncle asked with a raised eyebrow.

Before I could answer Kayson, Jaako and Omari walked in and they all were shaking their heads. I could already tell this was not about to be a good visit. So, I shut the door and headed to the bathroom.

"Where you going nigga, we don't got all day for this bullshit." Kayson fumed.

"I'm going to take a got damn piss, do you fucking mind?"

I continued to my room and shut and locked the door. I went in my drawer and pulled out my stash, I poured a line on the mirror and took that shit. I did coke from time to time but that shit didn't affect me one way or another. I threw my head back and enjoyed the high. Once I got my head straight enough to function, I was ready to deal with this bullshit.

I walked out of the room and they were in a full fledged conversation and the minute I walked in they all stopped and just looked at me. Whatever they were talking about Omari wasn't happy about it so I take it that it was about me.

"What happened the other day nephew?"

"I got arrested but you already know that, so what's up?"

"What did you get arrested for?"

"How could you be so reckless?" He folded his hands in his lap and then turned his attention to me.

"Man, I was just hanging with Jizzy and chilling, I wasn't hurting nobody."

"You were riding around with open bottles of white liquor in the fucking daytime." He stood up. "You don't take this shit serious, do you? Maybe you need to just fall back."

"Man, what the fuck does drinking have to do with me doing what the fuck I need to do in these streets?" He was starting to piss me off because had this been one of them he wouldn't even be saying shit, he only doing all of this because it was me.

"It has a lot to do with it, you causing unnecessary attention on yourself. Now if they're watching you, they're watching us." He pointed at me.

"You gotta start making better decisions D, stop thinking about yourself all the time." Jaako chimed in.

"If one win we all win, if one lose nigga we all lose and I ain't trying to lose." Omari said.

Kayson didn't say anything, he just sat there with a mug on his face. I didn't know what his problem was and I didn't give a shit, he would get over it.

"What the fuck is this, some kind of intervention?" I looked around and they all looked at me even Kayson.

"Denari, real shit if you don't straighten your shit, you out man." My uncle said with finality. "I built this shit by my got damn self and I be damned if I let yo' young, ungrateful ass fuck it up."

He stood up and walked out the door and slammed it on the way out. I sat down on the couch where he was sitting and laughed. His big ass was mad as fuck. Uncle Ray was Mama's half-brother that helped her raise us; he ran the most lucrative drug ring that Charlotte had ever seen. He was grooming us to take his place when he was ready to retire. I just didn't agree with the way he was going about it. He wanted us to work our way from the ground up, and I felt like he just needed to teach us to be boss ass muthafuckas. Fuck all this starting from the bottom shit. I wasn't built for this, I just wanted to sit back, watch the money stack up, and the bitches fall at my feet.

"Denari nigga you need to tighten up." Jaako shook me from my thoughts.

"Man, I'm just trying to live my life."

"At the expense of all of ours." Kayson finally spoke up. "You making dumb ass decisions like that puts all of us in a fucked-up position and the fact that you don't care lets me know that you ain't built for this." He started to the door.

"I'm just as capable as you are. I don't see what the fuck the problem is, nobody says shit when y'all out here partying it up and shit. Y'all just making a big deal out of this shit because it's me." I jumped up.

"Because you the only one out here going to fucking jail, dumb ass." Kayson fumed. "Yo ass been locked up twice in the last fucking month for dumb shit Denari! WHAT THE FUCK??" He yelled.

"Aight y'all chill out." Jaako intervened. "D, you gotta make better decisions."

"Man, I know, I just wanna have a little fun. Shit as much as we work we deserve that, right?"

Kayson laughed. "Nigga you don't work."

"I do just as much as you do."

"Nigga we both know that shit a lie. When yo ass ain't high out yo goddam mind sitting somewhere looking stupid, yo ass somewhere fucking up." He pointed at me.

"Fuck you Kayson." I yelled and he ran and got in my face. I pushed his big ass and he squared up. Jaako and Omari came over to get in between us. "Nah fuck that let him go."

"Shut up D, you know damn well Kayson will fuck you up." Jaako said pushing me back and he was right, I had tried Kayson a time or two and he beat the fuck out of me, but I was high off that coke and was feeling myself.

"That nigga can't beat my ass." I taunted.

"I'ma fuck you up." Omari was having a hard time holding his ass back. Kayson was beasting his ass trying to get to me.

"We brothers man chill out." Omari said giving Kayson a hard push which made Kayson run up on him ready to attack. Omari threw his hands up and looked at Kayson. "Bruh we ain't doing this." Kayson stared at Omari and turned to leave out the door. "Bruh don't leave."

"I'm out because if I don't, I'ma do some shit I might regret."

"All this because I wanted to party a little bit?" I asked and Kayson turned around again and Omari stepped in his path.

"No nigga because you don't give a fuck about anyone but yourself. You out here wilding and shit not giving a fuck about how it affects everybody else." He was pissed and I could tell because he was damn near yelling and Kayson hardly ever raised his voice unless he was pissed off. " Look at you sitting there with that shit around your nose like it's okay." I wiped my hand across my nose and noticed the residue on my fingers that was left behind from the line I did. I was slipping; I should have checked that before I walked out the room. Kayson shook his head and chuckled. "I'm out, I don't got time for this shit."

He walked out and I snatched away from Jaako and threw myself on the couch. I was tired of Kayson treating me like I was a damn child. I was a grown as man and could do what the fuck I wanted to do and I was going to do just that.

"Y'all can go too." I told Jaako and Omari. They both

looked at me like they wanted to kick my ass too but instead they both just left.

I sat there stuck in my thoughts; I didn't know why everyone was tripping. Hell, they do the same shit I do and I don't say shit. I let them do them. I wanted the same got damn respect. All the shit I had been through, I deserved to do what the fuck I wanted to do.

For some reason, I didn't want to be alone right now. I wondered if Heaven could get away from that bitch she called a boyfriend. I picked up the phone to give her a call.

"Hello," she whispered.

"Why the fuck you whispering yo."

"Cause I'm in the bathroom Denari, what do you want?"

"I need to see you."

"I can't, I'm at Ortiz's family's house and we are about to have lunch."

"So, fuck that nigga, it ain't like you like his ass anyway."

"Well Denari you ain't exactly ready to settle down with me, now are you?"

"Heaven I told you that I ain't about to stop fucking bitches now if you willing to jump on board, I will welcome you with open arms." I laughed.

"Fuck you Denari." She said before she hung up the phone.

Me and Heaven had been fucking around for about a year and she wanted me to be serious with her so she could get away from Ortiz bitch ass. Ortiz was the leader of the Ortiz boys that ran out of Fort Mill, South Carolina. They were some half ass gang bangers that dealt a little here and there, but they were mostly petty thieves and jack boys. We had a few run ins with them a few times and it wasn't pretty, but I think they got the idea and backed the fuck off.

Ortiz treated Heaven like she was his property, like she belonged to him. She hated it but wouldn't leave because she didn't have anywhere else to go. I always told her she was welcome to come here, but she would always say that at least with Ortiz it was all about her and with me she would be just another number and she was right. Since she didn't want to come play, I would call my number two. I picked up the phone and dialed a number.

"What do you want Denari?" she said with an attitude.

"Ya man just left." I laughed. "Come see me."

"I don't know, I don't want Jaako to see me." Krista said but I could tell she wanted to come get some of this dope dick.

"Man, he ain't. You coming or not?"

"Yeah I'm on my way."

"Well bring that ass on then." With that I hung up the phone and went to do me another line and get ready for her sexy ass to get here.

Chapter Six
KRISTA

I know what you're thinking but I love Jaako, I do. I just wanted Jaako to be the man I wanted him to be but he was just not willing to compromise. I thought that he was a man that I could mold into who I wanted him to be and that was working well for me until he started working with that fucking lawyer. I knew how he felt about that lawyer bitch, because I overheard a conversation he had with Kayson once but I wasn't worried because what kind of lawyer would date a fucking drug dealer. Defeats the whole purpose, right?

Jaako hated to be alone so I knew that he wouldn't leave me, especially if he didn't have a for sure chance with the lawyer bitch. He had been that way since he was younger and his parents died in that home invasion. He always tried his best to keep everyone at peace because he knew first-hand how it felt to lose someone you loved. His favorite line was "Life is too short," and I admit that I took full advantage of that.

I loved the life that Jaako provided for me and losing that was not in the plan. Hell, I thought my impeccable bedroom skills would keep him tamed but he wasn't like most men. Jaako wanted that fairytale love, but the hood version. I just wanted a man that would take care of me and do what the hell I said. Was that too much to ask? I mean my mom ran my dad for years and still did to this day. She handled all the finances and my dad just worked and brought home the money. That was how I grew up and that's how I wanted to live.

Now Denari was just something to do to pass the time. When Jaako wasn't available, I could call him and he would take care of me. I think I was just wrapped up in the thrill of being with him. I didn't want anything real or special with him I just wanted the dick whenever I could get it. As soon as Jaako started being the man that I wanted him to be, I would leave Denari alone. I would miss his dick action but I'm sure I could teach Jaako some of the things Denari does. I'm not saying that Jaako's sex is bad, because he had the tool and knew exactly how to use it. Denari was just better in my opinion. He was younger and liked to fuck. Jaako was into making love and all that sweet stuff. Sometimes a girl just wanted to be choked and slapped around a little you know? This was why I was knocking on his door as we speak.

"Damn why you banging like the fucking police Krista?"

"Because you knew I was coming so the door should have been unlocked." I said with much attitude. That was the one thing I hated about Denari though, he didn't know how to talk to women. At least Jaako was respectful.

"Don't come in here with that shit because you can leave."

"If that's the case why did you call me over here?"

"To fuck, not to hear yo' damn mouth."

"You know what, I can see that you're in a bad mood so I'm gonna go. Call me when you get your attitude together."

I started back out the door and he grabbed my arm and slung me in the house and slammed the door. He pushed me until I fell into the couch where he came and stood over me. For a minute, he just stood there and then he hiked up the maxi dress that I had on. Underneath I was naked because I knew exactly what I was coming for.

"Do that shit with ya legs." He said and dropped his pants.

"I will when you go grab a rubber."

"We didn't use one last time so what the fuck is the difference now?"

"Because last time we were in your car and it was spur of the moment and it won't happen again. Now go get a rubber." There was no way that I would let that shit happen again. The last thing that I needed was to get pregnant and not know who my child's father was because I was fucking brothers.

He smacked his lips and reached down in the pants that he just took off and grabbed a rubber. I watched as he slid it down his thick dick, my pussy jumped with anticipation. I guess he noticed the look in my eye because he smirked and then took his dick and slapped it against my freshly waxed pussy.

He took his shirt and pulled the front of it behind his head but not completely off, his arms were still in. I just looked at him. He was a little on the skinny side, he had muscles but they weren't anything to brag about. He had the darkest set of eyes I think I had ever seen on a human and his beard was always neat but scruffy if that makes sense. Denari's dreads were always neat and they brought out the strong features in his face. He was handsome and there was a mystery about him that urged you to want to figure him out.

"We gone do this or are you gone just stare at me?"

I smirked and spread my legs as far as they could go and that was far because I used to be a dancer so I was pretty flexible. Once he had a full shot of my pussy he placed his head at my opening, one hand around my throat and eased right in.

"Shit." He said as he got into a steady rhythm. I closed my eyes and enjoyed the ride that he was taking me on. He was touching things within me that I didn't even know were possible for him to reach. "Oh, we being quiet today?" He taunted.

"Just enjoying the ride." I barely got out.

I guess I wasn't making enough noise because he started putting in overtime and I was in heaven. I couldn't hold my screams in anymore. Right as I was getting into it we heard the door knob turn and open.

"Oh, shit my bad bruh." We both jumped and out of instinct Denari pulled out of me and stepped back and I balled up on the couch in an attempt to cover myself. "What the fuck? Krista?" I looked up and into the eyes of Omari. Fuck!

"It's not what you think." I hurried up and said, that was the only thing that I could get out in the moment.

"Then please tell me what the fuck it was because I think I just walked in on you fucking your man's brother wit yo' nasty ass." He growled. "And you," he pointed at Denari, "How the fuck you gon' be fucking Jaa's girl nigga. That shit is nasty as hell. What the fuck you think he gone do when he finds this shit out?"

"He ain't gone find out because you ain't gone tell him!" Denari said it more in an asking way than a threatening way because although Omari was usually quiet, I had seen him mad before and it's not a pretty sight.

"You ain't putting me in this shit D. Why you always gotta be the fuck up? I'm so tired of having to clean up your shit."

"Listen I don't wanna start nothing." I interjected.

"Well you should have thought about that before yo' ass decided to bust it wide open for the fam." Omari glared at me. I could hear the anger in his voice and I felt it was best if I got the hell out of here before shit got ugly.

"Look, just please don't say anything, I promise this is the end of it." I begged. "I would never want to come between brothers. I know I was wrong and I swear I will do whatever I need to do to make shit right just please don't tell him."

"Man, Jaa don't give a fuck about her and you know it." Denari said with the shrug of the shoulders.

"That ain't the fucking point man, we don't fuck after each other, that shit is nasty as fuck and you know it."

"Man, Jaa want that lawyer bitch that's been keeping us clear so shut that shit up." Denari laughed and I cringed at the thought that they all knew that he was feeling someone else.

"How long this been going on?" Omari ignored Denari's comment about the lawyer bitch.

"Why the fuck does that matter O?"

"Because I fucking asked." I was now at the front door ready to get the hell out of there.

"You won't see this again, I promise." I said to get him to agree to not tell Jaako.

"Just get the fuck out, you dirty ass hoe. I told Jaa not to trust yo' ass." Omari rolled his eyes and turned his attention back to Denari. "I can't believe you, her, of all people."

"Did you see that shit she could do with her got damn legs though?" Denari laughed.

"I'm fucking serious D." Omari yelled.

"This shit don't mean nothing." Denari waved his hands in the air to dismiss what Omari was saying.

Their conversation started to get a little heated so I made my way outside and headed home to shower and forget all about this. I hoped like hell that Omari didn't tell Jaako about this shit because I knew it wouldn't end up good. They were brothers so I knew that eventually he would forgive him but me, I don't know if him not wanting to be alone would be enough.

Maybe I should tell him before anyone else could? No I couldn't do that, then I would be pushing his ass right in to the arms of that lawyer bitch. I was just gone sit back and pray that Omari kept his mouth shut.

Chapter Seven

KAYSON

I was so tired of having to deal with Denari's bullshit. He was so fucking irresponsible and careless and his punk ass never fucking owned up to shit. Just listening to his aggravating ass voice had me on ten and I'd be damned if I was gone sit there and listen to his ass anymore. I could guarantee that them niggas was sitting there babying his ass. They were his fucking problem especially Omari's ass. I know they went through some shit, but got damn they couldn't keep leaning on that shit.

The fact that his ass was fucking tooting powder hurt me because his ass knew that shit affected me because of what my birth mother was. Although I never met the woman I resented her and that shit made it hard for me to trust women, which is why I could never settle down.

Having Jenacia in the house with me, made me want to

settle down. But I knew if I chose to do that, I needed to be completely ready. If I hurt her again, she would be out of my life forever and I wasn't ready for that.

With everything that was scrolling through my mind, I really didn't want to be alone. I was supposed to meet Jaako and Omari at The Oak Room tonight, but I didn't know if I felt up to it especially if they brought D with em. I needed a break from that nigga.

When I pulled up at home I saw that Jenacia's car was there and I was happy, I hoped like hell she didn't have plans because she was chilling with me today.

"Jen." I yelled when I walked through the door. "Jen"

She didn't answer so I walked to the back where I heard music, I walked in her room and she wasn't in there and then I heard the shower. I smiled and walked over to the door and just walked in.

"Ahhh!" She screamed and I doubled over in laughter. She had picked up her loofa like she was actually gone do some damage with it. "What the fuck Kayson."

"What the hell did you plan to do with that? Soap my ass up?" I laughed again and she threw it at me. "Man chill." I got myself together because I was still laughing. "What you got planned for today?"

"I was gon' go hiking at Crowder's Mountain and take some pictures for my portfolio. Why, you wanna go?"

"Niggas don't fucking hike, the fuck?"

"Shut up fool, yes they do, it's good for you. I don't wanna go by myself anyway."

"Fuck no Jen."

"Pussy." She taunted.

"I'll show you a pussy aight." I said and walked to the shower where she was.

"No! We slipped up once already and we are not doing that again. I need my sanity and you ain't ready for what I'm ready for yet." She said and then went back to washing up.

"You don't know what the fuck I'm ready for Jen." Shut the fuck up nigga is what I was telling myself in my head but my lips kept moving. "I miss yo' ass and I miss us."

"You trying to go hiking with me?" she said as she rinsed the soap off her body and turned the water off. I just stood there looking at her because she was everything that I could ever want. I just didn't know if I trusted myself to be what she wanted. I didn't really have the time to dedicate to her and I knew she was always busy with the magazine and doing her own thing so I didn't know how that shit would work.

When she opened the curtain, I started to salivate; her body was like a work of art. She wasn't skinny and she wasn't thick by any means of the word, she was just perfect. Her doe shaped eyes that were slightly slanted and her plump lips sat centered on her caramel colored skin. Her titties sat up just right, couldn't have been more than a C cup but that's all I needed.

"Helllllooooo" she snapped her fingers.

"Man, why you fucking up my wet dream." I smirked.

"Are you going with me or not?" she whined.

"Who the fuck gone give me mouth to mouth when I pass the fuck out?"

"You are being overly dramatic now, just come with me." She started that pouting shit and she knew that I would never be able to say no to that, so I agreed and went to dress in some ball shorts and a tank since it was the middle of May and hot as hell.

Once I was dressed, I went to the living room to wait on her and she walked out in some short ass, tight ass shorts and a fucking bra. I picked up the phone to call Jaako.

"What's good bruh?"

"Yo Jaa, if I come up missing Jenacia did that shit. She asked me to go to Crowder's Mountain with her."

"Nigga and you agreed? Black people don't do that shit." He laughed.

"Jaa this shit for real." I looked over at Jen who was shaking her head and laughing. "So just know, if you don't hear from me in about an hour come looking for me."

"Nah nigga you on ya own, you dumb as hell for going out there."

"Are you serious right now?" Jenacia finally spoke up.

"Hell yeah I don't know if I can trust you, you might be trying to kill me."

"If I was gone try to kill you Kay, I would have just poisoned your food."

I thought about that shit for a minute, she had been cooking for us lately. "Yo you heard that shit Jaako." I could hear Jaako laughing. For as long as I can remember he has been telling me to make shit right with Jen and that she was the one for me. Jaako ass was the hopeless romantic out of all of us so I knew this shit made his day. "Fuck you Jaako."

I hung up on him and Jenacia laughed and led the way out the door. During the drive, we talked about everything. That was the one thing I loved about her, I could talk to her about anything. She knew everything there was to know about my childhood. She accepted me for everything I was. She may not have agreed with what I did for money, more because it was dangerous than illegal, but she accepted it.

Jenacia was loving and caring and she always put everyone before herself. Which is why I never understood how in the hell she could ever come from a woman like Rose. That bitch was the spawn of the devil; it was like she hated her own daughter. I hated to be anywhere around Rose because of how she was. She used to make me pay her to see Jen when we were dating before. Like for real I couldn't step foot in her house unless I gave her $50. She knew what I did for a living and she used that shit to her advantage.

"Thank you for coming with me. I love spending time with you."

"Oh yeah? Where is ya little boyfriend when you need him?" I asked bringing up shit from the other night. She laughed.

"The same place ya little girlfriend is." She looked at me and then turned her head back to the road. "But for real, Julius is a male model who hires me to do his shoots because we work well together. I honestly believe he's gay but he won't admit it. He's tried to hit on me a few times but nothing serious." She paused and I was anxious to hear what the fuck else was coming. "The other night when I was mad at you I gave in to his advance but—"

"Jenacia you better not—"

"Would you shut up and let me finish." I smacked my lips and gave her the floor. "I gave in to his advance just to see what he would do. Just like I thought we got back to his hotel and he couldn't do it. Gave me this story about not wanting to ruin our friendship." She laughed. "So, me being me I came out and asked him if he was gay and he finally told me the truth. I always knew and like I told him, I would never think of him any less but he can stop all the acting around me." She glanced at me for a second. "So, that's what's up with my little boyfriend."

"So, that nigga like the same shit you do huh?"

"Yep! So, no action there for me."

"I got some action for you." I threw out there.

"Nope I already told you what the deal was. Hell, I feel dumb as hell sometimes for sitting around waiting on you to get your shit together. Well, kinda waiting."

"The fuck you mean kinda, Jenacia?"

"Exactly what I said, I mean you know I was with Roger for over a year. Before him I was seeing people, but I feel like I never give men a real chance because in the back of my mind I know they're not you and my heart only belongs with you and I hate that."

"Why do you hate that?"

"Because I know who you are Kayson and I know that you will never change."

"You don't know that Jen."

"Kayson I do, you are 25 years old and moving up in the drug game. There is no way that you are gonna tell me that with all the pussy that's gone be coming at you, you're gonna be able to settle down with me and be happy." I looked at her shocked. "Don't look at me like that I just want you to keep a buck and you know I'ma do the same."

"Honestly, I done fucked so many bitches out here looking for something that's been in my life all along. I will never be able to give another woman my heart the way you have it. I love you and you know that. I'm just scared that I won't be able to live up to person you have in your mind."

"Kayson, I love you the way you are. I just want the loyalty with the love. That's all I ask."

"That's some deep shit Jenacia," I said just above a whisper.

I understood what she was asking of me, and I knew exactly what she wanted. I just didn't know if I could fully give her that. But like I said, I done fucked plenty bitches and I swear there was no one out there like Jen. Our chemistry was out of this world. My biggest fear was disappointing her and I think that's where my hesitation was.

"Don't be trying to get all deep in this shit so you can get mad and push me off this got damn mountain." I said to lighten the mood of the conversation.

"Kayson, I get it. You don't want to fail." She said noticing what I was trying to do. "But you can't expect me to wait around forever."

I let that shit sink in, we rode the rest of the way to the mountain in silence, and both lost in our own thoughts. She wanted me, all of me and I wanted to give her that but in the same sense I was scared.

When we got to the mountain and got out the car, the mood lightened a little and we started up the mountain. I had never been hiking before but I must say that the scenery was beautiful and watching Jenacia with her camera in her element drew me to her, just a little more. The look in her eyes and smile on her face when she caught just the right picture made me smile. I knew right then that I needed to get my shit together before she made good on her little threat.

Chapter Eight
OMARI

I walked through the Oak Room with a Crown shot in my hand as the bass of Bounce Back by Big Sean resonated through the speakers. I was feeling good. After that shit I saw the other day I wasn't even in the mood to deal with anything but some liquor, a blunt and hopefully some pussy.

There were a few bad bitches in here half fucking naked throwing ass like they were trying to get paid, but I didn't want that tonight. I wanted something that I had to work for. I wasn't really one for relationships, them muthafuckas was too much work and I didn't have the patience. So, I just had fuck buddies and it would stay that way until I got old as hell or I found someone who was worth changing all of that.

"Heeeyyyy Omari," I heard someone sing from my right. I

looked in their direction and threw my head up and kept it moving. I wasn't in the mood to entertain a fan club tonight.

I walked around a little more before I found me a table, I knew when Kayson and Jaako got here they would flip shit about why I didn't get a VIP but I liked chilling with the people. Hell, even when I got a VIP I still spent more time out of it than I did in it.

I observed everything that was going on around me. All the thirsty niggas out here buying drinks and shit trying to get the next bitch that's willing to go home with them and the bitches sucking it all up knowing good and damn well they would be sneaking off with the next nigga. It was all amusing to me because I wasn't that guy. I didn't do all the buying drinks and shit just for some pussy. Either you were gonna give it to me or you wasn't, it was up to you.

"O" I heard Denari yell and my mood completely went left.

"The fuck you doing here Denari?"

"Shit I called to see what Jaako was up to and he said he was meeting y'all here so I decided to invite myself since this was a brother thing and all." He said sounding somewhat offended.

"Nah nigga be real, you called Jaako to see if I told him your disloyal ass is fucking with his girl."

"Who girl you fucking now bro?" Jaako asked as he walked up, I didn't even see him coming.

"Yeah who girl you fucking bruh?" I smirked and Denari

looked at me like he wanted to kill me but I didn't care, that nigga was wrong on so many levels it wasn't even funny.

"That nigga Ortiz girl, Heaven. I been sticking her for a minute." He laughed it off and I shook my head and walked off toward the bar. I wasn't with Denari's shit tonight and if I wanted to have fun, I couldn't be around him.

I sat at the bar and downed three more shots of Crown and just chilled for a minute. I looked around for my brothers and I spotted them in VIP, well Jaako and Kayson anyway. I got up and started off over in that direction but I noticed Kayson's first love Jenacia heading my way with this sexy ass woman with her.

I mean baby girl was stacked like a muthafucka, but she didn't have no waist and her thickness wasn't excessive or fake. Her light skin glowed under the club lighting and the red crop top she had on brought out the red hues of her skin. Her slanted eyes, small nose and mouth let me know that she was mixed with something and I swear it was a deadly combination. She had her hair in them twist shits that all the black girls were wearing so I knew she had some kind of black in her. I was hoping by the end of the night she had this black dick in her but I could tell that she was different from the hoes in the club.

"Hey O," Jenacia said and hugged me; I hugged her back but kept my eyes on her friend. "Kayson told me my favorite Barnes brother was here and I just had to come and find you."

"What's been up sis?" I asked still not taking my eyes off the beauty that stood before me.

"Well if you cared you would not be staring a hole through my Zemia." I finally looked her direction and she had an amused look on her face and I flipped her off. "Omari this is my friend and coworker Zemia, and Zemia this is the crazy ass Omari I was telling you about." She laughed.

"I'm only crazy when I need to be." I smirked and I guess Zemia knew what I was talking about because she returned the smirk. "How you doing Ma?"

"I'm good and it's nice to meet you. Jenacia has told me a lot about you."

"Don't believe that shit, sis a hater." Jenacia hit me on the shoulder and laughed.

"I'm sure." She said and then turned around and gave me a nice view of her plump ass. The nigga in me wanted to reach out and grab a handful, but if she was friends with Jenacia I already knew she wasn't about that shit.

"Aight O, I just came to holla at you. Me and Zemia about to explore the club a little bit. You going to VIP?"

"Yeah, that's where I was going when you came over." I said and then looked over to Zemia. "You may not want to explore too much because you wouldn't want to get a nigga fucked up, would you?"

"Excuse me?" She was taken aback by my forwardness but I didn't give a fuck. I meant what I said.

"You heard me, I don't like to share and I think you just stepped on my heart a little bit with them big ass heels." I chuckled. "I get territorial, you know what I mean."

"I'm sorry but I don't even know you and you are not my

man to be dictating my moves." She put her hands on her hips.

I shrugged my shoulders and looked her in the eyes. "You got one of two choices in the matter. You can fall in line and respect that you just walked into a trap called my life. Or you can go out here thinking you can do what you want, and then get mad and leave when I show my ass. It doesn't really matter to me, but the choice is yours."

With that I walked off, there was nothing else to say. I could hear her trying to go off but Jenacia stopped her and explained that it was no use that's just how we were, and she was exactly right. When I got over to the VIP section, Kayson was staring at me with a smirk on his face. I guess he was watching or he sent her over there.

"What the fuck you cheesing at nigga?"

"You." He laughed. "She bad as fuck though."

"Hell yeah, how long Jenacia been knowing her?"

"They work together at The Word, that local magazine shit. I just met her ass today when she came to the house. I invited Jenacia to come out with me and she said that she didn't want to be around all of us and be the only female, so she called her friend."

"Well she just got her friend in a lot of fucking trouble." I smiled.

"Don't be out here beasting nigga, I know how you do." Jaako chimed in, until that moment he was on his phone and shit smiling and keekeeing.

"I already told her if I catch her in a nigga face I'm

showing my ass." I sat back and threw my arms over the of the couch that I was sitting on and just watched as my future prospect move around the club like she owned that bitch.

"You can't be doing that shit O." Jaako laughed.

"I can do what the fuck I want, who in the hell gonna stop me."

And I meant that. I was a boss in every sense of the word. I was just waiting on my chance to show the world what I was made of. Me and my brothers had all proved ourselves but the decision was Uncle Ray's so we were just waiting on him to make his move.

We were just chilling and drinking, just enjoying life and shit. It felt good to just live with no got damn bullshit, and then I remembered that Denari was here and I hadn't seen him since earlier.

"Yo, where the fuck is Denari, I don't want no shit tonight."

"If you don't want no shit, don't even talk his ass up." Kayson said sitting up from the couch. I followed his eyes and seen that Jenacia and Zemia were dancing with some dude. I stood up and Kayson followed me. "Nigga that's Uncle Ray ass." Kayson laughed and I had to join in because all we were seeing was red so we didn't even notice that it was him.

We walked up and I jumped in his face, "Nigga you dancing with my woman?"

"Young blood you wouldn't know what to do with this beautiful woman right here." He grabbed Zemia's hand and spun her around and she was just a smiling.

"Nah yo' old ass wouldn't know what to do with her." He looked to me and furrowed his brow and then we all busted out laughing.

"I got yo' old nigga, my old ass will fuck you up." He pushed me. "My ass is tired, y'all wore me out." He said headed to where Jaako was still sitting.

"Told you yo' ass was old." I said under my breath and Kayson laughed.

We all sat down, Zemia sat on the other couch across from me while Jenacia sat beside Kayson. I wondered what was going on with them two now. Whatever it was I just hoped like hell he didn't fuck up because she was good for him and she was down for him.

"Why the fuck you all the way over there?" I mugged her and her pretty ass mugged me back which made me smile. "Come here man."

"I like it over here."

"I really don't give a fuck what you like, I'm asking you nicely." I licked my bottom lip.

"Why the hell y'all young niggas so rough? Damn y'all don't know how to caress women anymore. Y'all niggas be all aggressive." Uncle Ray shook his head.

"Because that's what they like." Kayson answered for me.

"Who said?" Jenacia and Zemia said at the same time.

"Come here sweet thang." Uncle Ray said and Zemia got up and walked over to where he was sitting and cuddled up beside him. I knew that shit was just to make me mad so I played along.

"Unc I will fuck you up in here, you know you ain't got yo' inhaler so you won't be able to keep up with me." Jaako and Kayson laughed.

"I'll just shoot you nephew, problem solved."

"Yo' old ass gotta get to it first." I said as I pulled out my gat from my waist band and he smiled at me.

"I taught ya well." He laughed and Zemia looked worried when she seen the gun in my hands.

All of a sudden, we heard this big commotion break out by the bar. Something told me to stand up and check it out and I'm glad I did because it was my brother getting jumped by three niggas.

"Oh shit that's D." Jaako yelled and jumped the rope that tied off our section and I did the same thing followed by Kayson. I could hear Uncle Ray going off and telling the girls to stay put.

We got through the crowd and they had Denari on the ground stomping his ass out. I swung on the first nigga that was close to me and hit him in the head with the gun that I still had in my hand.

"Oh shit he gotta gun." I heard someone yell and people started to scatter. But I didn't stop beating the fuck out of ol' dude until I felt someone pull me off and I turned around to swing and I realized it was Uncle Ray trying to get the gun out of my hand but I wasn't letting that shit go. I tucked that shit back in my pants and turned around to see that my brothers were all standing over top of niggas beating the shit out of them.

"Aight y'all that's enough." Uncle Ray said. Surprisingly there was still a crowd standing there even after someone said I had a gun. I guess being nosy was more important than muthafuckas lives nowadays.

"Pussy ass nigga, who the fuck you thought we were?" Kayson said and spit on the nigga he had just fucked up. "Muthafuckas better ask about us, our names ring bells bitch." He kicked the guy and headed back to where the girls were.

I grabbed Jaako and we helped Denari off the ground and headed out the door and to the cars before the police came. I knew it would be just a matter of time before they got there. We got that nigga Denari in my car and Unc said bring him to his house.

"Oh, my God Denari I'm so sorry. Are you okay?" Some light skinned girl came up and said. She looked familiar but I couldn't put my finger on it. Denari was so sneaky you would never know.

"Heaven let's go!" Someone yelled at her and she jumped. "If I have to call Ortiz, it's not gonna be a pretty sight." He said like somebody gave a fuck.

"Yo you alright?" I asked her and she looked at me and nodded her head but I could tell that she wasn't. "You sure?"

"Yes, just tell Denari I'm so sorry." She said and then walked off to the guy that was yelling at her. He was standing there shaking his head at her and she was walking in his direction with her head down like a child that was being chastised.

I didn't have time to worry about that though. I needed to get Denari to my uncle's house to get checked out by the doc.

I watched as Jenacia and Zemia walked to Kayson's car with him and Jaako hopped in his car. I got in my car and high tailed it out of the parking lot. I was happy as hell when I noticed that he was following me. I wasn't ready to let Ms. Sexy out of my sights yet.

I should have known that Denari was gonna be the one to mess this night up for everybody, which is why I didn't want his ass to come. But Jaako, old peacemaker ass, just had to tell him where the fuck we were going. I was gonna cuss his ass out if he made me ruin any chances with Zemia.

"Where's Heaven?" Denari asked from the backseat.

"Gone." Was all I said because I wasn't in the mood to talk to him about that shit.

"He's gonna hurt her." He managed to get out between moans.

"Well they could've killed you so I don't know what the fuck you want me to do."

He didn't say anything else probably because he knew I was pissed and how I got when I was mad. I kept driving until I got to Harrisburg, which is where Uncle Ray lived. I was pissed the fuck off because the more I drove, the more I thought about shit. I was gone lay into his ass once he was well enough to take it.

Chapter Nine
HEAVEN

I sat in the back of Cello's truck hating my life right now. I hated the day I ever met Ortiz. We had been together for the last two years and I honestly can't ever say that I ever had a happy moment with him. He has treated me like shit from the moment I met him.

Ortiz saved me from my father, who mentally and physically abused me every chance he got. My mother died from cancer when I was 14 and from that point on, he treated me like his own personal sex slave. Once I was 18, I left to never return. I was homeless, sleeping on the streets and in shelters. I got a job at Club Nikki's, which is a local strip club. I made decent money and I was able to get myself a little apartment off Nations Ford.

On my 19th birthday I met Ortiz, the owner of the club threw me a huge party that night and Ortiz was there with all his crew. He saw me and told me that I would never dance again and that I belonged to him and he meant every single word. I've been living in that hell ever since.

"Why do you do things like that Heaven? You know how he is."

"Cello, I'm tired of living like this. I'm 21 years old and he treats me like I'm 12. I'm not his daughter. I just wanna live my life." I whined.

"You think you are going to live any better with that thug in there?" Cello looked through the rearview mirror because I was in the backseat. "He's bad news." He warned.

"And Ortiz isn't?" I asked. "He steals from people for a living, I mean come on."

He sighed because he knew I was right. Ortiz sold drugs and guns from time to time but the most of him money came from his "jobs." He would visit all the big cities and rob the up and coming dealers and then come back home like nothing happened. He would go for weeks at a time just scoping them out and then he would strike. They would never know what hit them.

Ortiz had a crew of about 17 and Cello, who normally stayed behind to watch me just in case someone found out who they were and tried to retaliate. I knew he was due to leave for a "job" tonight, so I don't even know how he knew what the fuck I was doing.

"I thought he left for a job?" I said aggravated.

"Something went wrong and he had to leave before they could even get started. So, he's back until shit smooths out."

He said and then we got to a stop light. "You know he's never gonna let you leave him, right?"

"What if I don't give him a choice?" I said more out of anger than really meaning it but it was too late to take back.

"What is that supposed to mean Heaven? Don't go doing anything crazy." Cello said in his thick Dominican accent.

"I'm just tired that's all."

"Well you know he's waiting for you so it's gonna be a long night." He warned.

I sat back in the seat and stared out the window. I hated the situation that I had put myself in. When I met him, I thought that I would be living the good life. I mean that man was good looking and he had money, I just knew that I was gonna be treated like a princess. I thought totally wrong, he had money but that was HIS money and he made sure to let me know that every time I asked for something.

The nigga gave me an allowance every week like I was a fucking kid. Every now and then he would get in a good mood and take me shopping but it wasn't often. That's what I liked about Denari. He wasn't the sweetest man in the world, but he was generous and he let me know that he was a fuck up from the get go.

Denari had a way of drawing you in even if you didn't want him to. It was like the more you tried to stay away, the more he pulled you in. Like tonight, my plan was to go to the club and leave and meet him somewhere but no, when he saw me he wanted to make a scene and be all up on me. My mind was telling me to leave but I couldn't, my heart won the battle with Denari every time.

I met Denari about a year ago, I was out with Cello, and Ortiz gave him permission to bring me to the mall. I was walking around while Cello went to the shoe store and as I was walking out of Charlotte Russe, I ran right in to him. He cussed me dirty for making him spill his coke on his fresh all white forces and from that point on I was hooked.

Even though Denari always tried to down play us I knew that he really felt something for me because no matter what he was doing, if I was free he would make time for me. He loved me he just didn't know how to express it because of how he grew up. After tonight though, I'm sure that it would be a while before I got to see him again.

As we pulled up to the house I took the phone that Denari bought me and put it in the lining of my pocketbook so Ortiz wouldn't see it because I knew he would look. He had a habit of going through my things and my phone when I went out without him.

Before I could even get out of the car good he started. "So, you think you can make a fool of me?" I dropped my head and prepared myself for a night of him yelling at me.

"It was nothing, we were just dancing that's all." I tried to justify my actions which wasn't a good idea.

"You want to make a fool of me? Is that what you say?"

"Of course not Ortiz." I said as I tried to get past him but he shoved me in the house which made me fall face forward. I hurried and jumped up because I didn't want him to attack me. "Please don't do this." I begged.

"You should have thought about that before you went out whoring tonight."

"I didn't." I cried.

"You lie." He slapped me across the face. "My men tell me that you were all in his face smiling and laughing like you had something going on with him. You tell me the truth." He slapped me again. "What, you think you are going to leave me and be with him? Huh? Over your dead body." He slapped me again and I fell on the couch and cried. He kneeled in front of me and grabbed me by my hair and tilted my head back. "I was there when you had nothing, staying in that roach infested apartment wearing clothes from the Dollar Tree. When you were dancing for pennies at Club Nikki's. How dare you disrespect me like this." He threw my head back. "Go get cleaned up and pack a bag, you're going with me for this next job. I don't trust you here."

He walked off and I sat on the couch and just cried my eyes out. I hated this life and I hated him more. Why couldn't I just be happy with Denari? God help me, I can't live like this.

Chapter Ten
DENARI

"He's gonna be fine, sore, but fine." The doctor told my uncle that was standing on the right of me and Omari to the left. I couldn't see the other two but I knew they were there.

"Who did this to my baby?" I heard Mama say as she came tearing down the stairs.

"I'm alright Mama."

"You are not, you down here all bruised up and stuff." She looked at me and then up at Omari. "What happened?"

"Well Ma, you know your son, he can't even go nowhere and not start shit." He shrugged and walked off.

"Shit wasn't even my fault." I said and grabbed my side. "I was chilling with Heaven, dancing and shit then suddenly I was surrounded by three niggas. They started talking shit, and

I don't back down from nobody. I don't give a fuck if it's one nigga or ten. It is what it is."

"Shit ain't never yo fault, is it?" Kayson said from the corner. I couldn't see him but I could tell he had a mug on his face from the way the words sounded leaving his mouth.

"What the fuck would you have done Kayson? Just stand there and let them niggas talk shit to you."

"You know what the fuck I'm talking about D, who the fuck is Heaven?" He asked and I rolled my eyes. He got on my got damn nerves, nigga always thought he ran something and didn't run shit but them big ass lips of his.

"I don't want to hear that shit."

"Nah, tell everybody why the fuck them niggas surrounded you?"

"What he talking about nephew." My uncle asked.

"You know that nigga Ortiz?" I asked and he nodded his head. "Well Heaven is his girl but she ain't happy and I'm about to take her from him."

"You telling me that all of this shit was over a bitch?"

"Man, don't call her that!"

I defended her and I didn't know where that came from because hell I've called her worse. I didn't want to be in a relationship, but I did care about Heaven. She knew things about me that only my brothers and Mama knew, and she still accepted me. Can't nobody tell me that ain't love. Still didn't mean that I was ready to stop fucking around. That just meant that I was ready to make her my main and I just needed her to be okay with it.

"You in love with another nigga's girl?" Omari asked but I knew what he was saying had more meaning than what everyone else knew. I didn't give a fuck about Krista though, I just like to fuck her because of the shit she could do with her legs. Heaven was different and I could see long term shit with her, just on my terms.

"She won't be his girl soon nigga." I was getting aggravated. "Y'all niggas kill me, like y'all ain't never fucked a bitch that had a man already or was married." That shit was for Kayson. I knew for a fact that he had smashed a married broad before, because I smashed her fucking sister.

"But again, muthafucka our actions ain't affecting the muthafucking business or each other." Kayson yelled.

"Okay boys enough. I'ma have to go and get my oil and get to praying. Y'all down here cussing and shit." Mama said with a frown on her beautiful face.

"Ma you just cussed in the same sentence you talking about going to get oil in." Omari said and she threw the closed bottle of saline at him that was on side of the bed. My uncle had the basement of his house made up like a hospital room for times like this.

"Shut up Omari, I got this." She told him.

"Look I didn't ask y'all to help me, I was good."

"D, them niggas was stomping you the fuck out." Jaako finally spoke up. "What you thought we were gonna just stand there and watch you get fucked up? You know that ain't how we get down."

"I know man, but I swear I wasn't trying to start no shit." I really wasn't, hell I was kinda upset that they didn't even invite me out to begin with and I figured it was because I liked to get drunk and act a fool. "Hell, I didn't even drink tonight."

"Well I'm just glad that you're okay. I'm going back up there to entertain these beautiful ladies, I just wanted to check on my baby."

"Wait is Heaven here?" I tried to sit up but my got damn ribs were sore as shit.

"Nah some big ass dude came and told her to get in the car before he called Ortiz and she told me to tell you that she was sorry but she left with him."

"Fuck."

I knew that if she went with him that Ortiz was gonna hurt her and I didn't want that. I was really feeling her and I didn't want anything to happen to her. I looked around for my phone and grabbed it. I tried to call her but it went straight to voicemail. She must have turned it off. I needed to get to her and soon.

"You really feeling this girl?" Omari nosy ass pried.

"She understands that I'm a nothing ass nigga and she's okay with it." And that was all that needed to be said.

The doctor took a couple more vital signs and then left out. My uncle helped me to the downstairs bedroom where he suggested I stayed until I felt better. I agreed because I was a little fucked up but it was cool. A nigga was gone bounce back soon. Right before I dozed off to sleep I texted Heaven to text me and let me know that she was alright, and then I hit that pillow and was out like a light.

Chapter Eleven
JAAKO

It had been a couple of weeks since the shit at the Oak Room. Denari was getting around a little better and his face wasn't fucked up anymore. I felt bad that I even told him where the fuck we were. Nobody else wanted him to come because his ass like to get drunk and show the fuck out but that's our brother and I hated to leave him out. I just wanted everyone to be able to chill and have a good time together.

I had never seen Denari give a fuck about anyone if they weren't family until I heard the way he was talking about ol' girl. Even though he tried to downplay it a little, it sounded like he had some feelings for her. Maybe that's what he needed to get right.

"Hey babe, what you doing." Krista said walking into the living room with leggings on and a tank top with no bra.

Times like this made me want to give her more of me but then she would open her mouth. "Did you hear what I said?" See. "If you ain't have nothing planned, you could have taken your woman out on a date."

"Well if you shut the fuck up and let me speak, then you would know what I got going on." I snapped. I didn't mean to but she was getting on my got damn nerves with that demanding ass attitude. "I'm chilling right now but I know Kayson wanted to chill tonight at his house. He was gonna throw some shit on the grill, but yo' ass didn't give me a chance to ask you anything before you come in here with your got damn mouth."

Hell, at this point I didn't even want her to go. I would have had more fun by myself or calling Yameka to come with me. I hated I even told her anything, I should have just let her keep talking.

"You didn't have to cuss me, I was just asking a question."

"No, you weren't asking, you were telling me what the fuck I could've done. There's a fucking difference." Added the curse words just to piss her off.

"Look, I'm sorry." She said and then slid on my lap like that shit would make a difference. "I just wanna spend time with you Jaako, you always busy and never have time for me."

"Well Krista, yo' ass is going about it all the wrong way." I said and then tried to push her off my lap. She looked at me with a smirk and then hopped up and got on her knees. "Krista chill, I ain't even feeling you right now." I said and looked down at what she was doing. She had my dick out and her small hands were moving up and down my shaft. "This shit don't fix everything."

"Yes, it does." She said before she took my semi erect dick into her warm awaiting mouth.

I relaxed and stopped fighting the feeling she was giving me. I watched as she bobbed her head up and down, I could feel the back of her throat and that shit made my toes pop.

"Fuck, girl."

She popped my dick out of her mouth and then put just the head back in. I felt her tongue circling the head of my dick and then she would put my whole dick back in her mouth and she repeated that a few times. The sounds of her slurping and seeing the excess saliva drip from her lip and feeling that shit roll down my balls, had a nigga on edge. She licked, sucked and slurped until I couldn't take anymore.

"Shit I'm about to nut."

My whole body got tense and I exploded down her throat and she swallowed all that shit. My toes were scrunched so much them shits caught a fucking cramp. Once I got myself together I looked at her and she was slowly sucking my shit back to life.

"I'm still mad." I said and she winked and I grabbed her by her hair and pulled her up. She pulled down her leggings and like normal she didn't have on no fucking panties. I lifted her and eased her down on my dick. "Ride that shit until I ain't pissed no more."

"Umm your wish is my command."

She put her feet flat on the couch and started doing her

thing. I threw my head back and enjoyed the ride. Krista got on my got damn nerves one thing I can say, she made my ass happy in the bedroom.

"What up my brother?" I said as I dapped up Kayson when I walked in the back yard of his crib.

"Not shit, I just wanted to chill and have some fucking fun tonight without the shit."

"Feel ya." I nodded.

"What's up Krista?" Kayson hugged her and she hugged him back.

"Nothing, just chilling." She smiled. Krista was so beautiful, I just wished her personality and attitude matched her beauty.

"Well the girls are at the gazebo if you wanna go chill with them."

"Girls?" She said with a questioning look on her face. "You bringing your hoes around now Kayson?" She laughed and I knew Kayson was about to go in on her. I hated when she did that condescending bullshit.

"First off Jenacia is not a hoe, that's about to be my lady and if ain't no one here calling you out yo' name then I suggest you show the same respect." Kayson said with a straight face and a calm tone which let me know he pulled back out of respect for me. "Bruh I'm going over to the grill."

"I didn't me—" Krista started but Kayson just continued to walk away. Krista smacked her lips. "Tuh! That was rude."

"No, what you said was rude as fuck and if this is how you gone act we can leave right now." I said getting pissed all over again. "Why the fuck you think don't nobody like being around yo' stuck up ass. This is why the fuck I don't invite you to go anywhere."

"Jaako?" She whined like that was gonna make me take back anything I said.

"Nah fuck that, I meant what I said. Let me know now what you wanna do cause I can drop you back off at home." I gave her a look that told her that I meant business.

"I'll go talk to these girls." She said in a way that let me know that she thought that she was better than they were.

"I'm telling you now, if you show yo' ass I'ma show mine just so you know."

I walked off and went to join Kayson and Omari at the grill. I didn't see Denari so I take it that he wasn't invited and I was okay with that. Kayson had some big ass steaks on the grill with some ribs and chicken. My brother could throw down on the grill, his ass watched that Grill Masters show that comes on TV. Always talking about going on that shit. I told his ass they don't let real thugs on TV unless it was The First 48 and they asses was going to jail. He laughed and told me that he was gonna get on there.

"Yo the fuck wrong with that bitch bruh." Kayson said still pissed. "No disrespect, I ain't mean to call her a bitch but damn the fuck is her problem?"

"She thinks she run shit and the world owe her ass something and that's the furthest thing from the truth. Hell I wasn't gonna tell her, I was gonna invite Yameka instead."

"About that," Kayson said and looked at me and then turned his head with a smirk on his face. "I went to pay her today and kinda told her we were chilling tonight and she said that her and her receptionist Lisa was gone stop by."

"The fuck Kayson." Omari laughed. "When the fuck you was gonna tell me."

"Hell, I didn't know you were bringing the wicked witch of the fucking west with you. I was praying you were gone leave her ass at home."

Before I could say anything, Yameka sexy ass came walking through the door. My mouth dropped because I was so used to seeing her in her business attire but tonight she was dressed in a short ass purple looking t-shirt dress with some sandals that were flat but laced all the way up her chocolate legs. My dick immediately sprang into action and I guess she saw it because she started laughing when she approached.

"You are horrible, you know that?" She said as she hugged me and I inhaled her scent. I could smell that Coco Chanel perfume every day.

"You look and smell so damn good Yameka, why the fuck you out here like that?" I said still holding on to her.

"Um well you may wanna let me go Jaako, because someone is headed this way and she doesn't look too happy." I could sense the humor in her voice so I knew exactly who she was talking about. The smile on her face made what was about to happen a little better.

"Hey, how are you? I'm Jaako's girlfriend Krista." She latched on to my arm and stared at Yameka like she was supposed to be scared, Yameka just laughed.

"Okay and I'm Yameka, Jaakoooooooo—"

"Soon to be wife." Kayson said under his breath but I heard exactly what he said and I gave him the evil eye and he shrugged his shoulders.

"Yameka is a friend," I paused and looked at her. "And our lawyer."

"Ummmhummm." Krista said. "You know what I don't feel so well, I'm ready to go." That shit was music to my ears.

"Aight I can take you home." I hurried up and said which caused everyone standing there to laugh.

"Thanks for the invite Kayson, y'all know Lisa." Lisa waved at everyone.

"Yameka, the girls are at the gazebo if you want to go hang out with them."

"Yes, I would love that." She smiled and I knew right then that she is who I wanted to be with. "I'll see ya later." She said when she walked by me. I watched as she put an extra swing in her hips.

"I'm ready to go! NOW!"

"What the fuck I tell you about that shit Krista," I yelled and looked at her.

"Oh shit, look at bruh." I heard Omari say but I ignored him.

"Let's go so I can get you home." I said and headed toward the gate. "I'll be back bruh."

"What do you mean you'll be back?" Krista said with a shocked expression. "I said I was ready to go home."

"I heard you the first three fucking times you've said it. I said that I would take you home and that's what the fuck I plan to do, but that don't mean I'm staying at home with yo' ass." I said and she furrowed her brows. "Oh shit, that's what you thought? Fuck no." I shook my head. "Just because you got threatened because Yameka walked up don't mean shit to me. I'm good."

"Well I'm staying too."

I shrugged my shoulders. "That's on you but you ain't gone sit here and get on my got damn nerves either." At this point I was being mean in hopes that she would leave, I wanted to spend time with Yameka and I was going to whether she was there or not.

She just looked at me and went and sat on the patio by herself and pulled her phone out. I shrugged my shoulders and turned my attention to my brothers.

"Nigga you wild." Kayson said.

"What the fuck ever, she gets on my got damn nerves I should have left her ass at home."

"I don't like her sneaky ass." Omari said like he knew something that I didn't.

"Damn bruh is there something I should know?"

"Nah it's just something about her that I don't like."

"You don't like no damn body nigga." I laughed.

"True." He took a sip of his beer and looked over to where the girls were. "I like her pretty ass though."

"Nigga I bet you do." Kayson said.

"What's up with you and Jenacia?" I asked out of curiosity.

"I cut off my last bitch the other day," I looked at him like he had sprouted twenty heads. "The only one having a hard time is Brayla's ass, but I knew that shit was gonna happen."

"So, you trying to make it right?" He nodded his head.

"I'll be damned if I sit back and watch my woman dance off into the sunset with another man." He sounded serious as hell. "What's that shit you always saying, life is too short." I nodded. "Life is too short to be anything but happy and Jenacia's it for me. I think I'm ready."

Damn my brother sounded like he ready to chill out and do right by sis. That nigga growing the fuck up. I told his punk ass a long time ago to get his shit together, but I'm glad he listening to me now.

"I guess it's my turn to make my move then, huh?"

"Nigga, Krista gonna lose her fucking shit you go over there."

"Oh well she should have taken her ass home." I laughed and headed in the direction of where Yameka was sitting with the other girls.

I knew going over here was probably gonna start some shit, but at this point I didn't care. Just like Kayson said, "Life is too short to be anything but happy," Krista wasn't that for me. Her ass was a got damn headache. The proper thing to do is break up with Krista and then pursue Yameka, but I couldn't chance that. I knew it was wrong but I just couldn't be alone.

"If looks could kill, we would both be two dead niggas out here." Yameka smirked as I reached where they were sitting.

"She'll be okay."

"I don't think so Jaako; if I was her I would be mad too." Yameka shrugged her shoulders. "I didn't come here to have to beat a bitch's ass. I got way too much to lose." She gave me that keep that bitch under control look.

"You know I wouldn't let no shit like that happen."

I would never put Yameka in a position to jeopardize her career, that was the one thing that I loved about her. She was self-sufficient; she didn't need me for anything. She had her own shit going for her. Unlike Krista who use to be a dancer before we met, once she got with me all her dreams and aspirations just went away.

"You're looking good tonight." I complimented.

"You looking damn good yourself." The smirk on her face let me know that she was thinking the same thing I was thinking. I was damn sure gonna find a way to get the hell away from Krista tonight so I can dive into some of that goodness.

"Jaako, I don't think I've ever seen you like this in the what, six or seven years I've known you." Jenacia's smart ass butted in.

"Shut up sis and mind ya business."

She laughed, "I'm just saying, whatever you doing keep it up I like this on him." Her and Yameka high fived. "Hell, he been with that thing how long?" I rolled my eyes. "And this is the first time I've ever met her and I'm like a permanent fixture in the Barnes Brothers' life." She smirked.

"Yo Kayson!" I yelled.

"The fuck you want Jaako?"

"Come get yo' girl, she meddling in grown folks' business." I yelled across the yard and him and Omari laughed.

"Well you should have no business over there to meddle in." Krista said now heading my direction.

"Got damn, why don't she take her aggravating ass home?" I heard Omari say and it caused Krista to stop in her tracks. "You damn sure don't wanna go there with me." Omari threatened and the shocked expression on Krista's face let me know that something wasn't right and my brother knew about it and his ass was gonna tell me. I wasn't gonna go into that shit right now, but I was definitely gonna find out what the fuck was going on.

"Damn y'all just don't invite me nowhere." I turned to see Denari walking out of the back door. "I know I fuck up sometimes but got damn, I'm still yo' brother." He walked over to where Kayson and Omari stood.

"Fuck, let me go diffuse this shit." I looked at Yameka. "Am I seeing you tonight?"

"I don't think that's a question that you should be asking me." she giggled.

"That's all I needed to hear, I'll be back." I heard all of them giggle.

I walked back over toward the grill, passing a shocked and very uncomfortable Krista. I stopped and looked at her.

"The fuck going on?"

"Huh? Nothing, I just wanna know what you over there talking about with that bitch."

"Nah, I heard what O said to you and the minute D walked in you got real uncomfortable. Is there something I should know?"

She gave me that "I can't believe you would ask me something like that" look. I shook my head and tried to walk off. My gut was telling me that some shady shit was going on. I always trusted my gut, it had gotten me out of some sticky situations. I looked between her and my brother who was standing over there with a smirk on his face.

"Aye D, you fucking Krista?" I asked flat out because there was no need in beating around the bush.

"Oh my God, Jaako how dare you do that to me. Just because you out here trying to wife up the next bitch, don't mean you gotta throw me under the bus. I would never do something like that to you. I love you." She glared at me. "Can you stop looking at me like that?"

"Something ain't right and if I find out you fucking my brother I promise on everything you gonna regret that shit." I pointed at her. "Why don't you just go?"

"I'm not going anywhere without you."

"Yeah the hell you are because right now you about to piss me off and I want to have a good time tonight."

"All because you think I'm fucking yo' brother? Come on

Jaako, I think it's just your guilty conscience. I would never do no disloyal shit like that." I looked at her and walked off. Part of me wanted to believe her but her body language was telling a different story. I wanted to know what was up and I knew Denari wasn't gone sugarcoat shit.

"Bruh what's good."

"I'on know, sound like you tripping though. You know I ain't smashing her aggravating ass." Denari laughed but the look on Omari's face told a different story.

"I'm going to holla at Zemia." Omari said and walked off.

"The fuck wrong with him?" Kayson asked oblivious to all the shit going on around him. "Food almost done and we can eat, a nigga about to starve."

I looked at Denari and then back over at Krista who was standing in the middle of the yard with her arms folded. I didn't know what to believe but I notice everything and that shit didn't sit right with me. If they weren't fucking some other shit was going on and I was damn sure gonna find out what it was. One thing that I did know was that Omari knew whatever the fuck was brewing and he was gonna tell me whether he liked it or not.

Chapter Twelve
KAYSON

Everybody thought I wasn't paying any attention to what the fuck was going on but I was. I heard what the fuck Omari said and I saw what the fuck happened when Denari came in. I just didn't want to believe that my brother would be that fucking grimy. I knew he was a fuck up but got damn he wouldn't do that shit with his brother's girl, right? I mean we all knew that Jaako was secretly in love with our lawyer, Yameka but still him and Krista lived together.

"D, tell me you wouldn't do that?" I said when me and him was alone.

"Nigga, why y'all always on my case?" He whined like normal.

"Just answer the question." I was firm; he knew he could get by with that deflecting shit with the other two but not me.

"Man, I'm out of here." He said and walked in the house.

That right there let me know that it was true. He could lie to Jaako and Omari but he knew I would know which is why he left. How fucked up could you get, it wasn't like they just met a while ago they been at it for a minute so at that point it's just disrespectful. I was getting heated just thinking about it. I noticed Krista walking over and I had to get away from her because I wouldn't be able to hold my tongue.

"Is the food ready? I'm hungry and ready to go." Her attitude was the worst and to know that her nasty ass was fucking brothers, just turned my got damn stomach.

"It will be." Was all I said because any more conversation would warrant me to cuss her ass out and I didn't want to do that out of respect for Jaako. I looked around for him and I didn't see him, he must have gone in the house.

"You know I love your brother right?" Why couldn't she just leave well enough alone?

"Yo get away from me with all that shit."

"I didn't sleep with Denari; Jaako is just trying to justify pining over that woman all night."

"I'm a good judge of character usually and I know when someone is lying, just like when I asked Denari was it true and he got mad and left. You are just trying to find someone else to put the spot light on because you're guilty. I don't like you and if you are fucking both of my brothers, you are about to be in for a rude awakening." With that I took the last rib off the grill and walked in the house.

I let everyone know that the food was done and they

could eat. Everyone ate and we chilled for a little and then everyone left, I swear I was ready for everyone to leave. After that whole shit, I wasn't in the mood to be around anybody. Brayla's dumb ass kept calling my phone further pissing me off, hell she was calling right now.

"The fuck you want Brayla?"

"Why you answering the phone like that Kayson?"

"Because I don't know what the fuck you keep calling me for."

"So I can't call you now?"

"What the fuck." I took a deep breath. "No, that was the whole point of me coming by your house the other day to tell you that I had somebody in my life and I was trying to make it work with them. What part of that didn't you understand?"

"You can still have friends Kayson," she whined.

"No Brayla I can't, not ones I used to fuck."

"You are just talking to me like I wasn't anything to you." She sounded like she was starting to get teary eyed.

"You were a nut, the fuck?"

"We've been doing this for over a year and that's all I was."

"Uhhh yeah." I didn't know what else to say because she knew already what it was. I didn't want shit to do with her outside of a good fuck and she was good at that. "You act like I didn't tell you that I would never be with you."

"Yeah yeah because you waiting on that bitch." She said and I got pissed. I didn't even notice that Jenacia had come into the kitchen, she leaned over my shoulder. I'm sure she heard what Brayla said because she was on speaker. I just hung up the phone there was no need to keep arguing with her over something that was irrelevant. Either way I would never be with her and I was gonna be with Jen.

"So, did you mean that?" Jenacia asked me.

"Are you ready for that?"

"No Kayson the question is are you ready for that?" She came around from behind me and faced me. "I can't take being hurt by you again, so if you don't feel like you can handle this then let's just keep it how it is."

I smiled because her little ass was always trying to boss up on somebody. "I let all my hoes go so I need you to get yo' shit together so my nigga don't get lonely." I nodded toward my dick.

"Nah nigga we gotta date first." She smiled.

"And that's fine."

"So, no fucking for 90 days."

"You out yo' rabbit ass mind if you think I'm waiting 90 days to fuck." I gave her that nigga please look. "You better be glad if I wait 90 more minutes, I got half the mind to throw yo' ass on the island and make shit official." I was serious as fuck and she was laughing.

"Seriously though, I love you and I always have but my heart can't take another hit from you."

"I've thought about this for years. I wanted to make sure that I was ready before I stepped to you, because I knew what was on the line. When you moved in here and seeing you here every day, I swear that shit was confirmation like a muthafucka. Like I don't know what the fuck I would do if you weren't here with me. It's like I need you here and that's some real shit. I ain't never needed no one but my brothers." That was from the heart. "I love you Jenacia and I always have. I just wasn't sure how to show it and I still don't, but I'm willing to put my all in it."

"Like I've said before, I don't want you to be perfect. I know you won't be and hell I won't either, but I do want you to be loyal. I ain't with the community dick, I'm just saying." She said with her hands on her hips. "Just promise me that I will have all of you, I know I got your heart but I want all of you and I refuse to share."

"Selfish ass."

"You damn right, hell I earned my position in your life now it's time for you to earn yours in mine." She pointed her finger in my chest.

I stood and picked her little ass up and put her on the island. I opened her legs and stood in between them. I hadn't been this close to her since that slip up that we had a year or so back. I leaned in and kissed her; she grabbed the back of my head and deepened the kiss. I don't even know how to explain the feeling it gave me, I just know it felt right. She broke away from me.

"Please don't fuck this up." She said and I could feel the pain that I caused her so many years ago in those five words.

"Damn Jen, don't fucking count me out already." I mugged her playfully. "Give a nigga a chance."

"Shut up, you know what I'm saying."

"No, you shut up and give ya man a kiss."

"My man?" S,he smiled.

"What the fuck you think this is Jenacia? Some boyfriend girlfriend type shit? We grown as fuck yo."

"I hate you sometimes."

"Oh yeah show me how much you hate me." I winked and went back in for a kiss. We were about to consummate this relationship, right here in my got damn kitchen.

Her ass was trying to be all conservative with the kissing, hell I was a nasty nigga and she knew that shit. I took my tongue and parted her lips with it and got into that shit. I wanted her to feel what she meant to me. I wanted to show her, not just tell her.

I grabbed the helm of her tank top and pulled it over her head; she didn't have on a bra. I took her nipple in between my thumb and forefinger and rolled it around until it was nice and hard, just like I liked them. A small moan escaped her lips, I broke the kiss and lowered my head to her nipple and took it into my mouth and licked and sucked until her head fell back. Then I switched to the other one and showed it just as much attention.

"Ummm," she moaned. That shit was sexy and had my shit on brick.

I reached for the waist band of her shorts but her ass was to into what I was doing to her fucking titties to raise up so I could show her what else this tongue could do. I lightly bit down on her nipple, "Raise up." I said with it still between my teeth. She lifted her hips so I could slide off her shorts.

"That's what I wanted to see." I let go of her nipple and pushed her legs open. "Damn Jen." I smirked.

"I can't help it." She bit her bottom lip and smiled at me. Her pussy was so pretty, not a strand of hair in site and it wasn't all worn looking and shit. You know when a bitch been through it and her shit just lay open, nah baby girl shit was snatched and I loved it.

I attacked her lips again as I ran my thumb across her clit and down her center. She was wet as hell, I had to force myself not to just pull out and dive head first. I wanted to show her some things but her pussy was calling me something serious.

"Got damn I missed you." I said against her lips. "You gonna feed ya man?" I smirked and she nodded with her bottom lip tucked between her teeth. I took her by her shoulder and pushed back until her back was flat against the island. I grabbed the stool and positioned myself right between her legs like I was really about to have a damn meal. I leaned down and licked from her opening to her clit, nice and slow.

"Sssss shit." Her legs shook with excitement and that made me excited.

I twirled my tongue around her clit a few times and then sucked and she started moaning like crazy. After attacking her clit, I licked down to her center and moved my tongue in and out of her skillfully, slurping, sucking and licking. I replaced my tongue with two fingers and went back to my favorite place, her clit.

"Oh dear God." She cried out as I sucked on her clit and moved my fingers in the come here motion. "Shit Kayson you gonna make me cum."

"Umm hum." Was all I could say in my current state. I continued to work my magic until she started to throw her pussy in my face. I knew she was on the verge of cumming, and I wanted to get everything I could out of her. I stood up and dove all the way in.

"Oh oh yeah shit fuck baby I'm about to cum." She moaned out loud as hell. "Uhhhhhh," she moaned as she released into my mouth. I made sure to lick all of it up. Her little ass was spent but I didn't care I was just getting started. "Oh my God baby." She had her arms crossed over her eyes.

"Don't tap out on me." I said and she peeked from under her arms, I could see the smirk that was plastered on her face. "I got so much more in store for you tonight." I worked my way out of my ball shorts and tank. I stood there and admired her sexy ass naked body. I was a lucky muthafucka and I needed to make sure I didn't fuck up.

I put my dick at her opening and I could already tell it was gonna be a got damn struggle. I slid in nice and slow not wanting to hurt her. My thumb found her clit again to take her mind off any pain she may be feeling. She raised up and looked at me as if I was doing something wrong.

"I ain't no virgin baby." She smirked and I rammed my dick in her and she cried out. "Ohhh shit."

"You shouldn't have been talking shit." I chuckled.

"I forgot how big you were for a second."

"Clearly." We both laughed and I looked into her eyes as I moved my hips in a circular motion to stretch her out a little. Once I was in comfortably I started making love to her. Long, slow strokes that were driving her ass crazy and me too.

We stayed that way for about a half an hour before I came all inside her. I knew we didn't use a condom and we probably needed to be more careful next time, but tonight I didn't give a shit about any of that. I just wanted to make love to my woman and that's what I did. After the round in the kitchen, I carried her upstairs where we fucked in every position possible. If I wasn't sure before, this shit confirmed it, no doubt. Jenacia was my woman and there was nothing else left to be said about it.

Chapter Thirteen
OMARI

I swear I hated that nasty ass hoe, she was just fucking disgusting. Sitting up there making demands and she fucking brothers. I wanted to tell Jaako so bad that he should just go ahead and do what the fuck he wanted to do because her hoe ass was. She knew not to challenge me. The only thing holding me back from blowing up her spot was the fact that I didn't want to betray Denari, other than that everyone would have known what a slut she was.

I was so pissed at Denari for even putting me in the situation, while he sat unbothered. His ass didn't even give a fuck and I bet money on anything that he was still gone fuck her but just be more discreet about it. I wasn't believing all that bullshit about that being the last time, if I knew my brother he would be banging her ass out later tonight.

"Penny for your thoughts?" Zemia's sweet voice resonated through my E-Class Benz Coupe, for a second I was so lost in my thoughts that I had forgotten that I wasn't alone.

"Nothing to worry your pretty little head about." I glanced at her and then back at the road. I had volunteered to take her home after the cookout so that I could get to know her better but here my thoughts were consumed by my brother and my other brother's trifling ass bitch.

"I can't tell," she chuckled. "Whatever it is, it's got your face over there going through the motions." I had to laugh because Ma always told me that I wear my expressions on my face. It didn't matter what came out of my mouth but whatever I felt showed on my face.

"Whatever man." I laughed. I didn't know what it was about her but I felt comfortable around her. I didn't really trust people but with Zemia it was different and I hadn't even known her long. I wouldn't say she was the one and all that hoopla but she definitely had potential. I just needed to know more. "I'm not ready to go home yet, have a drink with me?"

"You promise to be on your best behavior?" I could see her staring at me out of the corner of her eye.

"Scouts honor."

"I don't know you well Mr. Barnes but I can almost bet my life savings that you are far from a boy scout."

"You have no idea beautiful."

I turned on to Caswell Dr. and pulled up to this little nice spot that I frequent. A little Irish pub that sold some banging ass food. They had a nice ass outside bar and sitting area and I couldn't think of a better place to take her to have a nice little convo.

"What you know about Kennedy's?" She said looking at me and smiling.

"Shit this my spot, I come here to chill when I need to just chill and clear my head. It's cool here and the women ain't thirsty." I chuckled. "So I can just relax and get my drink on."

"Maybe if you weren't so damn cute you wouldn't have to worry about all of that."

"Are you flirting with me missy." I pointed my finger at her. "I only give one warning, do that shit at your own risk."

"Duly noted." She laughed and opened her door.

We walked in and I went straight outside to the patio. It was end of May so it was kinda warm out. The tiki torches were lit and soft music played, there was just enough people there to set the mood for a bar scene but not enough to overwhelm you. The waitress walked over to get our drink orders.

"I'll have a whisky sour please." Zemia requested.

"A what?" I snarled my nose at her. "What the hell is that shit?"

"It's good you should try it." She smiled at me. "Make that two please." She told the waitress and I mugged her beautiful ass.

"How you know I'ma like that shit? It sounds weird as fuck." I wasn't a person to try new things. I liked to stick to my regular, which was Crown straight, no chaser. All my brothers drank Crown but Denari's ass was a gin drinker through and through.

"If you don't like it then I'll drink it and that round will be my treat."

"Ahhh shit look at you, trying to boss up and shit. Deal." Not that I would ever let her pay for anything while she was with me, that wasn't even my style. Even though I dibbled and dabbled with quite a few different women, Ann Barnes taught me how to treat them when they were in my presence.

The drinks came and I actually liked the whisky sour shit, for some reason I thought that it would be some sweet shit even though the name was whiskey sour. I guess she proved me wrong. We sat and made small talk until she brought up the tension at the house.

"Now stop stalling and tell me what had your mind in a frenzy."

"You nosy as fuck yo."

"Duh, you'll learn me." She smiled and I swear that shit made my heart jump. *Chill muthafucka we don't do this shit*, I coached myself. I had a feeling that she was asking from a genuine place, I just needed to decide just how much I was going to tell her.

"Have you even been put in a position where no matter what you do you will be betraying someone you love?" Staring her in her eyes, I could tell that she was really thinking about what I asked her. For a second there, I thought I saw a glimmer of sadness.

"To be honest, yes I have but I had to do the right thing so that I could sleep at night." She gave me a half smile.

"Care to elaborate." She laughed. "What's so funny?"

"It's just weird to hear you say that."

"What? Elaborate?" I furrowed my brows. "I'm a street nigga, not a dumb one."

"I wasn't saying that, you just so hard and it was weird to hear you say it that's all." *Shit I got something hard for you alright*, I thought.

"Hmmmhummm" I rolled my eyes in the top of my head mimicking a woman that thinks you're lying.

"Seriously." She smiled then got serious. "I had to tell my mom that my dad was taking me with him to see his mistress when I was 12."

That shit shocked the shit out of me, hell I spit my drink out. What kind of man takes a 12-year-old out to meet another bitch? I wanna beat her daddy's got damn ass and I don't even know the man.

"Yep." She nodded her head. "Told me that she was just a friend and that they needed to talk about some stuff in the room. I didn't know who the hell he thought he was talking to because I knew when I heard the moans and shit that they were doing more than talking." She shook her head and I could still see the hurt in her eyes. "He made me promise not to ever tell my mother. Said that if I did I would be the reason that our family broke up. I held that secret in for about a year. It destroyed my little 12-year-old heart until I couldn't take the guilt anymore. My mother was the sweetest woman in the world and didn't deserve what he was doing to her. After talking with my grandmother about it she explained to me that what my dad was doing was wrong, she encouraged me to tell my mother and I did."

"Damn that's some deep shit."

"Yeah but it honestly worked out for the best, the day I told my mom she went over there and caught them, left his cheating ass and found her a new man that loves her to death." She smiled. "The only thing that sucked was that my dad was pissed at me for telling it and refused to have anything to do with me, I hadn't seen him since the day he came and picked up his things."

"That's some punk ass coward shit."

"At first I was sad about it, but my step dad is an amazing man. When him and my mom got married, my dad signed his rights over and Justin Femster adopted me and gave me and my mom the best life ever."

I sat there and looked at her as she tried to mask the hurt that her dad caused. Even though she had a good life there was nothing like the love of the parent that created you. I could relate with her right there. I love Ma and what she did for me and my brothers, I appreciated the life that she gave us but in the back of my mind I can't help but to yearn for the love of my birth mother and even the bastard that killed her.

"Our scars show where we've been, not where we're going." I said remembering that's what Ma use to tell us when we first got with her. I remembered that and I even have it tatted on my calf.

"I like that."

"Ma always use to tell us that when we would act out because of what happened to our birth mother."

"What happened?"

"That's some sad shit and I really ain't trying to be crying and shit in front of you so if you don't mind can we save that for another time?" I asked lowering my head into my hands trying to wash the thoughts away.

I never understood how some people could just bury shit like that in their minds. I couldn't, I thought about that shit at least once a day which is one of the reasons I stayed either high or drunk.

"Of course," she reached out and touched my hand and the electricity that flowed through that one touch caused me to shiver. She laughed. "I seem to have that effect on guys." I looked up and she was pretending to be checking out her nails. I threw her a bird and we laughed.

We got to know each other a little better, she told me that she had a little brother that had been getting into some trouble, and he was in juvie now but was soon to get out. The way she talked about him let me know that she loved him like I loved my brothers. The more she talked the more I was starting to feel her and that shit was scaring me. I was telling her shit that no one knew, hell not even my brothers.

We talked about our exes, well her punk ass ex and my situationships. She thought that it was funny that I called them that but that's all I knew. They damn sure wasn't no relationships, hell I hated all them broads. I was just around for the fuck.

She didn't judge how I lived my life. The one thing that I didn't do was lie, I hated to lie which was why this shit with Denari was fucking me up so bad. I told Zemia what I was about and that it wouldn't change until I found someone that could change that. She told me that she understood and that she was working on her career and wasn't looking for anything serious, just a friend. I was gonna rock with that but something was telling me that it wouldn't last long, the attraction was there no doubt.

Our conversation just flowed; it was like talking to a friend that I've known for years. Hell, we were so into our conversation that I didn't even notice that someone had joined us at the table. I looked up at the chick and tried to remember if I knew her or not and nothing rang a bell. She wasn't my type anyway. She was super skinny and was dark skin with crossed eyes. I wasn't a superficial nigga or nothing like that but I did care about what I stuck my dick in.

"Can we help you?" Zemia asked with a questioning look on her face.

"You can't." The cross eyed girl rolled her eyes. "Well hello Omari."

"Hey?" I questioned. The bitch knew my name so now I was really confused. I swear I didn't know her and there was no way that anyone was going to tell me that I did.

"How have you been? Long time no hear or see." She looked in my direction but her eyes were crossed so I couldn't tell if she was looking at me or not.

"I know you?"

"Really Omari, yes you know me." She raised her voice which was the wrong answer because I didn't like scenes. "You know all of me and quite well I might add."

My facial expression had to be on ten because I was shocked as hell, I always remember who the fuck I slept with.

"I fucked you?" I put my hand over my mouth.

"Yes you did." She put her glasses that I didn't notice were in her hand until that moment on and put her hands on her hips. "Better?"

Hell no that shit wasn't better. "You sure I fucked you?"

"YES! Omari!"

"Nah, I'ma need some receipts cause I don't believe that shit. You got me fucked up this some kind of fucking joke, where the fuck my brothers at I'm getting punked."

"Really?" She snatched her glassed back off. "So you one of them niggas huh? Wanna hit it and then pretend I ain't shit." She yelled quite loud and she was starting to piss me the fuck off and I was trying my best to keep my cool.

"First off calm the fuck down because I ain't disrespect—"

"YOU ARE DISRESPECTING ME, I THOUGHT WE WERE GONNA HAVE SOMETHING!" She went off on this tangent and I just kinda looked at her like she was crazy. The antics were drawing a little crowd and I had to take a few deep breaths. I looked over at Zemia and mouthed the words sorry, she had to cover her mouth to keep from laughing but she got it together enough to tell me that it was okay. "YOU ONLY DOING THIS BECAUSE OF THAT BITCH!" That was it, she had just went too far. I slammed my hands down on the table.

"You looka here you cock eyed bitch, I don't remember fucking you and that's all there is to it and if I did I was drunk out of my fucking mind. I would never touch yo' ugly ass knowingly. Now you got one of two choices, you can stay here and keep pissing me off and end up floating in Lake Norman or you can keep it pushing and go on about your business. Your choice and you got about a second to make up your mind."

"Tuh!" She said before she turned on her heels and left. I just so happened to look down at her feet and I could see the dead skin flying off the back. What kind of shit is that?

"So Omari," Zemia said holding in her laughter. "The least you can do is take yo' situationships to get a damn pedicure." She busted out laughing and caused the table over from ours to laugh too.

"Ha fucking ha."

I shook my head still trying to wreck my brain, is there any way that I could have slept with—oh shit. I put my hand over my mouth. That's the bitch that Denari brought with him in the trap with ol' girl he was fucking from the Ford. I was fucked up and laying across the couch that night, hell I thought I was sleep when I noticed the bitch sucking the meat off my shit. I never looked at her because after that I bent her ass over the coffee table, strapped up and fucked the shit out of here and then went upstairs and passed the fuck out. I woke up by my got damn self so I thought that shit was a dream.

That night I drank damn near a whole fifth of Crown Apple by my got damn self and faced like two blunts from what I remember, it could have been more. So what ever happened don't even fucking count.

"Ewwww you fucked her, didn't you?" Zemia joked.

"I can't stand yo' ass, let's go man."

"Not until you tell me the truth Mr. I don't lie," The smirk on her face was sexy but I wanted to wipe it off.

"I don't know, I may have shit I get drunk and pass out and bitches take advantage of me." I shrugged. "Hell, if you ask me I didn't give consent so it was rape." I smirked and she busted out laughing.

"Man I can't with you Omari Barnes."

"You better learn too."

I got up so that we could leave, I wasn't exactly ready to take her home but I knew I had shit to do early in the morning. I had a new venture that I wanted to present to my brothers and Uncle Ray and I needed to make sure my shit was straight. I needed to be focus and I couldn't do that with Zemia's fine ass right in front of me. I was damn sure gonna see her again though.

Chapter Fourteen
YAMEKA

Jaako's little bitch was acting up tonight, she better be glad my degree saved her ass because she almost got fucked up because of her mouth. I knew that Jaako was seeing somebody but in my heart of hearts I didn't care. I wanted him but I knew that he was bad for me.

I knew all about the Barnes brothers and the fact that I have been defending their uncle and now them since I got out of law school, allowed me full access to their lives even when I didn't want it.

All four of the brothers were fine as hell but something about Jaako stuck out to me. Maybe it was his hopeless romantic attitude, even if it was just an act I loved it. I damn sure didn't know why he was with a woman like Krista though, that bitch was aggy and I just met her today. She better enjoy Mr. Jaako while she could because I was slowly letting my guard down.

From the moment I met him I knew that he was bad news, but he was the best bad news I had ever come across. I knew that me getting involved with a criminal wasn't a good thing, me being a lawyer and all but I couldn't help it. Just one look into his dreamy eyes erased all the doubt that I could ever have. My only issue right now was that I wanted to make sure that he wasn't about to dog me out like he was doing that Krista bitch. Before I took it there with him I wanted to make sure that he had all of that shit out of his system.

I wasn't that female that would allow him to do what he wanted. If he tried that shit with me I would be gone in a hot second. My phone rung jarring me from my thoughts, and what do you know it was the devil himself.

"Yes Jaako." I said trying to be hard but was smiling ear to ear; he was the only person that could make me feel that way.

"Open the door." I looked at the door as if I would see him standing there.

"You outside?"

"Nah, I just told you to open the door." He chuckled.

"Don't be a smart ass."

I got up and opened my door and there he stood in all his greatness. The gray sweatpants he had on hung slightly off his waist, showing his monster print and the black tank that hugged his chest had me ready to pounce on him. When he hit me with that million dollar smile I couldn't stop my nipples from getting hard as bricks, which he noticed right away. He reached out and pinched my right nipple, "Somebody is happy to see me." He whispered in my ear and my clit jumped.

"Back up homie I don't know where your mouth been." I stepped back to regain some of my personal space and he laughed.

"I know where it ain't been but I know where it's about to go." Fuck I just released a river, I would sure need to go and change my shorts, and they were soaked.

"You need to stop; I'm going to freshen up." I said and tried to take off to the back but he grabbed my arm and pulled me to him right before his hand found the inside of my thigh and made it up to my sacred place and he felt how wet I was.

"No need to change these." He licked his lips. "I'm just gonna fuck them up again." His sexy ass smirked as he moved his dreads from his shoulder to his back with his free hand.

"I hate you."

"This pussy says otherwise."

I tried to move from the hold that he had on my cat but he moved with me so that his hand wouldn't move. I cocked my head to the side, but that didn't move him one way or another. I just bit my lip as his thumb found its way into my shorts.

"Um," I moaned unintentionally.

"You are so fucking wet." He said as he released me and yanked my shorts down.

I was too weak from just the touch of his thumb to

protest so I just went with it. It wasn't like I really had a choice; Jaako had a way with my body that I didn't understand. No man had ever had control over my body like he did and that was dangerous. If I ever opened myself up enough to give him what he wanted, which was my heart, I'd be in a whole heap of shit if he ever broke it and that was my hesitation in the matter.

Once he had my shorts down, he pushed me against the wall by the door and put his knee in between my legs to spread them. His eyes never left mine and that was turning me on even more. He squatted down and placed my right leg on his shoulder and then licked from my slit to my clit and that shit felt good.

"Damn you always taste good."

He put his hand under my ass and threw my left leg on his other shoulder, when I was leveled he grabbed my ass and stood up.

"Jaako baby if you drop me I'm gonna shoot you." I said panting because he was attacking my clit as soon as he had me against the wall and my pussy dead in his face.

"Shut the fuck up and enjoy this fucking ride."

I looked down at him and he was looking dead at me with his tongue out and going to work. I bit my bottom lip and rested my head against the wall and enjoyed the powerful tongue lashing I was getting.

All you could hear throughout the whole room was smacking and slurping. I was about to cum off the sounds he was making alone. I swear this man was gifted. I loved that he liked to take his time with me and wasn't in to all that hardcore shit. I don't like to be slapped and all that, with my attitude I was liable to hit yo ass back in the heat of the moment.

"Fuck Jaako." I moaned on the brink of releasing buckets into his mouth.

"Feed daddy."

"Oh shit."

"Umhmmm." He said with a mouth full of pussy.

"Yesss yesssss right there. Oh God yess." I grabbed the back of his head and held in place until I released everything that I had built up from the moment he walked through the door. My legs were shaking and my chest was heaving up and down.

I could still feel him blowing and licking on my cat well after I came but I didn't have the energy to push him away.

"Give me one more."

"I can't." I panted.

"I think you can." He sucked down on my pussy; I was still sensitive so it didn't take long for him to take me there again. After that second orgasm I was through. I hoped like hell that he didn't expect me to return the favor because I couldn't, at least right now.

Jaako knew exactly what he did to me so he held on tight and carried me to my bedroom. He laid me softly on the bed and just stared at me.

"When are you gonna stop playing games with me?"

"When you get yourself together Jaako, I'm not about to be doing this back and forth with you and your girlfriend. If and when we get together, I want her out of your system completely. It's not gonna be some you jump right out of her bed to come live in mine. No I don't play that; you need to get her completely out of your life before you take it there with me."

"Me and Krista has been over for quite some time now." He tried to reason with me but I wasn't having that shit.

"But you still laying up with her and living with her. I'm not dealing with that Jaako." I tried to sit up but had to give myself a second because I was still weak. "You have the power to hurt me like no man has ever hurt me and until I am one hundred percent sure that you won't, I gotta protect me." I tried to read his eyes but I couldn't they were blank. I had a feeling that things were about to go left.

"I think I love you too." Was all he said before he laid down beside me on the bed and turned me where we could spoon.

The sounds of our breathing filled the room; his hands did most of the talking as he explored my body with them.

"I've always been so scared of being alone." Jaako said breaking the silence.

I knew what happened to his parents and I understand what was going through his mind but being with someone was not fair to him or her. He needed to get over that and get comfortable with himself if he plans on having a future with me. I wanted to tell him that but I needed to find a good way to say it and not be a bitch about it. But before I could say anything he finished.

"I know that's not an excuse and I know that to be with the woman who's in here." I could hear him tapping his chest. "I gotta come to grips with that shit and do what I need to do. I just ask that you be patient with me."

"As long as when you said patient you mean that you are getting your ducks in a row and you're not still trying to play house with the both of us. I need to know you're serious and until then things will remain how they are." I warned and he knew that I meant that I would continue to date, something that he hated. "I'm not built to be a side chick, I know what we're doing isn't right and I never meant to fall for you, but I did and there is nothing I can do about that now. Just know that if I find out you playing me, I'm out."

He didn't say anything else he just lifted my leg and slid into me from behind. I guess that was his way for telling me that he understood. I let a moan escape my lips and enjoyed the rest of the night with the man that lived in my heart but didn't yet have the key.

Chapter Fifteen
UNCLE RAY

I had been in the game since I was a little nigga, I was getting tired of the shit and I was ready to turn this shit over to my nephews. They were really doing the damn thing in the streets but they still had some work to do. I was not about to hand them over "the world" just for them to fuck it up.

I wanted them to work for this shit and show me what they were made of. Like today, Omari hit me up about a new business venture that he heard about that was sure to make us a lot of money. I also needed to tell them that we hit a snag and they was gone have to step up a little more.

I was okay with Jaako, Kayson and Omari; it was Denari that I was worried about. He wasn't even able to handle running a fucking trap house. I was trying to find something that was impossible for him to fuck up but I didn't feel like babying his ass.

"Raymond." I heard my sister Ann call out.

"I'm down here in the basement."

I waited until I heard her coming down the stairs. My sister was heaven sent. She was the only woman that I know that would take in four bad ass boys and raise them as her own. I loved her for it, one of the boys was closer to me than anyone knew but that was something that I would be taking to the grave. The only person that knew was Ann and I'm sure that she was coming to talk to me about it right now. Ever since she saw that DNA test that I had done years ago, she's been on my ass about telling him.

"What's up sis?" I asked when she reached the bottom of the stairs.

"You already know why I'm here." I sighed deeply. "That boy needs to know that he has family out here."

"He already knows he has family, we're his family whether he knows it's by blood or not. I don't understand why this has to be an issue. Just leave well enough alone."

"You're just afraid of what he will think of you."

I didn't say anything because she was right. I was worried about what he would think. I mean if I had a father out there that knew about me and didn't say anything I would take that personally. He looked up to me right now and I needed it to stay like that because when the respect is gone, so is everything else.

"You know how it is in this game, right now I need him to

be focused and not at odds with me. When everything is set into play and they are going good, then I'll tell him aight?"

"Raymond don't give me that slick shit, save that for them hoes out there." She pointed to the window. "You will not have me lying to my boys."

"I know but we gotta keep things how they are until we get shit right in these streets."

"Y'all shouldn't be in these streets, hell I raised all y'all different."

"How you raised me and we only ten years apart." I asked laughing.

"Because our mama wasn't shit and I had to do what I had to do for you that's why, so shut up."

My sister was turning 50 this year but she didn't look a day over 30, she made sure to take care of herself. She always said that she didn't want her boys to have to bury her. She worked out and ate right, and she worked at the children's hospital at CMC hospital.

"You better be watching my boys out in these streets." She warned me.

She already knew that I was, I couldn't let anything happen to them or she would surely take my life. Ann never wanted any of us in the streets but I had to do what I had to do. School wasn't for a nigga like me, I was street through and through. I tried the college thing, I went to North Carolina Central and played basketball but the streets had a hold on me. I got up there and got to hanging around these crazy ass white boys who introduced me to selling that "white girl" aka cocaine. Once that money started coming in, I was over school and ended up going home and hooking up with my partner and the rest is history.

In my defense, I did try and keep the boys in school and on the straight and narrow. I made sure that they had everything they wanted even after they got out of high school. I encouraged them to get out and open some businesses that I would invest in and get them started. Kayson tried it with a car wash and it did well, but like me he was a street nigga, through and through.

Even though we tried to keep them away they still gravitated toward it. Omari and Denari hooked up with some gang and started doing dumb shit that got them both locked up until their 18th birthdays. My sister was devastated, Jaako was the only one who didn't care about the streets as much as the other ones or so we thought. Jaako was arrested for distribution but got off scot free because of an illegal search and seizure. From that point on I knew that it was either put them on with me or let them kill themselves or end up six feet under.

I talked to my sister about it and it took some convincing but she finally understood where I was coming from. When I told them what was up they were happy as hell, even when I told them that they had to work their way to the top. Now here we are, I was waiting on them to come bring me a new venture that could make us all some money.

"Ann, you already know what would have happened if I wouldn't have taken them under my wing."

"Whatever Ray." She waved me off.

"Get yo' stubborn ass on up out of here." I laughed and she flipped me off.

"I'm going to be gone late, I gotta program at church."

"Down here doing all that cussing now you going to praise the Lord." I shook my head and she turned around and glared at me.

"The Lawd knows he's not done with me yet."

She turned to leave and I just laughed. That woman was my heart, if anything ever happened to her I don't know what I would do.

I sat back and relaxed on the couch and thought about calling one of my lady friends over but I knew I had to meet with my nephews so instead I just sat back and crossed my feet and turned on some ESPN.

About an hour later I heard the door to the basement open and voices heading down to where I was on the other side of the hospital area that I had set up.

"Unc!" Kayson said as he walked in with a smile on his face.

"The fuck you so happy about?"

"Life man." Was all he said and I left it at that.

"What's up what's up what's up?" Said Omari followed by Jaako who was so into his phone that he didn't even speak.

"Nigga you better say something when you walk in to folk's house." I told him and he looked up and walked over to dap me up.

"My bad Unc, I'm sitting here arguing with this dumb ass girl." He rolled his eyes into his head.

We all just shook our heads because we told him about that Krista girl when he got with her. You know she wasn't no good if Ann Barnes didn't like her and she liked everybody. He wouldn't listen though, he said that she had a good heart and that she wasn't as bad as everyone thought she was. His ass was about to see now though.

"We just waiting on Denari as usual?" I asked and no one answered.

"Let me call him." Omari said in an aggravated tone and then walked over to the other side of the basement.

"I'm sick of him, he's always holding us up. We ain't never gone get nowhere with dead weight."

"That's bruh." Jaako said.

"Don't remind me." That's the one thing I loved about Kayson, he was all about business and he thought that everyone should be like he was when it came down to it and that's not how it is. Everyone does things differently.

"Let's just go on without him, I'll just have to catch him up." Omari said and Kayson started saying shit under his breath. "Bruh just—"

"No stop making excuses for him, I'm sick of us having to pull his got damn weight." Kayson yelled pissed off and I understood they were trying to get somewhere and Denari was holding them back.

The basement door opened and we heard heavy boots coming down and I knew right away it was Denari, he was the only person I knew that wore fucking Timberland boots with fucking shorts.

"Bout got damn time, you need to get your fucking shit together! I'm tired of having to put everything on hold because ya retarded ass can't tell fucking time." Kayson yelled.

"Damn my bad I'm twenty minutes late, hell at least I showed up, right?" He looked around the room for validation but everyone was mugging him instead.

This showed me that what I was about to do was gonna be a good thing for all of them, I think they needed some space from each other before they killed each other.

"Aight my fault, I'ma do better next time." His smart ass smirked.

"Anyway," I interjected. "Omari, you had something you wanted me to hear about."

"Hell yeah," he stepped up. "I was talking to this cat that was telling me about some shit that's crazy and will bring in hella money."

"Talk nigga." I urged.

"So, you know them Vape shits?" I nodded, he was talking about them things that helped muthafucka stop smoking and shit. "Well they make pure THC juice for them now, and old dude told me how to make that shit and I'm telling you we would make a killing off the shit."

"Explain?" Jaako asked.

Omari pulled out one of the Vapes and started to show Jaako what he was talking about. He pulled out the juice that's supposed to go in there for the cigarette smokers and then he pulled out the pure THC.

"Instead of using that flavor shit that goes in there you just use the pure THC. Here hit this shit." He urged Jaako, he grabbed it and hit it and nothing happened and it caused Omari to laugh and Jaako to swing on him. "Nigga you gotta push the fucking button." Jaako tried again and hit that shit hard as hell and I swore I saw his eyes roll in the back of his head.

"Nigga yo, you aight." Kayson spoke up.

"Shiiiiiittttttttttt." Jaako said with his lungs full of smoke then he let a big cloud of smoke out through his mouth and nose then went into a fit of coughing. Once he got his self together he looked at Omari. "That shit is banging muthafucka, you a got damn genius."

"Let me hit that shit." Kayson said and hit it and did the same thing as Jaako, once he was done he just smiled and nodded his head at me.

"So how you get that shit in liquid form."

"One of two ways, we can buy that shit like that already from this nigga I was talking to, or we can extract that shit our self. I would just need somewhere to fucking set up." Omari shrugged his shoulders.

"How that shit sell." Kayson wanted to know.

"You sell it in vials, they come in 5ml, 15ml vials or a 30ml bottle. The shit ain't like rolling a blunt, as soon as the blunt gone you out. You just put drops in the tank of the vape so a 5ml vial will go for like $40 on the street but will last a nigga about 3 or 4 days depending on how much they smoke. Now a 15ml vial will go for $75 and last like a week and a half if the nigga don't share and shit." He laughed. "That got damn 30 will last a nigga fucking two or three weeks, maybe even more." Omari hit the Vape. "The Vapes cost about $90 but they last for fucking ever, I can actually buy them in bulk so we can sell them for less. But once you got the Vape as long as you take care of it and change the coils you good and you just need to buy the juice." He rubbed his hands together.

"You think this shit gonna hit?"

"Hell yeah, it's already big down there in Texas and shit but it's moving its way this way. I'm trying to be the first to have this shit on the market. I mean it ain't gone sell like coke and shit but I bet it pick up fast as hell."

"I think you're right nephew."

I nodded my head and agreed with him. I think this was gonna be a good thing. We needed to get on this shit and fast. I was gonna let Omari take point over this, it was time for all of them to gain some responsibility in the organization because it was time for me to sit back and enjoy the fruits of my labor.

"Aight so I'm splitting y'all up." I said and the only person that objected was Denari and that was because he would now have to pull his own weight.

"Why you wanna do that Unc, shit running smooth as fuck right now."

"You just scared yo' ass gone have to do some got damn work instead of riding our fucking coat tails." Kayson smiled, he loved the idea of not having to deal with Denari and I don't blame him.

"Shut the fuck up Kayson I'm about tired of you and yo' slick ass comments, just because everybody don't live and breathe this shit like you do."

"That's the fucking problem, to be successful in the fucking game you gotta live and breathe the shit. Yo' ass just think shit supposed to be laid at your fucking feet. Lazy ass don't wanna work for shit. What the fuck you gonna do now that you ain't gone have us to lean on?" Kayson prided.

"Fuck you man," was all that Denari could say because he knew that Kayson was right. Kayson was a born leader and it made me smile just to think about it.

"Chill." I broke up their little spat. "Omari, you taking over the operation for the Vape Juice so that's all that you are going to be responsible for, just let me know what you need. Jaako, you gone handle all sales for weed, molly and X. You think you can handle that?" He nodded his head because originally it was gonna be him and Omari, but I needed Omari to get that other shit off the ground. "Kayson, you got that white girl which is where most of our money come from, so you got the bulk of shit." Kayson smiled and nodded. He loved that shit.

"Yo I can just help Omari with his shit." Denari interjected. I knew what he was trying to do but that shit wasn't gone work. I needed to know if he was built for this shit or not.

"Negative." I said. "You gone run the house on Beaties

Ford by yourself. You will be responsible for pickups and drop offs, the crew and the way the house is ran. You won't have your brothers so the success of that house will be all on you, do you think you can handle that?" Instead of telling me that he could, he diverted the conversation to his brothers.

"Why they all get to move up and I still gotta be at the house?"

"Because Denari you ain't showed me shit but that you can party and smoke, that's it." I gave it to him raw and uncut. "This is gonna show me if you built for this life or not. 'Cause right now with all of your fuck ups, you showing me that this ain't for you. Prove me wrong."

This was his one and only shot, I needed for him to get his shit together and fast. He needed to show me that he could do what I needed him to do or he would sit back and watch his brothers become the kings of Charlotte. I'll be damn if I let him fuck this shit up for us.

"Aight, well meet me at the warehouse tomorrow and I will run down my expectations for each of you. 11 a.m. sharp, and not a minute later." I directed that last part to Denari. They all nodded their heads and headed out the door. I was ready to see if they could handle pieces of what I did daily.

Chapter Sixteen
DENARI

I can't believe that Unc just tried to play me like that. I do just as much as them niggas do, hell I put in work just like they do. They thought just because I didn't live in the fucking trap house that I wasn't working, shit I could make deals and shit too. Them muthafuckas get the cushy shit and I'm still stuck at the fucking house.

"Yo D wait up." I heard Omari yell from behind me but I didn't feel like talking to his ass either. He didn't even take up for me back there and we're blood.

"I ain't even in the fucking mood O."

"The fuck yo' problem man?"

"You! Yo' ass didn't even defend me when they were talking shit about me." I fumed.

"Nigga everything they said was fucking true. Tell me

what the fuck you know about running the trap? I'll wait." He folded his arms and waited for me to answer.

To be honest, I couldn't, I sat back and took orders from Kayson whenever he needed me to do something. When he wasn't telling me what to do I was partying or fucking. Didn't mean I didn't do shit just meant that I didn't have anything to do.

"I don't have time for this." I tried to open the door to my new school Camaro and Omari shut it back.

"No, you don't have time for it because yo' ass don't know, the only thing you know is what we told you. You never had time to sit down and learn the shit and Unc see that shit nigga. If you don't shape up, Unc gonna sit you down and I know you don't want that."

"Man, Unc ain't gonna do shit." I wasn't so sure about that so I know the uncertainty showed through my tone.

"Yeah nigga you don't believe that, you need to be at the warehouse at 11 a.m. sharp. Nah fuck that, have yo' ass there at 10:30 so you can learn this shit because I gotta feeling if you fuck this up, you out bruh." Omari looked me square in the eye, I could see the sympathy that he had for me and I could also tell that he was trying to hide it so he could show me how serious the situation was. Maybe I did need to shape up.

"Man, I'll be there." I waved it off like it wasn't nothing but I was gonna be there, and on time for once.

I hopped in my car heading in the direction of this little shorty I kick it with from time to time. It wasn't shit with her and she knew it, she was just happy to be in the presence of a Barnes whenever she could.

I really wanted to see Heaven but I hadn't heard from her since that night at the club and I wasn't about to be bugging and shit. She had that extra phone that I got her to call me and she hadn't, so I took it as she was trying to play house with that nigga. I understood after the first night or two she wanted to give things a chance to calm down, but it's been damn near two fucking weeks since that shit happened.

I wasn't a nigga that chased pussy, I cared about Heaven, I may have even loved her, but no one would know that shit but me. People use that LOVE shit against you. I mean just look at the shit my moms went through before my dad killed her. People would always ask her why she stayed and her response would always be because I loved him. I promised myself that I would never give anyone that much power over me. I would just stick to these bird brain bitches and keep it moving.

Speaking of bird brain bitches, I hadn't heard from Krista's ass lately. I guess she meant that shit about not fucking with a nigga anymore. I knew I was wrong as fuck for that shit but got damn the shit she could do with her legs was a fucking turn on and like I said, Jaako didn't give a fuck he didn't even like her ass, no one did. My phone rang and it was a number that I didn't know so I cleared it only for it to call right back.

"The fuck is this?"

"Denari it's me." Heaven cried. The way she sounded had

me alarmed and I didn't like it one bit, scared the shit out of me.

"Yo, the hell wrong with you?"

"Ortiz drug me with him out of town to do a job that night after the club. He wouldn't let me take anything, including my purse, which is why I haven't called. He takes all the cords to the phones when he leaves." She sniffled and I felt something that I had never felt before, sympathy for someone else. "He left two days ago to finish the job but he never came back."

"So you don't know where he is?"

"No," she broke down. "Some men came by here the other day beating on the door but I hid in the bathroom until they left. He paid for the room up until tonight, can you just come and get me I'm so scared."

"Man, where you at?" I heard shuffling and papers shuffling. "Emporia, Virginia?" she said in a questioning tone. I know it's right on the state line because I remember seeing the Welcome to Virginia sign."

"Damn Heaven, that's a long ass drive. What if I send you money for a bus or some shit?"

"I'm scared Denari, you told me that if I ever needed you that you had me." She cried. "I need you."

For some reason when she said that it broke my heart. I pulled over on side of the road and had her send me the address to the hotel that she was staying at and told her that I would be there in a few hours. I put the address in my GPS, stopped at the gas station and got me one of them Styrofoam coolers, filled her up with a 12 pack of Coors Light and hit the road. In a sense, I was making a commitment to her that I damn sure wasn't ready for. I just hope that her ass was ready to deal with what all came with my ass because I wasn't slowing down for nobody.

"Open the damn door Heaven," I was frustrated as hell, that was the longest fucking ride ever. Four fucking hours all on 85 North, it wasn't like I was able to site see or no shit like that, all I saw was fucking road. "You better open the got damn door before I leave yo' ass."

"I'm coming," she swung the door open and was standing there looking sexy as fuck, minus the black eye she was sporting. "I thought you were the guys again."

"Get ya shit and come on. I ain't trying to be caught slipping. I don't know what yo' punk ass man done got himself into."

She walked back in and got all her things and jumped in the car where I was waiting. When she got to the car I slid over to the passenger seat.

"Yo you driving, I don't feel like it."

"Okay," she said sadly and walked over to the driver seat. For a second I felt bad but then I remembered that long ass drive that I just made. Fuck that, her ass was driving or she could stay here.

I reclined my seat and cracked open a beer as I gave her

directions to the highway. She whipped my Camaro like a champ. Once we were away from the hotel I sighed a sigh of relief and relaxed and enjoyed the drive. I didn't even realize that I had dozed off until she was tapping me telling me that we were at my place.

"Um I—um."

"Look you can chill here with me for as long as you need to. You know what it is with us and I always keep it real with you. You know how I am and you accept that shit so welcome home baby girl." She didn't say anything at first, she just stood there and cried.

"Thank you."

"No thanks needed, but if you go back to him then yo' ass on ya own." She nodded.

We walked up the stairs and she said that she wanted to shower. I already knew that I wanted her sexy ass in the bed with me every night so I showed her where to place the little bit of shit she had. She told me that when they got to where they were going that he bought just enough shit for her to survive while they were there. She wasn't gonna be with me and looking like pure shit. We were going shopping asap.

She got out of the shower, she was wrapped up in a big ass towel with her hair in one of those messy buns. Her peanut butter skin tone was glowing, she was absolutely gorgeous and she didn't even know it. Ortiz had stripped her of all her confidence. I just hoped she got it back and fast because I wasn't trying to be stuck with no clingy bitch. That shit wasn't my style.

"Denari, someone is knocking at the door." Heaven snapped me out of my trance.

"Shit you live here too, go get that shit." I told her and headed to the bathroom to piss.

"Really?" she asked shocked.

"Look, I ain't about to say that I'm about to stop fucking other bitches but I will say that I won't disrespect you with the shit." I shrugged because I was gonna be one hundred. She dropped her head. "You know how I feel about you, but I'm young and I ain't trying to sell you no dreams. So, go get the door, if it's a bitch let her know that you live here now and that if she wants to get in touch with me she need to call my phone. No more stopping by." She lifted her head and had a devious look on her face.

She walked out of the room and I headed to the bathroom, as soon as the door opened all I could hear is Krista's fucking mouth.

"Who the fuck are you?"

"I live here who the fuck are you?" I hear Heaven say with a little sass. I smiled a little maybe there was more to her than I knew.

"Where the fuck is Denari?"

"I don't think that's your business, if you want some dick then you need to call like the rest of the hoes. There will be no more drive by dickdowns. It's a new bitch in town."

I decided to go and break that shit up before it got bad and then my neighbors started tripping. I did like this little fire that was emerging from Heaven though.

"The fuck you doing here Krista?"

"I came to talk to you." She looked Heaven up and down and then turned her attention to me. "Who is this?"

"She told you exactly who she was, what do you want?"

"So, you gotta girlfriend now?"

"What I got is none of your business, don't you live with my brother?" Heaven's face dropped when I said that. I forgot she was standing there for a minute.

"Can we not talk about my business in front of strangers."

"Heaven ain't no stranger, I know her really well." I licked my lips and Heaven blushed.

"Anyway, I need you to talk to him and tell him that we are not fucking around please." She rolled her eyes up into her head. "He won't even talk to me and he's talking about moving out, I need you to do something."

"First off, I don't lie and you know that." I laughed because I was lying right there. "Second, him wanting to leave you has nothing to do with us fucking, he don't like yo' ass and I don't blame him. The only thing you good for is putting them legs behind ya head, other than that you ain't shit."

"Fuck you Denari, you weren't saying that before this bitch got here. You were talking about how you were gonna get this pussy anytime you want."

"Krista shut up, if I wanted to fuck you right now you would. No questions asked."

"Are you going to talk to him or not?"

"He's not exactly talking to me either." I laughed.

"Fuck, what are we gonna do?"

"We?" I gave her a questioning look. "That's my brother he has to forgive me, but you on the other hand is a different story."

"Denari, I'm pregnant and I don't know if it's yours or your brother's."

My hand immediately went to my face and slid down. I knew I should have never fucked her raw but that shit felt too good not to. This shit was too much to talk about right now. I looked over at Heaven and I could see a glimpse of hurt in her eyes. She just shook her head and walked to the back of the apartment and shut the room door.

"I guess your little girlfriend ain't ready to be a stepmom." She laughed.

"Bitch you getting rid of that shit one way or another." I pointed in her face.

"No, I'm not killing this baby, me and Jaako are gonna raise this baby together."

"You don't think his ass gonna ask for a DNA you fucking idiot? And I'm telling you right now that I ain't father material so you can dead that shit right now. I ain't trying to be nobody's daddy."

"Well you need to help me get Jaako back in my good graces."

I thought about it for a minute and as bad as I hated to admit it she was right. She needed to make up with Jaako so he could take care of this baby whether it was his or not. Shit Ma did it with us, he surely could.

"Yo if this shit don't work you need to get rid of that

fucking baby and I ain't playing. You'll do it on your own terms or on mine."

"Just talk to him." She ignored my threat.

"I'll talk to him but I don't think it will matter. Jaako been looking for a way out." I hit her with some truth. "Yo' mouth and attitude make you so unattractive." I shook my head.

"I didn't ask for you to analyze me, I just need you to talk to your brother." She rolled her eyes and walked out. This shit was not gonna work. I knew my brother and he low key hated her, so this baby was not gonna make a difference. I had a feeling I would be getting rid of Ms. Krista sooner or later.

Chapter Seventeen
KRISTA

Leaving Denari's house I felt defeated. I just knew that he would have some sympathy for me, but his ass basically threatened to kill both me and the baby. I knew that Denari wasn't someone that I wanted to settle down with, but I thought that my sex game had him wrapped up enough that he would at least understand where I'm coming from. I was even hoping that if shit didn't work with me and Jaako that I would still have one Barnes brother under my spell but it ain't working out like that.

I pulled up to the only place that I knew that I could get solace from, my parents. My mom would have the perfect answer that I needed and my dad would baby me. I got out and used my key to get in and as soon as the door was open I heard the norm, arguing.

"Damn it Roman, why can't you just do what the fuck I say?"

"Chelsey I did, I don't know what else you want me to do." My dad said in his normal soft tone.

"I told you to take out chicken legs and here sit a sink full of chicken breast." My mom yelled.

"Chicken is chicken." He said under his breath but my mom had those bionic ears so she heard him.

"I'm so sick of your useless no good ass, I don't even know why I married you. I hate you, I should just go and run off with the fucking mailman. I bet he would know the difference between a chicken leg and breast." She went on and on until she saw me walk in, my dad had already left and went outside to his building, where he normally went when she got like this. "Well hello my baby."

"Hi mom."

"How are you?" She smiled.

"I'm okay, how are you?"

"Besides sick of your father, I've been doing good." She smiled and continued to season the chicken in the sink. "How are things with that rich Barnes man?"

"Not so good." I admitted and she looked at me like I had sprouted five heads.

"What do you mean not good, what's going on?"

"He thinks I'm sleeping with his brother for one and two, he is in love with his lawyer and is only with me because I'm assuming that she won't be with him." I shook my head on the brink of tears. "I don't know how things got so bad so quick."

"So his brother is rich too?" I nodded. "And you're sleeping with him?" I nodded again. "Well then you're set, what one won't do the other will." She turned back around like she had just solved the riddle.

"Denari is only 20 and he acts his age, he is nothing that I want to settle down with." I shook my head.

"Then why does he have access to your money maker?"

"Because he was fun and exciting where as Jaako was all about the love making and stuff. I wanted someone who knew what I wanted in bed and Jaako fell short of that just a little bit."

"Sex ain't gone pay yo' bills and keep you laced sweetheart. Sex is only there for you to secure the bag and then after that, you can worry about sex and stuff. Don't you listen to anything I say?" She had a confused look on her face. "See your father was good in the bed and he has money, but he's weak. When I want something strong I go out and find it, but I have my bread and butter when I get home. You never secured your bag before you went out looking for a substitute that was empty." She raised an eyebrow.

"I understand but that's not even the worse part." She turned completely around and gave me her undivided attention. "I'm pregnant and I don't know if it's Jaako's or his brother Denari."

"Who's do you want it to be?"

"Jaako's," I said like she should have known.

"Well then it's Jaako's baby." She shrugged and turned her back to me and finished what she was doing in the sink. "Just stick to the fact that it's Jaako's baby no matter what anyone says and eventually he will believe it. Your father did."

My eyes got big and I threw my hand over my mouth. I knew my mother was ruthless but I didn't know she was like that. I would have never thought that she could pin a baby on my dad that didn't belong to him but then again it was my mom.

"Dad's not my dad?"

"Of course he is, he feeds you and takes care of you." She never turned back around. "He's your father you just may not have the same blood through your veins or hell you might." She shrugged. "We will never know, now will we? All because I stuck to the story and that was what it was." She winked over her shoulder.

I honestly didn't know how to feel. I wanted to protest and ask who the hell my father was but I knew she wouldn't tell me. That little story was for teaching purposes only and not up for debate any further. I was gonna take her advice though, this baby that I was carrying was Jaako's and I didn't care who said what about it.

Chapter Eighteen
JENACIA

It had been two months since me and Kayson decided to make things official and I must say that it was everything that I had hoped for. We were still working on building trust and I still have some doubts about his fidelity, but until he gave me a reason to think otherwise it was gonna just be worthless doubt.

"Hey bitch." Zemia said coming into Olive Garden. The heffa was supposed to be here thirty minutes to go.

"Don't hey bitch me, you're late."

"Ah shit I'm always late, just love me hell." I laughed because she was right. She was always late; if she wasn't one hell of an editor she would have been fired from our job.

"I hate you hoe."

"Yeah yeah so you say." She rolled her eyes up in her head.

I met Zemia when I started working for The Word. Everyone told me that she had an attitude from hell and that she was rude. I was never one to go off someone else's opinion so I decided to get to know her for myself and boy was I glad I did. She quickly became the closest person to me. I loved every crazy personality and her smart mouth. She said whatever it was that came to her mind and didn't care how you felt about it.

She was with me through the abortion I had after me and Kayson slipped up last year. I wasn't in the best head space afterwards and she stayed with me until she was sure that I wouldn't kill myself and I was grateful. Zemia was loyal as they come and hell, she loved me more than my own mother. That says a lot.

"So, what you been up to girly? I don't really get to see you like that anymore since you been boo'd up with Mr. Barnes." She smirked and turned to the waitress who had a sour look on her face when she mentioned the name Barnes.

"Drinks?" the waitress said and rolled her eyes.

"Ooouuuu you gotta 'tude and I ain't feeling it. You can leave and come back when you feel better or matter of fact send someone else." Zemia scrunched up her pretty face and turned back to me. "Girlll bitches rude as shit though right?"

My attention was focused on the waitress who was staring me down. She looked so familiar to me. I just couldn't put my finger on where I knew her from. I looked at her name tag and it read Brayla, then I remembered that she was the bitch that came and picked Kayson up that first night I stayed with him. She was the chick that blew his phone up constantly. I guess she realized that I had figured out who she was because she smirked.

"Well hey sister wife." She laughed.

"Yeah, so I'm not about to play these games with you sweetheart. I got the keys, I got his heart so whatever you're about to try and say you can stop, it won't work."

"Is that what he told you?" She crossed her arms and put all her weight on one leg and popped her hip out.

"Nah bruh you ain't about to do this, don't yo' ass got some pasta or something to make? Where the hell is yo' manager."

"Anyway," Brayla rolled her eyes. She went in her pocket and pulled out her phone and started to scroll through it. She had this fucked up smile on her face the whole time. "This look like you got his heart?" She turned her phone toward me and my heart dropped to my stomach but I would never let her know what she was showing me was affecting me.

"Okay you just swallowed the babies he hadn't put in me yet." I clapped back, something about what I said changed her demeanor.

"Babies?" She damn near yelled. "You really don't know your man like you think you do." She laughed. "Kayson don't want kids boo boo."

"No sweetheart he just don't want kids with you." I pointed at her. I was starting to get mad but at myself. Why in the hell am I sitting here with her arguing about my man. I really needed to have a conversation with Kayson, I was not about to be in the streets arguing with every bitch that he's stuck his dick in. "Me and Kayson talk about starting a family all the time so I don't know where you are getting your info from but they are sadly mistaken."

"Girl stop arguing with this whorebanger, you know ya man and don't let no bitch tell you otherwise. She just bitter." Zemia mugged her.

"Bitch you don't know me." Brayla turned her attention to Zemia.

"No hoe, you clearly don't know me because if you did you would know that you getting mighty close to catching these hands. Try me." Zemia said in a calm voice that let me know it was probably time to go before shit got real.

Brayla rolled her eyes and turned to look at me. "Well our man was at my house last Tuesday when he said that he was at the club with his brothers, I made sure that he was satisfied because we knew you had to work." She laughed.

I laughed with her. "That's funny because last Tuesday Kayson and I rode to Cherokee and went to the Casino because I didn't have any shoots for the rest of the week." I raised my eyebrows and she stood there looking stupid. "I'm not about to sit here and argue with you about MY man, if you have an issue you need to take that up with him. I'm trying to keep my composure because unlike you I have a career to worry about. Now if you don't mind, we would like to speak to your manager." I said that with finality. She looked back and forth between me and Zemia and stomped off.

"That fucking picture had better be old as fuck." I said more to myself than Zemia.

"Girl you know it is, did you just not hear her say that she was with him Tuesday and it was a lie. That shit was probably something she snuck when he was high or drunk."

"I'm still asking him about it."

"Girl don't go causing trouble in your relationship on the strength of no bitch like that. I'm not playing with you." Zemia warned.

I knew she was right but in the back of my mind I knew that if I didn't talk to him about it the shit was gonna fester and I would turn it into something that it wasn't and I didn't want to do that. The key to every relationship is communication and we promised that if there was ever a problem that we would talk about it.

"I see your mind over there working, you bout to fuck up a good thing."

"Shut up and let's go, I ain't about to eat here knowing this bitch work here. She gonna spit all in our shit."

"Right! But I still wanna see her manager."

"Let that girl keep her little job. She needs it." I stood up and laid a ten-dollar bill on the table, but Zemia scooped it up.

"Fuck that bitch." She smacked her lips, I laughed and we headed out of the restaurant. I was gonna make sure that I talked to Kayson about this and soon. We walked out of the restaurant, "Where to, 'cause a bitch hungry."

"Let's go to the TGIFridays, I want that Jack Daniel's steak they got."

"Sounds good."

Both restaurants were in the same area as Northlake Mall so it wasn't a far drive. We actually could have walked but the heels we had on wouldn't let us be great. Let me stop I didn't want to walk any damn way. We pulled up and got out, the hostess showed us to a table near the bar because I was gonna need a drink after that bullshit I just dealt with.

"Girl that was some shit." Zemia said reading my mind.

"I know, I don't want to have to deal with that every time I run into one of his little bitches though."

"You may as well get use to the shit because being with one of them Barnes brothers, you got to have thick skin and if you ain't prepared for that maybe you need to take a step back."

"I've put in my time with Kayson and I'll be damn if I let him go over some bullshit."

"Okay, well shut the hell up and ignore the hoes."

I flipped her off and we ordered our drinks, me a glass of Sangria and Zemia ordered her norm, a Whisky Sour.

"Speaking of Barnes brothers, what's been up with you and Omari?"

"Nothing." She smiled. "He's really cool and I love spending time with him but I know what he's about. Hell, he damn near told me that he was a hoe and wasn't planning on settling down no time soon." She shrugged her shoulders and looked somewhat disappointed.

"You like him don't you."

"Bitch that's what I just said?" She tilted her head to the side.

"I can't stand you I swear." I laughed.

"Nah but seriously, I do like him. He's so sweet and attentive when we're together. We talk about anything. He even opened up about some things that happened in his childhood to me. I felt like we were getting somewhere but I ain't trying to get my hopes up because I know how he is. So, for now, we are just gone chill and be friends you know?" She finished off her drink and called for the waitress to order another one. "After what I witnessed with my mom and dad, I refuse to ever feel that way."

"Z you can't do that, their situation is not your situation. You can't keep pushing people out of your life because you think that they will do you like your dad did your mom."

I felt sorry for Zemia sometimes because that situation will be forever etched into her mind. She bases everything off what happened to her parents. Her ex-boyfriend Lan was like the sweetest person ever and he would do anything for Zemia but she wouldn't let him in out of fear. So, he got tired of waiting and broke up with her. She never let him in enough to feel anything so the breakup didn't bother her. I hated that for her.

"Girl I ain't got time to nursing no broken heart, I got

checks to run up." She waved me off and focused on the fresh drink the bartender had just put down.

"I know somebody who can break down them walls." I tried to lighten the conversation back up.

"I got some damn walls he can break down, humph," we both laughed.

About two hours later we were both full and tipsy, we were standing at the car trying to decide if we were going to call an Uber or not. We couldn't do anything without laughing so we knew for a fact that we shouldn't drive. I picked up the phone and called Kayson but got no answer, Zemia called Omari and got the same thing. We chalked it up as they were working so we submitted to calling an Uber. We stood by the car and talked while we waited when I noticed a familiar car pull in.

"Fuck, there's Roger." My high was blown that quick, I was praying that the Uber would pull up at any minute.

"He bet not come over here with that bullshit either." Zemia slurred, she had like six or seven Whiskey Sours so I knew her ass was blowed. I just shook my head and pretended to be busy with my phone.

"Damn ya man left you out here fucking drunk and shit?" Roger laughed but I didn't even dignify his question with an answer. "Oh, so because you dealing with a big ass drug dealer you can't talk to a regular nigga like me?" He walked toward me.

Roger was a supervisor at a local plant down here and he made decent money. I mean he took good care of himself. His problem was that he didn't know how to keep his fucking dick in his pants. He got caught up with them fucking twins he had on the way.

"How's Treyquisha?" I asked about his baby mama. "Your twin girls should be here any day now, right? Make sure you let me know, I would love to send them a gift." I smirked and Zemia started clapping.

"Good," clap, "Fucking," clap, "Answer." she slurred. I wanted to laugh but I didn't feel like making the situation any worse. This day was already a bust, running into both me and Kayson's exes was not what I was expecting.

"Oh you think you smart, huh?" Roger rushed me and I had never seen him like this before. He was usually easy going but something in his eyes was different. "Ya nigga ain't here to save yo' ass, now is he?" He gritted in my ear. I tried to push him off but he had my wrist really tight, and like a bitch his nails were piercing my skin.

"Muthafucka you better get the fuck off her." Zemia yelled and ran over to jump on his back. He knocked her off with one hand and I hauled back and slapped the shit out of him. He grabbed my arms so hard it felt like he could break something at any moment. I noticed a car riding by very slowly, I was hoping that it was the Uber or someone that could help but before I could cry he spoke again.

"Just so you know, be happy as long as you can because if I can't have you no one will." He whispered in my ear and pressed his lips against mine really hard and then slammed me against the car and walked in the restaurant like he didn't just assault me. I could have called the police but I had something better for his ass. I was gone let my nigga know, let's see what happens when he comes in front of Kayson Barnes.

I helped Zemia up off the ground, because she was having a lot of trouble getting up. I didn't realize that we had gotten that drunk. Lesson learned. Right as we were getting ourselves together the Uber pulled up and I had him take me to the trap where I knew they were, that was the only time that Kayson didn't answer the phone for me.

Chapter Nineteen
KAYSON

We had gotten a call that some shit had went down at the trap and Denari was of course nowhere to be found. I was pissed beyond measures. The whole time that we were running the fucking trap together it had never gotten robbed, but as soon as his little bitch ass take over shit go fucking haywire. I had yet to call Uncle Ray because I wanted to check shit out on my own.

"What the fuck happened?" I barked looking around the house at his workers. No one said anything so I pulled out my pistol from my waist band. "Aight cool, I'll start shooting a muthafucka every time I gotta repeat myself, until either I find out what the fuck I wanna know or all y'all muthafuckas dead. Your choice."

Denari's friend Jizzy spoke up. "We were in here chilling and counting up and niggas just busted through with gats telling us to give up everything." He shrugged his shoulders like that shit didn't matter to him and that shit pissed me off.

"And what the fuck did you do?" Jaako interjected it. His ass was so mad that he had turned red as a muthafucka. I wanted to laugh at his ass but now wasn't the fucking time.

"They came in here with guns and shit," he smacked his lips. "They could have killed us." He yelled like we were supposed to understand where he was coming from.

"Then muthafucka you should've taken that chance." Jaako said pulling out his damn gun so fucking fast and shooting Jizzy right between the eyes. Everybody fucking jumped including myself because Jaako was usually the calm one. It was me and Omari that was trigger happy.

"Damn nigga a little fucking warning next time." Omari complained because he was standing in the area that the blood spattered. "I just bought this fucking shirt nigga."

"Well buy a fucking nother one." Jaako barked. I didn't know what the fuck was wrong with him, but his hostile ass had been on one the last few weeks. I needed to talk to him about that shit.

"Where the fuck is Denari." I asked the three remaining dudes that were sitting there scared out of their minds but no one said anything. Jaako chambered another bullet and they all tried to tell us where he was at the same time. "Man, shut the fuck up." I told them then pointed at the one sitting next to Jizzy slumped body. "You, where the fuck that nigga at?"

"He said he had some shit to do that he would be back tomorrow."

Suddenly, we heard whimpering coming from the kitchen. "Who the fuck in here?" I yelled heading to the kitchen. There sat three half naked bitches. "You gotta be shitting me. Get the fuck in the living room," I ordered the bitches. I swear the one girl looked vaguely familiar to me. I wanted to ask her who the fuck she was but I wasn't in the mood to worry about it. When I got back in the living room they all looked like they had been busted. "Y'all some half assed dealers." I shook my head.

"What the fuck we gonna do with them?" Omari asked.

"Let me get everybody's fucking ID and if you don't have a fucking ID then yo' ass gone be slumped just like this muthafucka." They all pulled out identification and took a picture of every last one of them and then emailed them to my uncle so we would have them if any one of them tried to run their fucking mouths. "If I hear about what happened today from anybody, I'm coming to look for you. Don't think if you move it will make it hard to find you either, all I need is a fucking name and picture and I got both." I threw the ID's back on the table. "Y'all get the fuck out of here."

They all got their shit and ran out. "Oh, and don't come back either." Jaako added. "Your services are no longer needed."

"Man, come on, please this is how I feed my family." One guy begged.

"That's on you my nigga, we can't afford fuck ups like this." Omari shrugged and went to the back of the house to lock up. We were gonna have to shut this house down asap.

The guy looked at us begging for another chance, I wanted to feel sorry for the little nigga but O was right we couldn't afford fuck ups like that. We had just lost out on a quarter mil, in cash and drugs. Shit wasn't right, why now? I needed to holla at Unc so I could fill him in and see what we needed to do about Denari. He was starting to get in the way of the business. Brother or not, his ass just wasn't built for this.

"We gotta tell Unc." Omari said out of the blue.

"I was just thinking that." I said.

"Denari fucking up big time." Jaako said shocking the shit out of me, he's the one that likes to baby that nigga.

"Y'all don't start this shit."

"O, do you not see this shit? This is his fucking fault now we all gotta take the shit for it. I'm tired of his shit man." I yelled.

"I know but—"

"No fucking buts" Jaako said before I could. "He bringing us down O. His reckless bullshit is gone land us in jail or dead."

What he said made Omari think about shit. He knew he was telling the truth. Denari's ass needed a wake up call. He didn't take shit serious. I was over him and apparently Jaako was too. I already know when Unc get a hold of this information it's a wrap for him.

"We need to talk to him first." Omari said.

"That nigga ain't gonna listen." I shook my head.

I sighed deeply and then leaned up against the wall. Unc

had a cleanup crew but as soon as we called them we knew for a fact that Unc would be calling soon after. Jaako looked at me and I looked at him and nodded my head for him to make the call. I sat there and looked at my phone and waited of Unc to ring in and like clockwork, there he was.

"Clean up at the Ford?"

"Nigga's threw a party and shit got fucked up."

"Anything taken?"

"Everything of value."

"Got damn it." He yelled. "I'll see y'all in about three hours at the house. I got some shit to handle right now."

"We one short." I threw out there.

"Good." He said and then hung up the phone.

"Three hours at Unc's house." I told the other two.

"I just got a text that cleanup was outside."

We walked outside to let them muthafuckas do their thing. The block was hot and the fact that there were gun shots was normal. It didn't even phase the neighbors. I walked out and hopped in my truck I was gonna call Jenacia back because I see that she called me.

"Aye did sis call you?" Omari asked with a mug on his face.

Before I could answer my phone alerted me that I had a text message. I saw that it was Brayla texting and that it was a picture. My curiosity got the best of me and I opened it up. When I saw the picture my blood boiled, my breathing picked up and chest tightened. All I saw was red, there was the woman that I had changed for kissing all up on her ex-boyfriend. At that moment, I wanted to kill the both of them.

"Bruh the fuck wrong with you? You over there swelling up like the hulk or some shit." Omari looked concerned. "Z called me but she ain't answering her phone now, I ain't feeling that shit." He said looking down at his phone. "Oh shit, there they go right there."

I jumped out of the truck and rushed over to that car so fast. Jenacia was crying and making her way to me so fast and I didn't know why. I guess she didn't know about her little rendezvous with that bitch ass nigga that was cheating on her dumb ass.

"Oh my God bae he—"

I jacked her little ass up and brought her to my eye level. I had never put my hands on a woman but I swear seeing that shit had my heart in a thousand pieces, I could barely breathe. I couldn't even look her in the eye thinking of her betrayal.

"So you think you gonna make a fucking fool out of me Jenacia? Huh bitch? All the shit I've done for you, I let you live in my fucking house, do whatever you needed me to do and you still fucking with the nigga that had babies on you. You think that shit cool bitch." I threw her down and she hit the ground hard, landing on her wrist and she cried out and grabbed it.

"You muthafucka." Zemia swung her pocketbook at me and I went toward her and Omari stepped in.

"I don't know what the fuck yo' problem is, but you bugging bruh. You need to fucking chill." He pointed at me and I wanted to punch his ass in the fucking face.

"Bitch you go get yo' shit and get it the fuck out of my

house. I thought yo' hoe ass was different." I barked and Jenacia just sat there on the ground with tears flowing down her beautiful face.

She never said a word. I looked at her wrist that she was holding and it was bruised, I all of a sudden felt bad as hell. Then I looked at the other one and it was bruised as well, I traced her body with my eyes looking for more visible marks and saw an ugly bruise peeking out from under her shirt and I knew for a fact that I didn't do that.

"He attacked her you fucking dumb ass. Look at her fucking arms do you think she was with his ass willingly." Zemia yelled. "He walked up on us at the restaurant when she called yo' dumb ass for a fucking ride because we were drunk and—"

"Stop Zemia." Jen cried, I reached out for her and she slapped my hand away. I knew right then I had fucked up, but seeing that shit hurt me to my core. I guess that's how she felt all those years ago, when I did it to her. "O can you take me to get my things please?" she sniffled.

"Yeah sis come on," Omari said and I mugged the hell out of him and he mugged me even harder, I knew I was wrong but shit what was I supposed to do?

"Jenacia listen, I'm sorry somebody sent me a picture and I just lost it baby I'm sorry." I walked up on her and she cocked back and punched the shit out of me. I was a big nigga but I must admit that shit hurt. I had to grab my jaw.

"So, I guess the bitch was telling me the truth when she was feeding me all that bullshit." She laughed through her tears. "Something has got to be going on if you will take what she says and run with it, without even asking me." She finally looked into my eyes and the hurt I saw was enough to make me tear up a second. "And all that shit you did for me, I'll be sure to pay you back although I never asked for any of it." She started to walk off and then turned around. "You don't have to worry about me anymore, I never thought you were that man."

She jumped in my brother's back seat and him and Zemia got in the front. If looks could kill I swear Mama would be burying my black ass right now because the look Zemia was giving me was a killer. I watched as they zoomed off.

"What the fuck was that about?" Jaako asked walking over, he was still in the house so I guess he only caught the end.

"I just fucked up with Jenacia and I don't know if I will be able to fix it." I said walking to my truck.

"Where the fuck you going?"

"I gotta go pay somebody a visit." Was all I said before I jumped in and sped off.

I pulled in the drive way and parked right behind his black Impala. I jumped out leaving my car running, I knocked on the door and he swung it open immediately, so soon as I seen his face I hit him with a three piece that laid his ass out. I didn't even give him a chance to fight back and just fucked his ass up.

" I hear you like to beat women huh?"

"Fuck you." He got out between me punching his ass in the mouth. "It's a storm coming muthafucka and you Barnes bitches are in the center of it." He laughed and that pissed me off.

"Bring that shit on muthafucka they call me the fucking Rain man bitch." I cocked back and punched him in the mouth so hard that his teeth went flying across the room. I kicked and stomped that muthafucka until he passed the fuck out. "Y'all must not know who the fuck we are, talking about a fucking storm. Let's go then bitch." I said out loud.

I got in my truck and headed to the house to try and stop Jenacia from leaving.

Chapter Twenty
OMARI

"I can't believe he did this to me." I could hear Jenacia crying from the backseat.

"I'm sorry sis I don't know what my brother on, but he loves you and he was just acting out of jealousy." I tried to reason.

"That don't give him the right to put his hands on her." Zemia yelled at me. I had to bite my lip because I wanted to cuss her ass out for talking to me like that but I knew they were both running off emotions.

"I didn't say that, I was just saying that I had never seen him act like that over anybody. That nigga loves Jen with all his heart and to think of her—"

"What, doing the same shit that he's done to me? What, making a fool of his ass?" Jenacia got out through sniffles. "I would never do anything to hurt Kayson, I love him more than anybody. I would do anything for him and he knows it. So why come at me like that, why not just ask?"

"How the fuck did he know anyway?" Zemia asked and I shrugged my shoulders.

"It had to be that Brayla bitch because he said that he had a picture and when Roger was attacking me I saw a car slow down but I didn't think anything of it I thought it was the Uber driver."

"I'm beating that bitch's ass." Zemia yelled.

"Nah y'all chill, Kayson gone handle that." I told them both and they smacked their lips.

"I no longer trust your brother to protect me." Jenacia said before she broke down again.

really needed to have a conversation with my brother. He can't be out here wilding like that because some bitch told him something. He knows better than that and he better believe I'm snitching like a muthafucka too. I can't wait to tell Ann Barnes that he put his hands on a female and one that she genuinely likes too.

I got to Kayson and Jenacia's crib, her and Zemia jumped out and went into the house to get her things. I stayed out because I was sure that Kayson was on his way very soon. I needed to talk to him before he did anything else to make this situation worse. My phone rang and it was Jaako.

"Bruh." He yelled through the phone.

"Man, what the fuck is wrong with your fucking brothers today?"

"Nigga don't put them on me. I have no idea but they both fucking bugging." He said. "Where the fuck you at?"

"At Kayson crib, Jenacia wanted me to bring her to get her shit."

"I'm around the corner."

"Good 'cause you know this nigga is on theway, I'm surprised his ass ain't here yet."

"Nah he said he had to go handle some shit." Jaako said nonchalantly.

"Ah fuck nigga you didn't follow his ass?"

"Fuck no he was on that bullshit and you know how he get and I ain't trying to beat his ass today so I let his ass go, shit."

I hung up on him. Them niggas was scared of Kayson's big ass but I wasn't. We would go at it and I didn't give a fuck if he whooped my ass or not. I'll pick up something and knock the hell out of him. I hated when Kayson did that Hulk shit, get all puffed up and start doing dumb shit. His ass better be calm when he gets here. I reached in my car and grabbed a blunt that I was smoking on earlier from the ash tray, I lit that shit and prepared myself for the fucking storm to come.

Zemia walked out of the house carrying some bags, I popped the trunk to let her put them in. Once she had the bags down I went to grab her and she snatched away. I grabbed her again and this time turned her near me.

"This ain't our fight." I told her and she looked away from me. "What the hell Z?"

"Are you like that too? Huh? You hit on women? Tell me

now 'cause I ain't built for it. I'll stab you in yo' sleep and live happily ever after."

I was taken aback by her bluntness and for some reason I believed every word she said and to be honest that shit turned me on to the max. I loved a woman that could take up for herself.

"Look shawty, none of us hit women. In all honesty that was the first time I have ever seen Kayson act like that at all. He was hurt, I know that don't make it right but that nigga heart broke in two when he saw whatever picture he received. I could see that shit in his eyes. Kayson been through some shit too, again I know that ain't an excuse but it's gotta mean something, right?"

Zemia looked deep in my eyes and her expression softened a little, her feisty ass was still mad but she kinda understood and that's all I asked of her. Next thing we heard were tires screeching and we saw Kayson's truck whip in followed by Jaako's Escalade. Kayson hopped out of the car on a mission. I noticed the blood on his shirt and I ran up to stop him. I jumped in front of him and he pushed me hard as hell. I almost lost my footing but I regained my composure and pushed his big ass back.

"Nigga I ain't trying to go there with you but you need to chill the fuck out before you go in there. You already did enough. We can do this my way or I can call Ma and have her come over here, that's on you." I looked him straight in the fucking eye. After a minute or two, his demeanor relaxed a bit and he fell back.

"Fucking snitch."

"Call me what the fuck you want but that was some bitch shit. You know we don't do that." I yelled at him. "You know that girl loves yo' dumb ass and would never do no shit like that."

"I fucked up."

"You got damn right you did and you need to let her cool the fuck down and then y'all talk." I suggested.

"She can cool down but she ain't leaving this house. When we made this shit official that was it, there is no way out." He sent a soft threat that Jenacia heard because she had just come out the door. "Baby I'm sorry please just listen to me, please can we talk about this?" He begged and I swear I wanted to pull out my got damn phone and take a muthafucking picture so I could have fucking proof. Kayson fucking Barnes is pulling a fucking Keith Sweat move. "I was in a bad space when I saw the picture."

"But you know me!" Jenacia yelled. "You know I would never be on no shit like that."

"I know baby but—"

"Fuck that, no buts nigga." She hit him with his favorite line and I put my fist over my mouth to keep from clowning that nigga. I did notice that she didn't have any bags with her. "Then you gonna talk about all the shit you do for me when I didn't ask for any of this." She waved her hands around like a mad woman.

"I know, I know I was wrong."

"Yeah but this is how shit gonna play out." She wiped her

face and looked at that nigga. "I'm leaving because you don't deserve half the shit I do for YOU!" She pointed at him. "I'm moving in with Zemia until I find my own place which I'm sure won't take long."

"You ain't going no muthafucking where." Kayson had to open his big mouth.

"You wanna fucking bet?" She said and walked up on him and Kayson just stood there I wanted to clap so bad, somebody was finally putting him in his place.

"Can we just go inside and talk please." He begged.

"It ain't gonna change shit but we can." She turned to walk in the house.

I was finally able to release the laugh that I had been holding in and I wasn't surprised when Jaako joined in.

"Yo I ain't never letting that nigga live this down." Jaako said between laughs.

"Man, I wished I could have recorded that shit."

"I got ya bruh." Jaako smiled and we dapped up.

"So y'all laughing because he cares enough about his woman to beg." Zemia asked with her face scrunched up.

"Nah it ain't even like that, to know Kayson is to know that whether that nigga right or wrong he ain't apologizing for shit and he don't let no one tell him what to fucking do." I laughed.

"And he damn sure don't let muthafuckas talk to him like that, like for real he's killed people for a lot less." Jaako added.

"That nigga is fucking unbalanced like a muthafucka but I can tell you one thing, he loves the shit out of her because she just broke all his rules." I smiled because I was happy that nigga finally found that one.

We sat out there and talked and looked at the video that Jaako had on his phone for about thirty minutes before Kayson came out. I couldn't tell if shit was good or bad.

"Aye Z listen." He walked over to Zemia who twisted up her lips. "Chill here with her for a minute."

"Why should I?"

"Man please, I can't let her leave and we gotta make a move real quick."

"Ah shit I forgot about Unc." I said looking at my watch and we were late as fuck.

"What's in it for me?" Zemia asked.

"For all the shit I did today, I swear if I can make shit right we'll go on one hell of a vacation all on me." He threw out there and I could see her wheels turning but I was learning about little miss Zemia, nothing was that easy for her.

"First, you can't buy us nigga we got our own shit!" She spat and I could see Kayson's nose flare but there was nothing that he could do about it because he needed her. "Second, we want a damn good vacation like Maldives or Tahiti, some shit like that." Damn we had money but she wanted to break a nigga with these trips. "Third, if you ever put your hands on her again I swear I will shoot you with your own gun, now you try me." Zemia said and walked off.

"Damn that was sexy." I smirked and she looked back and threw me an evil glance. "I done told you this ain't our fight" She waved me off and headed in the house. "Damn I can't wait to taste that." I regretted it the minute it came out of my mouth.

"You ain't hit yet?" Jaako asked.

"Nah I'm just getting to know shorty, plus she knows how I move so I ain't trying to go there yet." I smiled thinking about the conversation we had about my lifestyle. It was crazy how cool she was. I was thinking about trying the relationship thing but I didn't want to hurt her so before I went there I needed to be sure. I wasn't trying to end up like Kayson's ass.

"Both y'all nigga losing it yo." Jaako laughed.

"I know you ain't talking and you dealing with two of em." Kayson said.

"And yo' ass driving for that fuck shit you just said." I slapped Jaako in the back of the head and climbed in the back seat of his black on black Cadillac Escalade.

Chapter Twenty-One
DENARI

It's actually been cool having Heaven at the house. I've been chilling out and not wilding as much as I normally do, I wasn't saying I was ready to settle down or no shit like that but I was feeling this shit a little. Hell, I'm usually out partying every night and fucking different bitches but for the last two months I've only been with Heaven and Krista's dumb ass. I know I should leave that hoe alone but I just can resist her sex game, that shit is A fucking 1.

Heaven has expressed how much she hates Krista but I don't really give a fuck about that. Heaven don't run shit, I told her ass to go and take some yoga or something and do that shit like Krista does and I won't fuck with her no more. She didn't care for my response too much but I don't know what else to tell her.

Right now, I was down in South Carolina trying to set

some shit up and possibly expand the family business. I knew that shit would impress my aggravating ass uncle, since he says I don't do shit. I'm making deals on my fucking own that could have us stacked like a muthafucka. Let's see what they'll have to say about that, bitch nigga will be singing my fucking praises by the end of it.

"So, you saying you can get me a key of coke for 16 grand?" Perry asked with a skeptical expression on his face.

"As an entry price, yes." I shrugged.

"Entry?"

"Yeah nigga I ain't trying to go broke supplying yo' ass." I didn't know who the fuck he thought he was fucking with but he wasn't about to fuck me over. I guess he thought since I was a little nigga that anything would fly and that shit just don't work for me.

"So, what the price going for? Cause I'm paying 25 now."

"Nah I can do better than that, and my shit is pure and uncut. Best shit North Carolina has ever seen." I tugged on my loose dreads. "20k nigga"

"What's the fucking catch nigga?"

"Nothing just trying to expand and shit, that's why I'm giving it to you so cheap at first so you can test that shit out. If you like, then we will enjoy a new business relationship." I cheesed.

"Yo' ass better not be not fucking cop." He barked. "This shit too good to be fucking true."

"Fuck you nigga you better ask around about me, my

fucking name is Denari Barnes and that shit ring fucking bells." I boasted.

His eyes got big and he acted like my name made him uncomfortable. *That's what the fuck I thought*, I said to myself.

"Yeah whatever." He said coolly. " I'll call you in a couple days to set some shit up?"

"Aight, don't be bullshitting either nigga."

He chucked his deuces and walked off in the direction of his car. I hopped in my Camaro and burnt out. My ass was feeling good as shit right now. I had actually done something right for a change. I reclined my seat and turned on some old-school Biggie and enjoyed the scenery back to the city. I was in my own little world until my phone rang through my Bluetooth. I was in a good ass mood so I didn't even bother looking to see who it was because I don't think anything could fuck up what I was feeling right now.

"Yoooo." I sang.

"I think you have something that belongs to me." Ortiz voice boomed through my speakers.

"I ain't got shit that belongs to you and if you talking bout my bitch then you better chalk that shit up because one man's trash is another man's treasure." I laughed. Hell, he left her out there for dead he couldn't want too much to do with her, so he can go somewhere with that bull shit. I wasn't trying to hear it.

"If that's what you think then more power to you but until you return her to me I will jack one of your trap houses every day. I've already hit your favorite one." Now it was his turn to laugh. I hit the steering wheel praying this shit was some kind of fucking joke. If he hit my shit and I wasn't there, then I would never hear the end of that shit. It wouldn't matter what kind of deal I set up, this fuck up would trump that in my uncle's eyes. His ass was looking for a reason to cut me out.

"You better not had touched my shit if you know what's good for you." I threatened.

"Your threats don't mean shit to me Denari. Like I said, you have something that belongs to me and I want it back, simple as that."

"Fuck you Ortiz, I ain't giving you shit. I'll let my brothers know that we gotta a problem though." I yelled through the car.

"I hear your brothers aren't too happy with you right now." He laughed again. "I mean you did cost them a quarter mil. Tell Jizzy I said good looking out." He said and then hung up.

Jizzy? What the fuck did Jizzy have to do with this shit? I know Jizzy wouldn't fuck us over like that, would he? Nah Jizzy wasn't like that and there was no way that he would betray me. He knew what the consequences was for that shit. I picked up my phone and called his number and didn't get an answer, I called again and again and got the same results. I called Joker to see if he had heard from him.

"Nigga why the fuck Jizzy ain't answering the phone fucking phone?"

"'Cause nigga, he dead and that shit is yo' fucking fault." He yelled at the phone.

"Who the fuck you talking to?" I growled. Muthafuckas

like to forget who the fuck is in charge when a nigga ain't in they face. He was about to piss me the fuck off.

"Yo' fucking brother killed him after some niggas ran in and jacked us."

"Jacked you?" I feigned stupid.

"Yeah muthafucka." I could hear the hurt in his voice because Jizzy was Joker's cousin and they were close as fuck. "I don't know who them niggas was but all I know is he said if you don't give him back what belongs to him he gone be back every day until you do."

"Did you tell my brothers about what he said?" I needed to make sure that they didn't know that part. If they found out that all of this was over a bitch they would have my fucking head.

"Nah they didn't give us a chance, they rushed up in there saying a bunch of shit and then Jaako ass flipped out and shot him?"

"Jaako?"

"Yeah nigga look I ain't got time for this, I gotta find me some fucking work."

"Nigga you work for me." I reminded him.

"Not no mo'," he said and hung up the phone.

What the fuck was going on? Jaako wasn't even like that, he didn't do spontaneous shit like that. If they would have said it was Kayson then I would have been like okay but Jaako? He always had my fucking back. I can't believe he would kill my boy like that. That shit kinda hurt. Jizzy was the only nigga I fucked with outside of my brothers and he knew that. Now who the fuck I'ma party wit and shit?

That nigga Jaako been feeling his self since that shit at the cookout at Kayson house. I done told his ass that I wasn't fucking that bitch, even though I was, he didn't have no fucking evidence that said so. I was pissed the fuck off I put my foot on the pedal and headed in the direction of his house. I was gone cuss his ass out. What the fuck was I supposed to tell Jizzy baby mama and family? I know Joker was gonna put all the shit on me and I wasn't trying to hear that bullshit especially when it wasn't even my fault.

Today was a good fucking day now I gotta deal with this shit. I already knew what the fuck Unc was gone fucking say, why wasn't I there. Like that shit would have made a difference. I wasn't trying to deal with that shit right now. But me and Jaako was about to have a conversation before I talked to anyone else.

I pulled up to the house he shared with Krista and noticed that his car wasn't there but hers was. I knew it wasn't a good idea to go in here when he wasn't here but I didn't give a fuck about that shit right now. I needed to know why my brother killed my nigga without talking to me about it first. I knew this was the best place to catch him because no one liked Krista's bitch ass so I knew my brothers wouldn't come here.

I banged on the door and she opened it with a face full of tears.

"What the fuck are you doing here Denari? I don't have time for this."

"Fuck you bitch, where the hell is Jaako?" I pushed past her and made my way into the house.

"He's not here and I don't know where he is, he doesn't talk to me anymore because of you." She rolled her eyes at me.

"How the fuck is that my fault? Ain't nobody tell yo' ass to bust it wide open for a real nigga." I smirked. "Hell, you were calling me not the other way around. You couldn't get enough of ya boy."

"Fuck you, you can leave." She pointed to the door but I walked around and sat on the sofa.

"I ain't going nowhere until I see him, so you better get fucking comfortable." I said realizing I had to piss and heading to the bathroom. I walked past the counter and something caught my eye. "What the fuck is this Krista?"

She walked over and snatched out of my hand. "None of your business." She grabbed it and stuffed it in her pocketbook.

"I thought I told yo' dumb ass to get rid of that fucking baby." I fumed. "I told you Jaako wasn't going for that shit and it's been two fucking months and you still fucking pregnant."

"He won't talk to me so I haven't had a chance to tell him Denari, no matter what anyone says this is Jaako's baby."

My hands found their way to my face and I breathed

deeply. I was two seconds from fucking her up. I was about over her shit.

"You know my brother ain't fucking dumb he gonna ask for a blood test right." I tilted my head to the side.

"He won't, he knows I'm faithful to him." She lowered her head and I gave her that bitch please look. "You know what I mean Denari."

"Actually, no I don't because there is a 50/50 chance that the baby is mine unless you were fucking somebody else too." I raised an eyebrow.

"Oh, go to hell." She waved me off.

"But you didn't say no." She smacked her lips and walked over to the couch and turned on the TV. I walked back to the bathroom, handled my business and washed my hands. I headed back in the living room and sat on the other couch. I just stared at her, she was cute as hell but her attitude made her ugly. Yeah, her sex game was off the fucking charts but I couldn't be with her ass unless we fucked 24/7 and that ain't fucking possible. Just staring at her ass though had my dick hard.

"Aye come handle this shit why we wait." I smirked. She looked at me and then at the door and shook her head.

"No, he may actually come home."

"Shut the hell up and come here, you act like we ain't did this shit before." I unbuckled my pants and pulled out my dick that was hard as a fucking brick. She licked her lips and rolled her eyes in the back of her head like she was trying to stop herself. "You know you want it."

"Let's get a quickie in because we don't know when he's coming home." She said biting her bottom lip.

"After you suck my dick, you can have what you want."

She looked at the door again and came over to where I was, she got down on her knees and started sucking the meat off my shit. Their walls and shit were thin so I know I would be able to hear when someone pulled up, so I wasn't worried. I threw my head back and enjoyed the fucking ride.

Chapter Twenty-Two
JAAKO

The ride to Unc house was quiet. We were all lost in our thoughts; Yameka was heavy on my mind. We had a little argument earlier today about the fact that I was still living with Krista, even though I'm never there. What she didn't know was that my condo would be ready by the end of the week and I could move.

I understood where she was coming from though. I wouldn't want my woman living with her ex, but I was working to get out of there. I was just taking my time doing it. The night that we talked about being together, I should have left. I just needed to get my mind right on the fact that I was gonna be alone for a while. Yameka was worth getting over my fears though.

Krista was making shit hard for me though, she called and texted all the time. She was constantly telling me how things would be better if I just gave her a chance to change. Then in the same sentence, she would turnaround and tell me what I needed to do in order for her to be happy. What she failed to realize is I'm gonna be me regardless and if she couldn't be okay with that, then we were no good together anyway. I swear I was too nice at times.

"Fuck, I forgot to change my shirt." Kayson yelled out.

"Stop by my crib, hell it's on the way. You got shit there." We all kept clothes at each other's house just in case some shit went down. "What the fuck you do anyway?"

"I went and fucked that nigga Roger up. I told that nigga to stay the fuck away from Jenacia, but all of a sudden that nigga got balls and shit. He did say some shit that fucked with me though."

"What?" Me and Omari said at the same time.

"He was talking about some shit storm coming and I was in the middle of it."

"The fuck? We ain't even got no enemies." Omari said.

"Exactly, I didn't know what that shit was about so I was gonna talk to Unc about it."

"Man, this better not have shit to do with Denari's ass." I threw out there and I heard O suck his teeth.

"Yo, why the hell you kill Jizzy anyway?" Omari asked me.

"Think about it, the only one that knew about the stash was us and Jizzy. Denari told me that he told that nigga where we kept our stash. When I went up there, the shit was empty. How the fuck they know to look in the back of the TV for money? Somebody had to tell them that shit, and it wasn't any of us." I said, and we were all quiet. "Exactly I—" I stopped mid-sentence when I noticed Denari's car in my fucking driveway.

"You got to be shitting me." Omari said under his breath.

I jumped out and headed to the door. I stuck my key in just in time to see Krista jump the fuck up from between Denari's legs. I saw nothing but fucking red.

"THE FUCK?" I yelled and grabbed my gun from my waist band.

"Jaako noooooooooo!!!"

Click! Click! I pulled my gun out and had it trained at Denari and Krista so fast that not even I knew what I was doing. I was flooded with emotions and I had no handle on the situation. On one hand, this was the push that I needed to get the hell away from Krista. I didn't love her, nor did I want to be with her, but that didn't mean that it was okay for my brother to fucking smash her. How long had they been doing this behind my back? And why in the fuck did Denari think this shit was okay. He knew that my heart was with Yameka, but damn he also knew I cared for Krista too. If he could do something like this what else was his disloyal ass capable of? I just wanted to cause pain; I was hurt by this shit. This shit was mad disrespectful. I kept waving the gun back and forth between the two.

"Bruh, don't do this man." I could hear the fear in Omari's voice as he watched my finger inch closer to the trigger as I waved the gun around recklessly. "This shit ain't even worth it my nigga."

"He right Jaako, chill." Kayson butted in and took a step closer to me.

They were right, I took a deep breath and got my mind right then I lowered my gun and placed it on the bar that was to the left of me. I looked at Krista who was standing there shaking like a fucking leaf. The level of betrayal was out of this fucking world and the smug look on Denari's face was elevating the level of anger that was fueling my body. It was like his ass didn't give a fuck.

"Jaako, it's not what you think please let's just talk about this," Krista pleaded.

"It looks like you were swallowing my brother's dick." I yelled at her and slammed my hand down on the bar where my gun was sitting. I was tempted to pick that muthafucka up, but I knew if I did someone was going to leave here in a fucking body bag. "But shit I could be wrong." I glared at the both of them.

"Damn chill bro." Denari said nonchalantly. "You act like I had her ass bent over the couch or something she was just wetting the whistle, you know how we do." He laughed and shrugged his shoulders like what he was saying made sense. That shit took me over the edge. I jumped over the couch and punched him in the fucking mouth. It was like the more I hit him the madder I got. He tried to fight back but I was too strong for him. I hit him over and over until I felt myself being lifted off him. "All that over some pussy yo' ass don't even want?" Denari yelled from the ground, through a bloodied mouth. "Fuck you Jaako."

"No bitch, fuck you! It doesn't matter whether I wanted her or not, that was my bitch and you are my fucking brother, which means this shit ain't supposed to fucking happen." My chest heaved up and down as I tried to get the hell out of Kayson's grasp and fuck him up some more. I was so fucking mad I was shaking. "You a disrespectful piece of shit, you stay the fuck away from me nigga." I was pissed. I wanted to send a bullet through his fucking skull, but I knew that Mama would have my ass for it and even though that nigga had me on ten right now, I would eventually regret it. He was still my brother. "Mama just saved yo' life bitch boy." I pointed at Denari and he just glared at me.

"Jaako, I just think we need to talk about this."

"Ain't shit to talk about. If you can do this shit with my brother, ain't no telling what the fuck else yo' ass been doing, so you can go to hell with that shit."

"You can't leave me, I'm pregnant."

I looked at the bitch like she was crazy, she was out of her rabbit ass mind if she thought that I was about to stake claim on a baby and I had just walked in on her sucking the gristle off my brother's dick. As far as I knew she was fuckin him too. I knew something was up at Kayson's house that day. I asked both of them muthafuckas what was up and they both stood in my face and lied through their muthafucking teeth. *Omari.*

"You knew nigga?" I turned to face Omari.

"Man look, I didn't want in the middle of that shit, bruh."

He shook his head. "Either way it went, I was gonna be fucking somebody over."

"Bruh, this shit is past fucking wrong, and you didn't think to tell me that shit was going down like that? I would have never kept something like that from you."

Omari shook his head. "Don't take it there bruh. I told that nigga to tell you, this shit has been eating me up, but I just couldn't be the one to cause this." He waved his hand around the room.

"Damn," was all Kayson said with a sympathetic look on his face.

"That's fucked up," I said. "I can't trust no fucking body, huh?" I let out a sarcastic laugh. "Kay, you knew too?"

"Nah, I just heard that shit O said at the cookout. I asked him about it and he said it wasn't shit, so I left it at that." He shrugged.

"Fuck all that, Jaako I just told you that I was carrying your baby." Krista said with her hands on her hips like she ran something.

"The fuck you telling me for, wrong brother." I grabbed my gun and turned to walk away.

"Jaako you know we don't use condoms, me and Denari do."

Kayson was still standing in front of me, blocking me from getting around him. If his big ass didn't get the fuck out of my way, I was gonna scoop his ass.

"So how long y'all been fucking?"

"The fuck does that matter?" Denari scoffed.

"Bitch, because I asked."

"I ain't gonna be too many more of your bitches though."

"The fuck you gonna do about it? Huh nigga? Get yo' ass beat like you just did?"

"Fuck you, nigga."

"I tell you what." I turned my attention back to Krista. "When the baby born call me and I will get a DNA test done. If it's mine, I'm taking it and killing you." I pointed at her and I meant every single word I said. The fresh tears that were now rolling down her face let me know that she knew that I was dead ass. "I'll be back to get my shit and you better not fuck with any of it. If a got damn sock is missing, I'm slitting ya throat."

"Jaako this is ya baby," she tried to reason with me.

"How the fuck do you know? I know that nigga and he nasty as fuck. So, you not about to tell me that he used a got damn rubber every time." I hit her with the yeah right nigga face. "And if you'll fuck my brother, there is no fucking telling who else you'll lay with. You heard what the fuck I said. Don't call me for shit; don't ask me for shit until that fucking baby is born, you got it?"

"Please Jaako."

"Fuck you bitch." I tried to walk around Kayson and he looked at me as if he were asking if I was gonna do anything else. "Man, I'm done with this shit. After we meet with Unc, I'm coming to get my shit and that's the end of it." He nodded his head and moved out of the way.

I looked at them one more time, grabbed my gun off the

bar and headed out the door with Kayson in tow. I could hear Omari going off on them when I was getting in the car. When he walked out of the house he was mad as fuck. I knew the shit wasn't his fault, but I still felt betrayed by him because as my brother he should have told me, but I understood that Denari was his brother too.

"I was wrong as fuck bruh, I can't take that shit back either. I just didn't wanna be the reason for the fall out. I told both to back the fuck off, but as you can see they didn't listen worth shit."

"How long have you known?

"I walked in on them at his house a few months ago, I flipped on them and they promised that it was over, but I guess they lied." I could tell that he was sincere, and it wasn't his fault, so I guess I couldn't hold that shit over him. "Don't think I'm on no snake shit because y'all know that ain't me. I was just put in a fucked-up position."

"You good bruh, this wasn't on you, just remember I'm ya brother too." That was all I needed to say about the situation and those few words spoke volumes.

Chapter Twenty-Three
UNCLE RAY

"I don't know where the fuck them niggas at."

"You know how these youngins are." Tate, my friend who was also the police chief, said as he sat back on the couch puffing on a Cuban cigar.

"They know I don't play that shit." I fumed, but before I could get another word in the front door came busting open. Kayson led the pack as usual. "The fuck y'all been?"

"My bad Unc, we had a..." Kayson's words dragged off as he looked back at his brothers, I knew something had happened. I could tell by the look on Jaako's face, "anissue." Kayson finished.

"What the fuck kind of issue?"

"Jaako, you take this one." Kayson said and came around and sat on the couch. "What up?" Kayson threw his head up at Tate.

"Well?" I said waiting for someone to say something, I didn't really care who it was. I just needed to see if this was gonna be an issue for the organization. "Talk, muthafucka."

"Walked in on ya nephew with his dick down Krista's throat."

"Oooooooo," me and Tate both put our hands over our mouths.

"Damn nephew, you good?"

"Yeah, it was some disrespectful shit because it was at my house, but I don't love that hoe anyway." He shrugged, and I believed him.

"Well shit, if that's the case, let's get down to business." I waved for the other two to sit down. I already knew who he was talking about; there was no need to ask because the only one that was disrespectful enough to pull this off was Denari. "So, what the hell happened?"

"Shit, we gotta call that a nigga ran into the spot on the Ford but when we got there Denari wasn't there. We searched the damn house and even the stash was gone. The only person besides us that knew that shit was Jizzy, so I shot his ass." Jaako said shocking me because he was usually the level headed one, always willing to give folks a second chance, but not today and for that I was proud. Some people weren't deserving of that and in this case, he did the right thing.

"Did they say where the fuck Denari was?" I asked then just remembered what they said and then threw my hands up. "My bad," Jaako chuckled. "So what y'all thinking, and before you answer that Chief Tate got something he wanna tell y'all."

Me and Deshon Tate went back as far as the playground in elementary school; we called him by his last name because he hated his first name. We ran the streets together for as long as I can remember even after he took the oath to serve and protect. He served alright; helped me serve the best coke, heroin, and weed that Charlotte and surrounding areas has ever seen. I helped him get to his Chief of Police position and he made sure that my crew stayed clear. We had a system and it worked for us.

Tate stopped by to let me know that Denari's fuck up has put him on the radar at the station and people are watching. That's what I needed the boys here for today to tell them that Denari was gonna have to step back until shit calmed down because we damn sure didn't need the heat right now.

"So ya brother has been a little busy bee." Tate started. "And the streets are talking and so is the station."

"So, what does that mean?" Omari sat up in the chair.

"It means that he gonna have to fall back before shit gets real." Tate broke it down really simple for them. He told them about all the charges that Denari had accumulated over the last six months. I could tell that they all were shocked because I didn't even know about some of them. I couldn't do anything but shake my head because I should have known.

"Nigga just keep fucking up." Kayson shook his head and Omari sucked his teeth.

"Look Omari, we got one of two choices." I started but waited until I had his full attention before I continued. "We can sit Denari down for a minute until he gets his shit together and get his nose clean." I gave him a look to say that I knew he was snorting that shit. "Or we can all go down for his fuck ups and I ain't going to jail for nobody."

"Who gonna tell him?" Kayson asked.

"I am. Y'all might be worried about that little nigga's feelings but I ain't. He did this to himself so it's up to him to make the shit right. You can't be a fucking boss running around the streets acting like a clown. He needs to grow the fuck up and until then that nigga gonna be looking in from the sidelines. If anybody has a problem with it, they can chill right along with him." I opened the floor to objections and just like I thought there were none. "Now that that's out of the way, Tate do you have anything else?"

"Yes!" He smiled; I already knew what the fuck he was gon' say. "Who in the fuck came up with that THC Vape shit?" I nodded at Omari who smirked. "That shit was fucking genius, you can barely detect it and you can't tell that shit from the vape juice that's supposed to be used. You putting us on the map nigga. Bra-fucking-vo," he stood up and started clapping. Omari started wiping imaginary dirt off him. *Cocky fucker.*

I had to laugh because it was true for that shit to just be getting started; I swear it was bringing in more money than regular weed. He had even found a wholesale nigga and was even selling the fucking vapes. Omari was smart; I don't know what happened to his fucking brother.

"'Preciate that, but who the fuck are you?"

"Ah shit my bad this is the Chief of Police that I was

telling y'all about. I thought it was time to meet the man behind the fucking badge."

"What up young bloods, the more low key y'all are the easier my job is just remember that and we will get along just fine." Tate smiled and they all nodded.

We talked about how shit would run, and we talked about everything that would have to be turned around now that Denari had fucked shit up. I needed to talk to that little nigga ASAP and that shit was happening today whether he liked it or not.

"Where D?" I asked as the fellas were leaving.

"Little bitch was at my crib but if he knows what's good for him, he won't be there when I get back over there." Jaako said and I felt that shit.

"Bet!"

I walked the boys out and I picked up my phone and text Denari 911. He literally had thirty minutes to hit me back, if I had to go find his ass it wasn't gonna be pretty.

Chapter Twenty-Four
DENARI

"Man, fuck!" I yelled.

"What the fuck am I gonna do now?" Krista cried. "How in the hell am I going to support me and this baby? Denari you're gonna have to help me."

"Fuck you, I told you to get rid of the little muthafucka."

"This could be your child, Denari." She placed her hands on her hips and glared at me.

"And you think I give a fuck? Shit, you see how fucked up I am. You think I wanna bring another fucked up nigga into this world? Hell no, go kill that shit."

"I can't believe you. One of y'all gonna take care of this baby." She said in a threatening tone. "Voluntarily or involuntarily, your choice."

"Bitch, threatening me is not good for your health." I

headed for the door. "Let me get out of here before that fool comes back, and I have to shoot his fucking ass."

"You ain't gonna do shit but what you did just now, sit back and get ya ass whooped."

I stopped dead in my tracks and just stared at the bitch. Who in the fuck did she think she was? I was tired of her and her fucking mouth. She needed to be taught a lesson, and fast. I walked over toward her and slapped the shit out of her. I hit her so hard that she fell to the ground. I stood over her daring her to say something else.

"You are nothing but a bitch, hitting women. I don't know what in the hell I was thinking ever fucking with you. I definitely lowered my standards with you." She just didn't know when to shut the hell up.

I raised my hand and I punched her in the face repeatedly, I got so mad that I blacked out. I was pissed that my brother walked in on this shit, that he fucked me over it when he didn't even want the broad, mad that she wouldn't shut up, that she was talking about keeping this baby, mad that my nigga Jizzy was dead, and that somebody had the fucking balls to rob me.

When I finally came to, Krista was lying in a pool of blood and was barely conscious. I freaked out and grabbed my keys and ran out of the house. I jumped in my car and sped off, just as another car was pulling in to the drive way. I didn't know who it was, and I didn't give a fuck, I just knew that I needed to get away from there as fast as I could.

It was a must that I get out of town for a minute, shit was

getting crazy as fuck. I drove like a bat out of hell until I reached my condo. I jumped out and headed up the stairs. I opened the door and Heaven was lying on the couch looking beautiful as ever, made me wonder why in the hell was I still doing the shit that I was doing.

"Pack your shit we gotta get out of town for a little minute." I told her.

"What's going on Denari? Is everything okay?"

"Stop asking fucking questions, pack a bag and let's go, or you can stay here and wait on that nigga Ortiz to find you."

That shit put some pep in her step. She got up from the couch and within ten minutes she had a bag packed and was ready to go. I made sure that I turned off all the lights and shit, and we were out the door. Right as I was about to pull out I got a text from my uncle that said 911. A part of me knew I needed to go see what he wanted, but the other part of me knew I needed to get the fuck out of dodge.

"Denari, talk to me baby." Heaven pleaded, as bad as I wanted to tell her the fucked-up shit I just did, I couldn't.

"Nothing, some shit went down and Ortiz on some bullshit." I gave her a half truth and she accepted it. That's what I liked about her. I could tell her anything but when I didn't feel like talking she would let the shit ride. She wasn't a an aggy bitch.

I cranked up the car and headed to interstate 77N. I remembered that my uncle gotta little cabin up there in Cherokee for when he wanna go gamble and shit. I'll just head there and hang out for a couple weeks until shit cooled down.

I needed to call my uncle to tell him what was up. I didn't want to hear his mouth, but I may need his connections to get out of this shit.

"Fuck!" I yelled and hit the steering wheel. I popped in some Old School 90's R&B and hit the highway. I would holla at Unc when I got there.

"Oh my goodness, this is beautiful." Heaven beamed as she stared out of the floor to ceiling windows that over looked the beautiful Smoky Mountains.

"You should see it in the winter time." I said as I walked up behind her.

"Maybe I'll get lucky enough to be able to come back out here with you sometime."

"No doubt." I kissed her on the cheek. "I gotta make a few calls, go ahead and make yourself comfortable. I'ma call in a pizza for tonight and we can go to the store tomorrow."

"Sounds good." She said sweetly and then headed back to the bedroom where I could hear her ooh and aah some more. My Unc really had this place hooked up and it was ducked away, just perfect for what I needed right now. I walked outside on the porch to prepare for this conversation with my uncle. I dialed his number and held my breath.

"So, you don't understand what the fuck 911 mean now?" His voice was so loud that I had to move the phone from my ear for a second.

"I had to get out of town." Was all I said because I knew I couldn't talk too much over the phone.

"You should've come here first Denari; you know what the fuck is up. I can't handle your fuck ups no more."

"Unc man, I just been going through some shit." I tried to reason with him, but he wasn't having it.

"No nigga, you just been on some rogue shit and you need to chill out for a minute."

I know I been on some other shit but damn it wasn't all that. Sounded like to me that he was firing me from the family organization. I wasn't about to lie down and take that shit.

"So, you saying I'm out?"

"Yeah for a minute until the shit calms down, they looking at you." I knew that was code for I was on the police radar but that's what the fuck we had police in our pocket for right? To handle shit like that. "Heat too high, so just chill."

"I'm gambling, but I'll be back in a couple weeks."

"Longer."

"How fucking long?" I was starting to get pissed.

"I'll come visit in a few days, just sit tight. Shit ain't good." He said that last part aggressive and that let me know that he was pissed and no matter what I said or did, this is what it was gonna be.

"So, I just gotta wait?"

"That's what the fuck I said." Was all he said before he hung up the phone. I laid my head back on the chair that I was sitting in. Shit was just crumbling around me and I needed to get a hold of it fast. I was fucking up royally and I knew it, but I couldn't help it. I would think of some shit to tell my uncle when he came down.

I really wanted to holla at my brother, but I knew that he wasn't fucking with me right now. I just needed to know how the shit with Krista looked. I didn't mean to flip out like I did but she just wouldn't shut up, it wasn't my fault. I just needed her to be quiet. I dialed my brother and waited on him to answer.

"WHAT?" He gritted on the first ring.

"Man, chill."

He laughed sarcastically. "You are a real piece of fucking work Denari; I'm over your bullshit." He stopped and said something to someone else. "You didn't even have to do that shit, bruh." I could hear the disappointment in his voice.

"It wasn't my fault, she just—"

"It's never your fault D, you can never own up to your shit. That's your fucking problem." He yelled. Omari had never talked to me like that before. "I don't have time for this shit, what do you want?"

"I wanted to know if she was pressing charges."

"We don't know, we here now, she lost the fucking baby, but I guess you happy about that right?"

"Fuck yeah! I told that bitch to get rid of that fucking baby!" I yelled, now getting upset.

"That could have been ya seed or your niece or nephew you fucking dumb ass. It don't matter how the baby was made, it was innocent. You need to get your shit together, real talk."

Damn, I knew shit was fucked up if O was pissed the fuck off. He was talking to me like I wasn't shit. If that bitch pressed charges, I would make sure that she didn't live to make it to the court date. Fuck her. Shit if she would have just kept her mouth shut then she wouldn't be in this situation and I didn't care what anyone said about it.

I needed to find a way to get Omari to handle that shit with Perry. He was supposed to call me in a week to set some shit up. It was already gonna be a task getting that much work and I only fuck with the house on the Ford. Now that I'm "out" how in the hell was I gonna get what the fuck I promised him. Lucky for me, O was always about a dollar.

"Fuck that bitch and all that shit, look I had set up some shit and I need you to run that for me."

"What shit, Denari? How you setting up shit without talking to us? That ain't how we roll, and you know it! That's how shit goes bad nigga."

"Here you go with all that, look this shit could bring in a lot of fucking money and I need you to stop being a fucking bitch and handle that."

"I got yo' bitch, ignorant ass muthafucka. You can fuck your life up all you want but I'll be got damned if I let you take me down with you. I was gonna try and talk Unc into rethinking shit, but now I see he made the right fucking decision."

This conversation wasn't going how I needed it to go.

Omari could be a stubborn son of a bitch when he wanted to be. I took a deep breath and looked to the sky.

"Look I need ya bruh, real talk. This shit could expand our shit. It could be just what I need to make Unc see that I can do this shit. If I can make a deal like this, I'll be back on top." I laid it out there in hopes that he would understand where the hell I was coming from, but to my surprise O didn't bite.

"No can do." He said dryly.

"The fuck you mean?"

"Exactly what the fuck I said, can't do it. You out man."

"O, man come on! This could be the fucking break I need."

"What's this nigga's name? Did you do the proper fucking research on this nigga?"

"Man, I know what the fuck I'm doing, that nigga's name Perry."

"Perry what?"

"I don't fucking know!" I was getting frustrated because he was acting like I was a fucking idiot or something. I didn't get the vibe that this nigga was on no fuck shit and who in their right mind would want to come against the fucking Barnes Brothers? So, what the fuck?

"Sounds like you ain't did what the fuck you were supposed to do." He said with disappointment.

"Nigga just trust me." He got quiet, like he was thinking about what I just said, I had his ass. There was no way that O would tell me no for some shit like this.

"Nah nigga, you need to take that shit up with Unc, because I want no parts of it. It ain't how I work."

"IS THAT HIM?" I could hear Jaako yelling in the background. "I'MA FUCK HIM UP, WHERE THE FUCK IS HE?" Next thing I know the phone went dead.

Fuck! What the fuck was I gonna do now? How in the hell was I gonna do this fucking deal? If I backed out, I will be the laughing fucking stock of the drug game and I wasn't trying to have that. Niggas would lose all respect for me and what the fuck did you have in this game if you didn't have respect? Nothing!

A nigga was stressed the fuck out and in need of some pussy, a drink and a line of that good shit. I needed to think of a way to get the shit that I needed to hook up with that nigga Perry.

Chapter Twenty-Five
KRISTA

I sat up in the bed and just let the tears fall from my eyes. When the doctor told me that they couldn't save my baby I didn't know how to take it, so I just broke all the way down. How could someone be so damn cruel? That baby was innocent, and he just didn't give a fuck. If it wasn't for my mother coming when she did I may have died too.

"Who did this to you Krista? Was it Jaako?" My mother yelled. She had been asking me that since she got here. I was not about to tell her who did this to me because I had so much more in store for him. He was gonna pay for this shit and in my opinion, jail was too fucking good for him. I wanted him dead and I was gonna do whatever I could do to make that happen.

"No Ma, Jaako was mad but he would never do anything like this to me."

"What was he mad about? That you're pregnant? How dare he treat you like that, just wait 'til I see him, I will make sure to give him a piece of my mind."

"No Ma," I rolled my eyes. "I did something stupid." I put my hand over my face and prepared myself for the lecture that I know was sure to come.

"What is it, Krista?!" she asked with more authority than I was prepared for.

"He caught me and Denari."

"What?!?"

"I didn't know that he was coming home because he had been making it his business to stay away. I messed up."

"What have I told you, Krista?" she damn near yelled.

"Never to get caught when I'm playing the field."

"So how in the hell did this happen Krista, I taught you better than that."

"I know." I put my head down while she lectured me on how to use and handle men. Unlike my mother, I did want to be happy one day with the man of my dreams, but until I found that man I wanted to be happy with Jaako's status and money. She went on and on until we heard a knock on the door. We looked at each other and my mom walked over to open the door.

"What are you doing here?" she scoffed.

"You fucking called me." I heard Jaako's voice and smiled inwardly. Just the notion that he came to see me made me feel like there was still a chance to get back on his good side. I needed to be close to him until I figured out exactly what I wanted to do with Denari's coward ass.

"Mom, chill." I said, and she smacked her lips and returned to her spot beside my bed.

Jaako mugged her all the way to her seat and then the look he gave me was mixed with hatred and sympathy. I turned on the water works as soon as he started to walk in my direction. I was genuinely hurt, I wanted my baby, but I needed to put on one hell of a show for him, if he was gonna forgive me for what he walked in on.

"Yo, you aight?" he asked right when there was another knock at the door, "it's Kay and O." He threw over his shoulder as he opened the door.

"Damn Krista, you good?" Kayson said as soon as he entered the room. Hell, that was more than Jaako did.

"So, you needed an entourage? Tuh!" my mother sneered.

"Look I don't like you, and quite honestly I'm here out of the kindness of my heart because I doubt the fucking baby was mine anyway." Jaako said in a calm tone and then he looked at me. "I can leave." I shook my head before my mama opened her damn mouth again.

"No," she stood up and pointed at Jaako. "This is your fault, who leaves a got damn woman alone with their psycho brother knowing that she's carrying their baby. You are a sorry excuse for a man and you should be ashamed of yourself."

Jaako laughed and I could tell it was one of those laughs

that he did when he was trying to control his anger. I tried to interject but Jaako held his hands up.

"Number one, you too got damn old to be trying to live through your got damn daughter. Number two, I don't know if that was my got damn baby or not. I see ya daughter didn't tell you that she was spreading 'em for the got damn family did she?" He yelled that last part. "And three, don't worry about my got damn brother, I got that handled."

"Umph, I bet you do." My mother rolled her eyes. "So, I take it you're paying for this little hospital stay, I mean it is your fault she's here."

"No, it's her fault she's here and if you're gonna be in here I'm leaving." Jaako started toward the door.

"NO!" I yelled to stop him. "Don't go, Mom give us a minute."

"Unless the conversation is about money, what do you have to talk about?"

"MOM!"

"What the fuck is wrong with you?" Omari blurted out with his face all screwed up. "Yo' old cougar ass probably told her to fuck both, didn't you? I bet if I threw a dollar at you, yo' ancient ass would bend it over bust it open, wouldn't you?" I was shocked that he was actually saying this to my mother. I looked at Jaako to try and get him to make him chill, but he had a stupid fucking smirk on his face. "I bet you don't even know who her daddy is, do you? Yo' ass was prolly throwing pussy to the highest bidder." He shook his head and headed toward the door.

"Jaako are you going to stand there and let him talk to my mother like that?" I was appalled that no one was saying anything, just standing there with stupid smirks on their faces "Jaako!"

"What? What do you want me to say?" he shrugged his shoulders.

"Check it shorty, you need to stop listening to your mother. Her ass gonna have you somewhere floating." Omari said and then headed out the door.

"Disrespectful hoodlums, all of you." My mother said with a nasty look on her face. "Krista, I don't think he has enough money for you to have to deal with all of this. Thank God you never fell in love with him. That would have been an epic fail for you." I gave her a look that told her to stop while she was ahead, but she didn't take heed to the warning and just kept going. "I'm glad you lost that bastard baby."

"Mother!" that shit hurt, because regardless of the circumstances that was gonna be her grandkid.

"What? Hell, now you can make it official with that other fella you've been dealing with. It was probably his baby anyway." She smirked and the look on Jaako's face was indescribable.

If I could have disappeared right then and there I swear I would have. I had been dealing with this dude that I met on a shopping trip with my mother out in South Carolina. His name was Perry and he was the sweetest thing ever. I just kept him at bay because I didn't know if he could take care of me like Jaako could, so I just dealt with him when Jaako was busy or I just needed to get away.

I did sleep with him around the time that I got pregnant, but this was gonna be Jaako's baby, regardless of what anyone said. But Denari fucked all of that up for me and I was definitely gonna make sure that he paid for all of this.

"Damn girl, you an all-out hoe." Jaako said with a laugh.

"Jaako, it's not like that." I reached out to him and he moved away.

"I almost felt sorry for you. Good looking out, Ma!" he nodded and turned to walk away. "Oh, and if yo' nasty ass gave me anything that's yo' ass, and I promise you that."

"Jaako, please I need you! I just lost our baby."

Again, he laughed. "Bitch that was the neighborhood baby."

He threw up the deuces and slammed the door on his way out. I was so furious at my mother. Why would she do that?

"Why would you do that?"

"He ain't no good Krista, I don't care how much money he got. He can't even protect you." She dug in her pocketbook and pulled out her phone.

"What are you doing?"

"Calling that detective to tell him that we know who attacked you."

"No you're not; I got something better planned for him anyway." I smiled, and she looked at me with a worried expression.

"Don't get yourself hurt over this, let the police handle it and move on with your life."

"No Mom, he destroyed my life and I plan to return the favor."

I laid my head back on the pillow and thought about what it would have been like to be a mother, and how it was taken away from me. Jaako acted like he didn't even care, and that shit hurt but I know he was just acting out about what happened. He would get over it eventually and come around. I was banking on it.

Chapter Twenty-Six
JENACIA

"Oh no, is she okay?" I asked Kayson, he had just got through telling me what happened to Krista. I can't believe Denari would do something like that. He was a selfish prick, but to beat a baby out of someone was crazy. "Is Jaako okay?"

"Jaako's ass is all over the place, he doesn't know whether to be mad or sad because from what her mama said, Denari wasn't the only one that she was sleeping with."

"Ohhhh damn!"

"Right," he said and then there was an awkward silence. "Tell Zemia that Omari will be there soon to pick her up, me and you will talk. Aight?"

"Okay." I said because even though all of this was going on that didn't mean that I didn't remember what he did just a few hours ago. I didn't forget that he put his hands on me and accused me of some shit that I didn't do, and I damn sure didn't forget all the shit that bitch said either.

"Jenacia, I love you and I'm sorry."

As bad as I wanted to reciprocate that I love you I couldn't, so I just hung up the phone. I understood how things looked, but he should have trusted me. I never gave him a reason to not trust me. How could he think that I would go back to someone that had a kid on me? Hell, I left him because he cheated, so I don't understand how that would even work.

"Jen, you good girl, what he say?" Zemia asked snapping me out of my thoughts.

"Krista slept with Denari and Jaako walked in on them, then somehow Denari beat Krista and made her lose her baby."

"Baby?" she screeched.

"Yeah girl, she was pregnant, and it could be Denari's or some other nigga's." I waited for a second to let the tea sink in before I continued. "I'm guessing that Denari told her to get rid of it and she refused, so he beat the baby out of her." I shook my head because I couldn't imagine having that happen. At least when I was pregnant I made the choice to get rid of my baby, and that shit still affected me 'til this day, and that shit happened a whole fucking year ago.

"Damn ol' Krista was getting around huh? She still didn't deserve that though."

"That's what I said."

"But what would make her wanna fuck Denari though? He ain't even all that cute, at least not compared to the other brothers."

"And he crazy as fuck, I hope her ass gonna be okay"

"I'm sure she'll be okay, but I gotta feeling this ain't about to go away. She gonna use this to her advantage." Zemia raised a brow. "I like that lawyer chick we met at the cookout, but I don't know if Krista about to let that happen, especially now."

"Yeah, but do you think he gonna fall for that seeing as though she slept with his brother and another nigga? That would be too much for anybody."

"True, but if that hoe spins it the right way, shit, it might just work," she shrugged.

"Bitch let me find out yo' ass be scheming."

"Ahhh bitch bye," she waved me off and took off toward the kitchen. "Bitch come cook, hell I'm starving."

" It's food in there, you cook."

"You already know I ain't domesticated." We both laughed because her ass was telling the truth. She didn't believe in catering to men. She couldn't cook to save her damn life, I tried to teach her once and we both got aggravated and went for pizza."

"Nah I'ma order in."

"Bitch I eat out every day," she whined. "I want you to cook."

"You make me sick." I fussed but got up and headed to the kitchen.

"Yeah yeah, I love you too."

I went to the freezer to see what we had; I ended up taking out shrimp and whipped up some shrimp and broccoli Alfredo. By the time I was done, Kayson and Omari were walking in the house. I was getting plates down and Zemia was messing over the stove.

"Damn babe." Omari walked in smiling. "You cooked this?" Omari was cheesing so damn hard that I didn't want to burst his bubble, so I wasn't gonna say anything, but my girl wasn't one to take credit for someone else's stuff.

"Awww how cute." She said as she turned around to face him. "You'll learn soon enough that cooking is not my forte."

"Say what now?" he said with a smirk on his face.

"Oh, you heard me, I don't cook." She tilted her head and he laughed and shook his head and walked over to the table.

"Well the shit smells good, sis."

"Thanks." I giggled.

I took down plates and fixed everyone some food. I sat it at the table. Kayson kept his eyes on me the whole time. I tried my best to keep my attention on what I was doing, but it was hard. He was sitting there in some stone washed Levi jeans with a plain white t-shit, with his dreads braided back. I didn't even notice that he had just got them done when I saw him earlier. His facial features were on full display and every time he licked his lips my pussy dripped. How in the hell was I gonna stand my ground with him sitting there looking like that?

"Let me holla at you real quick."

"Can we please eat first," I said and sat down. Kayson stood up and stood over me. I grabbed my fork and put a forkful of food in my mouth to ignore him, but he wasn't having it. "Kayson, just let me eat."

He let out a big sigh, lifted me from the chair that I was sitting in, threw me over his shoulder and carried me to the room like a cave man. When we reached the bedroom, he threw me on the bed and went back to shut the door.

"Damn, we couldn't eat first."

"That food ain't going nowhere."

"Neither is this conversation." I rolled my eyes and he lowered his head.

There was a chair that he kept in the corner of the room, he grabbed it and pulled it over to the bed and sat down in front of where I was now sitting up in the bed. He placed his hands on my thighs and looked me right in the eyes. I got lost in his beautiful light brown eyes, as bad as I wanted to look away I couldn't. It was like his ass had me in a trance.

"A nigga wasn't in his right frame of mind, it's not an excuse but when I saw those pictures I lost it. I know with everything we've been through, I don't have a right to act like that, but I did. I love you Jenacia and I always have, I can't lose you again. I went about it the wrong way, and a nigga apologize about that, but it happened and there ain't shit we can do about it. All I can do is promise you that nothing like that will happen again."

"You put your hands on me, Kayson."

"I know, and a nigga feels fucked up about that shit, but like I said, it will never happen again. I'm sure when Ann Barnes gets a whiff of it she gonna fuck me up and make sure it never happens again." He laughed, and I did too because that lady didn't play with or about them.

"I've never given you a reason not to trust me, so why now? Because of that bitch?" I tilted my head to the side and he cleared his throat. I could tell that the conversation was starting to get uncomfortable for him because he began to rub my legs a little harder.

"I was wrong as fuck to believe anything that bitch said." He laid his head in his lap and as if he had an epiphany he shot up and glared at me. "Don't even fucking think about it, I ain't been fucking with that bitch since me and you been kicking it. Hell, I ain't fucking with no one but you."

"That's not what she said." I raised an eyebrow.

"I don't give a fuck what she said; I'm telling you now I ain't seen that bitch. First time I heard from her was when she sent that picture. But don't even worry about it, I'ma take care of that." He nodded his head. The look in his eyes was pure evil.

"No, just leave it alone. You say you ain't fucking with her then you ain't fucking with her." I shrugged my shoulders. "Just stay away from her and we'll be good."

"Yeah, but I don't like people trying to break up my happy home and shit."

"Especially when you are doing such a good job on your

own." He sighed, and I looked at him. "You know what hurt the most though?"

"I don't wanna talk about this."

"You don't have a choice." I demanded. "How could you stand out there and talk about how you doing all of this and that for me when I didn't ask for any of that?"

"I was mad, man."

"So, every time you get mad I can expect that from you?"

"Man no, this shit ain't gonna happen again."

"I know because I'm getting my own place." I threw out there really quick.

"No the fuck you're not." I could tell that pissed him off, but so what.

"Yeah I don't want to be put in a position where I be left out in the cold if shit don't work out like with R—"

"Don't you ever compare me to that bitch ass nigga again." He heaved.

"I'm just saying." I shrugged. "I just want my own."

"Aight, cool." He said and stood up to leave out of the room.

"Really?" That shit was too easy it was something behind it.

"Yeah, I'll go add you to the deed to the house tomorrow, so this will be just as much yours as it is mine. Problem solved." He smiled like he just solved the million-dollar equation.

That's not what I meant."

"Well Jenacia, that's the only fucking choice that you got,

I won't let you get away from me again. I love you too much." He kissed me passionately. "Now, let's go eat, I'm hungry."

I just looked at him and shook my head. I needed to decide what I needed to do for me. I loved Kayson; I just needed to make sure that us moving this fast was the right thing to do. I would let him think that he won this round, but this conversation was far from over.

Chapter Twenty-Seven
JAAKO

Not only was that bitch fucking my brother, but she around here fucking some random nigga. I can only wonder what else her ass been up to. Even though I didn't love her ass, I still trusted her enough to live with her, and to know that she been doing all of this behind my back did something to me.

I wanted to slice her mama's got damn throat with her shady ass, but I'm glad I didn't. If I had done what I wanted to do, I wouldn't have found out just how scandalous she really was. Krista didn't know everything about what I did in these streets, but that hoe knew enough, so it made me wonder would she be shady enough to try and set me up. It would be foolish of her, but could she do something like that? Nah, that bitch wasn't that crazy.

This shit with Denari, the baby, and this other nigga was

just the push that I needed to get that bitch out of my life for good. I didn't want anything else to do with her. She could fuck the fucking President and I wouldn't give a damn.

I really needed to clear my head and let all this shit go, Yameka had been blowing me up all day, but I wasn't in the mood to talk so I didn't answer. I needed to see her but talking wasn't in the plans.

Pulling up to her house, I parked and got out the car, walked up to the door and laid on the door bell. I wasn't letting up until she brought her ass to the door.

"Who in the hell on my bell like that?" She yelled on the other side of the door and I still didn't let up. She swung the door open with a scowl on her beautiful face. "What the hell, Jaako?"

I didn't let her say anything else. I lightly pushed her in the house and stepped in shutting and locking the door behind me. I threw my keys on the floor and just stared at her for a minute. Yameka was beautiful, inside and out. I loved her spirit and her feisty personality; I also loved the fact that she had a real soft spot for me, even when I didn't deserve it.

"So, you gonna say something or you just gonna stand there looking like a fucking creep?"

I rushed her and backed her up against the wall, I covered her mouth with mine letting her know that I wasn't with the talking at all. I just needed her to know how I felt. I didn't want to say it, I wanted to show her. She was the only one that could help me take my mind off all the bullshit that I went through today.

She had on these little ass shorts and a tank top. I snatched that shit off so fast ripping the shirt. I didn't care; I would buy her a thousand more. I just didn't have time for the extras. I picked her up and carried her over to the table and sat her down and rushed her with kisses again.

"Whoa, Jaako." She said trying to escape my kisses and get off the table.

"Shut up!"

"Excuse me." She put her hands on my chest to try and back me up but I slapped them down and went to work on her neck. "Umm, are you gonna tell me what this is about?"

"No, I want you to shut up and let me show you." I looked her in the eyes so that she knew I wasn't playing with her ass. I really wanted her ass to shut the fuck up and let me have this moment, so I covered her mouth with mine again and this time she kissed me back. I pulled her legs to the end of the table and sat down in the chair that was closest to me like I was about to have a full course meal.

I pushed her back on the table and slid her up so that I was eye level with her pussy. I took a big whiff and I swear I got so lost in the essence of her smell and it instantly relaxed me. It was crazy how she had that effect on me, I don't know what I would have done had she decided not to wait around on a nigga.

Staring at her pussy had my dick brick hard, but I needed to paint my feelings with my tongue, and that's exactly what I did. I covered her freshly waxed pussy with my mouth and savored the taste. The shit had my taste buds on ten and I had to resist biting into it like a fucking peach. I moved my tongue around in a circular motion.

"Shit Jaa, that shit feels good."

The way she called out sounded sexy as hell. It wasn't like I hadn't heard it before, but something this time sounded different, it felt different, and I liked it. I ran my tongue down her slit and dipped it into her opening enough to make her squirm. I repeated that a few times before I moved up and attacked her clit like I was feasting on her for the first time.

"Oh shit ummm fuck, Jaako."

"Ummm" a moan escaped my lips; I was so into pleasing her that I was damn near on the verge of cumming myself.

"I'ma bout to cum baby, shit." She started to grind on to my face and that shit made me go harder. "Fuck, I'm cumming, shit," she screamed out and I lapped up everything she gave me. Shit was the sweetest thing I ever tasted. I nibbled on her button until she got herself together. I knew that she was sensitive by the way she kept jumping. "Ummm stop, you gonna make me cum again."

"Don't tell me to stop, you just shut up."

"You gonna stop telling me to shut up." She said between breaths.

"Or what?" I started going in on her clit again and she was screaming out of control. Once she gave me another one, I was satisfied. I leaned back in the chair that I was sitting in and pulled her up by her hands. She collapsed back on the table. "What you think you doing?"

"Shit, Jaako."

"Nah, get that ass up I ain't done."

She tried to get up but failed. I laughed and bent down and picked her up and threw her across my shoulder. I carried her back to her room and threw her on the bed. The look on her face was one of shock and excitement at the same time. I was the one that liked to make love and take my time. I was gonna take my time alright, but I wasn't in the mood for all that love making. I had a point to prove to myself.

I grabbed Yameka's legs, pulled her to the end of the bed, and then I spread them. I took my thumb and ran it down her slit and she jumped, that made me smile because that meant that I was doing my job. I undressed myself and let it all fall to the floor while never taking my eyes off her chocolate skin.

"I want this." Was all I said and before she could say anything back, I covered my mouth with her and placed my dick at her opening. I eased in, the way her pussy hugged my dick almost made me lose it. "Fuck!" I yelled out.

I lifted because I wanted to watch my dick slide in and out of her wet tunnel. Sex with Yameka was always great, but again, this time felt different. I didn't know if it was because I no longer had any baggage, or if it was because I finally knew what I wanted and where I wanted to be. No more holding on to bullshit.

Watching her face contort turned up something inside me and I gave her the dick like I never have before. I felt like I needed to show her that what she been waiting on was worth it. We went at it for a good two hours. I was exhausted and so was she, but I hated going to bed all sweaty. I got up and went into the bathroom that she had inside her room and ran a bubble bath.

"Come on, girl."

"You are out of your mind if you think I'm moving from this spot anytime soon," her voice was filled with exhaustion and it caused me to laugh. "Don't laugh Jaako, it's not funny."

"My bad." I laughed again, lifted her up, carried her to the bathroom, and placed her in the tub.

"Ummm," she moaned out as I lowered her into the bath.

"You gonna let me in?" I laughed as she took over the whole tub.

"You asking for a lot tonight." she laughed.

I ignored her and got in the tub behind her. I positioned her between my legs and leaned her back so that her back was on my chest. We sat there in silence for what felt like hours until she broke the silence.

"So, you ready to tell me what that was about?"

"No, didn't I tell you to shut up." I smirked even though she couldn't see me.

"Jaako!"

"Man, I'm fucking with you." I nuzzled my chin into her neck. "I just wanted to show you what I was feeling. I don't think words would have done it any justice."

"Well damn, if that's how you feel." she giggled.

"Seriously though, some shit went down today, and it made me realize some shit. I'm ready to be what you want me to be."

"Jaako, all I ever wanted you to be was you." She snuggled into me a little more. "I just wanted you to be you with me."

"You know I wanted that too."

"No you didn't, you were comfortable with your girl and you wanted me to be okay with it."

"I never wanted you to be okay with it; I needed to be okay with being by myself. I'm fucked up when it comes to being alone and shit. She was my comfort zone and I knew if I kept money coming her way that I wouldn't have to worry about her not being there. Today, all that shit backfired.".

"What happened?" I told her about all the shit that happened, it felt good getting that shit off my chest. I needed to talk that shit out. "Damn babe, she a hoe." I laughed.

"Tell me about it."

"I used to feel bad about dealing with you while you were with her, but now," she stopped and tilted her head back so that she could look at me. "Fuck that bitch." I kissed her on the lips and laughed.

"My words exactly."

"But..." she started.

"No buts, don't even think like that." I already knew what was running through her mind, but that's not the case at all. "This ain't no rebound bullshit. I wanted you way before I knew any of this. We been doing this, so stop it."

"I just want to make sure that you are done with her."

"She fucked my brother; you can't come back from that." We both got quiet again until she spoke.

"Are you upset about the baby?" she asked lowly.

"I don't know how to feel about that. In a way it could have been my seed so yeah, but to know that she was out here fucking like it was going out of style makes me okay with it in a sense."

"Do you want kids?" she asked out of nowhere. I smiled, because I knew that she did, she had mentioned it more than once.

"I want kids with you." I kissed her shoulder blade and she looked up at me and I couldn't read her expression.

She turned around and straddled my lap. She grabbed my dick that was already hard and slid down on it.

"Good, 'cause I want babies with you too."

I grabbed her hips and leaned back and enjoyed the ride that she took me on. This was the start of something amazing and I couldn't wait to see what we could be.

Chapter Twenty-Eight
OMARI

It had been a month since all that shit went down and I had barely heard from my brother. He was still on that help him with this deal he set up and I didn't trust it. I hated second guessing that nigga, but he had been on some other shit lately. Unc made him dip away for a little minute, because of all that shit with Krista, and so he could get his mind right, but something was telling me that Denari wasn't using his time away for that bullshit.

"So, you just gonna fuck and leave?" Jernisha's aggravating ass asked. I met her through that bitch Brayla that my brother used to fuck with. They were home girls and shit.

"Don't I always?" I looked at her ass like she was crazy.

"I thought we were building something." She pouted.

"How in the fuck did you think that? Did I tell you that?"

"Well no, but you keep coming back so I just thought that—"

"Thought what? That just because yo' ass can suck dick and throw the pussy that I was gonna wife you?" I laughed. These hoes were crazy as fuck if they thought that pussy made you eligible to be with a nigga like me. "Nah, to wife you, I would have to have respect for you and I don't."

"Wow you just gonna sit in my house and talk to me like that?"

"Hell yeah! What, you wanted me to sugar coat it for you?" I looked at her and she actually looked hurt. A part of me wanted to laugh, but now was not the time. I needed to school this bitch. "Every time I call, it's to fuck and you know that because when I get here you ass naked. When I leave, I drop a stack on the dresser, and not once have I taken you anywhere but to that back bedroom to fuck the shit out of you." I paused to let that sink in. "Now, where in any of that does it sound like I was interested in anything more?"

"I thought that's what you wanted."

"What, easy pussy? Hell yeah, what nigga don't like easy pussy, but if it's easy for me I can almost bet it's easy for another nigga." I waited on a response and never got one, so I laughed. "My point exactly. You don't even respect yoself shorty, so why should I?"

"Whatever." She waved me off and just like normal I went in my pocket and pulled off a band and left it on her nightstand.

Bitches were crazy as hell, why in the hell would I wife a

bitch like that. When I decided to settle down it was gonna be with Zemia, but right now she was on that we need to get to know each other bullshit and a nigga had needs. Shit, I was young as fuck and I wasn't trying to be sitting around with blue balls waiting on her to spread 'em. That was a fucked-up way of thinking but who gives a fuck? I was who I was, and I was a pussy man.

I must say that I did enjoy spending time with Zemia though; she was cool as fuck and knew more about sports than most niggas. I could sit with her and talk about football like I was with one of my brothers. We went to the bar to watch a preseason game and almost got thrown the hell out because of her mouth, that shit turned me on though. Her ass wasn't lying when she said she couldn't cook. She was gonna have to work on that, 'cause a nigga liked to eat, especially when I was high.

She had been on that take me out on a date shit and that wasn't my area of expertise. I was gonna try for her though. She deserved that and so much more.

I was on my way to the warehouse to check some shit out with the vape business. When I came across this shit I didn't think it would do this good, but I must say the money was rolling in. This risk wasn't that high because of the way it came, but the shit was potent and gave you a good ass high. I knew that shit because I kept my vape on me and full. Fuck rolling a blunt when I could just fill up my tank and have at it.

"Nigga, where you been?" Kayson asked as soon as I walked in the warehouse.

"Fucking with that bitch Jernisha that live off West Boulevard, had to school that hoe." Kayson laughed. "Hoe tried to hit me with that why I hit and run bullshit."

"Man, if Zemia find out you out here living foul and shit she gonna cut yo' ass off."

"She needs to get her head right then shit, how long does she want me to wait around on her?"

"Nigga with a woman like Zemia, you wait. They don't come around often and when you get her, you lock that shit down," Kayson preached. I looked at his ass like he was crazy.

"Say what now? Because I don't remember yo' ass locking sis down."

"And you see where that got my ass right?"

"But you got her ass now though, so it's all good."

"Nigga, that shit ain't been easy. I did a lot of shit to her and it's hard for her to trust me. If I had done that shit right the first time, I wouldn't be going through this."

"Yeah, yeah, yeah whatever I don't wanna hear that right now." I waved him off because it wasn't gonna happen like that for me. "What this money looking like?"

"I was going over some shit and something didn't look right." Kayson said with a perplexed look on his face. "Inventory was fucked up, I know what the fuck I counted last week but the shit is short like ten keys, but the money adds the fuck up. Shit is crazy as fuck and it's fucking with me, got me thinking I'm crazy and shit."

I already knew what the fuck was going on. Denari found somebody to give him the work he was trying to get from me.

That nigga found a fucking way to make that shit happen. In a way, I was proud as fuck but then again, I was worried because we don't know this nigga he moving with.

"O, nigga, you zoning out and shit, what you thinking?"

Here I was stuck in another muthafucking situation with my fucking brother. "Shit bruh, I don't know. If shit adding up, then I don't see what the problem is. You sure yo' ass wasn't fucked up when you counted that shit?"

"Now you know how careful I am with that shit."

That's true, he was the only nigga that I knew who liked to count money by fucking hand. I knew he didn't make a mistake, but I couldn't tell him what was really going on, not until I talked to my brother. I was so tired of being caught in these fucked up situations with him.

"You right bruh, shit maybe these niggas ain't signing shit out like they supposed to."

"That's what I thought too, I'ma have to have little meeting with these incompetent ass niggas."

"Yeah, looks like it."

"I'll holla at Unc about it and we'll get that shit together. I ain't really worried about it too much because the money adding up. Now if my money was fucked up then I would be acting a damn fool." He chuckled and so did I because I knew it was true. That nigga got real crazy when it came to the money. "Speaking of money, the vape business is booming."

"Fuck yeah and I love that shit."

"Me too nigga, Unc bout ready to hand this shit over and I'm glad."

"Shit's good, I just hope it stay that way."

"Right!"

I chilled with my brother for a minute and talked about Unc's upcoming birthday, we wanted to throw him the party of a lifetime. We had called Onyx and we were gonna rent that bitch out for the night and just have a fucking ball. We were still getting shit situated and all that shit, but it was definitely gonna be a good time.

Once I was done at the warehouse, I headed to my crib to chill. I just wanted to chill and relax a little. I needed to call my brother and see what the fuck his ass is up to. I had a fucking feeling that this shit wasn't gonna be good.

Chapter Twenty-Nine
DENARI

Everybody thought my ass was still hiding out in them damn sticks and I was okay with it. For what I was trying to accomplish, I needed them to think that. Unc always told us that money fucking talks, and I couldn't agree more. I got that nigga Joker that was night watch at the warehouse to feed me the product I needed to keep shit going with Perry.

That nigga hit me up while I was in Cherokee chillin' with Heaven and told me that if I couldn't come through in a week's time that he was moving on to another dealer, and I couldn't have that. I needed him so I could show them what I could contribute to the family business.

A nigga had to do what I had to do. I guess Unc told everybody not to fuck with me, because when I first showed up that nigga cussed me out and threatened to tell my brothers what I was asking him to do, but as soon as I showed him the bread it was a wrap and shit was good. I gave him the money up front, the first time from out my own pocket and then I used the money that Perry paid me to reup after that. I didn't want to do that shit, but I needed to get in with that nigga. Now the streets of South Carolina were eating off me.

Kayson would never know that I was taking shit out of the warehouse because the money would always come up right for the amount of drugs we had. Shit was a fool proof plan, and I was happy as hell about it. The trial run with that nigga Perry had come to an end, so now he was paying full price for that shit and I was living off the fucking profit.

I had got me a little crib out in Mooresville, North Carolina, away from everybody. It was cool as fuck out here. It wasn't Charlotte, but it wasn't the fucking sticks either. No one knew where I lived but Mama, I didn't even tell Omari and I was gonna keep it that way until I felt like they should know.

"Babe, I need pots and stuff to be able to cook." Heaven walked back in the living room where I was sitting on the couch.

"Aight, we can go to the store in a minute. I need to go to my condo and pick up some shit anyway."

"Good, I need to get out of this house." She said under her breath and it pissed me off. Hell, I was trying to keep her ass safe. That nigga Ortiz is on some other shit wanting her ass back and shit. I saved her ungrateful ass from that psycho nigga.

"I mean if yo' dumb ass feels like that then take yo' ass back with Ortiz, bitch. I don't need you here." I jumped up. All she did was complain about how bored she was just sitting here and shit. It wasn't my fault her ass was on the run.

"I didn't mean it like that, Denari." She looked in my direction with pleading eyes.

"Don't be trying to change it around now. You don't want to be here then get the fuck out." I pointed to the door. She was in nothing but a nighty seeing as though it was only ten in the morning.

"Baby please, I don't want to fight."

"That's all yo' dumb ass wanna do is fucking start shit." I walked up on her and mushed her in the fucking face. I knew it was wrong to be putting my hands on her, but she got on my got damn nerves sometimes. I walked in the direction of the room. Her got damn mouth just pissed me off and fucked up my high. I went to my night stand and took out my stash. I did a few lines and then laid back on the bed to let that shit take me to a better place.

I heard Heaven walk into the room and just stand there. I didn't feel like dealing with her right now, so I ignored her. I just looked up at the ceiling and enjoyed the high.

"Can I try it?" she asked softly.

"Try what?"

"That," I rose up to look at her and she was pointing to the dresser where I just took the hit.

"I'on think you can handle that shit baby girl, real talk." I chuckled, and she walked over to the dresser and picked up the rolled up one-dollar bill. I just looked at her because I didn't think that she would actually do it. Whenever she pissed me off she would always try and do something that she thought would impress me. To my surprise, she fixed a line that she had seen me do several times and she bent down and took half a line.

"Ahhh shit." she said as the potent powder burned through her nose. I laughed and coached her to hold her head back so that she didn't waste my shit. She stood there for a minute until she got used to the feeling that it was giving her, then she let go of her nose and looked at me with this goofy fucking look on her face. "Oh my goodness, I feel like I'm flying."

I laughed. "Bomb ass high ain't it?"

"Damn, this is what I been missing?" She asked and started stripping out of her clothes without taking her eyes off me.

"Yo, the fuck you doing, Heaven?" I said with a smile on my face.

"I don't know, I just feel like taking my clothes off." She shrugged.

Once she was naked, she came over to where I was laying and attempted to get me out of the ball shorts that I was wearing. I lifted my hips so that she could get them down. I reached for the hem of my shirt, but got side tracked when I felt my dick hit the back of her throat.

"Fuck, Heaven ssssss," I moaned out like a little bitch, but I didn't even give a damn that shit felt good as fuck.

Her mouth was extra wet and warm, I was about to lose my shit.

"Why does your dick taste so good today?" She asked while licking my head like it was a blow pop or something. She was feeling good as hell, but I know if her high ass fuck around and forget that she on my dick and bite me I'ma fuck her ass up, no questions asked.

She licked all the way down my shaft and then put both of my balls in her mouth while she jacked me off with precision. I don't know if I was just that high, but I swear it was like I was having an outer body experience with this shit. She had my whole fucking body shaking. Heaven's head game had always been A-1 but today she was getting extra nasty with it.

After she attacked my fucking nuts, she got back in my shit and went to work, slurping all loud and shit. I could feel her spit rolling down my nuts.

"Got damn Heaven, I'm 'bout to nut." I could hear my toes popping and I started shaking and shit. Heaven never swallowed but today she kept at it until I was shooting my load down her muthafucking throat. "Fucccckkkkkkkk!"

I must fucking say that was the best fucking head I have ever had. I laid there trying to get myself right, but I guess Heaven wasn't through with me yet. She stuffed my semi hard dick in her mouth and sucked me 'til I was hard again.

"What the fuck you trying to do?" I asked still spent.

"I need to feel what that shit feels like." She smiled and climbed on top of me and eased down on my now hard dick. "Ummmmm," she moaned and threw her head back.

Heaven rode me until we were both screaming out in pleasure. Once she was done she collapsed on my chest and just laid there while she got herself together. I wasn't used to this emotional cuddling shit, but for some reason I wanted to touch her in that moment, so I did. I wrapped my arms around her.

I cared for Heaven, she was the only person who knew everything about me and didn't judge me. She accepted me for me, no matter how many times I fucked up. I needed to work on being a better person for her. As soon as I get enough leverage with the Perry nigga, I'm gonna let my Unc and brothers know what the deal is, that way we can work on expanding more.

"I love you Denari, I don't need you to say it back because I know what you've been through. I just wanted you to know how I feel. I'm here for you and I'm riding 'til the wheels fall off."

I didn't say anything because the love stuff just wasn't in me, but I did care a lot about Heaven and I believed every word she just said. Hopefully in time I would be able to be that man for her, but right now I was just gonna be Denari. It felt good to know that she was gonna be there for me regardless though. We laid there in that position and dozed off; we would handle that other stuff later.

We ended up sleeping damn near six hours after that session

and would have still been sleep had my brother not been blowing me the fuck up. I didn't feel like dealing with his ass, so I told him to meet me at my old apartment in an hour. I needed to get my shit out of there and get it on the market anyway; I could kill two birds with one stone.

We both did a line before we left the house, so Heaven was over in the passenger seat in her own little world. Every now and then she would look over at me and bite her lip. I think this was the happiest I had ever seen her, and it was damn sure the most I ever heard her talk. I thought it was cute and funny at the same time. I didn't want her to get hooked on this shit or anything like that, but we could damn sure use it to have a good time.

"I'm hot." Heaven said and unbuttoned the little ass shorts she had on. It was late August, so the weather was a little humid.

"Keep ya damn clothes on girl." She laughed and proceeded to taking them off.

"I can't believe that shit is making me this horny, are you sure it's just coke in there?" she laughed.

"Yeah the shit just affects people in different ways."

"Well it's got me on one." She said as she relaxed in the seat with her bare ass. She better be glad that I had leather seats, or I would have slapped her ass. She was gonna clean my shit too.

"I see." I focused back on the road until I heard her playing with herself. I looked over and she had reclined in the seat and had her leg up on the dash, you could hear how wet she was, and that shit was turning me on. For a second there, I forgot I was driving until I heard a horn and I looked up and I was half way in someone else's lane.

"You should pay attention. Ummmm ssshittttt!" she moaned out. My dick was so hard it was about to burst through the zipper of my khakis. "Don't worry baby, I got you." She reached over and unzipped my pants and pulled out my dick and started jacking me off while she played in her wetness. I tried my best to pay attention to the road, but that shit was hard as hell because all I wanted to do was ease into some pussy.

We were almost to my condo in Charlotte and I was glad about that. I put a little more weight on the pedal to speed up the process. When I pulled up, I threw the car in park and didn't even bother getting out. I slid my seat all the way back and motioned for her to come and sit on me. She did as I asked her and eased down on my shit. I grabbed her by the neck and leaned her back, her feet were flat on the chair and her pussy was in plain view, and what a view it was. I took my free hand and applied pressure on her clit and she started bouncing on my dick. She laid on the horn a couple times, but I didn't give a fuck because this shit was feeling good as fuck.

"Bounce that pussy, baby." I said between gritted teeth. Right as I was getting in to it, I heard a knock on my window which I had rolled up when I parked. "Fuck," I yelled when I realized that it was Omari. I forgot that quick that I told him to meet me here.

"The fuck is you doing, bruh?" I could hear him say on the

other side of the glass. Heaven had yet to stop moving, I don't even think she knew that Omari was standing there. I rolled the window down enough for him to hear me. "You gotta be shitting me!" He said once he fully realized what was going on. My tint was dark as shit and you couldn't see shit from the outside.

"O man, what's up? You gotta key, go on up and I'll be up in a minute." I yelled through the crack. "Fuck, Heaven."

"Ummm shit, I'm 'bout to cum baby." I released her neck and grabbed her nipple and squeezed it and she moaned out.

"So, you just gonna keep fucking while I'm standing here?"

"Hell yeah, nigga you would too. You've done that shit, so what you saying?" I bit my bottom lip because I could feel my nut rising. I swear I've never came this fast on some coke before, but the way Heaven's pussy was hugging my dick I couldn't help it.

"Whatever nigga, I'm out; call me when you get a chance."

I didn't respond because I was about to nut and needed to concentrate on that. Right as I was releasing in her womb, I heard tires screech, and Omari yell fuck. I looked back, and I saw a black SUV roll down the street with a nigga hanging out the window with AK.

"Oh shit, Heaven get the fuck down." I yelled as I threw her in the passenger seat and reached for my gun that was under my seat but before I could open my door, I heard gun shots rang out and I saw my brother go down right before my eyes. Tears immediately started flowing and I jumped out and started busting back until they were no longer in sight. "Fuck,

O you good bruh? You gotta be good." Tears were rolling down my face and they wouldn't stop. "Heaven call 911." I yelled, I could hear her talking to somebody so I assumed it was the operator.

"Fuck D," Omari got out as blood spilled through his lips. I can't believe this shit was happening. I couldn't lose my brother; there was no way in hell that I would be able to keep going if my brother wasn't here with me.

"Hang on nigga, they coming to help you. I can hear those muthafuckas, just hang on." I could hear the sirens already. I don't know whether they were close by, or the neighbors had already called.

"I love you, nigga."

"Nah, fuck that. Don't talk like that, you gonna be good. Hang on O, shit." I yelled trying to cover the hole that was leaking in his chest. This shit was my fault; I knew that Ortiz had something to do with this.

About two minutes later the EMT's were piling out of the truck and coming to help my brother. I grabbed my phone and called Unc and told him what happened. He said that he was on his way to the hospital to meet them. They were taking him to CMC Main because it was the closest hospital and the best. Once they had him loaded up, I jumped in my car that was now full of bullet holes in the back and without a few windows. Right now, I didn't care about all that shit, I just needed to make sure that my brother was gonna be okay.

Chapter Thirty
KAYSON

Jenacia thought she was slick, trying to find a house behind my back. Sshe should know by now that I know everything and the fact that the realtor that she is trying to go through is my realtor and a really good friend of the family. Tracey knows all about Jenacia and the fact that she was looking for a place prompted her to call me.

Tracey used to try and get with me back in the day, and I was all for it until I found out she was one of Unc's many women. When he told me that shit, I cussed her ass out for trying to fuck in the family and then I told Unc, who cut her ass off too. We still kept in touch with her because she knew our family and she knew that when we came looking for houses, we came with cash and she knew how to handle that. We didn't have to worry about anybody looking at it or anything like that, so we kept her around for that purpose. I still think Unc hit that from time to time but that was his business, and he didn't have shit to worry about when it came to me.

Tracey told me the other day that Jenacia reached out to her to find her a place that was nice, yet affordable, and I wasn't having that shit. Her ass wasn't going anywhere and the quicker she understood that, the better.

I was currently on my way to the apartment that Tracey was showing her today. I told her to go ahead and act like she was gonna help her but let me know where they were gonna be. I pulled up to the apartments that she was looking at and they were cute, but they didn't have shit on the house that we currently lived in. I walked up the steps and into the apartment that Tracey told me about.

"So, this how we moving though?" I asked startling the both of them.

"Kayson, what are you doing here?"

"No, the question is what are you doing here?"

"I'm ju—just looking at—"

"What you doing is being fucking sneaky." I said louder than I anticipated. "I thought we talked about this shit?"

"No Kayson, you talked I listened," she said in a defeated tone, at least she knew this shit was a no go.

"You didn't object."

"You didn't give me a choice."

"Because I love you Jenacia and I ain't about to be living in two separate places. I refuse to sleep without you, so that means I'd be living out of a fucking duffle bag, and that ain't it for me."

"Kayson."

"Kayson nothing, I told you let's add your name to the deed so that you will feel like it's yours. Hell, if that don't work we will have your realtor here find us a house that we pick out together, but the end result for whatever you choose is gonna be me and you together in the same got damn house." I said in one breath.

She didn't say anything, just rolled her eyes in the back of her head and smirked. I don't know why she was trying to play hard ball. It had been damn near two months since that shit happened and I honestly thought that she was over it, but here she is still trying to move out and shit. The more I thought about it, the more pissed I got.

"If you fucking move out Jenacia, I'ma make yo' life hell. I just want you to know." She looked at me all shocked.

"You really love this one, huh?" Tracey words dripped with envy. I had forgotten that she was even standing here until she opened her mouth.

"Wait, y'all know each other?" Jenacia asked starting to put two and two together. "What, you fucked her too?"

"Hell no I ain't fuck her." I blurted out. "She was one of Unc's women." I said not thinking about how it sounded coming out. "I ain't mean it like that I was just saying that she and Unc had a thing."

"So, she called you to tell you that your girlfriend was looking for a place?" She had a questioning tone and I didn't like it. It was like she was trying to say something without saying it.

"You can stop right there with whatever crazy ass story you got floating around ya head. I ain't fucking her or nobody else. For the first time in my life, I'm only giving one woman the dick. I use her as my realtor. Everyone knows who you are and that you're mine, so if they see some shit like this they are gonna tell me. That's just how this shit works." I shrugged my shoulders but before she or I could say anything else my phone rang, and it was Unc.

"Speak of the devil and he shall appear." I said before I hit send on my phone. "What up Unc I was just ta—"

"Yo, get to CMC, O has been shot."

"WHAT!??!!" I yelled.

"You heard me, get here now!" He hung up the phone and it was like time stood still for a minute and I couldn't get my thoughts together. I let a lone tear slide down my face and I said a prayer to God to let my baby brother be okay.

"Baby, what's wrong?" Jenacia's voice brought me out of my trance.

"We gotta go, O's been shot."

"Oh my God." She said and threw her hands over her mouth before she headed to the door and I was on her heels. I could hear Tracey calling out from behind me asking questions, but I didn't have time to play twenty questions with her, I had to go check on Omari.

Walking through those hospital doors did something to me. I had to stop and get my thoughts together. The eerie feeling that I was getting wasn't making this shit any better, but I needed to get in there to check on my baby brother though. How in the hell did this happen? I hope like hell it didn't have anything to do with a bitch.

"Oh shit, Zemia." Jenacia reached for her phone but as soon as we turned the corner, I could hear her crying and I guess Jenacia did too because she headed her way.

The minute I saw Denari pacing back and forth covered in blood, all I saw was red. If he was there when Omari got shot, then I could bet my life on it that he had something to do with this. Fucking talking about this bullshit I rushed his ass and threw him up against the wall.

"What the fuck yo' dumb ass done did now? Huh? What did you do?"

"Bruh, it wasn't me, I didn't do shit," he cried. For a second, I felt bad for him, but deep down I knew that whatever happened to Omari was his fault. "They just shot him Kay. They shot my fucking brother, man."

He started sobbing and I dropped him to the floor and Mama went over to check on him. I had to attack the wall, so I wouldn't hit anybody else. I was so mad that I didn't know what to do, say, or think.

I felt Jenacia's arms circle my waist and for that brief moment, I felt calmness, but it didn't last long when I heard some bitch come around the corner with her mouth. I looked, and it was that Jernisha hoe that he was fucking with. She was loud and hollering and I got to her before she got any closer.

"Ohhhh Lawd, why didn't y'all call me, who shot my baby?"

"Bitch, O hated yo' ass. You wasn't nothing but pussy to him so it's in yo' best interest to hit the fucking door before your ass end up in the basement." That straightened her up real quick.

"I just wanna see him, I love him."

"Bitch, I ain't in the fucking mood, so you literally got three seconds before I disrespect my mama by putting my fucking hands on you." I growled.

"Is there a problem?" I heard Mama walk up and say before I had a chance to diffuse the situation.

"I just wanna know if my baby is okay that's all. I didn't come here to cause trouble." Jernisha said. I told O to stop messing with these dumb ass broads, but his ass don't listen.

"I don't know who you are, but I know for a fact that you are not in a relationship with my son." Mama was about to turn up because she put her hands on her hips. "Number one, I don't know you, and if you were any more than a piece of cat for my son he would have introduced me to you. Seeing as though I don't know you from a hole in the wall lets me know that my son used you as a dump for his, what's that y'all young folks call it nowadays, oh yeah seeds." Jernisha went to say something but was stopped by the hand. We all knew what the hand meant, but clearly, she didn't, but was damn sure about to find out.

"Just because we haven't got to the point where we are making family introduction, don't mean I'm nothing to him. He cares for me." She yelled and put her hand over her chest all dramatic. I was about to punch this broad all in her forehead in two seconds.

"That's a got damn lie and you know it. He just told me that you were tripping because he told yo' ass that you weren't shit but some pussy again." I was mad because I didn't know the status of my brother and this bitch was in here trying to show her ass. "Like I said before I'm not in the mood for this shit so it's best you get your delusional ass out of here. My mama raised me not to hit a female but bitch you tempting me."

"No worries son, that's what Mama is here for." She stepped in front of me. Mama was a feisty thing and would reach out and touch you in a minute then turn around and pray for you. "Interrupt me again," she pointed at Jernisha. "Now, secondly, you see that pretty thing right there with the braids?" Mama pointed at Zemia, who was looking dead in our direction with the look of fire in her eyes. "That's the woman that he's gonna marry. That's who he spends his time with and the one that he brought home to meet his mama. So, you see you don't know my son, you just know his anatomy."

"He's never told me he had a woman." She rolled her neck.

"You little bitch, that's because you ain't nothing to my son. Now this is a family situation and you are not and never will be a part of that. So, I need you to take yo' ten-dollar pack hair wearing ass on up out of here before these here hands come out of retirement." I smiled for the first time since I got the phone call, Mama was a G when she needed to be.

I guess Jernisha realized that everything she was saying was true because she turned on her heels and high tailed it out of there. Didn't have to say anything else to her. I looked at Mama and she hugged me tighter than normal and we walked back over to where everyone else was. She sat down beside Zemia.

"When he wakes up out of this I'm cussing his ass out."

It seemed like forever before someone came and told us anything. We were all antsy and getting fed up with the half ass answers from the hospital staff. About four hours into our wait, the doctor came out.

"Family of Omari Barnes please." We all stood and went in front of him. He looked at all of us, which was a good sign right? "Omari is a lucky man; the bullet missed his heart by barely an inch. We were able to get the bullet out. He lost a lot of blood, but he's gonna be fine."

"Oh, thank you, Jesus." Mama said and did a mini shout in front of the doctor who just smiled. "Can we see him?"

"You can but only two at a time. I need to tell you though, we had to intubate him because he coded on us twice, but we brought him back. He woke up for us and we tried to take the tube out, but he started to fight us, so we had to sedate him again. We'll try again in about two hours to see if we can keep him calm enough to take it out."

"Thanks, Doc." I said and nodded toward him.

"My pleasure. You all can go back two at a time please." He waited on us to decide who was going back. It ended up being Mama and Zemia. The only person that had any objections was Denari's guilty ass, but I shut him down real quick. Jenacia said that she was going down to the cafeteria and the Heaven chick went with her. I needed to talk to my brother anyway and find out what happened to O. I was gonna try my best to keep my composure.

"Denari, what the fuck happened?" Unc asked before anybody could say anything.

"I was going to clean out my fucking apartment; me and Heaven were messing around outside when O walked up to the car fucking with me. He said he was about to go and walked off from the car. I finished my shit with Heaven when I heard gun shots, and I jumped out right when I heard that shit."

"So, you mean to tell me that you were getting some pussy while your brother was getting shot? Typical fucking Denari, don't give a damn about nobody but your fucking self." Jaako spoke up for the first time since he walked in shortly after me.

"How in the hell I know niggas was gonna try and shoot shit up? If I had of known that I would have been right there with that nigga going to fucking war. I do some fucked up shit, but I'm there when it fucking counts, Jaako."

"Says fucking who?" Jaako barked.

"Aight aight chill, both of you niggas, we need to find out who did this to O. Fuck all that little girl arguing shit."

"Word on the streets is Ortiz and his boys are the ones

that hit the house." I said looking directly at Denari. I knew it was true because he couldn't even look me in the eye. "So, I take it this was him too?"

"Man, I'll handle it." he said like we were gonna go for that shit.

"Yeah nigga, we know how you handle shit."

"Look, he's pissed that Heaven's with me. He calls and threatens me all the fucking time but fuck him." He waved it off like it wasn't nothing.

"So, all of this because of a bitch?" Jaako said loud enough to get a few stares. "The fuck y'all looking at?"

"Don't fucking disrespect her like that man, real talk." Denari gave off a warning.

"Fuck you, nigga, you betta hope I don't fuck her ass." Jaako laughed and Denari balled his fist. We all knew that he was no match for Jaako so Unc stepped in front of him to keep him from getting his ass whooped. "I'm good Unc, where we find this nigga at?"

"I don't know."

"You don't know?!" I raised my voice. "You got niggas gunning for you and you don't know where they are? You fucking up, D."

"I'm on it; I gotta go. Y'all keep me updated on O." Unc said and walked off but before we were out of site he turned to look at me. "Speaking of the trap, I need to talk to you about some shit Kay."

"Bet," was all I said because that shit would have to be later, I wasn't leaving here until I saw my brother and I guess he understood that because he nodded his head and took off toward the elevators.

We all sat around and waited for our turn to go back. I waited 'til last because I knew if anyone could get him to stay calm long enough for him to get that shit out of his throat it would be me.

I walked in the room where he was laying on the bed hooked up to all that shit and I swear I 'bout lost it. Even the toughest thug couldn't handle this shit. My heart was in my fucking stomach seeing my little bruh like this. I sat down beside his bed; I made sure that I was able to come by myself because I didn't want anybody to see me like this.

After a few minutes the door opened and in walked a nurse. "We're gonna give him the medicine to wake him up, so if you could just stand near his head so that he can see someone he knows when he wakes up, it may keep him calm."

"Aight cool." I wiped my face as best I could before all the doctors and nurses filed into the room. I had never seen so many fucking people at one time before. I know good and damn well it didn't take all of them to hold his ass down, but then again that little nigga strong as hell, especially when he mad. They put the medicine in the IV and a little while later O's eyes popped open and landed on me and he immediately began to fight with the doctors because they were holding him down. "Aye nigga, chill man, so they can take that shit out ya throat. Don't make me get Mama." I yelled, and the nurses looked at me like I was crazy. Omari chilled out a little, he looked at me and then down at his hands. "Aye yo, let his hands go he ain't gonna flip out, but if you don't let them shits go you bout to meet the fucking Hulk."

"Sir, it's for his safety and ours."

"I'm telling you he will work better with you if you let his hands go," I looked down at O's hands and this nigga was counting. I guess that was the countdown for him to show his ass. "Y'all already got his ass strapped down, let go of his fucking hands."

Finally, they let go and Omari let them do what they needed to do so he could get that fucking tube out of his mouth. Once they got it out Omari mugged all their asses. I couldn't do shit but laugh, I knew his fucking throat was sore because if it wasn't he would have laid in on all they asses.

After they got him cleaned up and shit I let Unc know that he was up. They ended up moving him to another room where we could all see him. I was happy as hell that bruh was gonna be good. Now it was time to fuck some shit up.

Chapter Thirty-One
ZEMIA

They thought I didn't see that little shit with that hoe that came to see Omari. I knew we weren't together and all that, but damn I thought we was trying to figure some shit out. I guess not, 'cause he was clearly on some other shit. I was gonna stick around long enough to make sure that he was okay, but then I was out of here. He could call that ghetto rat to wait on him hand and foot.

I knew all that shit he was telling me was some bullshit. I mean I guess I couldn't blame him because I did tell him that I wanted to take shit slow. I mean we were young, I'm only 23. I knew that I had trust issues because of the shit that my dad did to my mom and the fact that he has never been in a relationship made me hesitant.

With all the red flags, I was still falling for him, how could I not? He was sexy as hell; his dreads were just scrumptious, his lips and eyes kept me in a trance. The way he walked, legs slightly bowed let me know that he was working with a monster. As sexy as he was that's really not what drew me to him. It was more his carefree personality. He was funny as shit and never let anything get him down.

Thinking about all of this had me thinking that maybe I should fight for him. Like I said we aren't together and it was my choice to just remain friends and see where things went. So it was kind of an open invitation to continue doing him. I just didn't think that he would, but his ass proved me wrong. I just needed to make sure that I wasn't about to get played, fuck that. If he still wanted to fuck with hood boogers, then he could do that shit by himself. Before I made any rash decisions, I needed to calm the fuck down and at least have a conversation with him.

"Girl don't you let that hot thot bother you." Mama Ann said beside me.

"Man get out of my head lady." I had started to fall in love with his mother too, especially after knowing their story. That woman was truly heaven sent.

"She just one of them women who thinks that just because she spreads 'em it means that she has rights to his life and that's not true. My son really cares for you, I can tell." She smiled.

"Oh yeah, how?"

"Well first off you met me, if he just thought that you were just some butt then you would have never stepped foot into my house. Second, you got this man calling his mama for ideas on dates for you." She laughed. "Omari ain't never took a woman out on a date or brought a woman home. I always told him to take his time and when the right one comes along that he would know. It looks like he found you."

I was speechless, so I didn't say anything. I just sat there looking at her until Kayson came out and told us that he was transferred to a regular room. We all hopped on the elevator and went to his new room. I was happy to walk in and not see him all hooked up to them tubes and shit. I took the chair on one side of the bed and Mama Ann took the chair on the other side. Everyone else filed in and settled.

"How you feeling?" I asked as I reached over and placed my hand over the bandage where he was shot.

"Better now." He smiled but that was short lived because Mama Ann went in on him.

"So, you good son?" he looked in her direction and nodded. "Well, who in the hell was that fire crotch heffa that rolled up here talking about she here to see her baby and shit, I mean stuff."

"Kayson already told me, and I promise I'ma handle that."

"You better because if I have to handle it, I'm getting in yo' ass too. Got this beautiful woman right here and you out here dealing with hot thots and shit."

"Ma what the fuck is a hot thot?" Kayson asked between laughing.

"Hell, I don't know, that thang that rolled up in here. You shut up; I got a bone to pick with you too." She pointed at him and I heard Jenacia laughed.

"Jen, you a damn snitch that was so long ago." Kayson looked at Jen and she shrugged.

"It don't matter when it happened. If you ever put your hands on her again, I'm gonna chop them thangs off ya hear me?"

"Yes ma'am."

"Back to you," she turned back to look at Omari. "You gonna mess around and lose this girl, and then what?" Omari dropped his head and then turned to look at me.

"I'm sorry, it wasn't nothing like that, she doesn't mean shit. She was just someone to pass the time with until your stubborn ass came around and gave us a chance. I know I should have went about it a better way, but ain't shit I can do about it now." He shrugged.

"Nigga that ain't no damn apology." Mama Ann yelled getting up. "Lawd, I ain't never cussed so much in one day. Please forgive me, Lord. All y'all need to get to church."

"Ma, I got this, I'ma take care of it, I promise."

"You better, I gotta get out of here and get some oil on me. Sitting around with you devils for damn near eight hours is enough for me." She grabbed her purse and was about to head out the door and then she turned around. "I don't want no shit out of y'all, ya hear me now?" they all nodded. "Don't give me that, I can see it in ya eyes it's about to be some shit." She shook her head and grabbed the door handle. "Just be careful, I don't want to have to deal with this again." She pointed at Omari and no one said anything.

Once she left, we all talked for a minute before they asked

for me, Jenacia, and Heaven to step out. We said that we would go down to the cafeteria and see what they had to eat. I didn't care to be in there while they talked about what happened next anyway. I wasn't green to the shit, but I damn sure didn't want my hands in it.

Chapter Thirty-Two
KRISTA

"So, you telling me that this punk ass nigga put his hands on you and killed my seed." Perry stood over top of me in my mother's living room.

"Yeah," was all I said. Perry didn't know that I was messing around with Denari, he knew about Jaako because I didn't want him to pop up whenever he wanted to.

"What the fuck were you doing with him?"

"I wasn't with him Perry," I whined. "He showed up to my house to talk about how he wanted to see his brother and he wasn't leaving until he did. When I tried to push him out of the house he snapped." I lied.

"So, what are you gonna do about it? If you can't protect my daughter then I don't think she needs you either." My mom interjected. I loved her to death but sometimes I just wish that she would mind her own damn business.

"Ma, I got this." She threw her hands up in mock surrender and headed for the kitchen. My dad was out back in his building as usual. When I told him what happened to me he didn't even seem surprised. If I didn't know any better I could have sworn I saw a smirk form on his face. All he said was I'm sorry baby and then left to go out back.

"Is there anything else that I should know about this and please don't lie to me? Just tell me the truth because regardless he should have never put his hands on you while you were pregnant."

I thought about just telling him what was going on. I mean what could he say, he's doing his thing I'm sure. I wasn't committed to him and we were just fucking around so it wouldn't mean shit if I was fucking both brothers or not. Before I could say anything, my mother stepped in, AGAIN.

"If you don't believe her then you can leave." She said as sweetly as she could then she gave me a look that said keep your got damn mouth shut.

"Ma'am with all due respect, it's my life and freedom I'm putting on the line to protect your daughter, so if I wanna ask questions I got every got damn right to do so. Now if it's alright with you, I'd like to talk to her please, alone." My pussy jumped from the way he talked to my mother. "Now if there is nothing to hide why in the hell did you wait until now to tell me about the baby?"

"Because I didn't know how to tell you. I didn't know how you would feel about it."

"And now?"

"I thought you had a right to know."

"Or you on some get back shit and need my help." He raised a brow waiting on me to come clean. "Yo keep it real with me or I'm out of here."

"Okay okay damn, I wanted to tell you about the baby either way, but I do want to get back at Denari for killing my baby. He deserves to pay for what he did."

"I agree." He said and then got quiet suddenly, he was thinking of something and I wanted to know what.

"What's up, what you thinking?"

"Don't worry about it; I got this I just need you to stay out my way. I'm about to take care of all of them." He smiled. "I need to get close to him alright, and he can't know that we know each other. Just trust me, when I'm done you won't have to worry about anything aight?"

"Yeah, I'm not one of those sit back and let a man handle everything for me type chicks, I like to be in the know."

"Well this time you don't really have a fucking choice now do you?"

I didn't say anything I just stared at him. Perry was handsome, but he wasn't Jaako. I would let him handle the Denari situation, but I'd be damned if I sit back and watch Jaako live happily ever after with some other bitch. That was not gonna happen at all.

"Okay I hear you."

"No, I need for you to be on the same page as me." He looked me in the eyes and I nodded. I didn't give a shit what he said.

"Stay away from them." He pointed at me and I just looked at him.

Without another word, he left out of the door and slammed it. I didn't know what his problem was, but I was glad that he agreed to get at Denari for me. I just needed to make sure that none of this could fall back on me because if they thought that I had anything to do with anything happening to him the rest of them would end my life no questions asked.

I was starting to regret what I had just set into motion and then my hand touched my stomach and I remembered what he did to my baby and that was all that it took for me to throw caution to the wind.

"Now that's the kind of man you need to be with." My mama came out of the kitchen wiping her hands. "Your biological father was just like him." I could see the smile in her eyes. She was in love with the man that helped create me.

"Why couldn't you just be with him?" I asked curious as to how she ended up with my daddy.

"Because my parents were hell bent on me marrying a man that made an honest living. They didn't care how much money Raymond made, they didn't want me with a drug dealer."

"Raymond?" I asked and looked at her with squinted eyes. It damn well better not be the Raymond that I think she is talking about. Because if so we were about to have a big fucking problem. Even though I knew that Jaako was adopted, it would still be weird that his uncle was my biological father. "Raymond Barnes?"

"Yes." She said and dropped her head. "He was my first love." She smiled. "And I never got over him. I was forced to be with your father by my parents, but I've never loved him." She looked at me like she had just remembered something. "You can't say anything to him because he doesn't know about you. Raymond hates me because I was forbid to be with him and instead of being honest with him , I just stopped talking to him. I never told him why or anything like that I just stopped talking to him and when I popped up pregnant with you he automatically figured that I was sleeping around on him. I let him think that and went on to marry your father. To this day if that man sees me he still mugs me."

"Wow!" was all I could think to say because that was a lot.

"Yeah, I know, my mama always said that a man like Raymond would only end up in jail or dead. She wanted me with a man that would take care of me and someone that I could mold into basically my father. I didn't want that though. I wanted Raymond and to this day I still do."

"That's why you wanted me with Jaako so bad." I started thinking about when I first told her about me meeting him. At first she was mad because I told her that he was a drug dealer but then when I described who he was she was okay with it and actually pushed for a successful relationship.

"No, I just knew that he was the kind of man that could give you the finer things in life and you wouldn't have to live all middle class like me." She looked around the house like there was something wrong with it when in reality, this was a nice ass house and my mother wanted for nothing.

"Well, all of that is gone now thanks to you." I rolled my eyes at her.

"I was a little mad that he didn't stick up for you, regardless of what was going on as your man he should have had your back."

What she was saying was true, he should have had my back. It didn't matter the situation, I was lying in a hospital bed, and he should have been there for me.

"I'm gonna have to do some damage control, and I know just the thing to do it." I smiled as I thought of a great plan to get Jaako to talk to me again. That bitch better enjoy him as much as she could because he was gonna be back in my bed and my life sooner rather than later. And with Denari dead and gone, things were going to work out just great.

Chapter Thirty-Three
OMARI

Sitting in this fucking hospital was driving me fucking crazy. I hated these people with a passion and every time they came in here to say something to me I cussed them the fuck out. I don't why they still found reasons to come in this bitch. Now they were talking about some got damn therapy, yep I need some therapy alright and that shit came right from my got damn vape. I called Denari three fucking hours ago and told him that he needed to bring my shit up here and he said that he was on his way, but I hadn't seen that nigga yet.

"How are you Mr. Barnes?"

"The same muthafucking way I was when you asked 30 minutes ago."

She laughed because she thought the shit was cute I bet if I whip out my dick again and piss everywhere she won't think that shit is funny. If I was a nasty nigga I would shit in the floor and call them to clean that up.

"I need to get your vitals."

"Nah they good."

"How do you know that if we haven't taken them?"

"Because I feel that shit but if you keep pissing me off I'ma give you a reason to come in here. Why can't y'all just leave me alone and let me do my bid."

"Bid?" she looked confused. "This isn't jail."

"Shitting me if it ain't, got this nasty ass food, no privacy and niggas wanting to wash my ass and shit. This is muthafucking jail." I yelled thinking about that male nurse they sent in here that time talking about he was gonna help bathe me, I flipped on his fruity ass. They had to call security on my ass and hoped and prayed they kicked me out of this bitch. The only reason I stayed is because Ann Barnes worked here and threatened my ass daily. Her ass was off today, and I planned to do what I needed to do to get kicked out.

"Will you please let me take your vitals?" she asked before the door popped open I looked to make sure it wasn't Ma. When I realized that it was Zemia dropping by before she headed to work I smiled.

"Is he giving you a hard time today?" She asked the nurse and I looked at her daring her ass to snitch.

"Well he refuses to let me take his vitals." She said with a smirk and I bit my lip and nodded. I was gonna make sure didn't none of them get any rest I was gonna be on the bell for every little thing, I swear fo God they were gonna hate me after today.

"Man take them shits and get out with yo' snitching ass." She and Zemia laughed and she did what she had to do and then left.

"Why is it so hard for you to do what you're supposed to do, huh?"

"I don't see the fucking point in this shit." I waved my right arm around because when the bullet went in my chest it damaged a few nerves and I had lost some strength in my left arm. Hell, I was right handed anyway so I didn't see the issue.

"You need to get your strength back in your left arm and they wanna run a few more tests to make sure you didn't damage anything else."

"Fuck that, you know just as well as I do they just wanna keep me here 'cause we paid cash!" I yelled hoping they heard me. My Uncle put money down for the best care and they are trying their best to run that shit up but I be damned, I'm getting the fuck out of here.

"Omari, I need you to behave while I'm at work." I looked at her and her slanted eyes were pleading with me and it was so hard for me to tell her sexy ass no sometimes.

"Man go on," I waved her off but then looked at her. "What I get out of it?"

"Weeeellllllll, if you do what you supposed to do while you are here, I got you when you get out." She winked, and my dick jumped.

"Don't fucking play with me Z."

"Ain't nobody playing but I gotta go, I'ma be late."

"You coming back later?"

"Yeah, after work." She smiled and then kissed me and left.

I knew she still felt some type of way about that bitch stopping by the hospital but after everyone left we stayed up and talked for a while. I wanted her to know where I was coming from with the whole thing. I didn't want her to feel like I was just playing with her or anything like that. I really liked her and was considering doing shit right. After the lil' talk she seemed to be in a better head space about us and agreed to give us a shot. She did tell me that if she had to deal with anything else like that she was done because she was not a woman that was gonna sit around and be treated any kind of way. And she wasn't, Zemia was a beautiful person inside and out.

I needed to make sure that I had all my ducks in a row when it came to her. She was worth more than the shit that I was up to and I was gonna make sure that I proved that to her. Starting by calling the Betty Boop looking hoe, Jernisha.

"Oh my God Omari are you okay?" She cried like she had any right to be worried about me.

"What the fuck you coming up here for bitch, and how did you know where I was?"

"Huh?" she paused. "The streets talk Omari, and I just wanted to make sure that you were okay."

"Why, I don't even like yo' ass. Didn't we talk about this shit? I told you all you were was some quick pussy. I never led you to believe that you were any more than that. So, what made yo' water head ass decide to show up here?"

"Omari, you don't mean that, you have to feel something for me. I mean look how many times we fucked."

"And! Hoe you were in rotation."

"Rotation?" She asked like she was shocked by what I was saying when I told her on multiple times that we were nothing.

"Yes, dumb ass, rotation, R-O-T-A-T-I-O-N! Got it that time? You were my number three so when the other two didn't pick up then I would call you. You were nothing to me and you never will be."

"Why are you being so mean, after all I've done for you?" I had to look at the phone because I was confused as hell because this bitch has never done anything.

"What the fuck you did for me?" I asked and waited on a response that never came. "You must got me mixed up with one of the other niggas yo' hoe ass got in rotation, but check this out," I paused to make sure that I had her undivided attention, "if you ever come anywhere near my girl or my family with that bullshit again, I will make your family pay for it aight?"

"Your girl?" out of everything I said all she heard was my girl. This dumb bitch was about to be fish food.

"Yeah, I got one of those now, so your services won't be needed anymore. I feel like you have been reasonably compensated for the work your mouth has done. I should not see or hear from you again, are we clear?"

"Damn you sound like you firing me from a job."

"I am you idiot, I no longer need to see what yo mouth do. You are fired! Are we clear?"

"Are you sure? I am good at being the side chick."

"How fucking dumb can you be, shit I need to start checking SAT scores before I fuck with bitches." I was getting frustrated because she wasn't getting it and I didn't want any issues with Zemia. "No, I don't want shit to do with you and if you come near me again I'm fucking you up. You understand that?"

"Fine you weren't all that anyway, I was just in it for the money." She blurted out.

"Well good then we shouldn't have any more problems."

"Whatever Omari, you'll be back." She hung up the phone and I shook my head and put the phone down. I didn't have time for her shit, I wasn't playing with her I would make her life a living hell if she fucked with me. I'm not one that likes to go after family members, but I would if the situation presented itself. Her dumb ass had been warned and I just wanted her to leave me alone and I would be just fine.

I really needed to be high right now because I knew these fuckers were about to come in here with the shit about physical therapy and unless I was high I was about to be a total asshole. I was gonna cuss Denari's dumb ass out and right as I was about to call his slow ass, he came around the corner.

"The fuck you been with my shit?"

"Man, I tried that shit and fell in love, so I had to go to the warehouse and get me one first. You know Kayson aggravating ass wasn't trying to give me shit, I had to tell him you sent me." He rolled his eyes and then looked at me. "You good, bruh?"

I knew that Denari felt like this shit was his fault but it wasn't that nigga was coming for him and if he was coming for him he was coming for me too. So, the way I see it, it was bound to happen. I was just glad it happened to me and not him. His skinny ass would have died.

"D this ain't yo' fault, that nigga gonna get his."

"You got damn right; the only way to make that nigga surface is for me to be out in public somewhere."

"Nah that shit ain't smart D, you could get killed. We gotta plan that shit out so we can take care of it quick and move the hell on you know?"

"Yeah," was all he said which meant that he was about to do some dumb shit. I hated when he got like that because more than likely it ends up bad. I decided to let it go for now, but I would be sure to try and keep an eye on him.

"Whatever nigga give me my shit, I need to float around this muthafucka." He handed me my vape and THC juice. I filled her up and hit her hard a few times until I felt my buzz. I laid my head back on my pillow and relaxed. Then I jumped up when I remembered what I was originally supposed to talk to his ass about.

"The fuck wrong with you?" Denari looked at me like I was crazy because I sat up real fast.

"Yo nigga, please tell me that it ain't you stealing shit from the fucking warehouse." I looked him in his eyes and the look that he gave me let know right then and there that it was him. He was the one doing that dumb shit and when Kayson ass finds out he gonna flip the fuck out.

"Aight well I won't tell you then." He shrugged his shoulders.

"Why in the fuck you think it's okay to fucking steal from your got damn brothers?" I yelled louder than expected.

"First of all, chill out with that yelling shit," he said in a threatening tone, I guess he thought since a nigga was a little fucked up I couldn't handle his ass. Denari knew I would fuck him up no problem. "I ain't stealing, I get the product, sell it and put the money back before anybody notice that shit." He really thought this shit was fool proof. "Y'all cut me out and left me no fucking choice."

"We cut you out because of dumb shit like this. You just keep fucking up and putting us at risk. This is why muthafucka, this bullshit right here."

"Man, whatever, I ain't hurting nobody and ain't nobody gotta know."

"That's where the fuck you wrong nigga, Kayson noticed it and asked me about it. He thinks it's just some nigga forgetting to sign shit out but he is looking for whoever the fuck it is." I told him and that changed his expression with his dumb ass. "I ain't gonna say shit because that ain't me, but if he asks me I ain't lying either." I put that out there just so that he knew I was done with his little bullshit ass secrets. I hated when he put me in these binds. "You don't even know this nigga, what if he the fucking feds and you don't even know the nigga last name." I looked at him because I figured he was talking about the nigga that he tried to get me to help him with.

"I got this, that's the problem now y'all always wanna find something wrong instead of just seeing what the fuck I'm doing right."

"D, yo ass don't fucking think shit through, you do shit off impulse; if it seems right to you then you do not give a fuck about the consequences." I shook my head because his ass ain't gonna ever change. "You don't even give a fuck about whether we get caught in the fucking crosshairs."

I threw that out there just to fuck with him and make him understand where we were coming from. I really didn't blame him for the shit but damn something needed to get through his thick ass skull.

"Oh aight," was all he said before he hit the door. I didn't even try and stop him because I didn't have the energy to try and get him to see shit my way. I grabbed my vape and took me a few more hits and got ready for these niggas to come and do this shit they gotta do and if they didn't hurry the fuck up, I was gonna decline that shit.

Chapter Thirty-Four
JENACIA

"Girl I don't know what I'm gonna do about Omari's ass." Zemia shook her head. "He up there giving them people at the hospital hell."

"I can only imagine. Why won't he just leave?"

"Ma Ann told him if he did that she was gonna kick his ass. He needed to be there to make sure that everything was okay with him. She didn't want him coming home and doing too much and end up right back in the hospital. So, she wanted him to wait until he was 100%."

"I understand that."

"His retarded ass doesn't. This nigga pissed on the floor on purpose because they tried to make his ass go to fucking therapy, how nasty is that."

I had to laugh at that because as long as I've known Omari he's been like that. He has never liked being told what to do and when you made him he would always make sure that you regretted that you did.

"He's a character for sure."

"Yeah I just don't know if I can handle that character." Zemia got the long face for a second.

"Stop Z, Omari is a good guy it's just with him you have to spell everything out." I knew she was scared to totally fall for him because of the bitch that showed up at the hospital but in his mind, they weren't together, and he could still do what the fuck he wanted to do and until she told him otherwise that's how he was gonna look at it. "He's not your father; you gotta stop looking at situations like your parents."

"I know but it's hard, shit my dad was my hero until he pulled that shit. I mean for my mom it was the best thing he could've done because she's happy now." She sighed heavily. I knew all about the things that went on with her mom and dad and how he shunned her out of his life because she told on him. What kind of man refuses to talk to his own daughter because she did what she thought was right at the time? Her dad was a coward, but I know it hurt her even though she tried to pretend that it didn't.

"It still bothers you that you don't talk to him, doesn't it?"

"It used to bother me a lot but now I just don't care," she shrugged, and I knew it was just her tough girl act that she was putting on. "I just hate that he got my brother in on this shit."

"Lyndon is home?" I asked shocked because I knew she

told me that it was time for him to be released but she never told me that he was home.

"Yeah, my dad went and got him like a month ago, they released him a little early. My dad has been keeping him with him in South Carolina."

"South Carolina?"

"Yeah that bastard moved and didn't even let anyone know." she rolled her eyes.

We dipped in the food court. We were just browsing around the mall because we were tired of sitting in the hospital. The guys were running around town looking for the dude that shot Omari so were kind of on our own. I was cool with that because I had time to focus on my photography. I had been saving for a place but since Kayson shut that shit down, I now had the money to look for a spot for my studio.

"That's some fucked up shit."

"Tell me about it, I finally got to talk to him at least. I told him that when things settle down for me I wanted to plan a day at Carowinds, so I can introduce him to everybody." She smiled. She loved her little brother and it pained her for him to be in jail, but she knew he needed it. Lyndon was out of control and I hoped like hell that he had gotten his shit under control for his sake and hers.

"You know I'm down."

"Good, now let's go eat. My ass is starving and you know that little Japanese spot got the best bourbon chicken around."

"Yes, they do." I agreed, and we skipped over to get in

line. I only had a few bags because I wasn't really in need of anything and although I liked to shop I wasn't a binge shopper. I didn't just go out and spend unnecessary money. Now don't get me wrong when I saw something I liked, I got it, but I didn't just go out spending money because I could. I didn't give a damn who my man was.

We got in line and got our food and went to find a place to sit. After we had gotten settled my stomach suddenly felt queasy. I jumped up and ran to the nearest bathroom. I entered the stall and threw up everywhere. That had been happening quite often lately and I didn't want to think that I was pregnant, but I knew that I was.

I went to the sink to try and get myself together. I splashed water on my face and then looked in the mirror, my face was pale, and it looked like I could use a good nap. I shook it off and went to walk back out to where Zemia was and ran dap smack into the Brayla bitch.

"Umph, look at what we got here."

"Bitch I ain't in the mood for your shit, so if you don't mind you can move to the side before I beat your ass." I told her straight up I owed her ass anyway for sending that got damn picture.

"Yo ass better not be pregnant, I'm telling you now. If you are you may as well say goodbye to the good life." She laughed and for a second what she said got to me but then I remembered who I was.

I smiled. "That's where you're wrong," I stepped in her face with throw up breath and everything. I didn't even give a fuck. "If I'm pregnant all that means is that I'm gonna get one hell of a ring, I ain't you; he actually wants more than a nut with me." She didn't take that too well because she acted like she was gonna do something so I punched that hoe in the mouth and dared her to do something about it. Instead she just stood there like she couldn't believe that I hit her. I shook my head and walked around her. "Stay the fuck away from me bitch. I promise you this is your last warning, pregnant or not I will fuck you up." I threw over my shoulder as I left the bathroom and went back to join Zemia.

"Girl you good?" she looked at me all suspicious.

"Yeah I just got sick." I said as I closed the box of food I just purchased and threw it in the garbage can.

"Is there something that you need to tell me?"

"Shit I don't even know myself." I said as I watched Brayla watch me from across the room. Zemia followed my eyes and jumped up.

"Do we gotta a problem?"

"Nah we good, I already popped that bitch in the mouth for talking slick. As long as she keeps her distance, I'm good."

"Aight." She shrugged. "You ready?" I nodded. "We need to go get you a test, so we can see if you are carrying my niece or nephew." She smiled, and I honestly didn't know how to feel about it to be honest. I had been in this situation before, so I wasn't sure if I was ready or not. I guess we would see and if the test was positive, and then I would have to deal with it because there was no way in hell that I was getting another abortion.

I was sitting in the living room on the couch just staring at the positive pregnancy test. Earlier, me and Zemia got one from Target and went back to my house to take it. The pregnancy line showed up faster than the control line, so I knew that shit was real.

At first, I was sad because I was just getting to where I was making a name for myself in the photography industry. I was getting more jobs than I could keep up with, and I also still had my job with The Word. Having a baby didn't mean that I would have to give all of that up, it just meant that I had more motivation to do more because I had someone to look up to me.

My biggest fear was that Kayson was not gonna want the baby like that bitch Brayla said, but his actions show me that he's gonna embrace this, and I needed him to.

"Baby?" I heard his voice calling me before I heard the door knob turn.

"I'm right here."

"Why yo' crazy ass sitting in here in the dark and shit?" He said flipping on the light switch. "I thought something was wrong, it was dark as shit in this bitch." He smiled and then walked over to where I was. The closer he got the more he started to pay attention to what was in my hand.

He raised an eyebrow and then leaned over me to see the results of the test; I moved my fingers so he could see. I made sure to never take my eyes off his face because I wanted to see his expression. It would tell me what I needed to know. The fact that he was showing no emotions at all was freaking me out. His face was even and his body language gave me no indication of how he was feeling about the situation. I hated when he did that.

He swung his dreads that were hanging freely out of his face and he looked at me in the eyes then all a sudden, the corners of his mouth turned up and I even saw a glimmer in his eye.

"So, you giving me my first baby boy?"

Tears immediately started to fall from my eyes because he was actually happy about it or he seemed to be.

"Or girl." I smiled through my tears.

He shook his head. "I had a dream the other night I had a son. I just didn't say shit." He got on his knees and positioned himself in between my legs and kissed my still flat belly. "Hey baby, this ya daddy, hurry up and grow so you can come out here and holla at cha pops. I got some shit I need to teach you." I smiled so hard I thought my face would crack. "So, you know if you try and move out of here I will chain yo' ass up right. I mean I would have before, but now you carrying my seed, it's official." He threatened.

"As long as you keep your word to never hurt me again, I'm here." I promised.

"I promise you that, baby."

He leaned up to kiss me and I had to close my eyes to savor the moment. I just knew that things were gonna go up from here. I was happy that I was about to get my happily ever after.

"Oh, I punched your bitch in the mouth today." I said after he broke the kiss.

"Huh?" he asked and then it clicked. He frowned up. "So, you think that shit cool to be out here fighting while you pregnant? The fuck wrong with you, Jenacia."

"Well I didn't know I was pregnant, and it wasn't a fight, I hit that bitch in the mouth and she stood there like I knew she would." I rolled my eyes. "She walked in the bathroom while I was throwing up and was talking all slick about how you gonna leave me if I'm pregnant, because you always said you didn't want kids and shit like that."

"I told her I didn't want kids because I didn't want them with her."

"I know, that's what I told her, and she kept on, so I felt the need to shut her the fuck up, and I did." I shrugged.

"Well, let that be the last time. Don't worry about her because I warned her ass once and she don't listen, so I'll handle that shit. You just worry about carrying my son." He went back to kissing on my belly. "Why you got this little shit on with no underwear on."

"Why can't yo' ass focus." I laughed. "We were talking about the life that we are about to bring in this world."

"And I'm happy about that but I heard that sex was very good for the baby, and helps with delivery, so let's get started on being healthy." He smirked and pulled me to the edge of the couch and spread my legs as far as they could go. "Thank you for giving me a son."

"Kayson don't get caught up in that, you very well may be blessed with a baby girl."

"Nah, God never gives us more than we can bear." He was serious as hell; I just couldn't help the laugh that escaped my lips.

"You got issues."

"Yep and I'm about to show you just how many." He bit his bottom lip and those light brown eyes of his bore into my soul. If I wasn't wet then, I damn sure was now. "Damn just look."

He took his finger and moved it up and down my slit. I let a soft moan escape my lips. Even the smallest touch from this man lights me on fire. I could hear him unbuckling his pants and I anticipated the feeling of him.

"I love you, Jenacia."

"I love you too, Kayson"

He placed his dick at my opening and forced his way in. I shivered from the pressure, and released the breath that I didn't even know that I was holding in. My eyes rolled to the back of my head as I enjoyed the feeling of him moving in and out of my treasure box. This is one of the many reasons I loved this man like I did. He knew exactly how to make me happy. Now that our little family was growing, things could only go up from here.

Chapter Thirty-Five
YAMEKA

*L*aying here with Jaako is like a dream come true for me. I never thought this would happen. I just knew that he would never leave that bitch, Krista. I hate that it took all that for him to leave her, but so long as he did, I was good. She hadn't gone away completely, she still called him, like now, and he was on the verge of blocking yet another one of her new numbers.

"This bitch is starting to piss me off, I'm just gonna change my number." He blurted out. He snatched up the phone and yelled into the receiver. "WHAT THE FUCK DO YOU WANT?" He put the phone on speaker so that I could hear every word that she said.

"We need to talk Jaako; you can't just shut me out of your life like this." She whined on the other end of the phone. "You at least owe me a conversation."

"Owe you?" He looked at the phone with his handsome face all scrunched up. "You sure you called the right person, because if my memory serves me right, you were the one that was fucking around with my brother and some other nigga, please tell me what the fuck I owe you?"

"Don't act like you were innocent, you were fucking with the lawyer bitch."

Jaako put his finger up to tell me to let him handle it. "Krista, don't disrespect her like that again. I'm trying to be nice about the shit, but you are making it hard. You fucked up, whether you want to admit it or keep throwing the blame on everybody else; the ending is still the same. I'm done with you; I don't want anything to do with you. I want you to stop calling me; there is nothing that you can say to me that would change anything about this situation. From the looks of it you won't have any issues finding a man. I left the house, I let you keep your car, what the fuck else do you want from me, Krista?"

"A fucking conversation." She yelled.

"That's not gonna happen so now what?"

"Damn it Jaako, if you want me to leave you alone you'll be at the house in an hour." I could hear the desperation in her voice.

"I have ways to make you go away, trust me that's not an issue." He let out a sinister chuckle. I looked at him like he was crazy because he was crazy. Being a lawyer, his lawyer, I damn sure didn't need to hear him say that. He winked, and I rolled my eyes.

"Jaako, just give me a conversation and if you still wanna walk away I will let you no problem." She pleaded. I shook my head because she was really pathetic after all she did, and she expected him to go out of his way to accommodate her needs. He didn't respond he just hung up the phone and turned it off.

"So, are you going?" I asked because I needed to be sure that he wasn't about to fall for this bullshit.

"Hell no, there is nothing that she can say to me that will change the way I feel. I saw that shit with my own eyes. I saw my brother's dick popping out of her mouth. There is no way in hell that I could ever consider anything with her." He shook the thoughts away and then smiled and looked at me. "You ain't got nothing to worry about baby, I'm all yours." He leaned over and kissed me.

The kiss was nice and soft but there was a lot of meaning behind it. He was making sure that I knew that he was where we wanted to be. Jaako was a hopeless romantic and that was one of the things that I fell so hard for. He didn't always say how he felt, but he always showed how he felt and that meant more than anything that he could have said.

He rose up and climbed on top of me, his lips were still attached to mine. He wedged himself in between my legs and positioned his monster at my opening and eased in. Looking me in the eyes, he didn't move or anything he just stared at me.

"Have I ever told you that I loved you?" I didn't say anything because I was stuck on what he was gonna say next.

"If not, I love you, Yameka Tate; I've loved you from the moment I walked into your office. Even if you didn't wanna give me no play then." I smiled and then I laughed.

"I try not to get involved with my clients that could be trouble for me." I ran my hands through his dreads, "but it was just something about you Mr. Barnes that I just couldn't resist." I said honestly.

"I hope it's always like this." He started to move slowly in and out of me, making sure that he teased my spot every time. "I could live in this pussy." He said as he concentrated on making me cum.

"Shit baby, that feels so good."

"Umhummm." He snuggled his nose in my neck and continued a slow and rhythmic pace. He slid his hands under my ass so that he could go deeper, and I thought I would pass out from pleasure right then and there.

My nails slightly dug into his back as he slowly grinded into my most special place. I moaned out of control as he moved his hips in a circular motion not missing a thing. I could feel the tingling feeling in my toes; I knew it would be much longer before I came.

"Shit yo' pussy hugging." He said into my neck as he sped up his pace a little. Jaako could go for hours if he wanted to, but it was times like this where we both got so wrapped up in the feeling that we just let our bodies do what they want.

"Goooddddd, I love you." I said, and I meant it, and not just because he was performing magic tricks on my body. I really did love Jaako and I have for a while. I just didn't trust him or myself to be what we needed to be for each other. "Shit!" I yelled out and I came all over his dick and it was the best orgasm that I've had to date.

"I'm 'bout to nut." He lifted enough to place his lips on mine and we both rode the wave of ecstasy together as one.

"Hey Daddy, what are you doing here?"

"I need a reason to see my baby girl?"

"Well no, but I know you're a busy man and all." I got up from my desk and walked around to hug my daddy. I was the definition of a daddy's girl for sure. There was no one in this world that could tell me that my daddy could do anything wrong.

Deshon Tate was the epitome of the word father, not only was he a stand-up father but he was also a stand-up guy in the community. My dad was the police chief of Charlotte; I know it's crazy that I was in love with a drug dealer while my dad was the head nigga in charge down at the police station. You can't help who you love.

"Who's been occupying all your time? I never see you anymore."

"No one, Dad, what are you talking about?" I blushed like a little school girl. In my dad's eyes, no one would ever be good enough for his little girl. I didn't know how he would take the fact that I was dating a client either, so I didn't think that now was the right time to divulge who held my heart's interests.

"You can do that shy thing if you want to but I know better." He smiled. "I'm gonna give you a couple weeks to get him in shape to meet me and if you don't bring him around by then, I'm gonna go out and find him myself, deal?" I nodded, and I knew he was serious.

"Okay Daddy, I got you." I winked.

"You need to call your mother too, she's been complaining about not seeing you and you know how she is." he laughed and so did I.

"Lawd, don't I know it." I smiled thinking about my mom, she was one of the sweetest people you would ever meet until you made her mad or she didn't get her way. Dad always said that I acted just like her and I could see that.

"Well I'm gonna let you get back to work, I have a few things I need to deal with myself." He kissed me on the cheek and just like that he was gone as fast as he came.

I needed to get myself together so that I could introduce Jaako to my dad. Jaako had been in a little trouble before, but not enough to ring bells in my dad's ears so I think we will be okay. Now to just convince Jaako that he needed to meet my dad.

Chapter Thirty-Six
DENARI

Living out in Mooresville wasn't as bad as I thought it would be. It was a little get away from the city living and I liked it and I actually thought about staying out here for good. I hadn't been in any trouble lately, I'm still doing my shit with Perry behind everybody's back, but I didn't classify that as trouble. I was doing what I needed to do for me and to get my name back out there. As soon as I got where I needed to be I would let them in on it, and hopefully they got with the program.

That nigga Perry been calling like crazy talking about needing to up his shipment. It was already hard enough for me to get what I was getting, and to ask Joker to up the shipment was gonna be a fucking task. His scary ass was already talking about Kayson asking questions and shit like I gave a fuck. He could ask all he wanted, if the money was right there shouldn't be a problem, now should it?

O had been calling me too, but I didn't even feel like fucking with him right now. He was popping all that hot shit about me stealing from them, like I wasn't a part of this shit too. Like I didn't help build this shit. They all in their feelings cause that shit happened at the trap, but that could've happened to anybody, they just wanted to fuck with me.

"It's so pretty out here." Heaven said from the passenger side of the car.

"Yeah."

"What's wrong with you?" she asked.

"Nothing, just thinking about some shit." I said and then my phone rang. "Yo." I answered without looking to see who it was.

"Nigga, you thought about what we talked about?"

"Yeah nigga I thought about it, and I don't know if I can do that. The risk is too fucking high."

"And I thought you were supposed to be some big-time nigga." Perry taunted. I don't know why my ass didn't check the caller ID, I had gotten good about it, but this time I was in my thoughts and didn't even fucking think before I picked it up. "Well if you can't do it point me in the direction of the nigga who can, 'cause I ain't got time to be playing with you."

"Muthafucka I put you on, what you mean?"

"Right and I thought you were the nigga to see about this work. Shit, these muthafuckas blowing through the supply. I need more to follow the demand on the street."

I couldn't even front, I understood where he was coming from, because if you couldn't supply the demand they went elsewhere no matter how good yo' shit was. I knew I needed to find a way to get more shit, Joker's ass was gonna have to man the fuck up, and fast.

"Man, I got you, I get it."

"Good!"

He said before he hung up, I was gonna cuss his ass out when I saw him. I don't know who he thought he was hanging the fuck up on me like he ran something. He was slowly crossing boundaries, and I needed to put a fucking stop to that shit fast.

"Everything okay?"

"Yep," I said as I sat back and marinated over how in the fuck I was gonna get this shit done. I was gonna have to figure out a way, my name depended on it.

"Man, what the fuck you doing here?" Joker's scary ass said as he looked around to make sure no one saw me.

"I need a favor my nigga."

"I already told you, I can't fucking do it. Kayson's ass already triple counting shit. You know his ass notices everything and just like I thought he noticed that right off."

"Kayson don't give a fuck as long as the money right."

"Nah that nigga talking about that's how muthafuckas mess up by not knowing what the fuck going on under their nose." He shook his head. "I ain't trying to lose my life over this shit. My girl just gave birth to my fucking daughter."

"Shit nigga, you already in deep as fuck." I shrugged. When he mentioned his daughter, I found my way in. "If you don't do it then I'ma tell that nigga that you the one been helping me in the first place." I looked at him and he looked like he wanted to fuck me up, but he knew better. "It's in your best interest to go ahead and do that; your little girl needs you."

"That's fucked up, man." He shook his head, he knew he didn't have a choice and I knew he didn't have one either.

"Yeah, I know, but it is what it is, I'll be back in two days for the shipment and have my shit ready I don't wanna have to fucking wait."

"Yeah," was all he said. I chuckled because that nigga was in his feelings. Hell, it ain't like that nigga ain't getting paid so I don't know what the big deal is. He just better have my shit that's all I know.

Chapter Thirty-Seven
KAYSON

Shit was still coming up missing at the warehouse and it was starting to piss me off a little. Even though the money was right the product was off. I prided myself on being an organized muthafucka and this shit was fucking with me. I needed to get a handle on that shit and soon. I talked to Unc about it and he said that as long as the money matched up then I shouldn't worry about it. That's how muthafuckas got caught up, not knowing what the fuck was going on in they own shit and I was not about to be a part of that at all.

"Yo, so we heard anything from that nigga Ortiz yet?" Jaako asked at the desk beside mine that was located at the back of the warehouse.

"Nah not yet, but I got the fucking word out, whoever see that nigga; bring him to me alive."

"I can't wait to set my fucking eyes on that nigga." Jaako gritted his teeth, I hated when he did that shit.

"I can't believe that nigga doing all of this over a bitch though."

Yes, Heaven was beautiful, but her ass wasn't Beyoncé or nothing, she was definitely expendable. Then again, I can't even say that because if a nigga came at me wrong about Jenacia then I would damn sure shoot up his whole got damn family. That nigga just chose the wrong family to run up on.

Me and Jaako did a little business before we got ready to go and meet Omari at the hospital. His ass was finally getting the fuck out. He was in there giving them people hell because he was ready to go home. They were trying to tell him that he needed some physical therapy on that one arm, but he wasn't having it. He said he could do the physical therapy at home.

Two weeks later they were sending his ass home, the only reason his ass stayed that long was because Mama threatened his ass. He was feeling better and ready to put in work. He had his main man, Ice looking after his part of the business and that nigga was doing a damn good job of it too. I needed to find me somebody that I trusted to handle shit when I needed to dip out.

"I'm hungry as shit my nigga." Jaako said leaning back in his chair.

"Feel you; I could go for some Chicken Coop." I looked up and that nigga had the biggest fucking smile on his face. That place was small as hell on the inside, and trying to get food from there was like trying to pull blood from a turnip, but the shit was worth it. I'm an impatient nigga so I didn't go there often, but today I was in the mood for it.

We finished up and headed over to South Charlotte to order and fucking wait. Once we got there it was stupid packed, and I was starting to regret that decision.

"Fuck!" I yelled out in frustration.

"Nigga we here now and it took me forever to fucking park, so we staying."

I didn't argue because I really wanted some damn chicken. We hopped in line and gave our order and stood back for that shit to be called. I kept feeling somebody looking at me but when I looked around everyone seemed to be in their own world or staring in the back hoping the next order called was theirs. I went to grab my phone and just so happened to look up and I caught the eyes of a young girl who was staring me down. The more I looked at her the more she was starting to look familiar.

"Aye bruh, ain't that the freak hoe that was at the trap with no clothes on when them niggas ran in?"

"Where?"

"Right there trying not to look in this direction."

"Hell yeah that's her with her cute ass." Jaako licked his lips and I shook my head.

"She looks familiar as hell though." I took a good look at her and then she finally looked up at me and her light brown eyes danced beneath the light that she was standing under. He thick lips and light skinned made me shiver.

"Nigga she looks like a miniature version of you." Jaako said now focusing on the girl too.

He said what I was thinking but I didn't want to say that shit out loud. I was getting freaked the fuck out. I've always had access to my birth certificate anytime I wanted to know who created me, but I never felt the need to look. So, this chick could very well be of some kin to me, but hell to be honest I didn't want to know that either.

"Numbers 156 and 157," the worker yelled letting us know that our food was ready. I walked up and grabbed my bag and Jaako did the same. I looked at the girl one more time and I turned to walk out the door, but I bumped into this little frail woman who looked to be in her fifties. She had fair skin with light brown eyes like the girl and puffy lips that weren't the pink color they were designed to be. She looked at me for a second and I looked at her. Before I could excuse myself, she spoke.

"Son," was all she said, and I looked at her a little more and I didn't know what to say. "You don't even know me," she dropped her head. "Your father told me that when you were old enough that he would tell you the truth and let you decide if you wanted to see me."

"What the fuck you talking about, yo?" I was getting frustrated because she was talking all this shit about my father like I was supposed to know who he was and shit. Hell, as far as I was concerned the only "family" I had was my brothers, my ma and Unc. "Man, I gotta go you talking crazy."

"My name is Chelley Ford." She smiled like that shit was supposed to mean something to me.

"Okay and?" I was two seconds from getting rude.

"Mama come on so we can get home." The young girl that had been looking at me all weird since I got here.

"Mama?" I asked looking back and forth between the two of them.

"Oh fuck." I heard Jaako say from behind me.

"Will somebody tell me what the fuck is going on?" I said a little louder than I intended.

"I'm your mother." The little frail lady said, and I looked at her like she was crazy.

"Ann Barnes is my mother."

"She didn't birth you, I did." She had a little too much bass in her voice when that came out of her lips than I liked.

"Hell yeah you birthed my ass, full of fucking crack." I yelled out and she dropped her head. "Excuse me because I ain't even in the mood for this shit right now."

"Mama just let him go, he'll come around eventually." The young girl said.

"Kaylin, I know baby, I know." She looked up at me. "I was in a bad space back then but eventually I straightened up, it took a while, but I did it. It was too late to come for you then, you were happy, and Ann gave you a life that I couldn't. Your father told me to stay away until you were old enough to make your own decisions. If you don't believe me just ask him. I've always loved you; I just want you to know that." She said before she walked in the restaurant and over to Kaylin.

Right as I was about to leave I had to stop because she kept mentioning my father, I didn't know who the fuck he was. No one ever talked about him, so I knew nothing about him. I turned to her once more. "Who is my father, you keep saying it and you never said his name?" She gave me a look of confusion, like that was something that I should have known. Was I missing something?

"You don't know?" she asked, and I shook my head to refrain from cussing her out for asking that dumb fucking question. "Raymond, Ann's brother."

I could not think, speak, move, or nothing at that moment. All I could do was stand there and look at her like she had sprouted twelve heads. I felt Jaako's hand on my shoulder and he slightly pushed me out the door. When we got outside he just looked at me with sympathetic eyes. He wanted to say something so bad but just like me he didn't know what to fucking say. All I could do was shake my head and hop in the car. Somebody owed me some fucking answers and I was getting that shit today.

Chapter Thirty-Eight
UNCLE RAY

"So, you know for sure that it was Ortiz that shot you?" I asked Omari who was up and dressed waiting to be discharged. I wanted to make sure that I was raging war on the right muthafucka.

"I saw his face," was all he said and that was all I needed to hear. I had men everywhere looking for him and anyone associated with him was gonna die. Starting with his parents who I had my men going to pick up now.

"Aight then that's what it is. I think you should come to stay at the house until this shit blows over."

"So, you want me to run?" he laughed. "You know I ain't even built like that, Unc."

"Nigga I know, but I want you to lay low and I know you." Again, he laughed, because he planned on doing anything but lying low.

I should have known better than to ask him to do anything but what he knows how to do and that's survive. From the time he was a kid he had to teach himself how to survive and even more so he had to teach his brother. I needed to have a conversation with him to see what the fuck all this beef was about. It had to be over more than some pussy, right?

We waited around for another hour before the nurse came and finally discharged him. I didn't know where the hell his brothers were, but this nigga was anxious as hell to get the fuck out of here, so we left and headed to the house. They would just have to meet us there.

"Hello." I heard O answer his phone. "Nigga they gave me them papers and my black ass ran the fuck up out of there. Fuck that, y'all were taking too long, we headed to Unc's house," he said into the receiver.

The drive was quiet; we were both in our own thoughts. I knew my sister was at the house cooking all this nigga favorites, so his ass was gonna be excited when he walked in. I just needed to get all this bullshit behind us, because when I did I was planning on giving this shit up. Them niggas earned this, and they knew the business inside and out especially Kayson. He was almost better at this shit than me. So, handing it over in his hands was the sensible thing to do.

Pulling up to the house I could see his girlfriend and Kayson's girlfriend was here but no one else had made it yet. So, I helped him out of the car and ushered him into the house. As soon as he hit the door that nigga started grinning from ear to ear and then all a sudden, he got serious.

"Zemia!" he yelled. "Zemia!"

"What? Is everything okay?" she ran out of the kitchen followed by the other two.

"Why the fuck you in the kitchen man?" he narrowed his eyes at her. "You know yo' ass can't cook, I swear if you fuck something up I'ma hold you down and make you eat it." He was serious as hell which made all of us laugh and she flipped him off.

"Leave that girl alone, she in here trying to learn for yo' punk ass. If I was her, I wouldn't do shit for you." Ann said heading back into the kitchen.

"I'm just saying."

"You ain't saying nothing," Ann said. "Go wash up, the food almost done."

We went and got cleaned up and headed to the kitchen. We all looked around and still no Jaako and Kayson. Where the fuck was those niggas at? I picked up my phone to call when the door busted open and in walked Kayson with the look of death on his face.

"Who the fuck is my father?"

His question caught me by surprise because I had no idea how to answer it without pissing him off further. I just never thought that he needed to know. Ann just stood there and mugged me. I already knew she was pissed but what's done was done. She had been on me for years to tell that boy the truth, but

I just wasn't in the place to do so. When he was younger, I was too busy running the streets chasing ass to settle down and focus on raising a son. I know that shit sounded selfish as fuck, but it was the truth. By the time I settled down a bit to help Ann out with the boys it was too late, we had fell into the *Uncle* and *Nephew* role and I didn't want to fuck with that because it worked.

"Kayson have a seat." Ann finally spoke up.

"Nah I don't need to sit down, I need somebody to tell me something." I watched how his chest rose and fell. I could tell that he was hurt and felt betrayed, but it really wasn't that deep.

"Look, shit was crazy back then. Ya mom said that I was ya father, but she was a crack hoe and I didn't believe her. After a while you started growing up and shit, I saw my mannerisms in you and that's when I had you tested." I lied. I knew he was my son because I was the reason that his mother was on drugs so bad. Hell, I use to dab in the coke myself, but no one will ever know that.

Me and Chelley had our thing and I was actually in love with her, but she was wild back then, so I used the coke to keep her "tamed." That worked for a while until her addiction grew out of control and she wanted the drug more than she wanted me. When I found out she was pregnant, I cut her ass off. I thought her ass had gotten some business about herself only to find out that she was just getting her supply elsewhere. Hell, I was always in the streets so it's not like I wouldn't have known what she was doing anyway. The day

Kayson was born, and Ann called and told me that he had coke in his system, I felt bad as shit.

"So, is this why you adopted me?"

"No baby, I adopted you because you needed to be in a good home with people who love you."

"Love me, you mean people who lie to me."

"Kayson, now that's not fair," Ann pointed at him with tears in her eyes.

"What, you felt bad because ya brother didn't want my ass, so you took me in because we were family, huh?"

"Stop Kayson, right now." She now had a full face of tears and this was all my fault.

"You want some truth little nigga?" Wasn't nothing little about that nigga, he had a build like I did but I still had him by a good fifty pounds. "I was young and fucking dumb, me and ya moms was out here living reckless and shit. I wasn't ready to be a daddy and ya mama damn sure wasn't ready to be a mother. When she had you, you were fucked up and needed a lot of care. There was no one better to do that than my sister. You were headed to foster care where you may never have gotten what you needed. Whether you were my son or not she was gonna take you in, that's just the kind of woman she is." I threw out there. "This ain't her fault, it's mine, so if you wanna be mad at somebody, be mad at me. She always told you that when you were ready we could tell you all about your birth parents, but you always said that you didn't need to know." I added that because it was true. He always said that he didn't want to know about them because as far as he was concerned we were his family.

"Fuck all that you still kept that shit from me. I had to find out shit from some skinny bitch and her daughter. When y'all could have told me a long time ago."

"You seenChelley?" Ann asked him with her face turned up. Ann made Chelley promise that when the time was right that we would tell him together and the right way.

"Yeah we were at the Chicken Coop when she stopped me talking about some son."

"I'm your mother!" Ann yelled out. "Always have been and always will be and don't you forget that shit."

"Let's go somewhere and talk about this shit." I told Kayson, we needed to have a heart to heart because I didn't need this shit getting in his head.

"Nah UNC." He put emphasis on Unc. "I'm done with this right now."

"Please don't do this Kayson."

"I didn't do anything, y'all did this." He said looking between me and Ann. "Let's go Jenacia."

"Kayson—"

"Let him go Ann, the man needs time to process this shit." I told her, and she rolled her eyes at me.

"I told you to tell him a long time ago, Raymond!" She threw the spoon down that she was scooping out the potato salad with and ran out the kitchen. She was hurt because she felt like Kayson was putting the blame on her. When he got out of his feelings we would talk about this shit, but until then I was gonna give him his space, as long as it didn't affect business, I would let him be.

He gave me one more look and left out of the Kitchen with his girl in tow. I wasn't tripping over it, he would come around. He was my son, and just like me he was a processor, he needed time to let things sink in before he came around.

After a while Denari and his girl came, and they were all sitting around like they had lost their puppy, so I got up and fixed me a damn plate I wasn't about to let all this good food go to waste. Shit would work out, it always did.

Chapter Thirty-Nine
ORTIZ

"This little bitch is starting to piss me off." I yelled to no one in particular. I was really getting upset with the fact that Heaven thought it was okay to just run off with that little fucker, Denari. I was hoping that it was him that got hit that day at his apartment, but when I found out it was his brother I was pissed.

"She'll be back, when he starts showing his true colors she'll come back." Cello said trying to reason with me.

"I don't want the bitch back; I want her ass dead for pulling that fucking stunt."

"We did leave her at that hotel to fend for herself."

"I went back to get her, didn't I?" I looked him in the eye with a questioning look. I knew that he looked at Heaven like a little sister, but she betrayed me, and she knows what happens to people that betray me."

"Right boss." Was all he said. "So, what's next?"

"I'm waiting to see what these niggas about to do; I shot one of theirs, so I know they are looking for me. I need to play this smart so I'm gonna chill for a minute."

"Out here in this country ass town."

We were currently chilling in a little town called Troutman, it was country as hell. I swear I could count the number of stop lights on my fingers. There was one fucking store here; you had to go clear into the town north and south of it if you wanted to shop. I was aggravated by that, but when it comes down to it, this was the best place to be in this situation.

"Yo, what if they come after your family and shit?"

"Them niggas ain't that smart. Plus, my dad a muthafucking G, he got them no doubt." I didn't even think of the fact that they would retaliate by going to my family. I had never known them to be those kinda niggas. They usually go to the target and destroy, they weren't one for hurting innocents and I needed to bet on that.

"I hope you right."

"Yo Cello, you starting to act like a bitch, is there something that you need to tell me?"

"Fuck you, Ortiz." He flipped me off and walked back inside the little house that we got in the country.

Even though it was country as fuck I must say the shit was nice. We had so much land, the little realtor bitch, Tracey, found this shit for us. She came highly recommended from some associates of mine, and I must say she came through for a nigga. I called her one day and she had this property the next. The fact that she knew how to work with people who paid cash was great, I would definitely be using her again.

Being out here all secluded and shit made me want some pussy and bad. I pulled out my phone and I started to call the realtor bitch, but she seemed like she would be too much work for me. I just wanted to fuck and call it a day, so I picked up the phone and called this bitch that I kick it with from time to time.

"Hola papi"

"What's up?"

"Nothing, what you up to?"

"I need some pussy." I was straight forward with her. I just wanted her to know that all I wanted was to fuck and that's it. I didn't want all that extra shit that she liked to bring. "And bring ya girl, Cello's here."

"Aight shoot me the address."

"Cool," I texted her where we were.

"Why in the hell you all the way out there." She asked. Her ass was nosy as fuck.

"Don't worry about all that, you coming or not?"

"Yeah, we'll be there in a couple hours."

"Aight!"

I hung up the phone and went to tell Cello that we were about to have company, but when I went in the living room he was standing in the middle of it with his phone to his ear just staring off into space.

"The fuck wrong with you? We got pussy on the way. That bitch Brayla and her friend Jernisha bout to roll through." I rubbed my hands together. "Ay Cello, you heard what I just said nigga?"

"Ortiz, shit ain't good my nigga." He handed me the phone.

"Who the fuck is this?" I yelled into the receiver. "HELLO!" all I could hear was breathing.

"It's the muthafucking grim reaper bitch, you fucked with the wrong family." The voice on the other end of the phone spat.

"Ortiz, what did you do?" I could hear my father in the background. "Who are these people?" My heart sunk to my chest. This couldn't be happening right now. There was no way they found my parents. I could hear my mother in the background praying in Spanish.

"You better not touch my fucking parents."

"Why should I give a fuck about your family when you didn't have any regard for mine?"

"Denari has something that belongs to me, if you steal from a man you get your fucking hands cut off." I gritted.

"You didn't shoot Denari, bitch."

"Wrong place wrong time." I was talking tough, but I was silently praying that he didn't harm my parents. I would never be able to forgive myself if he did.

"Same goes for them." *Pow! Pow! Pow! Pow! Pow! Pow!* "Damn the old bitch just doesn't want to die." He laughed on the other end of the phone. "Say goodbye to your son." He said, and I could hear my mother struggling to speak. That broke my heart into a million pieces; I let the tears fall freely down my face. Fuck being tough, this shit was eating me alive. I was witnessing my parents' demise and it was all my fault, all over some bitch. *Pow*! "You're next bitch." He said right before the line went dead.

I threw the phone across the room. We bought burner phones so that we could keep in touch with our families. We disposed of them every time we used them, so it didn't make a difference that it broke into a million pieces.

"THEY KILLED THEM!" I screamed out.

"Time to clap back." Cello said, and he was right it was time to show them Barnes bitches I wasn't anything to fuck with. They wanted to take everything that I loved, well I was gonna return the favor.

Chapter Forty
OMARI

Damn it felt good to be home, I hated that fucking hospital. If I ever got sick to the point I had to be in there for a long period of time I was just gonna kill myself, fuck that shit. I don't see how people did it. I refuse to.

I wasn't expecting that shit to come out at my welcome home dinner though. Unc being Kayson's daddy was a bit much for him, hell for everybody. I was gonna give bruh a minute to calm down before I talked to him about it because that was some heavy shit.

"I'm so glad you home." Zemia said coming into the room where I was laying down.

"Shit me too." I laughed because I knew that she was tired of coming up to the hospital with me showing my ass. She hated that shit, but she did it and that made me feel a little something more for her.

"How you feeling?"

"I been feeling good, a little sore but that's to be expected. Ready to get back to work."

"Nigga, that can wait." She rolled her eyes and I laughed.

She didn't understand. The streets were all I knew. I plan to stack my money so after I retire, I won't have to work 'cause I ain't good at shit else.

"What's gonna happen after the streets?" She asked like she was reading my mind.

"Shit, I don't know, I plan to stack all I can while I'm in these muthafuckas, so I don't have to worry about it."

"Can you really picture your antsy ass sitting around the house all day with nothing to do?"

"Fuck no, I'll aggravate you or my brothers."

"Homey, I planned to keep working."

"So, you wouldn't stay home with me, even if we had money?"

"Um no, I have a career that I love and there is no amount of money in the world that would make me stop what I'm doing."

That's what I liked about her; she was so driven and smart. She knew where she was going and why, the best part about it is that she wanted the same things for me.

"I think you should open up one of them smoke shops and sell your vapes and the legal juice." I laughed at how she said legal juice. "I'm serious."

Shit that wasn't a bad idea, hell I could do that now and sell my "green juice" under the table. I could make this illegal business legal as shit. Then when I was tired of the street life I would have this to fall back on.

"You on to something baby." Smiled and grabbed her by the arm and pulled her to me and kissed her lips. "I might get started on that now."

"I didn't tell you that for you to have a way to sell your illegal juice legally." She rolled her eyes again.

"I'ma give you a reason to roll them eyes if you keep on." I whispered in her ear and she shivered under my touch.

We had been kicking for a few months now and I had yet to hit the pussy and for some odd reason I was okay with that. Don't get me wrong, I wanted to fuck her in the worst way; I was just okay with waiting until she was ready.

"You're not well enough for that."

I looked at her like she was crazy and went in my ball shorts and pulled out my already hard dick. Her eyes got big when she saw it and I smiled. I was definitely blessed, and I was ready to show her just how much.

She was leaned across my lap; I pushed her so that she could move so I could get this show started before she could say no. I positioned myself on top of her and just looked into her eyes. I didn't want to pressure her if she wasn't ready, but in the back of my mind I was praying like hell that she was.

"You good?" she nodded her head. "You sure?" She smacked her lips and rolled her eyes again. I leaned back so that I could pull off the shorts that she had on. Once I had them off, I reached for the hem of her shirt and pulled it off too. She wasn't wearing any underwear because she had just gotten out of the shower when we got to the house. "Damn you don't know how long I been waiting for this." She smiled and leaned up and connected her lips with mine.

This kiss went from sweet to downrig ht nasty in a matter of seconds and I embraced that shit. I broke the kiss and attacked her perfect nipples that were staring right at me begging for attention. I circled her areola and then slightly sucked on her nipple until a soft moan escaped her lips. With my other hand, I slid my hands between her legs so that I could see how wet that pussy was.

"Got damn." I said once her juices soaked my fingers. I was all for foreplay, but after feeling that, I couldn't take it anymore. My dick needed to feel that gushy, not my got damn fingers. I placed the head of my dick at her opening and looked down at her. She was looking dead at me. "You sure you ready for this." She bit her bottom lip and grabbed my hips and guided them toward her. I took that as a yes and began to inch my way into her. "Damn you tight as fuck."

"Ssssssss," she shut her eyes tight and endured the pain that I know she was feeling, her ass was super tight, but that was okay. I liked it like that. I moved my hips in circular motion and at a slow pace until I was all the way inside of her.

"Fuck!" I moaned out like a bitch.

I kept my slow and steady pace, I wanted her to get used to my size and enjoy it at the same time. Her pussy juices had my dick covered, thank goodness, she didn't make me wear a condom because I needed to feel all this.

"Ummm ahhhhh," she moaned out and let me know that the pain had subsided and the pleasure had kicked in.

I cupped both of her legs in my arms and spread them as much as I could, I got down in that "go deeper" position and I grinded into her. I made sure that I hit everything that I could to make sure she'd cum long and hard.

"Omari," she cried out and that shit sounded so good I had to bite my lip to keep from calling back out to her. "Shit Omari."

"Damn baby, you got some good pussy." I had to put some kind of thug in it because I really wanted to cry out how good she was making me feel, but I wasn't trying to lose the fucking thug card, at least not yet.

"Just like that, baby."

"Like that?"

"Yes, just like that, oh fuck."

"Shit, you choking my shit." I had to bite my lip and turn away from her. The fuck faces she was making were turning me the fuck on, and I wasn't trying to nut all early. I had some shit to show her.

"Oh God, I'm cumming," she cried out, her body started shaking and I looked up and she had tears coming out of her eyes. That's how you know you hitting the pussy right when that one lone tear fall.

I moved nice and slow while she got her self together, and when her breathing became somewhat normal, I grabbed her right leg and threw it over her left leg so that she was on her side. I lifted myself to my knees and I watched as I slid in and out of her. My dick was covered, and I loved every minute of it.

"Shit!" I yelled out, I had to move, or I was gonna be filling her up with my seeds. "Turn over and don't let my dick fall out or that's your ass." And I meant that shit too. She turned over in the direction I already had her until she was on all fours with her ass in the air. I pushed down on her back a little until I got the arch that I like and then I went to work on her. "Ummm shit this feel good as fuck." All that thug shit was out the window, all you could hear was our skin slapping, me moving around in her wetness and both of our asses moaning.

"Ohhhh Omari, shit."

"Let that shit go." I moaned while slapping her on the ass.

"Shittttt." I felt her walls clamp down on my dick again and that was it I couldn't take anymore.

"I'm about to nut." I sped up until I felt my shit build up, shit was feeling too fucking good to pull out, so I said to hell with it and let off inside of her. "Uhhhhhhh," I yelled out as I dropped off the last bit of special sauce up in her womb.

"Oh my God." She said as she collapsed on the bed on her stomach. I pulled out and rolled on the other side of her. We just laid there in silence while we got ourselves together. "You know I ain't on birth control, right?"

"I don't give a fuck about that," and I didn't. It was what it was, if it was my time, it was my time.

"Just thought I'd let you know." She mumbled. "Are you okay?"

"Hell no I ain't okay; I'm hurting like a bitch." She lifted up and looked at me. "But I swear that shit was worth it and don't say shit, because as soon as I get my shit together I'm diving back in."

"Noooo, my shit sore as hell already."

"I'll make it feel better first."

She mumbled something, but I didn't give a damn about what she said, soon as I got my shit together I was definitely fucking the shit out of her one more time. I reached over and grabbed my vape and took a few hits and let that shit marinate. I could hear her lightly snoring, but I didn't give a damn. I reached for her shoulder and rolled her over on her back, climbed back in between her legs and slid down until I was face to face with her pussy. I latched on to her clit and lightly sucked until I heard her moan and I knew I had her. I hope she knew that she was stuck with my ass.

Chapter Forty-One
ANN BARNES

I was headed over to have a few words with Cheryl, I felt like her intentions were bad with how she told Kayson about things. I had never seen him look so betrayed and hurt. Everything I did for him was for his own good. Now here this witch comes along trying to fuck up what I worked so hard to build within my son.

When I pulled into the projects where she stayed I just looked at the surroundings and thanked God that he placed Kayson in my life. He wasn't the best person in the world by far, but I think he would have ended up much worse with her here. I got out and went to knock on the door.

"Who is it?" she sang.

"Ann Barnes." I stated sternly to let her know that this was not a social call.

She swung the door open and we just had a nice little stare

down. I was there to give her a piece of my mind and I planned on doing just that. I must admit I did feel sorry for her for a second. She was younger than me but look like she had a good ten years on me. Them drugs did not do her body good.

"Can I help you?" She said nastily.

"We need to talk about MY SON," I put much emphasis on the my son part.

"You mean my son." She smirked. "You never could have kids, could you?"

That was a sore spot for me and nothing to joke about. "No, any bitch can have a pup, but it takes a mother to raise it. All you did was give birth to a drug infested baby. I nursed him back to health when he almost died as a baby, and you didn't even stick around to see if he was okay. You ran out to go and chase your next high." I rolled my neck 'cause she had me heated already and I hadn't even stepped in the house. "I raised him; made sure he had the best of everything. I made sure that he is the man that he is today; I did that, not you. All you did was hug that got damn glass pipe and whatever else you could get in your system to make you feel better about your miserable life." I went off.

"You don't know what I went through."

"It doesn't matter what you went through; when you have a child that child becomes your priority, and you work through your shit with your child." I pointed at her. "I been through some shit in my day, some shit that would bring the strongest woman to her knees and I almost let it get me. But

I decided to pull myself up and make a change. So, don't give me that, I been through this and that bullshit, because I know the song and dance and the shit don't mean nothing to me."

"Why are you here?"

"Because we need to talk about the little stunt you pulled. I don't know what your motive is, but you need to back the hell off. I have never told Kayson not to have a relationship with you and if he wants to that's his business, because no matter what I'm his mother and I know my place in his life." I had to throw that in there, just so she knew that I was not afraid of being replaced in his life because that was not possible.

She laughed. "If you weren't worried then you wouldn't be here."

"I'm here because I need to know what your motives are."

"He's my son and I want to get to know him."

"I don't believe you Chelley." I simply stated.

"You don't have to believe me, I really don't care what you think to be honest, I just want to get close to my son."

"If I find out that you have ill intentions, you are gonna regret it." I threatened.

"Did you just threaten me?"

"Yes, I did." I said in the calmest voice I could muster up.

"Aye, what's going on here?" I didn't even notice that Kayson was walking up until I heard his voice. I wanted to ask him what the hell he was doing here but I didn't want to make the situation worse.

"Nothing, Ann just came by to make sure that I had your

best interest in heart." She smirked, and I glared at her and Kayson picked up on it. I didn't want him to think that I was trying to get in the way or him getting to know his birth mother, I just wanted to know that she wasn't gonna hurt my baby.

"Mama?" He questioned me, I looked at him and then back up at Chelley who now had a sour look on her face because he called me mama.

"Yeah, son?"

"What's really good cause I know yo' little feisty ass." The look on his face was serious but I could hear the humor in his voice.

"Come walk me to my car, I'll let you and Chelley have some privacy."

"Aight," he said and then turned his attention to Chelley. "Let me walk my mama to her car and then I'll be back. I hope it's not a problem that I stopped by."

"No not at all son, take your time and the door will be unlocked, just walk on in."

"Cool."

Kayson put his hand on the small of my back and led me down the stairs and to my car. When we got to the car I went to grab the handle and he turned me around and hugged me, he gave me one of those hugs like he used to give me as a kid and I embraced it.

"I'm sorry for how I talked to you the other day; I was just mad and hurt."

"I know baby, and we should have never kept something

like that from you, baby."

"I know why you did it, I don't like it, but I understand." He said and then looked down at me. I loved how mature he had become. He was far from the little reckless teenager who stayed on punishment more than not. I knew I had raised him right and I wasn't worried about him falling for anything that she may throw at him.

"We'll talk about it later; you go in and talk to Chelley. And baby," I paused because I was looking for the right words to say without being a bitch. "Be careful okay?"

"Don't worry I only got one mama." He smirked being a smart ass.

"You ain't got to tell me that, I already know."

"Man, take yo' feisty ass on somewhere."

"Keep it up Kayson Barnes, I got a belt with yo' name on it." I pointed at him.

"Save it for your grandson." He threw out there, I had to let it process for a minute, and then I gasped and threw my hand over my mouth.

"Jenacia's pregnant?" He nodded his head with the biggest smile on his face. "Oh my goodness, I'm so happy, I'm gonna be a grandma." I couldn't describe what I was feeling at the moment, but it trumped any ill feelings that I walked away from Chelley's door with.

"I knew that would make your day. But don't say anything, we got an appointment today and after we get some info from the doctor I'll tell everybody."

"Now damn it Kayson, you know I don't like to hold shit

like that in, I wanted to damn celebrate." He laughed but I didn't find shit funny.

"Chill man, the appointment is in a few hours so I'm sure you'll be fine until then."

"Fine."

"I love you, Ann Barnes."

"I love you too, son."

He helped me in the car and then he walked back in the house with Chelley. Kayson was a smart boy, so I knew he would be okay. I just hoped that bitch didn't try and use him. She didn't want to see me mad.

Chapter Forty-Two
KAYSON

As bad as I wanted to mad at Mama I knew I couldn't, she was only trying to do what was best for me and at the time telling me that Unc was really my daddy wasn't the best thing for me. I hate that they felt like they had to keep that from me. I loved and trusted the both of them, so I knew there were no ill intentions.

Seeing mama here raised a whole bunch of red flags. I knew how she could be when she felt threatened, so when I pulled up and saw her neck going I just knew she was about to cause a scene. I knew she was worried about how I felt with all of this because that's just how she was. She loved her boys and she was gonna do whatever she needed to do to protect us.

I was still trying to figure out why I was here in the first place, in a way I wanted answers as to why she just left me in that hospital to fend for myself and on the other hand I didn't give a fuck, because her doing that placed me with Mama. I didn't even know if I was gonna be able to handle the answer that may come out of her mouth, but I was here now and there was no turning back.

I looked through the ID's we got from that day at the trap, found who I now know as my sister's and that's how I got the address. Even if I never had a relationship with Chelley, I would like to get to know my sister. She was just as innocent in this as I was. I would see how everything goes, I knew deep down I still harbored some ill feelings towards her, but not enough not to be here if that makes sense.

I got to the door and I turned around to see Mama still sitting in the parking lot looking at me. I shook my head and laughed, took a deep breath and knocked on the door.

"It's open." Chelley yelled.

I walked in and looked around, it was your typical hood apartment, it had the bare necessities, but it was clean and that was a good sign. I put my hands in my pockets and just kind of stood there in an uncomfortable silence.

"Have a seat, son." I didn't know how I felt about her calling me son, but I would just let her have that. I just didn't want her to expect me to call her mom or no shit like that. I already gotta mama and she was a fucking handful. "I'm so glad you decided to stop by, I've been thinking about you since that day at the Chicken Coop."

"Oh yeah?" my eyes were glues to the ground.

"Yeah, I have, I know I left you all those years ago, but I

was in no position to take care of you, so I did the best thing for you. I walked out of your life. Now things are different, and I want us to have some kind of relationship, if that's okay with you?" She said softly, and I looked up at her for the first time since I stepped in the apartment.

"I guess I understand that." I shrugged and completely ignored what she said about wanting to have a relationship. I didn't know if I was ready for that. This was a big step for me and I needed to adjust to it first. The room fell silent again.

"Well, tell me about you." She picked the conversation back up.

"Nothing really to tell, I'm 25 my birthday is in November."

"I know when your birthday is Kayson."

I shrugged my shoulders, hell I didn't know what she knew about me. From my understanding her ass was high out her mind when she had me, so she might have forgotten.

"Go on," I could tell that she felt some kind of way, but she would be okay.

"I got three brothers and I got a beautiful girlfriend named Jenacia, no kids, yet." I smiled so hard when I said that just thinking about the baby growing inside Jenacia.

"You said yet." She raised her eyebrows. "You telling me that you're about to make me a grandmother?"

"Nah I ain't saying that because my son will only have one grandmother. No offense, but I don't even know you. Ann Barnes is the woman who raised me into the man that I am today, so if anyone gets those bragging rights it's her."

She didn't care for what I said, I could tell by the look on her face but when she noticed that I was staring at her she changed it up.

"I guess I understand that."

"You really don't have a choice in the matter." I was starting to get upset how she just thought that she was just gonna interject her way into my life that fast. I should have never come here. I thought and then I stood up to leave until the front door opened and one of the main reasons that I was here walked through the door.

"Hey, Ma." Kaylin said as she walked in the house. She was looking down at her phone, so she didn't even realize that I was in the house, when she looked up and saw me her eyes got big.

"Say hey to your brother."

"Hey," she waved. "Nice to meet you." She walked over and sat down beside Chelley.

I couldn't help but to stare at her, she looked so much like me it was crazy, "You look like me." I couldn't take my eyes off her, my sister was beautiful.

She laughed, "I know, that day I saw you at my friend's house, it freaked me out. I knew I had a brother so when I saw you, I knew exactly who you were."

"You knew about me?"

"Yeah."

"Why didn't you say anything?"

"Well, I wasn't exactly in the position to do so, you know with you and your brothers waving their guns around and shooting people." She shrugged her shoulders and Chelley gasped and put her hands over her mouth.

I chuckled because it was who I was so the fact that she saw that didn't bother me, I'm just glad that she knows what I'm capable of now, so we won't have an issue later in life when we do build a relationship.

"You mean when you were damn near naked in a room full of niggas." I got mad just thinking about what they were doing to her or how many times she had been there. Now that I know she was my little sister some shit is gonna change whether she liked it or not.

"I was hanging out with my friends."

"Maybe you need to find new friends." I raised my eyebrows 'cause that shit ain't nowhere for a—"How old are you?"

"17."

"Oh hell no." I said louder than I intended. "Some shit about to change and quick."

"You are not my father, you didn't even know about me 'til a few days ago." She sassed.

"I never said I was your father, but I know how them niggas work and trust me they were gonna fuck you and throw you to the wolves. And you right, I didn't know about you, but I do now, and I promise you that shit is gonna change whether you want it to or not, that just how shit is. You'll get to know me, and you'll hate me but that's okay, you'll love and respect me though." I smiled at her pretty face. "I can't wait 'til my brothers meet you."

She didn't say anything she just kinda sat there. It was crazy how just a few days ago it was just me and my brothers and now I have a little sister. The big brother role came easy to me because I've had to do it all my life; it's just now I was throwing a girl into the mix.

"I gotta go take Jenacia to the doctor, give me your number and I'll hit you up. Maybe you can come hang out with me one day." She handed me her phone and I put my number it and called myself so that I would have hers. Chelley sat on the couch with a smile on her face at the exchange that just happened between me and Kaylin. I didn't bother getting her number because I knew that it was gonna take me a minute to warm up to her. "Here." I said as I dug into my pockets and pulled out a wad of money and threw it at Kaylin. "Go get you some clothes and shoes, whatever girls blow money on." This shit was so new to me it was crazy. "I'll get at you later and aye," I turned to look her in the eye. "Stay the fuck away from the trap house and as soon as I get over there they will all know that you are my sister and they are to stay the fuck away from you."

"Don't do that." She said with her pretty face all scrunched up.

"Watch me," was all I said before I walked over to her and pulled her up from the couch and pulled her into a hug. "I love yo' little ass already." She hugged me back and I kissed her on the cheek. "I'll see y'all later, and call me if you need anything, aight?" She nodded her head and I headed out the door.

The feeling that I was feeling right now I couldn't explain it. It was like I had an instant connection with her. It was like she had been in my life forever already. I jumped in my car to head to Jenacia; I was ready to hear more about my seed. This was a good ass day. I don't think anything could ruin this day.

Chapter Forty-Three
JENACIA

We were sitting in the office of my doctor waiting to be called back, and Kayson was telling me all about the visit that he had with Chelley, his birth mother, and his sister. He bragged about how cute she was and that she looked just like him. I just wanted him to be careful, because he didn't know them like that and I didn't want him to get hurt. I knew how Kayson could be with family. He would go all in for them, and with Kaylin being a girl she would have him wrapped around her finger. I just hope their intentions are pure.

"Did you hear what I said Jen?"

"Yes baby, I heard you, I'm happy for you and I can't wait to meet her."

"Why you say it like that?"

"Like what, don't you start with yo' paranoid ass." I laughed.

"For real, tell me what's on ya mind."

"I just want you to be careful until you get to know them."

"You sound like Mama." He rolled his eyes in the back of his head and I laughed.

"When has Ann Barnes ever been wrong?" I raised a brow and he didn't say anything. "Exactly, I'm not saying don't get to know her, I want you to do that. I just want you to be careful while you do, until you know them like you know your brothers." I shrugged.

"I know; I just love her little ass already. I don't know what it was, but I felt an instant connection with her." He stopped and looked around. "I sound like a bitch." He said loud enough for everybody to look in our direction. I laughed and then the nurse called us to go back.

I had been going to the same doctor for years; he had been seeing me for as long as I had been seeing a gynecologist. I was comfortable with him and I was excited that he would be handling my pregnancy. We got all my vitals and I gave her the urine sample and she told us that she would be back shortly so that we could get started.

"So, what they about to do?" Kayson asked looking around messing with shit.

"He's gonna examine me, make sure I don't have no diseases or infections that could harm the baby—"

"You better not have shit, 'cause I know my dick clean, Jenacia don't make me fuck you up." He pointed at me.

"Shut the hell up Kayson, they have to do it. It's procedure."

"Oh." He said finally sitting down in the chair beside the bed, I just shook my head.

A little while later the nurse came back and said that we would do the ultrasound first because the room would be in use later and we needed to see how far along I was.

"Alright, Jenacia when was your last period?"

"End of July around July 23rd." I nodded my head remembering when the last time I had to buy pads.

"Okay, so that would put you right at about 9 weeks so we will have to it transvaginal."

"Trans what?" Kayson yelled, and I gave him a look that warned him not to embarrass me and of course he ignored it and continued his questioning. "The fuck you mean transvaggy or whatever the hell you said." The nurse laughed.

"We take this." The nurse picked up the wand that was already covered with the finger condom thing with the jelly. "And it's gotta little camera on the end and we insert it into the vagina so that we can see the baby."

"Nah that shit on TV, they just do it on the stomach."

"Yes, later in the pregnancy after 12 weeks we will do it that way, but right now the baby is too small to be seen without getting a transvaginal ultrasound. The little one is still tucked away in the pelvic area."

Kayson gave a skeptical look but finally nodded his head. The nurse went to get Dr. Miller and they came back in.

"Hi Jenacia, how are you?"

"I'm good, Dr. Miller."

"And you are dad?" He reached his hand out to shake Kayson's.

"Yep." He smiled big.

"Alright, well let's get started, if you would put your feet in the stirrups and scoot all the way to the edge of the bed." I did what was asked of me and I could see Kayson mugging Dr. Miller from the chair beside me. "Okay, now I'm gonna go ahead and get your pap okay."

"Okay."

"You're gonna feel some pressure."

"If that's what you're using she'll be fine, she's used to much bigger." Dr. Miller and the nurse laughed, and I just glared at him. Dr. Miller got what he needed for the pap.

"Okay now let's look and listen to baby."

I smiled and got excited at I watched the nurse turn on the big screen that was directly in front of me so that I could see what they were seeing. He inserted the wand in me and moved it around a little.

"There we go—oh," Dr. Miller said and both me and Kayson sat up.

"What's wrong?" I was scared that something was wrong.

"Well it could be good news." He smiled. "I see two fetuses."

"What?" Kayson and I said in unison.

"You are pregnant with twins. Now let me get a few measurements, listen to their heart beats, and then I'll get you a few pictures."

I looked at Kayson, who had a smile on his face. I was terrified. I was already scared to become a mother, now I would have to carry two babies. And this fool was sitting here laughing. I wanted to cry but I held it in.

"Baby A's heartbeat." Dr. Miller instructed us and once I heard that beautiful sound it brought tears to my eyes and every doubt that I just had went out the window. "And Baby B," he said as we listened to the heartbeats. Kayson grabbed my hand and kissed me on the forehead.

"Thank you, baby." He whispered.

Once we were all done in the ultrasound room we went back into the regular room so that we could we could talk about everything else. I was still a bit nervous, but I was starting to get excited too.

"Is it okay to discuss your medical history with dad?"

"Yes," we said in unison and I rolled my eyes at Kayson because I could have sworn that was a question for me.

He went through all my medical history and I answered all his questions and until he got to the dreadful question that I forgot all about. I knew there was a reason why I didn't want Kayson at the first visit, FUCK!

"This is your second pregnancy correct?" Dr. Miller asked because he was the one who checked me out last year when we had that slip up.

"Nah, first." Kayson answered for me and Dr. Miller looked at me sympathetically.

The tears started to roll down my face immediately. I knew I should have told him a long time ago, but me and

Kayson were in such a bad place. I was not in the position to be a single mother and I knew he wasn't ready to settle down to be a father. So, I did what I thought was best for the both of us.

"Jenacia, do you two need a minute?" That's what I liked about Dr. Miller, he wasn't one of those doctors that was always in a rush. He actually cared about his patients. I nodded my head at him and he got up and walked out of the room. I said a silent prayer that Kayson would understand where I was coming from.

"What the fuck is going on Jenacia? You were pregnant by that bitch nigga and didn't tell me? I told yo' ass to always strap the fuck up." He was mad because he thought that I was pregnant by someone else, so I can only imagine what he would do if he knew that the baby was his. My first mind was to lie, but I couldn't do him like that I loved him too much.

"No Kayson, remember last year when—"

"You got pregnant?"

"Yes, but let me ex—"

"So, where is the baby?" He stood up and faced me and I lost it. I put my face in my hands and I just sobbed uncontrollably. Kayson was beyond mad because he did not once try and console me. I got myself together enough to talk to him, when I looked in his eyes I saw nothing, not one ounce of emotion. "Where is the baby? Is that why you dodged me after that?"

"I had an abortion." I said barely over a whisper.

"Come again?"

I raised my head and looked him dead in the eye. "I had an abortion." This time I spoke loud and clear. I had been holding that secret in for a while and I felt somewhat of a relief walking in that truth.

He shook his head. "You're no better than her." He put his hands in his pockets; I knew that to mean that he was trying not to flip out. "You are no better than Chelley."

"Kayson that's not fair, you don't understand. I was not in a position to be a mother and you were running the streets fucking like 40 going north. I was not trying to be a single mother."

"You think I would have done that to you?"

"Back then yes I do." I stood by that revelation. Kayson was hell on wheels and he wasn't trying to slow down for anybody.

"You couldn't at least have a conversation?" He looked hurt and that was tearing me apart.

"I should have and for that I'm sorry, but I knew you would have tried to stop me."

"You damn right I would have." He slammed his hands down on the counter. "That was selfish as fuck."

"It wasn't the right time Kayson, I'm sorry." I broke down again and he walked out of the doctor's office. I knew that the conversation wouldn't go well, but I at least wished that he would have understood where I was coming from.

The doctor walked back in and we talked about all the different things I could and couldn't do and eat. We talked about my caloric intake and how much weight I should gain with twins. We set my next appointment and I walked out to the lobby expecting to see Kayson but instead Zemia was standing there with a sympathetic smile on her face.

"He hates me."

"Girl that man loves you, he just hates what you did, give him a minute to grasp it and he will get it together."

"I hope so." I sniffed.

We walked out the door headed to Zemia's car. I was on my phone texting Kayson cussing his ass out; just so happen to look up and there was Roger and his baby mama getting out of the car going in the same office I just left from. I hurried and got in Zemia's car trying to make sure that he didn't see me. I looked in the rearview mirror and he was just standing there staring at the car with a fucked-up grin on his face. This was not the Roger that I thought I knew, and I was going to make sure that I stayed away from his ass.

Chapter Forty-Four
UNCLE RAY

I called Kayson and told him to stop by so that me and him could have little man to man talk. I could tell when I talked to him that he wasn't feeling it, but I didn't give a damn about what he was feeling. We needed to talk about this, and we were going to.

"Ray, you hear anything I said, man?" Tate's voice boomed through the phone speakers.

"My bad, nigga. Just chill I don't know much about ya daughter outside of the work she does for us, but if she's anything like you she's smart and the nigga about something." I gave him advice about meeting his daughter's boyfriend.

Tate's daughter was our lawyer, a damn good lawyer at that. I knew that Jaako had a sweet spot for her, but I also knew she shut him down on more than one occasion. She always said that she would never date a client. Even though

Jaako was a good man, he was also a drug dealer and that was bad for her business, so I knew it wasn't him that she was seeing. Whoever it is I hope he does good by her, she was a good girl.

"You know I'll be conducting my research." He laughed and so did I because I knew he was telling the truth. "I'll hit you later, man."

"Aight Tate, and don't piss my lawyer off."

"She better not piss me off."

We chatted for a minute or two longer and then hung up. I felt for him, there is no way that I would be able to do the whole daughter thing. I swear I would've been done killed somebody. With my nephews, I let them live their lives. I didn't get involved unless they asked for my advice. They never introduced me to girls unless it was serious, and I was good with that.

I sat back and chilled, hitting a few female friends back; you know sold a few dreams and then waited on Kayson to get here. I had prepared myself mentally for this conversation because I knew it could get ugly. I raised him to not trust words but actions, and my actions were foul in a way. I just hoped that we could talk this out. About an hour later, he came strolling in the house like he owned it. The more I looked at him and how he acted; I don't see how people didn't know that he was my son.

"What up, Unc?" He walked over and dapped me up and sat down on the love seat across from me. "What's good?"

"What the hell wrong with you?"

"Jenacia man." He ran his hands through his dreads and slumped in the seat. "So, we found out that she's pregnant with twins." He smiled slightly.

"Congrats, man."

"Thanks." Then his smile disappeared. "Then I also found out that she killed one of my seeds."

"Damn."

"Yeah I know, then gave me that, well I did what was best for me bullshit and I wasn't ready. That shit ain't no excuse. The least she could have done was tell me about it." He was upset, and to be honest I knew that I didn't have a right to speak on the matter seeing as to why I called him over here.

"You ain't been home?"

"Nah, I got me a room at the Ritz for a few nights."

"Nigga take yo' ass home, regardless of what's going on she still pregnant with your kids, what if something happens to her?"

"I know but—"

"Nah nigga no buts, that girl loves you. She even took you back after you fucked up all those years ago. Had yo' ass crying and shit everyday talking about how much you love her and how she needed to forgive you."

"I wasn't fucking crying." He mugged me.

"Hell, you might as well been." I shrugged. "Listen, people mess up and they make rash decisions when they are scared. I'm not saying what she did was right; because that should have been a decision made by the both of you, but she did what she thought was best for you. I mean look at the situation we in now," I looked at him as he thought about what I was saying. "Would you want your child to go through this? What if she would have had the baby, given it up for adoption, and not even told you and the baby going with a fucked-up family? You gotta think about it from all angles."

"Still don't make that shit right."

"Didn't I just fucking say that? Look I somewhat understand where she was coming from. I didn't do shit the right way with you, but that was a decision that I made and that was a decision that she made. If you love her you wouldn't be punishing her for it, you would be there for her. Did you even ask her how she felt about the shit?" I waited, and he just looked at me. "I'll answer it for you…No, cause yo' ass stubborn as fuck."

"Look who's talking."

"Yeah, but we ain't talking about me, now are we?"

"Man, you right." Was all he said. Things got quiet and awkward as fuck.

"Look, I called you over here to tell you that ain't shit got to change. I've always been that father figure for you, I helped raise you and made sure you had shit. I've always been all y'all daddy but my title was just Unc and I'm good with that if you are?"

"Shit would feel weird as fuck calling yo' ass pops." I laughed and so did he.

"But them my grandbabies." I pointed at my chest, so he would know I meant that.

"Ain't that shit gonna be weird cause you know Ann

Barnes ain't about to give up her Grandma title." We both laughed.

"That's true we will work all that shit out later, just know them gonna be some bad ass, spoiled ass kids." I smiled.

"I already know." Silence fell again and I didn't like the shit.

"We good?"

"Yeah, we good, I trust you and Ma with my life, and I know that everything y'all did for me was for my own good, there were no ill intentions." I nodded my head.

"I don't want none of that weird shit." I raised a brow.

"Fuck you, nigga." He smiled.

"My nigga." I stood to dap him up. "So, what business looking like?"

"Man, I been wanting to talk to you about that shit for a while now, but so much shit was happening I kept forgetting." I sat up in my seat to give him my full attention. "Shit been weird as fuck at the warehouse. Inventory been off for the last couple months."

"Fuck you mean?"

"Meaning product count been off, but the money been right, like somebody selling shit out from under us."

"I don't like that shit at all, that's how muthafuckas get caught the fuck up."

"Tell me about it."

"I'll look into it."

"Yeah I got people checking some shit out too."

"You know I got at Ortiz's parents for fucking shooting O, right?"

"Nah I didn't know that shit, but good move, I hate fucking with the families but when a nigga touch mines he makes his expendable."

"My thoughts exactly. Nigga moving like a fucking ghost, can't find him anywhere. He didn't even show up at his parents' funeral. Can't track that ass for shit."

"I'm sure he will flush out soon, we might need to use that little bitch, D fucking with."

"I was thinking about that too, I need to see where his head at, you know how his ass is."

"Right, I ain't really talked to him but he knows I ain't for his shit, so he doesn't call me like that." I laughed because it was the truth. Those two stayed into it.

"Aight Unc, let me get the fuck up out of here and go holla at Jenacia, her pregnant ass about to give me hell."

"You better know it."

We hugged and he left. I sat back down on the couch and flipped through the channels on TV and ended up stopping on SportsCenter as usual. I was chilling until my phone rang, I looked down and I didn't really care for the person that was on the other line. I debated on hanging up the phone but then I answered.

"Hello?"

"We need to talk."

Chapter Forty-Five
KRISTA

"I don't think this is a good idea Krista, it's been years since I saw Raymond." My mom pouted from the other side of the table.

"This is not about you, it's about me. All these years I could have been living the life, but you wanted to hold on to this little secret. I deserve to know him." I rolled my eyes.

I had been begging my mother for days to allow me to reach out to Raymond to let him know that he had more than just his precious nephews in the world, he had a daughter too. And I deserved all that he gives them and then some. I called him earlier today to see if he would meet me and when he said that he would, I was happy. He didn't want to, but I told him it was something about Jaako. When I said that, he said he would be here in an hour.

"I don't think you understand, you don't know Raymond. This is not going to go the way you think it will go."

"Well I guess we will have to see then, huh? If you will excuse me I need to get this." I held up my phone that was going off. It was Perry.

I got up from the table and walked outside the restaurant. I wanted to have total privacy when I talked to him.

"Yes, Perry."

"I've been calling you for like an hour."

"I'm sorry, I've been caught up with my mother."

"I want to see you."

"Do you think that's a good idea seeing as though you are about to do what you're about to do?"

"I don't care; I'm doing this for you so if I can't see you then I don't need to do it, right."

I rolled my eyes in the back of my head because I knew sooner or later the bitch was gonna come out of him. I swear men would do just about anything for some pussy. Especially mine and that's why I did half the shit that I did.

"Awww you miss me?" I said in a sweet voice.

"Yeah I do, so I'm in on my way to Charlotte later and I gotta pick up from Denari tonight, so I'm just gonna see you then."

"Okay, just tell me where."

"Your house." I was hesitant to have him at my house just in case Jaako decides to pop up, which I doubt or Denari's dumb ass pops up.

"I don't know if that's a good idea."

"Well that's the only choice you have, so I'll see you later. Oh, be naked."

Perry was starting to get on my fucking nerves something serious, but I needed him right now, so I was going to have to deal with it. I put my phone in the back pocket of my jeans and turned to go back in the restaurant and noticed that Jaako's car was pulling into the parking lot. I wondered what the fuck he was doing here. I strutted over to his car to see why he was here, but I didn't need him to be fucking up my meeting with Raymond.

"Jaako?" I asked like I didn't already know that it was him. He sighed deeply like he didn't want to see me. He looked down at his watch and then looked around the parking lot.

"What, Krista?"

"I thought that was you. Look, I really think we need to have a sit down and discuss some things."

"Like I told you before, there is nothing that you can say that will change how I feel." He shrugged.

"Can you just have a conversation with me or not?"

"Not." He said and then walked to the back seat of his car. "Can you please go?"

"I'm having lunch here."

"Damn it okay well let me call Yameka and tell her to choose another restaurant."

"What you scared to have your precious lady around me?"

He laughed, "No, not at all because she knows what she is in my life. It's been months Krista, why don't you just move the hell on I'm just saying."

"Because I was here first, Jaako."

"And she'll be here last." His phone rang, and he answered it like I wasn't even standing there. "Hey baby, yeah I'm here but we have an issue."

"So, I'm an issue now?"

"Yes, you hear that," he laughed at something she said on the phone. It was like I was butt end of the joke or something. "You sure baby, okay fine, I'm on my way." She must have said something because he smiled hard as hell. "I love you too, Yameka." He hung up the phone and reached for his door handle.

I slammed my hands down on the top of his car. The look in his eyes told me to run, but I wasn't fast enough. By the time I stepped with my left foot, I was being dangled from the air by my collar that he had in a tight fist.

"Let me go, Jaako."

"Look bitch, I tried to be nice but you just keep on with your shit, so I tell you what, this is your last fucking warning. I will not hesitate to put a fucking bullet in your head. You don't want to piss me off; it's in your best interest to stop fucking with me." He looked me in the eye and I wanted to piss on myself. I had never been so scared in all my life.

"GET YOU HANDS OFF MY DAUGHTER." My mom came up and swung on Jaako and he pushed her back and dropped me from the hold he had on me.

"I'm telling you now if you say anything to me or Yameka when we get back, I swear you will regret it." He pointed at the both of us and we were both terrified.

He got in his car and backed out of the parking space not even caring that he came inches from running me over. I stared at him as he drove off, and I had fucked up with him beyond repair. I guess my next move is gonna be trying to get close to my father.

"Are you okay, Mom?"

"Yeah, I'm fine, are you?"

"Yeah let's go in, I'm sure he'll be here in a minute."

Me and my mom walked in the restaurant and ordered our drinks and food. I was still a little shaken up, but I was trying to relax. Things didn't get any better when Ray walked in the building and over to our table. He had the look of death on his face.

"What's this about?" Hsaid without even saying hey.

"Well hello to you too." I told his rude ass. My mother didn't say anything she just sat there and dropped her head.

"You said you needed to tell me something important concerning my nephew. I ain't here for no bullshit, so tell me what you need to tell me, so I can fucking go, I got shit to do."

"That was the only way to get you here," I rolled my eyes.

"Fuck this, I'm out."

"I'm your daughter." I blurted out and he stopped in his tracks, he turned around slowly and glared at my mother who had yet to lift her head.

"Chelsey, tell her to stop fucking lying."

"Why would I lie about something like that?"

"Shut the fuck up I'm not speaking to you, Chelsey." He said a little louder and it made the both of us jump.

"Yeah Raymond, she's yours." He laughed.

"You sure you wanna do this with me?"

"Raymond, I'm positive she's yours, I was already pregnant when I got with Roman." Again, he laughed.

"I'm positive that she's not, after I had my son, I had my shit clipped. I knew I didn't want kids and I made sure that I wouldn't have any more."

My eyes got big and I looked over at my mom and she was just as surprised. "I don't believe you."

"You ain't got to, but I know for a fact you ain't got my blood running through ya veins. You need to go back to her rolodex of niggas she was fucking at the time to find out who ya daddy is." He shrugged. "Do you think if I thought you were my daughter that I would have let you fuck my nephew? I knew you were a hoe the minute I found out who your mother was." He shook his head. "Y'all have a nice day."

He turned to walk out of the restaurant and I turned to look at my mother. She had some explaining to do.

Chapter Forty-Six
JAAKO

Every time I saw or talked to Krista I got pissed off. I don't know why she thought I owed her a fucking explanation or anything for that matter. In her twisted little mind, what she did was justified because I was with Yameka and that's not how this shit goes. I was frustrated but I needed to get that shit out of my head because I wanted everything to go smooth with Yameka's parents.

"Hey baby, I'm sorry about that, I don't know what the hell is wrong with my car. It was working just fine earlier."

"It's cool, I called my guy on the way over here and he's gonna pick it up and take it to his shop and see what's wrong with it."

"Thank you, baby." She leaned over and kissed me. "What's wrong?" It was like she could sense when anything was bothering me, and I loved that about her.

"Krista and her fucking mama."

"Don't let that bitch ruin our day." She pointed her freshly manicured nail at my face and I pretended to bite it.

"I ain't, I just wish the bitch would go away, before I make her."

"Jaako!"

"My bad." I laughed, she hated when I said stuff like that because she was my lawyer and she didn't want to hear anything that would jeopardize her defending us if she needed to. Sometimes I just did shit to get on her nerves.

The drive to the restaurant was full of laughs and jokes. All it took was for me to be around her to get all that negativity out of my head. I just hoped Krista didn't try and start shit when we got there. Pulling up to the restaurant I noticed Unc's car immediately.

"What the fuck he doing here?" I said under my breath.

We got out of the car and walked hand in hand in the restaurant, and the first thing I see is Unc arguing with Krista and her bitch ass mom. My first thought was to go in the opposite direction, but I wanted to know what the hell he was doing here with them of all people. I walked in his direction just as he was walking off from the table. He ran right into me.

"Unc, what the fuck you doing here and with them?"

"That little bitch called me talking about she needed to talk to me and it was about you."

"The fuck?"

"Exactly and I get here, and she was on some straight up

bullshit talking about she was my daughter and shit. What they didn't know is I had my shit clipped right after Kayson." Well damn this bitch just didn't know when to quit did she. "So, I just cussed the both of them out and now I'm going to find me some pussy—" he stopped mid-sentence when he noticed that Yameka was standing here. "You got to be fucking kidding me."

"What the hell is going on here?" I heard Tate, our connect with the police, say from behind me.

"Hey, Daddy." Yameka went up and hugged him and I stood there looking stupid. I never knew who her father was. I just knew that he worked in the criminal justice system and I didn't ask too many questions. "This is the man that I was telling you about, his name is Jaako and Jaako this is my dad."

"I know who the fuck he is." Tate hissed and then looked in the direction of me and Unc. "What the fuck are you doing with my daughter?"

"Wait, you know each other?"

"Yes!" We all said in unison.

"In my defense, I didn't know that she was your daughter, I mean not that it would change anything because I love her."

"This is not gonna work for me." Tate shook his head and then looked at Unc. "You knew about this?"

"No I didn't, I don't get in my nephews' business because they are grown, but I can tell you now that Jaako is a good man, so you have nothing to worry about."

"I don't want to hear that shit, you know what he does for

a fucking living." He said loud enough for people to hear. Well this wasn't going how I expected it to go.

"Tate, no disrespect, but we do the same shit." I gritted through my teeth. I was getting pissed the fuck off.

"Daddy?" Yameka screeched. She looked back and forth between me and her daddy and then ran out the door with Tate following behind her. I headed for the exit to go and see what the fuck was the problem.

When I got outside Yameka was standing there crying her eyes out. Tate was standing there with his hands folded across his chest. I could hear him saying something about me to her and I didn't like that shit, we were grown and Yameka was 32 years old.

"Do you know what this could do for your career?"

"Daddy, do you know what it could do to your career?" She came back. "And you, why didn't you tell me?" She looked in my direction.

"Baby, I didn't know he was your father and I don't talk about my business with you remember."

She didn't say anything, she just looked around and continued to cry. I didn't know what I could say to make it any better, but I knew that she was hurting and whether I agreed with it or not I was a part of it. I walked over and enclosed her in my arms.

"This is some bullshit, my daughter the successful lawyer is fucking with my business associate, a fucking drug dealer."

"Yo, I may be a drug dealer Tate, but I can fucking promise you that there is no one out here that could protect her like I can. Ain't a damn soul gonna be there for her like me. It doesn't matter what I do, as long as I don't bring that shit home to my woman." I laid it all out there. I'm over all his smart-ass comments like his crooked ass wasn't in the same business as me.

"I just need to go." Yameka said.

"I can take you to the house." I volunteered.

"No, I'll take her," Tate interjected, and I gave him a look that said don't fuck with me.

"I need to talk to my dad." Yameka placed her hands on my chest.

"Don't let this come in between us; we worked too hard for this." She stood on her toes and kissed me on the lips. She gave me a half smile that wasn't convincing at all, but it would have to do. I would give her time to get things together with her dad, but I wasn't going anywhere and the sooner the both of them get that through their thick heads the better.

I watched as they climbed into Tate's SUV and pulled out of the parking lot and sped off down the street. I don't like to get into family drama, but I swear if he tried to come in between me and Yameka he is gonna have fight on his hands and I bet my life on that.

"Ain't this some bullshit?" Unc said from behind me.

"Why didn't you tell me she was Tate's daughter?"

"I didn't think she would ever fall for your shit and that shit wouldn't have even mattered to you anyway, now would it?"

"Hell no." I laughed.

"Exactly but I wished I would have known though so I could've given that nigga a heads up or something."

"That muthafucka will be alright, the only reason I let that nigga slide with all that slick shit was because of you, you know that, right?" He nodded his head. "I don't know if I'll be able to do that again."

"It won't happen again."

"Good!"

Chapter Forty-Seven
KAYSON

"Jenacia, listen to me."

"No Kayson, you listen to me." she fussed. I was sitting in the warehouse waiting on my brothers to get here.

"Go ahead, I'm listening."

"I can't do this anymore; I can't trust you to be here for me. Every time you get mad what you gonna do put your hands on me and then leave? No, I'm not going for that. The only thing I want from you is for you to take care of your kids." She yelled out in one breath.

"Shut the hell up."

"No, you shut up I'm sick of your shit. You so caught up in the shit you got going on that you think everyone is disloyal like you."

"Don't do that, don't go drudging up the past because you mad, Jenacia."

"I'll do what I want to do."

"I'ma let all this slick talking slide because I know ya hormones out of whack from the twins, but I'll be home later, and we will talk about this face to face. It sounds like yo' ass need some dick or something 'cause I swear you doing the most." I laughed but she didn't see anything funny.

"I changed the locks."

"If you changed the locks, I'm fucking you up." I sat up on the edge of the chair, she was starting to piss me off I ain't been gone but three damn days. "Jenacia."

"What!"

"Did you change them locks?"

"Sure the hell did." She sassed, and I ran my hands through my dreads. "Go lay with the bitch you been with for the last three days Kayson, fuck you. I knew you were gonna do this."

"I wasn't with no bitch, I told you I ain't on that shit no more, so stop."

"I can't tell, 'cause you still being the selfish, childish asshole that I remember."

"Is that why you killed my baby?" I don't know why I asked that but I did, and I needed an answer from her, but she didn't say anything. I could hear sniffling, but she wasn't saying anything. "Jenacia?"

"I did what was best for me; I wasn't in a position to be a single parent."

"I would've been there."

"When you wanted to Kayson and you know it. You were too busy trying to move up the ladder that the only thing that mattered to you was your money and your dick and you know it."

She wasn't lying, if you would have told me a year ago that I would be trying to settle down and raise a family I would have laughed in your face. I didn't have time for that I just wanted to do me and get money.

"I get it, but that shit still don't make it right."

"I never said it did."

"Can we talk about this later?"

"Whatever, Kayson."

"For real I'm sorry for leaving and not coming home. I just needed time to process shit."

"Well, I need time to process shit too."

"Aight cool, I'm giving yo' ass three hours and I'll be home."

"Call before you come so I can open the door."

"Stop fucking playing with me, you better not had changed the locks."

"Okay." Was all she said before she hung up the phone.

I really needed to work on my patience and shit like that. I can't run away from shit when it gets bad with her. I needed to get my feelings in check and learn to work shit out. I had kids coming and she needed me, they needed me.

I did a little bit of work while I was waiting on everybody to get here. Numbers were still fucked up and the shit was baffling. I asked around and of course no one knew anything. What they didn't know is that I put in cameras that I planned on watching later to see who the fuck was fucking up, so we could dead them niggas.

I heard the door to the warehouse chime and it was Denari which was weird because his ass was never on time for shit. I was against inviting him to this, but Unc thought enough time had passed and we needed to talk to him and see where his head was at. Plus, we needed to find a way to flush Ortiz out, and him and Heaven knew more about him than anybody.

I was about to get up and go holla at him until he headed to the back of the warehouse. I watched on the monitors as he went to holla at Joker who was looking around like he was guilty and shit. They exchanged a few words and Denari handed him a wad of money that Joker accepted and put in his back pocket. I wondered what the fuck that was about. Something was telling me that I just found out who was fucking up the count. I was gonna try my best to remain cool, but I swear I wanted to fuck his ass up. He was never gonna learn.

To be able to keep my cool long enough for everyone to get there I just stayed up in my office and watched from the monitors. I decided to come down to see what everybody was up to. I noticed Jaako looking all crazy.

"Jaa the fuck wrong with you."

"You'll never guess who Yameka's daddy is."

"Who, nigga?"

"Tate!" Shit that ain't good at all, can't be fucking the police's daughter. I didn't even know what to say so I just looked at him and I could tell that the shit was eating his ass alive. He loved Yameka and had for some time and to think that this may be the end of their relationship.

"What the fuck you gonna do about it?"

"I'ma let her work that shit out with her pops, but I ain't about to let her go. She it for me." He shrugged, and I understood where he was coming from.

"Well since we sharing and shit, I got some good news." I couldn't contain my smile. "Y'all niggas gonna be uncles."

"Bullshit." Omari said as he came over and dapped me up. "Congrats bro."

"Thanks man, check it though, we are having twins."

"Got damn super sperm." Omari laughed.

I dapped up everybody else except Denari who kept his distance. I wasn't tripping because I was cool with that. I didn't even want him here, but I was about to bust his fucking ass in just a little minute.

"And I got a sister, but that's a story for a different time."

They continued to congratulate me on the twins and then we got down to business. Unc told us about the move he made with Ortiz's people.

"So, I need y'all to keep an eye out cause I'm sure that nigga gonna clap back." He said once he was done telling us how it went down.

"I'm ready for him for ass this time, and I promise I'm not the one that's gonna end up with the hole in my chest." Omari rubbed the place where he had gotten shot just a little while ago.

"Ortiz gonna get his, know that." I assured. "But I just wanted to talk to y'all about the way the fucking count been coming up all fucked up." I looked at Denari and he was staring straight at me. "I put cameras in so I could find out what the fuck been going on and—"

"Cut the bullshit, it was me." Denari blurted out.

"The fuck you mean it was you?" Unc said and I just stood back waiting for him to say something stupid so I could swing on his ass.

"Y'all cut me out and I needed to do what I needed to do to keep my name in the streets too." He said like the shit made sense.

"We cut you out because you were fucking up, nigga." Jaako said.

"Like you ain't ever fucked up," Denari waved Jaako off. "Nobody said nothing when yo' ass shot Jizzy."

"Jizzy was a fucking snake, dumb ass, how the fuck you think the niggas that hit the spot knew about everything?" He didn't say anything. "That's what the fuck I thought, yo' ignorant ass ain't built for this life."

"Fuck you, I'm just as good as you muthafuckas."

"Who you been selling my shit to, man?" I asked calmly because I was two seconds from whooping his ass.

"My nigga, Perry," was all he said.

"Perry who?" Unc interjected.

"Man, I don't know all that I just know he doing big things

in South Carolina, and the shit he was working with was watered down as fuck and he was paying way too much for it. So, I made him an offer he couldn't refuse."

"You really are a dumb muthafucka." Unc said shaking his head. "How the fuck are you wheeling and dealing, and you don't know shit about the nigga?" Unc spread his arms and waited for Denari to say something, when he got nothing he continued. "Where he live? Who his people? Who work for him? Is that nigga the middle man? Does he work for somebody else? You got to have some kind of fucking answers."

"If that nigga was the Feds, don't you think they would have got me by now?"

"Muthafucka, no!" Jaako yelled. "They watch until they got enough to put you and everybody around you behind fucking bars! A couple of sales don't hold no weight in the court system."

Denari didn't say anything, he just stood there looking around. This nigga just didn't care about nothing, he damn sure didn't give a fuck about the fact that he may just put us all at risk of getting locked the fuck up.

"Who helped you?"

"That shit don't matter."

"Yeah it does, because they had strict instructions not to deal with you at all. So whoever did it not only stole from me, but they were disloyal as fuck."

"Nah, that nigga didn't have a choice."

"Did you pay him?"

"Yeah for his troubles."

"That makes it voluntary because even if you threatened him he could have still come to me." I walked to the back and called for Joker and he walked out already knowing what it was. He looked at Denari like he wanted to fuck his ass up. "So, you know I told y'all not to deal with his ass for any reason, right?"

"Yeah I know."

"This nigga said he threatened you is that true?"

"True or not, I knew better. Just take care of my baby girl and my girl, that's all I ask."

The nigga had heart and I didn't want to kill him, but I didn't have a choice. If I let him get away with this shit, then other muthafuckas would think that it's okay for them to do it. If I fired his ass, he might wanna get froggy and clap back and I couldn't risk it. I pulled out my heat and dropped him where he stood.

"You didn't have to do that shit yo."

"Yeah, I did, it's called being a fucking boss and yo' ass ain't ready. Stay the fuck out my warehouse, Denari. I ain't fucking playing. Enough is enough and I ain't doing time for you. I don't know where you gonna supply this nigga from now, but it won't be from here and if anybody try that shit again they will meet the same got damn fate."

"Unc, man, don't let him do this shit."

"You did this; you went about all this shit the wrong way. This is your fault."

"Man fuck this and fuck y'all." Denari stormed out the

door and for once Omari didn't follow him. I think he was starting to understand all our frustrations.

"Shit should be smooth sailing now, right?" Unc asked and we all nodded. "Well I'm going to jump in some pussy, a nigga need it with y'all drama filled asses." We laughed, and he dapped us all up and headed out the door.

"Denari just don't know when to quit, so now we got to switch shit around. We need to find a new warehouse and everything. I don't trust this Perry shit I'm getting a bad vibe—"

BOOM!

We all dived to the floor as debris and glass fell on top of us. I tried my best to shield my face, but I could feel the small pieces of glass in my arms. I looked around and I saw Jaako moving around and Omari was peeking out from under his arms. I knew that they were okay; we were the only ones here besides... Fuck!

"Oh shit, Unc!" I could see the flames from the widows, and I jumped up and ran to the door. As soon as I got to the fucking door, there was Unc's car engulfed in flames and he was nowhere in sight.

Chapter Forty-Eight
DENARI

I don't know what the fuck else I got to do to show these muthafuckas that I can do everything that they could do and better. I made that deal on my own, I been putting in work and the shit was paying off. We were slowly taking over South Carolina; business was booming so much that the nigga was trying to double his order. Why in the fuck would they try and shut that shit down? All they keep talking about is unnecessary shit, his last name, what the fuck did that matter if the nigga's money was green he was good in my book. If he was the FEDS I would know that shit.

I can't believe Omari's ass just stood there while they were tearing my ass a new one. I had no idea what his problem was as of late, but he was being disloyal as fuck. We were all brothers, but me and that nigga shared the same fucking

DNA, so that should mean a little more. A conversation with him was definitely needed.

Boom! Boom!

Looking in my rearview mirror, all I could see was a big ass cloud of smoke and it had to be coming from the warehouse, because there was nothing else around. The U-turn I busted was illegal as hell, but right now the only thing that was on my mind was going to check on my family. My Camaro pushed 120 easy and I was pulling back up in no time.

"Oh shit!" was the only thing that I could say at the scene that I was witnessing. Jumping out my car, I ran down to the warehouse, I watched as my Uncle's car became engulfed in flames. I spotted Kayson standing in the doorway with his hands on his head. It looked as if he had tears running down his face. He disappeared into the warehouse and I followed him. "What the fuck happened?" I yelled and they all pulled out on me. "Whoa, nigga it's me." I threw my hands up.

"Did you do this?" Kayson said walking toward me with a scowl on his face. When he got within arm's reach, he took a swing at me but I backed up enough for him to miss, and Jaako jumped in between us.

"Kay, calm the fuck down, you know good and damn well D ain't did no shit like that." Jaako's voice trembled, the pain he was feeling could be felt with every word he spoke.

"Where Unc at man?" I asked on the verge of tears myself, but no one said anything. "Come on man, where the fuck Unc at?"

"He walked out to the car man, that's all we know." Jaako admitted.

"FUCK!" I screamed and then I just broke down. We had our issues, but I swear I loved that nigga more than I would ever be able to explain. He was my father, and no one could tell me any different and to think that I may never see him again was taking all the thug out of me, out of all of us.

"Bruh, chill," Jaako tried to calm me down. "He could have gotten out."

"Ortiz." Kayson said out of the blue and then turned toward his office. We all followed him in there and he pulled up the cameras that he told us he had just installed. "Unc got at that nigga's family, so this has his name all over it and I swear on my unborn shorties, his ass is gonna feel all my pain." He said as he did something with the tape.

He pressed play and I watched as we all filed into the warehouse. After we were all inside, you could see a figure walk out of the woods. He looked up at the camera, pulled out a gun and shot that muthafucka down.

"I'ma fucking kill 'em." Kayson said through gritted teeth.

"That was that nigga Roger, that used to fuck with Jenacia wasn't it?" Jaako asked.

"Yep, and that nigga just guaranteed himself a spot in hell."

"We need to find that nigga and fast." Omari finally spoke up sounding just as hurt as the rest of us. "How in the fuck he know where we do business at anyway?"

We all looked at Kayson, and he gave us that don't even

fucking think about it look. The only person with any ties to Roger was Jenacia. I hated to think like that but shit, if it was me they would be thinking that shit.

"Don't even think about that shit, Jenacia would never do no shit like that. Hell, that nigga probably working with Ortiz, we need to call Tate." He said getting up and running outside with his gun in his hand. We all followed. It wasn't likely that that nigga was still out there, but just in case.

Kayson was right though, we had all known Jenacia for years and she was like a sister to us. She got on my got damn nerves sometimes, but I knew she was loyal to us. This shit was really fucking with me. Kayson was trying to be hard, but I could tell that he wanted to breakdown, but he was trying to be strong for us.

"Who gonna tell Ma?" Omari asked after we searched around the building making sure that we wouldn't get any more surprises.

"I will." Kayson said and just stood and watched as Unc's car burned to nothing. "I will call the clean up crew to come empty this out and take it to the backup spot, just in case someone calls the cops." We all nodded, it was just like Kayson to handle shit, and it was times like this that I appreciated his ass. "We all need to get out of here."

"We can't just leave Unc like this, man." Omari said.

"He's gone, O." Jaako tried to reason with him.

"WE DON'T KNOW THAT!" O yelled jumping in Jaako's face.

"Calm down man, we all need to just calm the fuck down."

Kayson said wiping his eyes. "We gotta get out of here O, I'll call Tate so he can get his people out here before anybody else can get down here aight?" He looked in Omari's direction. "He will be able to tell us if a body is in there or not." He grabbed Omari's shoulder.

"I gotta get out of here." I said to no one in particular, shit was too heavy for me and I needed a fucking hit and bad.

"Nah bruh, we need to be together right now." Kayson said, and for once his words were sympathetic to what the fuck I was feeling.

"I'm good, I just need to go and grab Heaven, and I'll meet you back at the house."

"What the fuck did I just say!" There was the Kayson that I knew. "The last thing we need right now is to get caught slipping by this nigga. We stick to fucking gether point blank period! We don't know who the fuck he working with or where the fuck he is and until we do, we stick together."

I understood where he was coming from I just wasn't feeling how the fuck he was trying to handle me. He always thought he was the leader, above us and shit. I looked at him and before I could say anything a car came down the long driveway. We all drew our pieces until we saw that it was Unc's clean up crew. Kayson walked over to holla at them.

I called and told Heaven to stay away from the doors and that I would be there to get her soon. I could tell that she was high by the slur of her voice. Once Kayson got everything squared away we jumped in the car to go get Heaven and the other girls. Shit was about to get real and fast.

Chapter Forty-Nine
ORTIZ

"You get the job done?" I asked Roger as he sat on the sofa in the living room of the house we had in Troutman.

"I told you I did, didn't I?" Roger said with a bit more bass than I allowed. I jumped up with the knife that I was using to cut my steak, and placed it at his throat.

"Who the fuck you think you talking to, I don't like you anyway! The only reason I put up with you is on the strength of my sister."

I knew Roger from way back when his family used to live in Rock Hill. We were tight and ran in the same circle. When I started the Ortiz boys he came to me wanting to earn a little bit of money, so I let him in on my shit. Things were going good with our little arrangement until I found out that he knocked my muthafuckin sister up. He knew just like everyone else that she was off limits.

You see my sister Maria, had a little reputation on the streets and I was trying to help her clear up her name, but the more I tried to keep her away from everybody the more she snuck and did her own thing. Had me out here shooting niggas over talking shit about her and the shit was true after all.

To make matters worse, Roger had a whole live in bitch at the time and he tried to give Maria a hard time about the baby. He even asked her to get rid of it, but we grew up Catholic, so we didn't believe in that. He tried some fuck shit for a while, then all a sudden, he was all for being with her and the kids. Come to find out his girl left him for Kayson Barnes. I lost all respect for him after that, now I just tolerate him for Maria's sake.

"Come on man, I thought we were better than that?"

"Ortiz, no!" Maria's voice snapped me out of my trance. I would do anything for her including putting up with this clown. I shook my head and returned to my seat to finish my food. Cello thought the exchange was funny.

"No one saw you?" I asked.

"They had cameras nigga, you didn't tell me that, but I took them shits out as soon as I seen them."

"Fuck!"

"It's cool, hell the blast probably took that shit out, so I wouldn't worry about it."

"Do you know who we fucking with?" It wasn't like I was scared of their asses or anything like that, but I wasn't dumb either. They were as ruthless as they come. If you were coming for them, you needed to come correct or the end result would be deadly.

"Fuck them Barnes bitches, they will be alright."

"Tell me that when they got yo' ass hemmed up somewhere."

"Sounds like you scared or some shit," he smirked. See this is why I didn't like his bitch ass. I pulled out my gun and fired a shot past his head and the little pussy screamed and ducked.

"Now who the fuck scary?" Me and Cello laughed.

I got up and went to sit on the deck. I needed to clear my mind a bit before Brayla got here. Because of the situation that I was in I wanted to make sure that the people around me that I let into my space right now were legit. I couldn't risk having someone around that could possibly fuck around and lead them muthafuckas right to me. It was only a matter of time before they realized that I was connected to that dumb ass Roger. I didn't give a fuck what he said, if they had cameras, they already know who did that shit.

These niggas thought they could just go around touching people's families and shit and not have any consequences and that was the furthest thing from the truth. When they touched my parents, they opened up something in me that I didn't even know existed. I was going to take my time and kill each and every one of them and everything they loved. Especially those beautiful women, starting with Heaven.

"Hey Papi," Brayla announced as she entered the room.

"Take your clothes off." I needed her to be at her most vulnerable point when I get at her about Kayson.

"Damn it's like that, I thought we were better than that." She sounded hurt but at this moment I didn't give a fuck. I just needed to have this conversation with her, so I could see where her head was at. If I found out she was playing me I was gonna slit her throat right then and there.

"I just missed you, that's all." I tried to soften it up, but my tone was still harsh.

I had been feeling that way since I had my guys do research on her and found out that she use to fuck with that nigga Kayson. A part of me wanted to believe that she wouldn't do no shit like that, but nowadays women weren't shit so I needed to make sure for myself.

Once she was naked, I looked at her butter pecan colored skin and traced the curves of her body with my eyes. She was beautiful, there was no doubt about it. She definitely gave Heaven a run for her money and I could see her replacing Heaven in my life, but I couldn't do that until the bitch was dead. So, I kept my feelings at bay for the time being. Plus, Brayla's eyes were sneaky and my mom always said that eyes were the window to the soul.

Standing up and in front of her, I ran my arms down the length of hers and just stared at her in the eyes. Fear and lust radiated from her eyes. I turned her around and lightly pushed her on the bed and nodded telling her to slide up on the bed. Once she was where I wanted her to be, I grabbed two sets of handcuffs and cuffed her to the bed. I was a man that loved to be in control of any situation and we had been dealing with each other for a few months, so the cuffs didn't raise any alarm.

"So, it's one of these kinds of nights." She licked her lips then tucked her bottom one in between her teeth.

I climbed in the bed; I was only dressed in my boxers when she came into my room, so I climbed in between her legs. The heat coming from her pleasure spot made my dick rise. I was hoping like hell that I didn't have to kill her, but if I did I may as well get some pussy first. I smiled at the thought as I worked my way out of my boxers.

Placing my dick at her opening, I eased in and she let out a sexy moan. Her eyes rolled back into her head and she spread her legs more to give me better access.

"How do you know Kayson Barnes?" Her eyes popped open and she tried to scoot back but I grabbed her legs, that was the first sign of deceit right there. "Are you working for him?"

She gave me a confused look and then she rolled her eyes at me. "I thought he sent you to kill me since I fucked with his little girlfriend." She let out a huge sigh and then relaxed under my hold.

"Why the fuck would you think that? I would have killed you a long time ago if that was the case."

"Shit I don't know, that nigga ain't got it all and I never know how to take him. He stopped fucking with me months ago when he started fucking with that bitch he with now."

"So, you don't have no communication with him anymore?"

She laughed. "Why are we talking about Kayson with your dick in my guts, that's a little weird." I gave her a serious stare and she stopped laughing. "Man, I ain't with that setting niggas up and stuff, I just like to have my fun and live my life, Ortiz."

It was my turn to laugh, I didn't need her to set anybody up, I had them niggas in a vulnerable state right now and it would be nothing to just get at them if I wanted to, but I wanted to make this fun. I needed them to suffer. I didn't trust her ass anyway.

"Were you ever in a relationship with him?" I needed to know how deep shit went with them because I couldn't risk her having a change of heart and risking everything that I had planned.

"Let's just say I was in a relationship with him and he was in one with my pussy, make sense?" She rolled her eyes like I was getting on her nerves.

"So, I ain't got shit to worry about when it comes to you and him."

"Hell no, I wouldn't care if that nigga died tomorrow."

"Okay." Was all I said because I would be keeping a real close eye on her, I didn't trust her worth a shit. But I didn't want to kill her right now; she may come in handy later. I grabbed the back of her thighs and watched as my dick slid in and out of her while she screamed bloody murder.

I had a lot of shit I needed to do but right now, I was gonna fuck the shit out of Brayla.

Chapter Fifty
ANN BARNES

I sat staring off into space as I listened to my boys and Tate tell me about everything that happened tonight. I couldn't move, my body wouldn't respond to anything, I couldn't cry. My brother wasn't dead, he couldn't be dead. There was no way that he would leave us here. The only emotion that my body would allow me to feel was anger right now.

"HOW COULD Y'ALL LET THIS HAPPEN?" I jumped up and yelled. I didn't know why I was angry at them or why I was blaming them, but that's what was happening and for some reason I couldn't control it. "YOU WERE SUPPOSED TO PROTECT EACH OTHER." I pointed at all of them and they lowered their heads. I wanted to comfort them so badly, but my body wouldn't let me. I was frozen where I stood, and I shook, that's how upset I was.

"Ma, we didn't know." Jaako said looking up at me. I could see the pain in his eyes, I knew they were hurting and it took me seeing that and to hear Omari sniffle to break me out of my trance and at that moment, I lost it.

"Nooooo, not my brother, God bring him back." I cried. "Why him Lord, I need him here."

All the boys came over and threw their arms around me and we cried together. I swear I had never seen Kayson cry until this very moment and it was then that I knew that things would never be the same.

"We found no remains." Tate said from his seat on the couch and I looked at him.

"So, he could still be alive?" I said with hope trying to release myself from the boys hold they had on me.

"That's not what I'm saying, the body could have disintegrated. They are still processing the scene right now."

"But he could still be alive?"

"There is a possibility, but there's a problem." Tate said and then looked in the direction of my boys. "They are investigating why he was out there in the first place."

"And?" Kayson said.

"And there is no explanation as to why he was out there so they are gonna be looking into everything, including his family." He raised a brow. "I more than likely won't be around just to keep suspicion down, but you know how we operate, Ray gave me specific instructions on how to proceed if anything ever were to happen to him. So, Kayson we need to pick a spot to meet so I can keep you up to speed with the investigation, you are in charge now."

"You can make this shit go away right; I mean you are the chief of police." Omari asked him with red eyes.

"I can as long as they don't bring in the DEA, then it's out of my hands and we are all gonna be in some shit." He gave us a serious look then he pulled Kayson to the side and talked to him about some things and then he left.

"Are y'all in trouble?" I asked Kayson when he joined us in the living room. We all had taken our seats back on the sofa.

"Nothing we can't get out of, they just digging right now." He shrugged trying to keep it together, but I could see the worry in his eyes but just like his father you would never know what he was feeling.

"You sure?"

"Yeah Ma." He walked over and bent down and kissed me on the cheek. "We need to plan Unc's memorial or something."

"But he just said there is a possibility that he is alive." I was grasping at straws, but what was life without hope.

"Ma you didn't see that car." Jaako said reaching out to rub my back and I leaned into his shoulder. "We need to plan the memorial." I nodded my head, I would do it because it's what they want but something was telling me that my brother was still alive.

Chapter Fifty-One
KAYSON

Today was the day of the memorial and to be honest I wasn't feeling this shit at all. I didn't want to face the fact that Unc was gone. I had just found out that I shared the same DNA as this man and we didn't even have a chance to explore that. I know I said that I wanted to keep things the same, but after I found out that I was gonna be father some shit clicked in my head and had me wanting to do things differently. Now, I would never have that chance.

Finding and killing Roger was something that I lived and fucking breathed. I needed to get my hands on him something serious. I would not rest until maggots feasted on his rotten corpse. I needed to feel the life slipping away from him as I watch him take his last breath and until then I won't be okay with everything that has happened.

"Hello," I said as I picked up the phone on the third ring.

I was so lost in my thoughts that I didn't even realize that my phone was ringing. I didn't even bother looking on the caller I.D. because Tate was the only one with this number.

"I ran the information on Roger and I found out something very interesting."

"Speak."

"After running his known affiliates, you will never guess who came up."

"Tate, I honestly ain't in the mood for this right now. We gotta get to my uncle's memorial and I ain't feeling this shit so just tell me."

"Ortiz." Was all he said.

"I knew his bitch ass was behind this, he just opened up some shit his ass ain't gone be able to handle." I gritted my teeth in anger. "You coming today?"

"You know I can't do that, and as bad as I want to, I just can't."

"I feel that." We talked a little business and he hung up.

I stood up from my bed that I had been sleeping in at Mama's house. Jenacia was serious when she said that she was tired of my shit and she changed the locks on the doors. After the night Unc got killed, she came and stayed with me over here, but told me that if I wanted my family that I was gonna have to prove it to her because she was tired of the back and forth with me. I didn't have the energy to argue with her about that. We had too much going on with Unc dying and trying to find Roger, so I let her have that, but after today I was moving back home with her whether she liked it or not.

It wasn't safe for her to be there by herself. Even though I had someone there around the clock keeping an eye on her, she needed me and right now I needed her something serious.

I made sure my green tie that matched the green and brown Gators that I had on was straight and I put on my suit jacket and headed to the house to pick up Jenacia. I took one more look in the mirror and then headed out the door.

When I got there, she met me at the door. She was dressed in a black dress that stopped mid-calf and hugged every curve that God gave her. Her belly was still flat because she was in the early stages of her pregnancy, but just knowing that I had created the life that was growing in her stomach excited me.

"You look beautiful." I told her, and she smiled.

"You don't look too bad yourself; it looks like you were peeping through my window though." She looked me up and down and I did the same and I noticed that her shoes where the same green as my tie and gators.

"Our chemistry is just that strong." I grabbed her by the waist and kissed her lips.

"If it was so strong, we wouldn't be staying in separate locations." She broke away from me and headed to the passenger side of my truck.

"It won't be that way after tonight." I followed behind her and opened the door before she could and helped her in. Once she was seated, she looked at me and then rolled her eyes and I chuckled and shut the door.

I walked around the car making sure to take in my

surroundings. Neighbors were out, and I noticed the guy who watched the house for me. I nodded at him and then disappeared into the car. I put my seat belt on and backed out of the driveway.

"You know you can't keep doing this to me, right?" She said, and I didn't want to argue but I also didn't want to blow her off, and by the sound of her voice she needed this conversation.

"I'm sorry, a nigga was thrown by that shit Jen, to hear that you didn't think a nigga was good enough back then to be a father hurt."

"That's not it Kayson, it's not that you weren't good enough, it's that you weren't ready. You were out here with all different types of bitches, running crazy with your brothers. On top of that I wasn't ready. I was still trying to get my career up off the ground and a baby would have gotten in the way of that."

"That sounded selfish as fuck." I said before I could stop myself. I didn't want to take the conversation in the wrong way, so I took a deep breath, got my thoughts together and continued. "I understand where you are coming from, but I still feel like I at least deserved a conversation. The way you went about it was selfish."

"You're right I was selfish, because I did what I thought was best for me," She stopped and then turned toward me, paused before adding, "and you. I should have talked to you, but I know you Kayson, and you would have tried to talk me out of it and it wasn't the right time for either of us. I did what I thought was best and that I won't apologize for, but I will apologize for how I went about it."

I sat and thought about what she said, and she was right. Neither of us were ready to be parents and I damn sure wasn't trying to be nobody's man at the time. Had she had the baby, I would've expected her to stay at home and take care of the baby while I ran the streets and did whatever the fuck I wanted to do. In a sense, a baby would have trapped her, and she didn't want that, and I guess I had to respect that. I really didn't have a choice, it was done and over with.

She had forgiven me for all the shit I did to her and it would be crazy for me not to forgive her for making a decision to better her life.

"You right," was all I said.

"Okay?"

"I forgive you and I understand why you did what you did. Just promise me that there are no more secrets." I glanced at her and she just sat there, she didn't say anything just stared straight ahead. "Jenacia!"

"Where were you when you didn't come home?" I knew she was gonna ask that even though I had already told her where the fuck I was, she didn't believe me.

"Where did I tell you I was?"

"So, you were at Ma Ann's house? You weren't with no other female?"

"Jenacia I may do some dumb ass shit but when I told you that you are it for me, I meant that shit. The one thing that you will never have to worry about is another woman, and I put that on my unborn seeds." I reached over and touched her belly and she covered her hands with mine.

"I believe you."

"Okay, so stop questioning my loyalty to you, I love you and this is forever."

She smiled, and we continued on our way to the memorial. I grabbed her hand because knowing that I had her by my side gave me the peace that I needed to get through the day. I needed to work on my temper though because I didn't want my quick temper to be the reason that I lose the woman that was meant for me.

I had been thinking about running off to get married because I wanted all of us to have the same last name. I needed to talk to Jen to see what she felt about that after we get all this mess out of the way.

Pulling up to the church, I spotted Ma standing out in front looking lost. I parked and helped Jenacia out of the car, she ran over to where Ma was standing and comforted her. I headed in their direction right as my phone rang again, this time I looked at the caller ID because it was my personal phone and I wanted to make sure that it wasn't one of my brothers that were in trouble.

"Kaylin?" I asked because I hadn't heard from her since the day I threw her them bands and gave her my number.

"Yeah, it's me."

"What's wrong? Why you sound so down?"

"I need a favor." She said right as I made it to where Mama and Jenacia were standing. "I need money." That sent alarms up like crazy because I had just hit her off nice the last time I left, and she shouldn't need money already.

"Money for what, Kaylin" When I said that, both Jenacia and ma looked at me with raised eyebrows.

"The lights will be cut off soon, Mama doesn't have the money to pay the bill and we have no food."

That sounded a little strange to me because when I was over there the last time, Chelley seemed to have everything together, but now all a sudden, the lights are getting cut off and they need money for food. That wasn't sitting well with me but the one the thing that I refuse to do is turn my back on my sister. Chelley wasn't high on my priority list but Kaylin was, and I was gonna make sure that she was straight.

"What happened to the money I gave you last time I was there?"

"I ahhh—I umm spent it." I could tell she was lying to me and I didn't like it. She didn't know how I operated just yet, so I wouldn't hold it against her, but before I handed her any money, we would have a conversation about how I felt about liars.

"Kaylin that's bullshit, but right now I'm at my Uncle's memorial I will get with you later and make sure you straight."

"What about Mama?"

"Kaylin my concern is you, you are my priority."

"But-"

"No buts," I cut her off. It was starting to sound like Chelley put her up to this and it was starting to piss me off and I didn't need that right now. "I gotta go, I'll call you later."

"Okay." Was all she said before I hung up the phone. I looked at it and shook my head.

"Son, be careful." My mom looked at me with sympathetic eyes. "Chelley ain't never been who she pretends to be, she has an agenda."

"Ma-" she held up her hand to stop me.

"I won't say anything else, but just be careful."

I nodded my head and we headed into the church to get this over with.

Chapter Fifty-Two
JAAKO

The memorial went by like a blur; I didn't feel like being there. I didn't want to believe that Unc was gone but realistically, there was no way that he could have survived that. There was no way. I sat back in the pew and looked to my right and into the face of Yameka. Even though we hadn't really talked about what happened at the restaurant with me and her father, she didn't hesitate to be there for me when all this shit went down. I knew the conversation was near but right now, I was just grateful for her being there.

The pastor had just called for everyone to come up there and say what they had to say and me and my brothers decided that it was best if we all went up together. Once we were at the front, we just kind of stood there looking at each other trying to decide who was gone do the talking. Of course, Kayson stepped up because that's who he was.

"Unc was a damn good man." Kayson started, and I nudged him with my elbow and he glared at me. "Man look y'all gone have to bear with me because a nigga ain't all polished and shit." I nudged him again and a few people in the congregation giggled. "Just pray for me." He looked at me to get my permission and I just shrugged. "Unc, along with Mama, took in four bad ass boys and raised them like they were their own. There aren't many people in the world that you can say would do that. They loved us and groomed us to be the men that we are today. It's a shame that someone took his life in the manner that they did. They took a piece of all of us when they took him," he paused and looked at the huge picture that we had at the front of the church. "If you ever got the chance to know him, then you should consider yourself lucky." Kayson stepped down and kissed his hand and placed it on the picture and we all followed suit and returned to our seats. The rest of the service went by relatively fast and we were grateful.

Afterwards we all stood outside the church as everyone came and gave their condolences. My blood started to boil when I saw one person in particular. I released Yameka's hand and headed in her and her mother's direction.

"What the fuck are you doing here, Krista?"

"That is no way to talk to my daughter." Her aggravating ass mom said. Her fucking voice reminded me of nails on a chalk board and every time I heard them I just wanted to fucking scream. I hated that woman with a passion. Hell, I think I hated her more than I hated her daughter.

"I don't know if Raymond told you, but he was my father." She said with a smile on her face. I knew the bitch was lying because I talked to Unc about the shit in the restaurant that day so I don't even know why she trying to pull that shit right now.

"Bitch shut the fuck up, you know good and damn well that Unc told me about that shit you tried to pull so lie a-gotdamn-gain. Yo' ass just looking for a fucking payday and you won't get it here, so get your money hungry ass away from here."

"HOW DARE YOU COME TO MY BROTHER'S MEMORIAL TRYING TO SMEAR HIS NAME." Ma yelled from behind me, I didn't even notice that she had walked up until she started yelling. "My brother would never produce something as nasty and evil as you."

"Wanna talk about evil," Chelsey, Krista's mom started. "Let's talk about that evil thing you raised that goes around killing innocent babies." She pointed at Denari and I put my hands over my mouth because we purposely left that part out when we told Mama about all the dumb shit that Denari had been up to. She snaked her head around and glared at me and then focused her attention on Denari, the look in his eyes read nothing but terror. Ann Barnes had that effect on us and no matter how thugged out we were, when she hit us with that look, we knew what it was. I did not want to be present when they had that conversation.

"Whatever that little bitch got, I'm sure she deserved it." Mama said shocking the shit out of me. I think that she was just mad at what was going on right now because she would never wish ill on a baby.

"How dare you speak to my daughter like that, you filthy piece of trash. You are all no good, every last one of you and I hope that you all end up just like your no good uncle."

I don't know what she said that for because before anyone could stop her, Mama had punched Chelsey dead in her mouth. She didn't stop there either, she knocked her down and climbed on top of her and commenced to whooping her ass. Krista thought she was gonna jump in and try and help her mama out, but Zemia was there so fast she didn't know what to do.

"Aye, y'all cut this out, we in front of the church." I said trying not to laugh and split them up at the same time. "Y'all niggas gonna help me or what?"

"That bitch need her ass beat." Omari said walking very slow to help get Zemia off Krista. "Come on bae, wit' 'cha mean ass." He pulled Zemia up and wrapped her in his arms. "You fucked that bitch up." He kissed her on the cheek and backed up her up away from the crowd. "You can't be doing all that though."

"Fuck that hoe, they were gonna try and jump Mama Ann." She said trying to catch her breath.

"I'm good baby, them hoes can't see me." Mama said dusting off her dress as we got her up from off Chelsey where she was just throwing down. "Lord please forgive me for my actions, they got me out here acting a complete fool in front of the Lord's house, but she deserved it out here bashing my late brother's name." Just thinking about it must have pissed her off again, because she lunged at them and they backed up. "Just get out of here, why are you here anyway?"

"We just wanted to pay our respects." Krista said finally getting up off the ground.

"No, you came here to start some shit with that Unc was yo' daddy shit. Get the fuck out of here before yours be the next memorial we go to." I threatened and then walked off. "I'm sorry everybody." I said to my family and the nosy people who thought it was okay to just stop and watch.

"Oh, you are haven't began to be sorry because I need all of you at the house, so we can talk about this baby situation." Mama said and jerked away from me and headed over to Denari. She got right in his face. "If what the bitch said is true, just know you gonna have to deal with me." Then she walked off like she didn't just threaten him in front of everybody.

We all looked at him and his eyes pleaded for help, but he was definitely on his own with that. I shrugged and headed to my car with Yameka in tow. We got in and headed in the direction of my mama house.

"That was crazy." Yameka said breaking the silence that had filled the car since we left the church.

"Yeah, I know, I'm sorry about that."

"She just doesn't give up, do she?" I didn't know where she was going with the conversation but I didn't like her tone at all.

"Don't do that."

"Don't do what? I just wanna make sure that this won't be a constant issue; I mean I gotta career and a lot to lose. I can't be out here fighting that bitch every time we see her out."

"And you won't."

"Just like today right? I mean this was your uncle's memorial and this happens." I could tell that there was something else bothering her, but she didn't just want to bring it up.

"This is about your dad," I broke the ice. "No need in beating around the bush, let's get it all out on the table so we can talk about it and move on."

"That too."

"Did you talk to him?"

"Yes and no, he told me what I needed to know but he didn't want me a part of it, so he cut it short."

"Listen, I didn't know he was your dad."

"If you had known would you have told me?"

"I don't know."

"Wow!"

"I'm saying this shit is another ball game, I would never want to interfere with another man's family life, that shit can get you killed." I shrugged. I was rambling trying to give her enough to drop the subject, but not enough to put her in the middle. "Shit is complicated, but I promise to keep it as far away from you as I possibly can. I want to build with you and I hope this shit don't fuck up what we could have."

"I love you Jaako, and you know that. I just don't want to have to give up everything I have worked for just to be with you."

"You don't, and you won't, you act like I'ma do this forever." I glanced over at her and she was staring me in the face. "What, you thought a nigga wanted to slang dope for the rest of my life?"

"I didn't know what you wanted to do because we don't talk about it."

"Because we can't."

"My point exactly, I can only know certain things about you, because not only am I your woman, but I'm your lawyer too."

"I can find a new lawyer."

"Not one that can do what I do Jaako and you know it."

She was right, she was great at what she did. Being a lawyer was definitely her calling, but I'd be damned if I give her up because of it. I wanted her, and I was going to have a life with her no matter what she said.

"Well I guess we gonna have to find a way to make this shit work, because being without you is not in the cards for me." I shrugged and turned up the music to signal the conversation was over. I said my piece and I listened to hers and I was over it. We would just have to figure the shit out.

Krista

I was not expecting that at all, for the years that I was with Jaako, Ms. Ann had never even raised her voice better yet her hand in my presence. I understood that we may have gone too far with it being the memorial and all, but that didn't give them the right to put their hands on us.

"Filthy animals, I have the mind to go take out papers.

Who do they think we are?" my mother ranted. I knew I should have left her at home, had it not been for her mouth, things wouldn't have gotten so out of control.

"We are not taking out papers." I sighed.

"Look at my face, what the hell is wrong with those people? I see why her sons are so fucked up, she is too."

"We should have never come; I should have never let you talk me into it." I rolled my eyes.

"I was just trying to help, I mean the man is dead, how in the hell would they prove that you weren't his daughter now that he was dead? I was trying to secure our future."

"Our?"

"Yes, our, what, you thought you were the only one that was going to reap the benefits? Absolutely not, I was gonna make that man love me again and be set for life."

"Speaking of Raymond, who is my real father?" She didn't say anything, she just sat there quiet like she had to think about it.

"I honestly don't know, the night that I was forbidden to talk to Raymond again I went on a rebellious streak and just had fun for a whole two days before I retreated back home to live my boring life with your father."

"Wow!"

"Wow nothing, you were raised in a good home and you were given the best of everything, I made sure of that. It doesn't matter who your biological father is." She yelled, so I decided to let it go.

We pulled up at her house and I wasn't in the mood to be

around her anymore, so I just let her out and headed to my house. Jaako hadn't been back since he left, so I just settled in and changed the locks. Perry was at the house right now waiting for me to get back.

Things with him had been okay, I just wished that he had the money that Jaako had. He was sweet and made sure that I was satisfied in the bedroom, he was what every woman would want. I was gonna try and do things the right way with him, but like I told him, to keep me he needed to get his money up and he promised that he had things in motion, I just needed to let him work. If one of those things didn't involve handling Denari then I wasn't really interested.

I pulled up to the house and just sat there for a minute. I needed to reflect on some of the shit that had went down. How did things get this bad that quick? One minute I was living the life with Jaako and the next I'm here plotting to kill the man that killed my baby. I hated Denari because if it weren't for him none of this would be happening to me right now. I would still be living with Jaako, reaping those benefits and still doing me. He was so busy he would have never known. I told myself not to deal with him, but I did it anyway, all for the love of dick.

My mother ruined me, and I blamed her for some of this too. Had she not been running her got damn mouth in the hospital, Jaako wouldn't have just thrown me to the wayside. He probably would have forgiven me for the shit with his brother but finding out there was yet another man in picture threw him over the edge. Now he hated me and to be real I missed him, but he clearly didn't feel the same seeing as though he was living it up with black Barbie. I rolled my eyes at the thought of her.

"So, you just gonna sit out here like a fucking creep." Perry said knocking on the window. I was so lost in thought that I didn't even realize he had joined me outside.

"My bad, I had some stuff on my mind."

"What the hell happened to your face?" I looked up at him and he was wearing a scowl. I figured I would use this to my advantage. He opened my door and I got out and stood in front of him.

"I went to Jaako's uncle's funeral and evidently I wasn't welcomed because when he saw me, he punched the hell out of me." He looked at me suspiciously and I really started laying on thick. "I have never seen him like that and they all just sat back and watched as he hit me like I was a man."

"I've done research on them niggas and you telling me that he hit you and left those scratch marks?" He gave me a yeah right bitch look. "From what I hear out here in these streets ain't no bitch in their blood, but this," he rubbed his hands down my neck, "this was a bitch move. You sure he did this to you?"

"If you don't believe me, that's on you." I yelled at him. "But I know what happened, I was there." I pointed at him and stormed off in the house.

"Calm the hell down, I was just asking because yo' story ain't adding up. You told me that he had never put his hands on you before, and now you telling me that he hit you in the face for merely showing up at his uncle's funeral? Excuse me for asking questions." He slammed the door and walked to the bathroom.

I loved when he talked to me like that but there is no way that I could back away from my story now. He would think that I'm a liar and I needed him on my side. I was not going to be satisfied until Denari was six feet under and Perry was the only one that I could trust to do that.

"Wait, where are you going?" I asked when I saw him pick up his keys.

"Out! You done pissed me off."

"I'm sorry, let's go out and grab some food and chill. I promise to make all of this up to you."

He looked me from head to toe; I made sure to pop my hip out, so he could get a view of all my curves. He licked his lips and I knew that I had him. Shaking his head, he told me to come on. I smiled and followed him to his car. When we got to his car he stopped like he had remembered something.

"Aye, let's take your car."

"No, I don't want to ride in my car. If Jaako sees me riding around with you in that car, he would flip fucking shit." I lied. Jaako didn't give two shits about who was in that car or not. I just didn't want to drive my car, his was much nicer.

"If y'all ain't together and you ain't fucking with him anymore, what does he care about somebody else being in your car?"

"He bought the damn car Perry, what the fuck is wrong with you?" I glared at him.

"Okay, okay cool. But we need to make this quick so that we can park this bad boy because it's hot." I nodded my head because I didn't really give a fuck about what he was talking about right now; I just wanted to ride in this bad ass Mercedes coupe.

We hopped in and headed out, he thought we were gonna make this shit quick, but I was gonna make sure that I was seen in this car. I wanted muthafuckas to hate. This is the first time he's driven this car down; he's usually in his Tahoe so I was going to enjoy this ride. I smiled and sat back in the seat and enjoyed being chauffeured around.

"Sir, I need your license and registration please?" the cop said from the driver's side window.

Perry threw me a look that let me know that he was pissed the hell off. Not only did I have him take me to dinner, we went shopping too and then took a stroll around Charlotte. Every step of the way he kept saying that he needed to park the car and I would give attitude and he would give in. I was enjoying myself until this cop stopped us.

"Exactly what are you stopping us for, officer?"

"Because that sign back there says stop not yield, this gentleman rolled right through it."

"Sir, that was an accident, we promise to be more careful." I batted my lashes and smiled at him. He smiled back, and I knew I had him until he laughed.

"I'm sure it was, but I'll still need your license and registration, sir."

Perry reached in his pocket and pulled out his wallet and went for the dash to get his registration, when a gun fell out of the dash. The officer immediately drew his weapon on us.

"Shit!" Perry yelled as he hit the steering wheel, he followed by putting his hands up in the air to surrender. The police jerked the door open.

"Get out of the car slowly, both of you, and keep your hands where I can see them."

"Take it easy, officer." Perry said slowly getting out of the car. "I don't have a gun so don't shoot."

"Officer Milton, now ma'am get out of the car slowly with your hands up." I did as I was told and then he instructed me to walk over to the other side of the car where they were standing, and I did that too. "Do you have anything on you or in the car that I should know about?"

"I'm invoking my right to remain silent." Was all Perry said and then turned his head to stare down the road.

I was freaking out, but I knew one thing, I was not about to go jail for anyone. I sat and I thought about everything that I would stand to lose if I went to jail. Hell no, I was about to snitch until I couldn't snitch anymore, fuck Perry, this shit was his and I had no knowledge of it.

I immediately got scared because I knew that Perry had a bag of weed in the middle console and I was not about to get in trouble for that bullshit.

"There's weed in the middle console." I blurted out and Perry just shook his head.

"Who does it belong to?" before Perry could say anything I spoke up again.

"Him! This is his car, I was just on a date with him." I'm sorry, but I am not about that jail life. I would sell out my mama if it meant keeping me out of jail.

"Have a seat on the curb while I call for backup." I hesitated but the officer warned me that I could follow directions or he could cuff me and put me in the back of the police car. I quickly sat down and prayed that this was over soon, and I was back in my house in my bed.

"Fuck, man!" Perry yelled out making the officer turn around and look at us. He was at his car more than likely running his plates. "This is all your fucking fault."

"How is this my fault?" How dare he blame this shit on me, his ass should have been paying attention to what he was doing instead of running stop signs, we wouldn't be in this mess.

"I told you the car was fucking hot, now we both about to go to jail." He said through clenched teeth.

"I'm not going to jail, that gun and weed is yours." I clenched my chest.

"Yeah, but the shit that I got in the trunk could get us both life, even if I say it's mine they won't give a damn."

"The trunk?" I said loud enough for the officer to hear, he shook his head and then looked at the trunk.

"You stupid bitch!"

"Is there anything that I should know before my backup gets here? Cooperating might do you some good."

After a few more minutes, his back up showed up and they brought the K9s. They went straight to the trunk and removed the floor board where the spare tire usually goes and just started pulling stuff out of it. I had never seen that many drugs in one spot.

The officers called something in on the radio and more officers came along with a big van that read DEA. I knew this shit couldn't be good. Perry put his head down and took deep breaths.

"Don't say shit, if you do I swear I will make sure that you take yo' last breath." He glared at me and the look he gave me had me wanting to piss myself. I had gotten myself into some shit that I had no way of getting out of.

"Mr. Roman and Ms. Jacks, my name is Special Agent Milgram from the DEA or Drug Enforcement Administration. You got a lot of drugs here." he said and then just looked at Perry. "Listen, I can tell that you are just the middle man in this, because otherwise you wouldn't be riding around with this shit in your car. Let me help you."

"Tell him, Perry." I nudged him, and he glared at me.

"What's in it for me?" Perry asked, and Special Agent Milgram laughed.

"Not receiving life in prison."

Perry looked at me and I looked at him and I knew right then what we were gonna do.

"So, if we help you take down the biggest drug ring Charlotte has ever seen, we will be good?" I asked.

"Let's go have a chat." Was all Special Agent Milgram said and then loaded us up in his van and we were off to tell them what they needed to know.

Chapter Fifty-Three
DENARI

I was not looking forward to going to see Mama. I already knew what was gonna happen, she was gonna tear my ass a new one. I was wrong as shit and I knew that. I should have never put my hands on that bitch while she was pregnant, but I told her on numerous occasions to get rid of that fucking baby, and she didn't listen. Then she started to run her fucking mouth and I felt like she got what she deserved.

Surprised was an understatement when I was told that she didn't tell the police, but that left me wondering what else that bitch had up her sleeve. I needed to make sure that we get someone on her and quick.

"Are you okay?" Heaven asked as we pulled up to Mama's house.

"Hell no, Mama don't play that putting yo' hands on

women shit, but that bitch deserved it. On top of that, the bitch was pregnant."

I shook my head and reached for the stash that I had in my dash. I pulled out the mirror that I had and fixed a few lines. I took two and then held my head back and enjoyed the rush. I could hear Heaven sniffing so I knew that she was finishing off what I fixed. She had become somewhat of a regular user. I didn't mind because she did that shit with me and hopefully that's how she kept it. When she started going outside of me to get that shit, that's where the problem would come in.

"Hopefully, she will understand where you were coming from." She leaned over and kissed me. It relaxed me a little.

"Let's go get this shit over with, I already know ain't nobody in there gonna have my back." I was already prepped to do this shit on my own. I knew these niggas didn't give two shits.

I got out of the car and waited on Heaven to get out S me at the front of the car. I grabbed her hand and we walked in the front door and it was like I was walking the green mile or some shit. Everybody was just sitting there looking at me. Mama was sitting in her favorite chair just staring at me. I wasn't stupid, so I was going to make sure that I sat the furthest away from her.

I grabbed the chair that was nearest to the door and sat down and pulled Heaven on my lap. Not as a shield or anything, but more as a comfort blanket because I knew Ann Barnes was about to go in on my ass.

"So, what's this I hear about you putting yo' hands on women while they pregnant?" She sat up in the seat and then looked at Heaven. "Little girl, go on in the kitchen with the other women before I get mad and slap the shit out of you. What kind of woman thinks it's okay to be with a man that likes to put his hands on women?" she fussed.

"I—I—"

"I don't really give a fuck what you are about to say, just do what the hell I said." Heaven looked back at me. "What the hell you looking back at him for? Sit there if you want to, you about to see a side of me that you won't like, now try me."

"Bae go on." I nudged her, and she slowly got up and made her way out the living room.

"And go clean your got damn nose. Sitting up here high as hell." Mama shook her head. "I hate a weak woman."

Heaven didn't say anything just kept walking. She had been here before, so she made a quick right before she got to the kitchen and made her way to the bathroom to clean herself up. Thinking about what Mama just said had me wiping my nose to make sure there wasn't shit on it.

"You made sure you didn't leave any evidence this time." The disappointment in her voice had me feeling like shit. "What happened Denari? Huh?" She bit her lip. "Were you high off that shit when you did it?"

"Mama it wasn't like that."

"Then how was it like, because I know I taught you better than that." She put her hand on her knee, a clear indication that she was about to get up.

"I didn't think she was really pregnant, I just thought that this was another way for her to try and play Jaako."

"Pregnant or not, what I tell you about putting yo' hands on women?" she growled.

Whenever Mama got mad her voice got real deep like something evil was about to come up out her ass. I didn't know how to answer her question. If I said something she didn't like, more than likely something was gonna be flying at my head and I was too high for my reflexes to kick in.

"I was wrong, I—" before I could finish my statement, just like I thought, the $500 vase that she cried for last Mother's Day, came hurling at me head and before I could move out of the way, it crashed against my forehead. That lady had an arm on her. It didn't matter if you ran or not because whatever she threw was gonna reach you.

"You wanna put your hands on a woman put your got damn hands on me, Denari." She said, and I didn't even realize that she had made it over to where I was sitting until I felt her slap me in the back of the head.

"I'm sorry, Mama."

"You damn right you sorry, I don't know what the fuck happened to you. You doing too got damn much." She hit me again. "All this shit yo' fault, my brother ain't here right now because you wanted to be a fucking idiot." She screamed and then broke down where she stood.

I lifted my head and I could feel the blood trickle down the side of my face from where she hit me and for once I didn't give a fuck about what happened to me, my heart was hurt for my mama. I fucked up and it's causing her pain and I couldn't take that. I jumped up and went to grab Heaven.

"Denari, don't leave man, she didn't mean that shit." Omari tried to stop me.

"Yeah she did, and she was right. All of this was because of me."

Kayson let us know about the conversation he had with Tate about Roger being hooked up with Ortiz. I knew right then they were gonna blame Unc's death on me. I was just waiting to hear it. For once in my life, I take full responsibility for this shit and I was going to make sure that the nigga paid for all my family's pain, even if it cost me my life.

"I'ma make this right, Mama." Was all I said before I hit the door and I meant every single word.

After I left Mama's house, I drove around trying to get information on where Ortiz's bitch ass was hiding. I needed to find that nigga something serious. My phone rang, and I wasn't in the mood to deal with this shit.

"Look Perry, now ain't a good time, my uncle just died and shit ain't right."

"Sorry for your loss, but work don't stop because someone died."

"I tell you what, go find another fucking supplier then, bitch." I yelled.

"Aight, aight look. You know when shit gonna be back up and running, because shit getting tight around here."

"I don't know, soon."

"Maybe I need to talk to your brothers and see if I can move things along."

"Nah nigga, I say what goes!" I yelled. This nigga was getting out of hand and he was starting to piss me off. He was getting too pushy and that was sending up red flags.

"Just hit me up when you ready, but don't leave me waiting too long."

"Nigga, I ain't." I hung up the phone and continued my search to find Ortiz's bitch ass. Niggas on the streets were saying his ass pushed it up 77 north near me. Perfect, shit shouldn't be too hard then, right?

Chapter Fifty-Four
KAYSON

With everything going on I had completely forgot about my sister calling and asking for money. Shit was starting to make me wonder if Chelley put her up to it. I would hope not, but I was damn sure going to see. Mama kept telling me to be careful because Chelley wasn't everything she pretended to be. I knew Mama was just looking out for me, but I didn't want to find out for myself which was the main reason I was pulling back up at her house.

Knock knock knock!

"Who is it?" I could hear Kaylin yell.

"Kayson." I could hear her running through the house to open the door. When she did the look in her eyes wasn't the same as it had been when I first met her. She was sad and looked a little lost. "You good?" I asked and then hugged her, and she collapsed in my arms.

"I need money." she cried into my chest.

"What the hell is going on, Kaylin?"

I would give her whatever she needed, but I needed to know what was going on. I wasn't just gonna be out here dropping stacks and not know what the hell was going on.

"Mom is really sick, and I don't have any money to get her medicine and take care of her."

"What's wrong with her?"

"We found out that she had Breast Cancer a few years ago, she beat it once but now it's back and has spread. She has Medicaid, but they won't pay for some of the medications that she needs to keep the pain away."

"Why didn't you tell me when I was here before?"

"That's why she was so hell bent on telling you who she was, she wanted a chance to know you before she—before she —you know."

She couldn't get the words out of her mouth and I don't blame he, I don't know if I would ever be able to come to terms with Mama dying like that. Hell, I can't even deal with Unc not being here, that's why I was blocking that shit out. I didn't know how to handle the situation, so I just didn't deal with it, so I knew what she was going through. Her situation was worse because she had to sit there and watch her mother slowly die. Unc's death was sudden and unexpected.

"I'm sorry, Kaylin." I hugged her again. "Just know that I'm here for you with anything you need. I'm just a phone call away aight?" she just nodded. "How much y'all need." She shrugged her shoulders. "Tell me."

"Her medicine is $267, and I need money to pay the bills, her check paid the rent but that's it. She usually works part time at the stadium, but she can't since she's been sick. I used the money you gave us last time on bills." She dropped her head. "I'm sorry I have to ask you again."

"Don't you ever be sorry to ask me for anything. That's what big brothers are for." I scolded her. "I hate that we are just meeting, but now that I'm in your life you will never have to want for anything." She dropped her head again. "And stop doing that, don't drop your head when you're talking to people, it makes you look weak."

"It's just been so hard, I take care of her and go to school. I get money from my friends to help out around the house." That pissed me off because it made me remember the first time I saw her half naked in that trap house.

"That shit ain't gonna happen again." She looked at me because she knew what I was talking about. "If you need anything you get it from me, do you understand?" she nodded. "I don't want to ever see you hanging around people like that, they mean you no good."

"You mean people like you?"

"Yes, people like me! Stay the hell away from them. You go to school and prepare to go to college. That's all you should be worried about. I'll talk to Mama about possibly getting someone to help with Chelley, she's a nurse so she knows a lot of people in the industry and she will point us in the right direction."

"Thank you so much." She hugged me.

"I don't need thanks, just don't be afraid to ask me for anything." She nodded her head. The first time I met her, her little sassy ass had so much to say, but now she was quiet as a church mouse. "Let me step out and call Mama."

I stepped outside and reached for my phone to call Mama. I knew that she was gonna talk shit, but I needed her help. I don't know why I was so eager to help Chelley, I think in my mind I made myself believe that I was helping Kaylin, and that's how I rationalized it.

"How's my big baby?" Mama said on the first ring, I swear even in the worst situations she could brighten my day with just the sound of her voice.

"Hey Ma, I need your help."

"Anything for you."

"It's Chelley she—"

"Now got damn it Kayson Barnes, I done told yo how I felt about her, just because you wanna get to know her, don't mean I do." she started going off. Every time I brought up Chelley's name this is what happens, and I always laugh. I don't care what this woman said, she was worried about being replaced and I thought it was cute even though she didn't have anything to worry about.

"Mama she got cancer, and Kaylin been taking care of her by herself. She's a kid, Ma."

"Well Lawd, lift her up in the name of Jesus." She said and I shook my head. I was convinced Ann Barnes was crazy. "What you need son?" That's what I loved about her, if someone was in trouble she was always down to help. She just didn't play that taking advantage of people, it brought out the Hulk in her.

"Can you come over here?" I held my breath.

"Kayson."

"Ma."

"Fine, I'm on my way."

She hung up the phone and I waited on her outside. I knew she would be right over because that's the kind of person she was. She didn't care for Chelley, but because she was in need she put those thoughts aside. I met her at the car when she pulled up about an hour later.

"Thank you for coming."

"Anything for you." She kissed my cheek and we went in the house. By this time, Kaylin had helped Chelley out of the bed and into the living room. She looked very different than the first time I saw her. I could tell that something was wrong with her.

"Hey Kayson." She said with a weak smile.

"Hey Chelley, how you feeling?"

"I'm making it, I told that girl not to bother you with this mess." She looked over at Kaylin. "Hello Ann."

"How long have you been sick?" Ma wasn't about all the pleasantries, so she went straight into nurse mode.

"I've known for a while." She started to cough, and Kaylin brought her water. "I beat it last year and thought I was in the clear. I never thought it would come back this fast."

"Cancer is a sneaky bastard, you never really know what's going on with it."

"Tell me about it." they shared a laugh.

"What stage?"

"A very aggressive 3."

"Radiation? Chemo?"

"Both, but it doesn't seem to be working." She sounded so sad.

"Well, I got some people that are very good at what they do. I'll call in some favors. In the meantime, we need to get you some help."

"Kaylin helps me, don't you baby?" She smiled, and Kaylin joined her at her side on the couch.

"But that baby needs to be a baby. Let us get you somebody in here to help you out and take some of the load off this baby?" Mama was asking but there was force behind her words.

She was hesitant, so I butted in. "We'll let you choose who and I'll pay for it. Kaylin needs to be in school, not home taking care of you." The words came out harsher than I intended. "I'm sorry but I want nothing but the best for her and I think this would be best. Plus, you need the medical help so you can get better."

I could kind of tell that she was not gonna get better, but I wanted to give Kaylin a little hope. I could tell that she was bothered by this. I just wanted her to have a good life and I was going to make sure of it.

"So, it's settled?" Mama asked and Chelley nodded her head. "Okay, well let me check you out really quick." She grabbed her nursing bag that she carried everywhere and checked Chelley over while I went and picked up the medicine with Kaylin.

During the ride, I learned a lot about her. She loved math and wanted to be an accountant. I told her all about Jenacia and the twins and she was excited to be an auntie. I told her once we got a nurse in place for her mom that I would bring her to the house to spend some time with us and she was excited. We talked for the rest of the day while my mama made a few calls to start the process and got Chelley back to bed. I promised that I would visit more often and made her promise to call or text me at least once every day.. Once everyone was situated I headed back home. Today turned out not to be so bad. Now it was time to get back to business.

Omari

It's been about a month since Unc died, and shit just wasn't the same. He was the one that we all looked to for shit, and now we didn't have that. Kayson was trying to be that for us, but he had so much shit on his plate that he was stretched thin as fuck. I felt bad for bro, because he was trying his best to keep everything together for us. He was working day in and day out to get the operation running, plus dealing with his home life, on top of trying to find Roger and Ortiz. He never complained, but I could tell he was going through it.

"Bruh, let me know what I can do to help you. You ain't got to do this shit by yourself."

"I'm good O, just make sure you get the shit for the smoke shop settled."

Ever since the day me and Zemia talked about me opening

a smoke shop, I was on that shit. She wanted me to do it so that I would have a business to fall back on and I wanted that too, but right now I needed it to help me clean up my THC vape business.

"I got that shit under control, now let me help you." I put my hand on his shoulders and he took a deep breath.

"Aight, get everybody at the new spot tonight so we can let them know what's going on. I know they are freaking out about not knowing shit."

I laughed because I couldn't count the number of text messages that I've gotten from our guys wanting to know when they were getting back to work.

"I can do that, anything else?"

"Nah, I got the traps set up and this shit straight," he said talking about the new warehouse his ass had set up. "Oh shit, some of that shit you had for the THC got broke cause them niggas was careless as fuck so you need to go and see what you do and don't have."

"Got ya, I can damn sure do that."

"Bet! A nigga hungry as shit, I could go for some Cheddars." He rubbed his stomach.

"Nigga, yo' ass always fucking hungry you gonna be fat as shit by the time Jenacia have them got damn kids." I laughed.

"Who the fuck you telling, her ass almost four months and I already gained ten pounds, I need to get my ass in the gym ASAP." He shook his head. "But right now, I want some got damn food, you in or what?"

"Yeah, man."

We finished up what we were doing and then hopped in his Silverado and headed to Cheddars. About half way there, Kayson pulled in the gas station to gas up. He walked in the store and I climbed out to pump the gas. I noticed this nigga kept fucking staring at me; I patted my back to make sure that my piece was there and looked toward the door to make sure that my brother was straight.

"Excuse me." the nigga with the eye problem called out.

"I know you?"

"No but I know your brother, Denari." I pulled my gun from my waist band and tapped it against my thigh. Dude laughed like he wasn't worried but the perspiration collecting on his forehead was saying otherwise.

"I don't know you."

"I know, and I want to change that." He said walking closer like his ass was invited.

"We got a fucking problem?" I turned to look, and Kayson was quickly approaching with his gun in hand.

Dude threw his hands up, but he still had that dumb ass smirk on his face. "Nah, no problem, I just wanna talk business. I had been working with Denari and shit was booming but I can't get that nigga to answer for me and when I saw y'all pull in I figured I may as well holla at the head, you know?" he shrugged.

"Nah, I don't know shit." I said replacing the gas nozzle and walking around the other side of the truck in case he tried some shit with my brother. "The fuck you want, dude?"

"Shit dried up and I ain't trying to let muthafuckas come

in and take over my shit and you know that's what will happen if I don't produce."

"What's ya name?" Kayson asked. I could see his ass wheeling and dealing in his head.

"Perry."

"Perry?" we both said at the same time.

"You that nigga from South Carolina?" dude nodded. "Oh yeah we shut that shit down and quick. We don't know shit about you and as far as we know yo' ass could be the Feds." I said with a mug on my face.

"What you mean shut it down?"

"Exactly what the hell he said." Kayson barked.

"We had a deal."

"You ain't had no deal with us. Denari ain't in a position to make deals like that homey."

"Ain't this some shit," he rubbed his hands down his head. "What I gotta do to make shit right?"

"Desperate niggas usually come with an agenda." Kayson narrowed his eyes. "Know what I mean?"

"You got shit wrong, I can get work anywhere, but everybody around know the Barnes brothers got the best shit this side of the country ever seen."

Kayson didn't say anything he just glanced up at me and shrugged. This was the part that Unc usually handled. We never really had any dealings with setting up business deals and shit, but seeing as he ain't here, we didn't have a fucking choice.

"Let me get ya info, if you check out we will call you." Kayson said pulling out his phone.

"How long is that gonna take?"

"You ain't 'bout to fucking rush me. If you had done yo' research, then you would've known that Denari ain't got shit to do with the business like that." Kayson threw out there.

"Aight man, you right, you right." He nodded and then headed back to his car.

"If you on some shit, I promise I will kill everything you love." I threatened, and he didn't say anything, just got in his car and burnt out.

We got in the car and headed to Cheddars to eat. Something about that meeting didn't sit well with me. I needed to hit the streets to find out about that nigga. He was too eager, and that shit is always an epic fail.

Chapter Fifty-Five
JENACIA

Kayson had been so occupied with what he had going on that he barely had time for me. I don't know if it was my hormones acting up or what, but I swear all I did was cry over the lack of attention he was giving me. Like tonight, he called and told me that he had a meeting with his crew and he would be home after, but when he walked in the house the first thing he did was grab his laptop and head to his office. I was starting to feel so alone in all this and this is what I didn't want.

One person that I could always call on was Zemia. She has listened to me cry about this for weeks now. I picked up my phone and I called her. Before she even answered the phone, I was already bawling.

"He still being a dick?" Was the first thing out of her mouth when she answered.

"Yeah, he came straight home and went right up to his office. It's like he doesn't even care about me or this pregnancy. I don't know what to do." I whined and reached for the tissue that I kept beside the bed. I blew my nose into the tissue. "I was so scared that this would happen and that I would be left all alone in this and he's proving me right. I can't do this, all this stressing ain't good for the baby."

"You right it ain't, so chill out before my nieces or nephews come out all jumpy and stuff, then I'ma kick yo' ass." I giggled, she always knew what to say to make everything better.

"I just want my man back, Zemia." I whined.

"I know, and I can't imagine how that shit feel and you pregnant. But right now, they trying to make shit right, so we can live good."

"I knooooowwwww."

"Well you just gonna have to give him a minute. In the meantime, I'm here to listen to your spoiled ass."

"I'm not spoiled."

"Yes the hell you are." Kayson said from the room door, I hadn't even realized he was there. I wonder how much he had heard. "You can hang up now." He said calmly.

"Umph, Daddy has spoken." Zemia said giggling.

"Shut up hoe, I'll call you back later."

I hung up the phone and just stared at the sexy ass man that I had the pleasure of calling mine. He had his dreads up in one of them man buns but his was masculine as hell, it brought out his facial features, especially those lips that I secretly wished were wrapped 'round my clit right now.

"Why didn't you just tell me you were feeling like that?"

I don't know why but I just burst out crying, not a little whine I mean full-fledged bawling, snot bubbles and all. He walked over and wrapped his arms around me and hugged me tight enough for me to know that he didn't mean to hurt me but not enough to cause harm.

"I di—didn't wan—want to nag you." I got out between sobs.

"You ain't nagging me by telling me how you feel. I would never want you to feel like you are alone in this, because I will always be by your side. If you need me, I'm never too busy for you just say it." He lifted my chin so that I was facing him. "Okay?"

"O—okay."

"Good, now go clean ya face, I know what yo' problem is. You need some dick."

I tilted my head like I was offended but, in all honesty, I was jumping for joy inside. It had been a couple days and I needed some TLC. I went in the bathroom, slammed the door and locked it, and then I walked over to the mirror to get myself cleaned up all while doing a little happy dance. I swear my hormones were all over the place right now, one minute I'm crying my eyes out and the next I'm happy as shit.

"Bring yo' ass out of there." Kayson yelled from the other side of the door.

I opened the door, pretending to have an attitude. Kayson

grabbed the helm of the gown the I had on and lifted it over my head and threw it to the ground. He grabbed me by the waist and laid me on the bed. I was starting to get a little bump, it wasn't huge, but you could tell it was there, he looked down at it and smiled.

"I don't want you to ever think that I don't love you or have time for you and my kids. Everything I do is for y'all." He leaned down and kissed my little belly. "I love you, Jenacia." He slammed his lips against mine. The electricity that flowed through that kiss was enough to bring me to my first orgasm.

"Uhhhh I love you too." I couldn't help the moan that escaped my lips

He kissed me again, but this time a little more rough and nasty, getting my juices flowing, and I honestly don't know how much foreplay I could take. Ever since I found out I was pregnant, I swear my sex drive was through the roof, and if I didn't get it I was mad as hell. I was liable to take over if I didn't feel that pressure soon.

Releasing the hold on my lips he traveled to my neck and sucked like he was looking for blood. Once he was satisfied with the passion marks he left, he landed on my nipple where I wouldn't let him stay long because they were sore. Normally they were my pleasure spot, but not now, them things hurt too touch.

"Damn Jen, I can't even kiss 'em?"

"Nooooo, they hurt," I whined, and he laughed. He

already knew what it was, so I don't know why he was tripping.

"Fine, there's something else I wanna lock on anyway." He looked up and smirked at me and dipped his head in between my legs and feasted away.

"Fuck, baby." I cried out, he was making circular motions with his tongue around my clit that was sending a tingling feeling through my toes. Kayson always knew how to handle my body and that was one of the many reasons I fell for him.

The sounds of him slurping and sucking on my center heightened every feeling in my body and before I knew it, I was releasing my nectar into his mouth.

"Oh shit, oh shit, oh shit." Was the only thing I could get out.

"One more." He said coming up for air.

"No!" I hurried and said which made him laugh, but I didn't see anything funny.

"Fine." He lifted up and released himself and placed his dick at my opening. I closed my eyes in anticipation of him entering me. When it never happened, my eyes popped open and I looked at his ass like he was fucking crazy.

"Kayson why you gotta play?" I was getting pissed because my hormones were raging, and I needed to feel him in the worst way and he was playing with me.

"Tell me you want it."

I looked at him like he was fucking crazy, leaned up, and put his dick in myself. He laughed and shook his head, but he definitely got the picture. Spreading my legs as far as they could go to give him all the access he would need to fuck this attitude right out of me.

"Ummmmm," I moaned as he started to move in and out of me with precision.

"Shit, Jen." Kayson bit his lip and gripped my hips for a little more leverage. "Pussy juicy as fuck, got damn."

"Ummhmmm," was all I could get out.

"Whoever said pregnant pussy is the best pussy wasn't fucking lying." He grinded into my pussy hitting shit that wasn't supposed to be touched. Whether he was supposed to touch it or not, it was igniting things in me that was sure to drive my ass crazy if he kept it up.

I don't know if it was the connection between the two of us or if it was my hormones, but it was like I was having an outer body experience. The way he moved inside of me and the way he bit down on his juicy lips made everything so much better.

"Shit I'm 'bout to cum baby."

"Fuck I'm cummin with you." He moaned in my ear.

He sped up the pace and within seconds we were both exploding. My body was so relaxed that I didn't know I dozed off, but I woke up to Kayson lowering me into a tub full of warm water. He slid in behind me and we talked about our babies, and then headed for round two.

Chapter Fifty-Six
DENARI

I can't believe that I was the cause of all the shit that my family was going through right now. Just sitting back and thinking about all the shit that I had done, I see why them niggas ain't want nothing to do with my ass. I needed to make this shit right and fast.

"Why ya face all scrunched up?" Heaven asked breaking me out of my thoughts.

"Man, shit all fucked up."

"Yeah this has been a fucked up month."

"And this shit is all my fault."

"Why would you say that? It's not your fault. Who knew that Ortiz would do something so crazy?"

"Because he said he would, he told me that if I didn't return what was his, then he would keep coming after me and my family."

I looked down at her and she had the saddest expression on her face, which made me feel some kind of way. I wasn't good with the mushy shit, but I didn't want to make her feel like I blamed her or anything like that because I didn't. I knew this was all on me and I fucked up.

"Why didn't you just send me back?" She asked in a faint voice. "Looks like I just made your life harder than what it should be if you ask me."

"Do you know what he would have done to you if I would have sent you back to him?" She just looked off into space. "Exactly, Heaven I would never be able to live with myself if some shit like that happened to you."

I don't know where all this shit was coming from but for some odd reason I meant that shit. I didn't show that shit all the time, but I did care about her something serious. I could almost say that I loved her, but I would never let that come out of my mouth.

"But he killed your uncle because of me." I wiped the lone tear from her eye.

"Stop crying and shit, you know a nigga ain't good with that kind of shit. There is more to it than that." I stopped.

"What do you mean?"

"Nothing, just know that a lot of shit went down, and Ortiz just wrote a check his ass can't cash."

She didn't say anything else, she just sat there looking all crazy and shit. I didn't want her to think that any of this was on her because it wasn't. I made the decision to go after her, I made the decision to go and get her and I made the decision not to send her back. That shit was on me and I was gonna make sure that the nigga paid for all the heartache he caused my family, especially my mama.

I had been keeping my distance from everybody because I didn't know what to say to them. They never flat out said they blamed me, but I could tell they did. Even Mama blamed me, and that shit was a hard pill to swallow. Speaking of family, O was calling me right now.

"What up, bruh?"

"Not shit, where the hell you been? Ain't nobody seen yo' ass."

"Just been chilling trying to get my shit together, you know?"

"No nigga, I don't know, at a time like this we supposed to be rocking this shit out together."

"I know, but that shit eating a nigga up, real talk."

"This shit ain't on you D, there is only two niggas to blame and they are Roger and fucking Ortiz. We need to be getting at them niggas and separating ain't a good look right now."

"I know."

"Well, get yo' retarded ass down here then before I come and find yo' ass. Just 'cause you moved to that country ass town don't think we don't know how to get to you."

"Shut the fuck up." I laughed for the first time in about a month.

"Nah, real shit though, Tate need to holla at us about something."

"Ah shit, that ain't never good."

"You know that nigga don't talk over the phone, so just get ya ass down here, we gotta be at the new spot at seven sharp, nigga."

"Man, I'ma be there."

"On time nigga, you know how yo' ass do and shit. We ain't got time to hear that nigga mouth about you being late."

I laughed again because he was right, I was on my own time, always had been. My biological mother used to tell me all the time that I thought I owned the world. She would always laugh about me coming late then getting stuck and them having to cut her open to get me out. I don't know why I remember that, but I do, and I've been living by that for all my life.

"Aight, man."

"Oh, one more thing, that nigga Perry stopped us at the store talking about getting into business because yo' ass dodging him."

"Oh word?" I could feel my blood boiling, I told that nigga not to go over my fucking head with that shit. "I told that nigga to fall back."

"Kayson having him checked out to see if he legit, if he is I think he gonna make yo' ass run point on that nigga."

"Oh, so it's okay to work with the nigga now?" I said sarcastically.

"Don't go there nigga, you know why the shit was an issue." Here he goes with the bullshit. "You know good and well that ain't how we do fucking business. You gotta do ya fucking research and shit and you can't just go taking shit without talking to us. You should have done the shit the right way and it wouldn't have gone down like that." He fussed.

"Yeah, aight nigga."

"Denari—"

"I said aight, I'll see y'all at seven."

I hung up the phone. I was so mad that I had smoke coming from my ears. I hated shit like that, and they could throw all that bullshit on it to make themselves believe that all they wanted. They didn't want to work with Perry before because it was something that I came up with, a deal that I did. That's all that was, and it was fucked up but now all of a sudden Perry approached Kayson, and it was all good in the hood. This was the kind of shit that made me resent his ass, he thought that he was somebody important and now that we found out he was Unc's real son he thought he ran shit. He needed to calm the fuck down. He ain't the only one that can make shit happen.

Chapter Fifty-Seven
TATE

Some funny shit been going on around the station the last few months or so, I told Ray about the shit before all that shit went down and he told me that he would investigate it because he had a connect in the DA's office too. I don't know what the fuck was going on, but I could feel that something wasn't right.

I had a few guys that worked under me and knew what kind of shit I was into. They were with it because it put extra money in their pockets. Just last week they were all transferred out and a new set of officers were assigned to the precinct. That shit was weird on its own because I was the one that did the hiring and transferring, but that shit was done over my head and when I asked them about it, they played the shit down.

I was careful with my shit and how I handled it. There was

no way that they could tie me to anything that I could think of, but I was meeting with the fellas to let them know that I was falling back for a minute until I knew what the fuck was going on.

"Chief Tate." The police commissioner knocked on my door and I motioned for him to come in.

"Sir." I nodded toward the chairs that were in front of my desk.

"I won't be here long." His tone was condescending and the look on his face had me ready to shoot his ass in the face, but I smiled and remained cool. "I know you have noticed the changes that have occurred around here lately."

"Yes, I have, and I would have appreciated a heads up."

"Well they were under my instruction not to say anything to anybody."

"And why is that?" Now I was getting upset. I sat up in my seat so that I could see exactly what he was going to say.

"We got word that there is some corruption amongst the precinct and we need to get down to the bottom of it. Internal Affairs will be combing through some things trying to get things sorted out." he warned. "Is there anything I should know?" He asked like he already knew something.

"The question is, is there something I should know?"

Instead of answering me he looked around the office and smirked, then turned around to walk out. Pompous bastard, he never liked the fact that a black man was in this type of leadership position anyway. He probably been doing everything in his power to knock me off my shit. I wasn't about to let him.

I sat outside of my car for a minute just to think, I must say that Kayson is really stepping up to the plate with everything. I didn't expect anything different seeing as though he had Ray's blood flowing though his veins. He was born for this; this is what he was meant to do. I just hoped that he took it well that I was gonna have to fall back from everything for a minute but I trusted that he would be able to handle it all.

I got out of the car and walked in the new spot they found on the north side of Charlotte. When I walked in I swear I was impressed with what they had done. Kayson had upgraded some stuff including the security. That shit was perfect.

"Tate, my nigga." Kayson came out from the back to greet me. I swear he reminded me so much of Ray it was crazy.

"Youngblood, what's good?"

"Shit ain't been right you know." I just nodded my head because I hated that they were going through that, I knew how they felt though. Ray was my nigga.

"I feel ya, but you got shit looking good right now." He smiled and looked around.

"Unc taught me well." He looked up and then put his hands in his pockets and looked at me. "What's up Tate, you didn't sound too good on the phone."

He could read people like Ray too. Shit was starting to freak me the hell out. I could already tell that he was expecting bad news, and I hated to give him that shit, but I had to do it.

"Where everybody else, I need to say this shit one time."

"Yoooooo." I heard Omari come through the doors followed by Jaako and to my surprise Denari. His ass was never on time, but here he was. The only thing that I didn't like was that he had his girl with him and he knew that was the number one rule, don't bring your women to work. Before I could say anything to him he spoke up.

"I know she ain't supposed to be here and that's my bad, but I wasn't leaving her all the way down there and not be able to get to her if something happened."

I was shocked as hell that those words came out of his mouth. First, he took responsibility for his actions, and second he actually gave a damn about someone other than himself. I couldn't even scold him I just nodded my head.

"Ah shit, look at you lil nigga." Kayson said giving him dap. "Sound like you trying to grow up."

Denari didn't say anything he just told his girl to go and wait in the back and he would be done soon. She put her head down and did what he asked her to do.

"Aight, now that y'all here, we got a problem."

"Fuck, I knew this wasn't gonna be good." Jaako said and I glared at him. I still didn't know how I felt about him fucking with my daughter, especially now that shit was getting crazy.

We still needed to have our talk and I had to remind myself to do that before I left there today.

"Anyway, shit at the precinct been weird. They are going over my head doing shit, they transferred all my men out from under me last week and now IA in the building."

"Oh shit, so they looking at you?" Kayson asked.

"I can't be for sure, but I think so."

"What you gonna do?"

"I'm going to talk to my daughter to get her advice. I got people in high places that can make certain stuff go away if they are making a case against me. I might have to turn in my shield but I'm good with that, I'm 'bout over this shit anyway. I just need to fall back so they won't tie us together."

"What if they already have?" Omari asked.

"That's a good possibility." I said and then looked around. "Y'all need to move as carefully as possible. Keep shit tight and don't fuck with nobody you don't trust." They all nodded. "Shit gonna work out and Kayson you got everything in that shit ya uncle left you to keep shit going the way you need it to. I'll keep the burner but only call if you absolutely have to." he nodded again. "Shit gonna get back to normal real soon."

We chopped it up a few more minutes, and then I asked to see Jaako for a minute to talk about my daughter. He was hesitant, but he agreed. I knew they were grown and it was really none of my business who she dated, but I didn't want her mixed up in all this shit either.

"You probably already know what I wanted to talk to you about." He nodded his head. "When I first found out I was pissed as hell. I won't lie, I told her that she had to stop seeing you, but she pretty much told me to kiss her ass." We both chuckled.

"I love Yameka, more than you will ever know. She makes me a better person. I don't know what I would do without her."

"I see." I put my hands in my pockets. "I just want to make sure that you keep her away from all of this. If shit go bad, I don't want her career and shit in jeopardy. She worked too hard for it."

"You don't have to tell me that Tate, I already know that. I would never put her in a situation that would cause anything bad to happen to her."

"What if you can't help it?" I let that question linger a little and he didn't have anything to say back he just kinda stared off into space for a minute. I just wanted him to know that sometimes things happen that are out of our control and maybe them being together could cause more problems for her than they are ready to realize. "Just think about that. I gotta go though, so y'all take care and be careful. When shit die down, I'll be in touch and if the shit pop off, I'll reach out. Other than that y'all won't hear from me." He nodded and then turned to head to the back of the warehouse and I headed out the door. My next stop was Yameka's office.

Chapter Fifty-Eight
JAAKO

I never thought about shit that way. I mean, what if some shit went down and I couldn't make sure that she was out of harm's way? What if some shit popped up and it fucked up her career because she was with a drug dealer like me? Maybe I needed to talk to her and see where her head was in all this because I didn't want to put her in a situation that she may not be able to get out of.

"What the fuck he want with you?" Kayson asked walking up on me while I was thinking about the shit he just said. "He still on that bullshit with you and Yameka?"

"Yeah man, but the nigga starting to make sense."

"The fuck you mean? You love her, and she loves you, end of fucking story. Can't shit he or anybody else say change that shit Jaako, so stop letting that muthafucka get in ya head." He was right, hell he always was, but I still needed to have a conversation with her.

"You right, bruh, I'll talk to her about what he said when we have dinner tonight."

"Nigga, don't be causing unnecessary issues in ya relationship." He warned.

"Who the fuck are you, Dr. Phil or something?"

"Fuck you, nigga." He laughed. "I've fucked up enough for all of us and if I can help y'all niggas not make the same mistakes I've made, then I will do that."

"I feel ya."

We headed to the back to do counts and make plans for the upcoming week. We ran this drug business like a legit business, which is why we were so successful. We had plans and goals and shit and we stuck to them. Just like a normal business would.

"Shit looking good on my end." Omari said rubbing his hands together. "Oh, and I think I found a building for the smoke shop." He beamed.

I loved that he was excited about something other than the drug game. I knew that he was going to use the shop to sell his THC, but eventually he would just focus on the legal side of things.

"Cool, that would be good for you to wash up some of that money coming from the THC." Kayson said. "What y'all think about the shit Tate said?"

"I don't know what the fuck to think, I mean shit is weird as fuck. One minute everything good and then suddenly shit all fucked up. We been easy though, outside of Unc getting killed, we ain't had no issues."

"Right, but that's what them muthafuckas be wanting you to think."

"That's true Kay, but we been doing this shit, if the FEDS were watching don't you think they would have been rushed us?" I gave him a questioning look. "We don't need to start playing scared now, that's how muthafuckas get caught. Yeah, we need to move silent but keep doing what the fuck we are doing. Just need to keep an eye on who the fuck we deal with."

"Speaking of that." Kayson said and turned his attention to Denari. "What's up with ol' boy? His ass seems desperate as hell."

Denari shrugged, "Shit you tell me I heard that you were taking over that deal for me." Here we go with the shits.

"I ain't taking over shit, I was just trying to see what was up with him seeing as though you were sneaking behind everybody back dealing with him. We need to make sure he ain't on no bullshit. Hell, it looks like he ain't about to stop pushing and we need to find out why and if he is legit we need to make this deal."

"Aight, so I went about it the wrong fucking way big fucking deal, I was—" his selfish ass started but was surprisingly cut off by Omari.

"Big fucking deal?" He scrunched his face up. "It's shit like this that puts you on the FEDS' radar D, you can't just go Rambo with this shit. You gotta let us know what the fuck going down. I ain't trying to go to fucking jail for nobody, nigga."

"Y'all wouldn't have listened to me anyway." He waved him off.

"If you would have come correct, we would have." I chimed in. "Find out who the nigga is and what he about. Bring that shit to us so we know it's good. Don't just up and meet some nigga and do business with him without knowing who he is. All money ain't good money and we only want that good shit."

He rolled his eyes like a bitch and just stood there looking dumb. I shook my head because no matter what we said it was never gonna get through to him.

"So, am I back in or what, because if not there is really no reason for me to be here."

"You are one selfish son of a bitch." I was getting amped. I hated his attitude. "I'm so sick of your fucking entitled attitude; we don't owe you a got damn thing." I pointed at him. "We worked for this and to get where the fuck we are right now, and you just want us to hand a part over to you and you not have to work for the shit?" I was so confused with his thought process.

"So, you saying I didn't work for shit?"

"Denari, nigga what the fuck have you done to contribute to this shit besides get us robbed?" He gritted his teeth like that shit meant something to me.

"You just mad 'cause I fucked yo bitch, that's what this is

all about." He smirked, and I wanted to punch that nigga in the mouth, but I laughed instead.

"Says the nigga that's running around putting his hands on women like a little bitch." I spat, and his nostrils flared. "What you thought, talking about fucking Krista was gonna piss me off? Nigga, I'm so over that bitch, and have been for a while. I actually owe you a thank you. That was just the push I needed to get that bitch away from me." I smiled.

"I bet I could get ya new bitch too, nigga." Kayson stepped up in front of me, I guess thinking I was gonna whoop his ass or something, instead I continued to laugh.

"Denari, you going too got damn far." Kayson warned him.

"Nah, he good because I know for a fact that my lady would never go for a fucking coke head." That got his attention because he started wiping his nose all paranoid and shit. "Just fucking pathetic." I shook my head and went over to where my desk was.

I honestly wasn't bothered by anything he was saying because I knew how childish he could be, but the fact that he thought it was okay to brag about something like that made me look at him in a whole new light. When the shit first went down I told myself that I should just let it go because that's just how he was, but he didn't even deserve my forgiveness.

"Man, I'm sorry, bruh." He tried to say.

"You can save that shit, I'm good on you." I didn't even look up from my computer when I said it. "Kayson, so what we doing about this nigga, Perry?"

"Shit I don't know, we looked him up and took a ride out

to his place of business and shit seemed legit. I asked around on the streets about him and he seems to be rocking the shit out of South Carolina." He shrugged.

"So, you think we can trust him?"

"From what I see we can, but that's what I wanted to talk to Denari about, because he's the only one that has had any personal contact with the nigga, but seeing as though he got his ass on his shoulders, I say we hold off on it until we see what the fuck going on with Tate."

"I agree."

"Aight man look, the nigga cool as fuck and he had never sent up any red flags with me. We always did business, just the two of us. I'll handle him."

"Can we trust you to do that without fucking up though, because with the shit going on with Tate, we can't afford any fuck ups."

"I got this, man." I chuckled and grabbed my phone I needed to go and pick up Yameka and I didn't have time for this clown to be sitting up here telling us what he was gonna fuck up basically because that's all his ass was good at.

"You out, Jaako?" Omari asked.

"Yeah, I told my girl I was taking her out, seeing as though we been busy as hell trying to get this shit up and running smoothly again."

"I feel you, I had to fuck the attitude out of Jenacia the other day. Her mouth was getting reckless on the phone talking shit about me like I wasn't right in the house." Kayson said, still feeling some kind of way.

"Oh, I know she been had Zemia's ass tied up in that shit, and then when they get off the phone she looking at me sideways. I'm glad you handled that, shit let me take my ass home and maybe I can have a good night with my lady."

"Well shit, we going to the EpiCentre if y'all wanna join us." I suggested. Yameka had expressed wanting to get to know the girls a little better. They all text and call each other but they all had careers, so they rarely got to hang out and shit.

"Let me see if Jenacia's lazy ass got clothes on, if not count us out because I don't be wanting to sit there and watch her ass try on 30 fucking outfits finding something to cover her got damn stomach."

"Leave my sis alone, she ain't used to be pregnant yet."

"Why the hell not?"

"You just mean as hell, Kayson." I laughed at him. He thought everything should happen when he wanted it to happen. He couldn't tell that woman how to feel.

"Whatever." He looked down at his phone. "She said she still got on her work clothes, so I know she got on something decent 'cause she doesn't go to work in just anything so we're in."

"Zemia do what the fuck I tell her to do." Omari said grinning.

"Aight, I'll make sure to tell her that shit too." Kayson said pulling out his phone and pretending like he was gonna call somebody.

"Nigga, yo' bitch ass better not." Omari jumped and tried to get the phone out of his hands.

"Nah nigga, you run shit remember." We all laughed. I missed times like this where we just enjoyed each other and shit. I pray we can get back to this and soon.

"Fuck you, we going too." He said grabbing his phone and calling Zemia. "Baby whatever Kayson say he a got damn lie okay?" He hurried up and said. "Aye, you feel like going out for a bit?" I guess she said something because he was concentrating, I looked over at Kayson and he was texting away at his phone and suddenly Omari glared at Kayson. "Nah baby, you know I ain't said no shit like that. Kayson just trying to start some shit cause Jenacia ain't fucking with his ass like that. You know how we do." He covered the receiver of the phone with his hands and laughed. "Aight baby, I'll be there in about an hour." He said a few more things and then hung up the phone. "You a bitch ass nigga, Kayson." We all laughed.

"Aight, well let me go pick up my woman, let's meet at Strike City I know I said dinner but I'm in the mood to have some fun."

"Yeah, I don't wanna sit and stare at y'all muthafuckas all night any got damn way." Omari said as he walked out of the door but not before he shoulder bumped Kayson.

"Aight, one hour nigga, don't be trying to get no pussy." I yelled at him and he flipped us off and headed out the door.

I didn't bother to invite Denari, if he came he came if he didn't he didn't, and I was okay with that. I wasn't his biggest fan right now anyway.

Yameka

Jaako had been on mind all day. I don't know what it is about that man that has me so head over heels for him, but I am. Finding out that he was working with my dad had me in a bad head space, but the reality of the situation is, they were both grown men and could make their own decisions.

I was excited about the date that I had with Jaako tonight. We need this time together. I had been so busy, I retained a few more clients and my workload was over the top but I was good at what I did so there was no use in complaining about it.

"Baby girl." I turned my head in the direction of my father who was standing in the doorway of my office smiling. For my dad to be in his late 50's he looked damn good. His age only showed in his salt and pepper hair, but in my opinion it made him look that much more handsome, especially against his chocolate skin.

"Hey Daddy," I got up from my seat to greet him, "to what do I owe the pleasure?"

"Well, I need some legal advice and I wanted to talk to you about something."

I didn't like that last part because it appears every conversation that we had since that day at the restaurant has been about me rethinking my relationship with Jaako, and that was not an option with me. I knew the risk of dating a drug dealer and I was willing to take all responsibility for whatever happens, but I felt that this was worth it and if Jaako was the man that I knew him to be he would never let anything happen to me.

"Daddy?"

"Okay, legal advice first." He smirked so I already knew what the other part was about, and I was not about to sit and listen to it. He would just be sitting there talking to himself.

"I'm listening." I sat there while he told me about all the stuff that was going on in the precinct, and how the men that worked with him illegally had all been transferred out. He told me how they brought internal affairs in and how weird things were. He wanted to know what he should do. "Dad, that's not legal advice." I chuckled.

"I know but you've dealt with this kind of thing before." He was right, he was there when I defended this police officer when he was up on corruption charges and we won the case and the officer went on to sue the city of Charlotte and won. When I said I was good at my job, I wasn't just blowing smoke, I knew what the hell I was doing.

"That's true Daddy, well number one don't quit that is like admitting guilt. Just run the precinct as you have been. Keep your nose clean and let them do their investigation. If something comes up, we will handle it accordingly. Don't let them rattle you, they don't know who they messing with." I said with confidence.

"That's my girl, all that money spent on ya education was well worth it." He smiled.

"Really Daddy?" I folded my arms over my chest. "So, you put me through school so I could clean up your mess?"

"No, I put you through school because your ass could argue that the sky was green and have people believing it." He laughed. "I knew that you were gonna be something the day you came out hollering like somebody was trying to kill you. I swear that was the happiest moment of my life and you have been making me proud ever since." He paused, and I knew that the Jaako speech was coming. "Baby, I just don't want you involved in all this mess. If he is ever caught, and you are involved with him, then you can lose everything."

"Not if they can't prove I knew anything about his activities. This is the reason we don't live together right now, we don't share anything of value, and we aren't married. As far as they are concerned he is just someone that I'm sleeping with."

"Yameka." My dad said sternly.

"I'm just saying." I giggled. "Me and Jaako have talked about this, and he don't plan on doing this shit forever, but until he decides to chill out then this is what it is. I got this all figured out. "

"I sure hope you're right." Was all he said. We talked a little more and then he said he had to go and meet someone and that he would talk to me later. I kissed my old man and told him to be careful.

I needed to start coming up with a plan just in case shit hit the fan, because I refuse to live my life without my dad or the love of my life.

Chapter Fifty-Nine
OMARI

We were all chilling at Strike City having a good ass time. I don't think I have laughed this much in a while. Watching Kayson's non-bowling ass cuss out the lane, because he swears it was crooked, made my fucking night. Zemia seemed to be zoned out and I didn't know why, she was fine when I picked her up, but for the last hour or so she had just been staring at her phone.

"Baby, what's good?" I asked her.

"Oh, I'm fine." She gave me that little half smile shit. I didn't believe that because I knew her, and something was up.

"So, we lying to each other now?" I asked her, and she smiled.

"You see that guy over there in the green polo?" She pointed to one of the regular lanes. We had paid for the private bowling so we could chill and talk freely.

"Yeah, what about him?" I folded my arms over my chest.

"That's my dad."

"Oh, that's that nigga, I need to go holla at his bitch ass." I started that way and she grabbed my arm.

"No Omari, that would just make everything worse."

"Fuck him, he ain't gonna say shit to you. I will fuck his ass up with no problems." I was starting to get pissed because she was acting like she feared the muthafucka. Just seeing the look on her face made me want to kill his ass and I might just do that shit.

"LYNDON!" She screamed ignoring what I just said. I followed her eyes and looked right into the eyes of the male version of her, down to the chinky ass eyes.

"Zee!" He smiled and ran toward her and swinging her around off her feet. I smiled at their reaction because I knew how much she missed her brother.

"Oh my God, it's so good to see you." She leaned back to look him over and then hugged him again. "I've missed you so much."

"I missed you too sis, but can you let up on a nigga, I swear you gonna suffocate my ass." He laughed and so did I.

"Shut up punk." She hit him in the chest and then looked at me. "Baby, this is my little brother Lyndon, and Lyndon this is my boyfriend Omari."

"I'm ya got damn man, ain't nothing boy about me." I mugged her ass. She knew I hated that shit, I was starting to think she did that shit on purpose.

"Anyway," she rolled her eyes. "What are you doing here?"

"Nothing," he said looking around avoiding eye contact with Zemia.

"Oh, you're with him." He nodded. "Okay I will let you go, but here take my number and keep in touch." They exchanged numbers but right before he could walk off, up walked her bitch ass father. Now Zemia asked me not to approach him and I didn't, because those were her wishes, but he was in my space now and I was free to do what the fuck I wanted.

"You are here because?" I asked when he got close enough, I wanted to make sure that if he said something I didn't like I could reach out and touch his ass.

"What I'm doing here is none of your concern," he said in a calm tone. "My beautiful daughter," Zemia immediately froze when he said that, and I didn't like that shit. She told me that they stopped speaking because she told her mother about him cheating but her facial expressions and body language were telling a whole different story.

"Zemia, what the fuck is wrong with you?"

"Nothing, I'm just not feeling well, can we go?"

"If you—" I started but this muthafucka had the nerve to cut me off.

"What, this man ain't taking care of my princess?" Tears immediately started to stream down her face.

"What the fuck, Zemia?" I yelled and grabbed her arms and made her focus on me. I looked her in her eyes and what I saw broke my fucking heart. I knew there was more to the story because she was too nonchalant about the whole thing. It was like she had blocked something out and whenever the subject was brought up, it would threaten to bring those thoughts to surface.

"I hate him." she whispered. "I fucking hate him."

I don't know where the hell she got the strength from, but she broke away from me and started swinging with everything in her at her father. Zemia's fists were small but when she connected you could hear that shit. It was like she was taking all the anger and rage that she had in her out on him and I just sat back and let her. I felt as though she needed it. It wasn't until he acted like he was gonna hit her back that I jumped in and hit him dead in his fucking jaw.

"Muthafucka, I will kill you if you ever fucking touch her."

"What the fuck is going on, Zemia?"

She just started shaking her head and saying no with tears clouding her face. I wrapped her in my arms and just held her. She was shaking and the more she broke down, the more pissed I became. I looked at her bitch ass daddy with murder in my eyes.

"I see nothing's changed, she's still trouble. Lyndon stay away from her." Her daddy said as he picked himself off the ground.

"I'm trouble because I kept your secret all these years?" Zemia finally spoke up.

"What's going on Fin?" The woman that was with her father approached and asked.

"Your man here likes to rape little girls." Zemia yelled and my body shook. Lyndon's eyes grew wide and so did everyone else's who were within earshot.

"You're delusional, you were nothing but a troublemaker then and you're one now. Let's go honey, let's go Lyndon." He blurted out, but Lyndon didn't move, neither did that woman that was with him.

"No! The reason I told mom that lie all those years ago was in hopes that she would leave you and you would hate me enough to leave me alone. The day you walked out of my life was the best thing that ever happen to me. Oddly enough, I still loved you because you were my father and somewhere in the back of my mind I wanted to have a relationship with you. So, I buried all those things you did to me in the back of my mind so I wouldn't hate you." She cried. "I was your daughter, bad enough what you did to mom, but you had to ruin me too." She then turned to the woman whose mouth was covered with tears streaming as well. "If you have little girls you may want to keep them away from this sick bastard, people like him can't stop at one."

"Why didn't you tell me?" Lyndon walked over to hug Zemia.

"I didn't want you to hate him because he actually loved you, I never told anyone—"

"Because it never happened, you lying bitch." Her dad yelled out and I hit him in his muthafucking mouth this time. "Fuck."

"Keep fucking talking and the next thing yo' bitch ass

gonna feel is a fucking bullet piercing your fucking skull." I said calmly. Zemia grabbed me and pulled me back.

"He's not worth it." She cried.

"No, but you are." I looked her in the eyes. "Get the fuck out of here real talk." I warned, and he took heed to what I had said because he took off, but he was by himself. The woman he was with and Lyndon both stayed there with Zemia. The woman whose name was Susan asked Zemia a few questions and the more she told her the more she cried. Turns out the lady had three daughters ages 10, 12, and 15. I hoped like hell he hadn't done to those girls what he did to my baby.

"I'm ready to go." She said leaning on my shoulder.

"Yeah 'cause we got a lot to talk about." I looked her in the eyes and she nodded her head. I invited her brother to come with us and he accepted. I told my brothers that we were out, and I apologized for fucking up their night and they assured me that it was all good. I grabbed my girl and we headed to the house so we could talk about everything.

The whole ride to the house I couldn't help but think about how Zemia felt holding all that shit in. I knew the shit I witnessed as a child fucked me up, so I can only imagine what she was going through right now. I wanted her to know that I was here for her. Her brother was quiet as fuck, I wondered what the fuck was going through his head. The man that he idolized was a fucking child molester. I shook my head at my thoughts and turned up the music. The only thing that was on my mind right now was murder and I was trying to drown that out, but it wasn't working.

When we got to the house, I showed Lyndon to the guest room and Zemia went straight to the bathroom. I was gonna follow her, but something was telling me that she needed a minute to get her mind right. So, I headed to the kitchen to fix me a drink.

"I'ma kill em." I heard Lyndon say from the living room, I didn't even hear his ass come in here.

"You didn't know?"

"Nah, if I would have known something like that I would have deaded his ass way before now." The anger in his voice was evident and I knew exactly how he felt. "How could he do that to his own daughter?"

"Your guess is as good as mine." I shook my head. "Beer? Shot?"

"All of the fucking above."

I grabbed two glasses down and filled them with Crown Royal Black, grabbed two Coors Lights from the fridge and joined him in the living room. Nothing was said we just sat there and let the alcohol numb us. Once we were done I went and grabbed the whole bottle and sat it in between us.

"You love my sister?" Lyndon said out of nowhere.

"More than I care to admit." I laughed. I was never one to do the relationship thing, better yet the love thing. The only women I've ever loved were my mothers. But I loved Zemia and I couldn't see my life without her. I don't think I ever told her that, but I knew my actions showed it.

"I love you too." I heard from the hallway and there she

stood, puffy eyes, tear streaked face even after the shower which let me know that she had been crying nonstop.

"Come here." I told her and she walked over to me. She was dressed in some grey leggings and a big white t-shirt that I was sure belonged to me. "You good?" She nodded. "Don't lie to me woman." She shook her head and then placed her head in her hands. "Why didn't you tell me?"

"I convinced myself that it didn't happen. When I told my mom that he was cheating and she left him, that was my out. I made myself forget, until he opened his mouth tonight, then it all came rushing back."

"You should have told, Mom." Lyndon said letting a lone tear run down his face. The love that he had for her reminded me of the love that I had for my brothers. "You could have told me, sis."

"I couldn't Lyndon; I didn't want to even think about it. I was disgusted, I was ashamed, I blamed myself. I couldn't live through those thoughts again."

"I'm gonna kill him." Lyndon told her.

"No, you are not, you will not get into any more trouble, and he's not even worth it."

"He hurt you, Zee." She nodded.

"And it would hurt even more if you got to jail over him." she told him.

He nodded his head, but I could look in his eyes and tell that he was not about to let this go. He was going to avenge his sister and if he let me, I was going to be right there with him. There was no way that I would be able to let that muthafucka live with what he did.

I pulled Zemia into my arms while she told us about the bastard she called father. The more she talked the more I knew that her dad wouldn't be breathing too much longer, and I put that on both my moms.

Chapter Sixty
PERRY

I hated the position that Krista put me in. I didn't know what the fuck I was thinking driving that fucking car around knowing I was dirty as fuck. Trying to please her ass and I didn't even know if she was worth it. Now look, my ass about to be labeled as a got damn snitch. I didn't have a choice though, if I took this charge it would have been my third strike and I knew it would have been over for me and I wasn't ready to live my life behind bars. So, if all it took was telling on some niggas that I barely knew, then I would just have to do that.

I didn't even know how big the fucking Barnes brothers were until I went to check into Denari, and when I did working with him was a must. I knew that with his name in my pocket I would rise in no time. I was making noise in South Carolina, but it wasn't enough, I needed to really get with it and they were the way to do it. I had every intention on working with them but now I got to do what I got to. Maybe after I get them gone, I can take over.

I heard that they had been asking around about me and shit, but I knew that was coming. The niggas were smart, and I knew that I had to make shit look good for them. I couldn't let them know that I was working with the cops, because that would be the end for me and family.

They finally called me to meet up and that shit was music to my ear. I was starting to think that they would never call, and my ass was gonna be up shit's creek. If I could get Krista to stop calling my ass, shit would be okay. I don't know why she felt the need to keep calling me. If I didn't answer the first time, why in the hell you gonna keep fucking calling? Aggravating ass bitch.

"What the fuck do you want?" I yelled into the phone.

"Why you gotta be so got damn rude?"

"Because you on my got damn nerves that's why. What do you want?"

"I'm calling to see where everything is at?"

"Why?"

"Cause my life is on the line too."

"You think I give a fuck about that?"

"You got me in all this shit and you gonna say something like that." I had to pull the phone away from my ear and make sure that I was talking to the right person. This bitch had lost her got damn mind, if she hadn't of been running her got damn mouth and demanding that we drive my car, shit wouldn't be so fucked up.

"You are a piece of fucking work."

"Look, let's not act like this, we need each other."

"No, that's where you're wrong, I don't need you for shit. I could run and leave yo' ass for dead." And that shit was the reality of the situation.

"Okay okay, let's just talk about this."

"Nah, right now I gotta go, I'm meeting with Kayson and I don't need you in my ear. I need to have a level mind."

"Okay," she said sadly. "Just call me and let me know how it goes."

"Yeah, aight." I said with no intentions of calling her back. Fuck her!

I turned my ringer off so that I could concentrate on the task at hand. I needed to make sure that I said all the right things when it came to them. If I said one wrong thing that could be it for me. I drove to the place where they told me to meet them. The more I drove I noticed it was in the middle of nowhere. I turned on a long ass driveway and drove until I saw a building that was all fucked up, like it had been burnt or something.

I sat in my car for a minute until I saw Denari pull up. He smiled at me and I knew he was gonna be on his shit about me going over his head but his ass was playing too many games for me and like I said this was strike three and I wasn't ready to live that prison life.

"Perry, what up nigga?" He said approaching my car.

"Nothing much." I shrugged. "Where everybody at?" I looked around and I was starting to feel uneasy.

"They inside, come on." He waved me inside.

I followed behind him and there the rest of the brothers were just chilling the middle of what I take as the warehouse. Something was telling me that this was not where they did business, but they were testing me first. I get it.

"What's up fellas?"

"What's good?" Kayson greeted me.

"Not shit, I didn't think y'all were gonna call."

"We almost didn't." He shrugged; the streets said he was the asshole. "So, we checked you out and you seem legit."

"I heard, my people were wondering why niggas was asking personal shit about me." I smirked.

"We needed to know where yo' family lived and shit just in case." Kayson smirked. I nodded my head and had a seat. "So, what you talking?" I looked at the other two that were just sitting there not saying shit. I didn't trust niggas that didn't talk.

"They gonna say something?" I asked and Denari laughed.

"Perry, that ain't what you here for." Denari said. I folded my arms across my chest. "You still wanting what you were getting from me?"

"Nah I need more, my people blowing through that shit I need to up it, I need 20 keys."

They all looked at me, but shit was true though, the shit I got from them flooded the streets and flooded it quick, I had niggas coming to cop from me all the way from Georgia, so I needed that much weight.

"You can handle all that?" Kayson asked.

"Yeah."

"You pay up front."

"Of course." I don't know who these niggas thought I was. I didn't need them for shit, I had money. They were starting to piss me the fuck off.

"Aight we will call you and let you know about pick up and drop off times and places it will change every time and you won't know until one hour before it's time to meet and you will have exactly one hour to get there. Call this your probationary period. Denari will be handling your account, you good with that?"

"I ain't really got a choice do I?" I laughed but no one else thought the shit was funny.

"Yo, I don't trust that nigga." Omari finally spoke.

"I don't really trust you either."

"Difference is I don't give a fuck, and we don't need yo' ass, you need us." He glared at me.

"Cool it, bruh." Kayson smiled. "You can leave." He looked at me.

At first, I thought he was joking until he asked me if I heard him. Who in the hell did these niggas think that they were? Just dismissing niggas like they some Dons or some shit. I got up and shook my head and headed for the door. I was starting to feel better about what I needed to do. They needed to be knocked down a few notches.

I got in my truck and pulled out. I grabbed my phone and called Special Agent Milgram.

"I'm in," was all I said and then hung up the phone and headed back to my neck of the woods to wait on these cocky bastards to call.

Chapter Sixty-One
DENARI

"Yo, I really don't like that nigga." Omari said when Perry was out the door.

"Yeah, it's something about that nigga." Jaako chimed in.

"Y'all chill, Perry cool as hell and he's a money fucking maker. Just watch." I tried to get them to see shit my way for once.

"All money ain't good money, he has an ulterior motive." Kayson said.

"So why the fuck did you decide to work with his ass then." I was getting pissed because I was confused as hell. It was Kayson's call to bring him in, so now he saying he ain't with it? What the fuck?

"Because, nigga you already brought that nigga in behind our fucking backs. He knew us, he stopped us out in fucking public. I brought him in so yo' ass can keep an eye on him. I don't got time to deal with another enemy and who knew what kind of problems we would run into if we would have turned that nigga down. I checked him out, he's moving in South Carolina, and right now we don't need no shit. But this is on you; you need to make sure this nigga is who he says he is!"

"I got ya."

"No nigga I'm serious I ain't talking about no half ass shit like you normally do, I mean yo' fucking job is to check up on that nigga and often. Know who he deals with and all that."

"I said I got ya."

"Yo D, this real shit." Omari said.

"I know that, nigga."

"I hope you do." He raised his voice. "Yo I'm out, I'm meeting with this chick about this building."

"Bet, call me and let me know how that goes so we can get Yameka to look into it." Jaako said and Omari agreed and left.

"Look Kayson, I know I fuck up sometimes, but I swear I got this, bruh."

"I'm holding you to that, baby bruh. Shit serious."

"Huh!" I heard Jaako say.

"What the fuck is your fucking problem?"

"You, you a fuck up nigga. That's all you do, just like I'm sure you gonna find a way to fuck this up."

"Fuck you, I got this." I said and then turned my back and walked out. I was over his salty ass, he been had his ass on his shoulders since I fucked that bitch. I hadn't heard from her ass either. I would have thought that she would have been on some shit about that baby situation, but she hadn't.

I hopped in my car and headed to the house. I wanted to see Heaven for some reason. Whenever I was stressed the fuck out she was who I wanted to see. I sent her a text for her to be naked when I got there, and she replied with a picture of her already naked. My girl!

I pulled up to the house and jumped out of the car, I was ready to release some stress. I walked in the house and she was sitting on the couch playing in her pussy. Her inner thighs were coated in her juices.

"Damn baby, you started without me?" I bit my lip and she motioned for me to come to her. I knew that she was high because she was the freakiest after she had done a line or two. When I got to where she was she unbuckled my pants and they hit the floor, then she worked on my boxers. Once they were down I stepped out of them and pulled my shirt over my head and stood in front of her with my dick standing at full attention. "What you gonna do with that?"

"Ummm," she moaned as she took all of me in her mouth. I gasped when my dick hit the back of her throat. I had to lean back on my heels to keep from moaning out like a bitch. With my dick still down her throat, she stuck her tongue out and started massaging my dick.

"Fuck Heaven." I picked my leg up and put in on the couch to give me leverage. I grabbed the back of her legs and she turned so that she was sitting straight up. She brought her little hands up and wrapped them around the base of my dick and started moving them in a circular motion, while she sucked and slurped on my head. "You gonna make a nigga nut, fuck."

I could tell that she was smirking because her high ass cheek bones were showing. She moved one hand to my balls and started massaging them. I knew right then and there that I wouldn't last too much longer.

"Fuck Heaven." She looked up at me and I thought that shit was sexy as fuck. I loved a bitch that could look me in the eyes while she sucked my shit. "Got damn I love this shit." I moaned out and she started going in. "Umhuh, fuck I'm 'bout to nut." I bit my lip and curled my toes and released down her throat and she sucked all that shit up. "Oh shit." I yelled out because she was still licking my shit and I was sensitive as hell. "Stop that shit." I backed up and she laughed.

"I thought that dick was mine, you telling me I can't do what I wanted to do with it." She smiled. I smirked at her and got down on my knees. Her eyes got big because I never did this, but right now I had something to prove to her ass.

"Don't get scared Heaven, spread em."

She spread her legs and I went to work licking and sucking on her clit and it drove her crazy. I really didn't know what the fuck I was doing, because like I said I never really did that eating pussy thing but I watched the hell out some porn, so I was doing what the fuck I saw and it sounds like I was doing a good job because she was moaning all crazy.

"Yes baby, I love you, I love you." She panted.

I went even harder. I wasn't about to tell her I loved her.

The closest I had ever been was telling her ass that I loved what she did to me and that's all that she was gonna get.

"Oh oh shit I'm cummin." She moaned, and I put two fingers inside her and worked them around while I attacked her clit. I could feel her walls clamp down on my fingers and I knew she was releasing and I sucked on her while she rode the wave. "Ah ah stop, Denari." She tried to push my head away and I slapped her hands.

"Nah, you thought that was funny when you did it to me."

"You gonna make me cum again."

"Cum on then." I still had my fingers inside of her and her shit was pulsating, and I thought it was sexy as hell and I was ready to feel her. I removed my fingers just as she cried out that she was hitting another orgasm. I wiped my mouth with the back of my hand and slapped her thigh. "Turn over." She opened her eyes and looked at me like I was crazy, and I laughed. "Turn yo' ass over Heaven, I ain't done." Sluggishly she turned over, put her knees at the end of the sofa and bent her head in the crease of the couch, and put that arch in there just like I like.

"Just like that." I stood up behind her bent down a little and slid into her. "Sssssssssss damn." Heaven was wet as fuck and her shit was squeezing my dick. I moved in and out of her slow until I got my shit together. After that I tore that pussy up until we both screamed out in pleasure and collapsed on the couch. "Got damn."

"Why you do that?" she whined.

"That shit felt good as hell." I smiled, and she rolled her eyes.

My phone went off alerting me that I had a message. It was Omari telling me that he was doing Oak Room for his birthday and I was hype as hell, I wanted to turn up and have some got damn fun.

"What you smiling about?"

"Oak Room Saturday for O's birthday."

"Cool." She said and then dozed the hell off.

I wanted the whole city to come out and party with us, so I put that shit on my Instagram. That was sure to get everybody the fuck out. Time to have some fucking fun!

Chapter Sixty-Two
BRAYLA

Dealing with Ortiz hasn't been the best situation that I've been in, true he laces me with money and shit, but I swear he was the most controlling person I had ever had to deal with. I see why the other bitch left his ass, who wants to deal with that shit? Nigga got people following me around and shit, talking about it's for my protection, I knew better though. He just didn't feel right unless he knew where I was always.

The shit with him and Kayson was starting to drive his ass even more crazy, he lived and breathed revenge against them for killing his parents. Hell, he already got rid of the uncle, what the fuck else did he want? I wasn't with all this shit, I didn't want to get caught in the crosshairs of this little war that was brewing.

"I think I love Cello." Jernisha broke me out of my thoughts.

"Girl you ain't known that nigga but a hot minute, how the fuck you in love already?" I rolled my eyes 'cause she swear she in love with every nigga that throw her the dick.

"It doesn't matter bitch, he makes me feel like more than a piece of ass." She gazed off. "He said when all this shit is over we gonna move away and start over."

"So, you just gonna up and leave my ass?" I asked her.

"You would do the same thing to me, but more than likely Ortiz will come too."

"I don't know if that's something permanent." I mugged her.

I wasn't trying to live my life in prison. Fuck that! I was beautiful and young, so as soon as I found another sponsor I was probably gone. Call me what you want, but life too short to be anything but happy and Ortiz didn't make me happy. With his mean ass.

"You are not about to let another bitch ride that gravy train, so stop."

"That's the only reason I'm still around, that nigga mean and controlling. Who got time?"

"Anyway, you see ya boys gone be at the Oak Room Saturday?" Jernisha said showing me her phone. Denari had put up a blast for his brother's birthday inviting everybody to come out and celebrate with them.

"Oh, let me call Ortiz and let him know what's up. Maybe

he will back the hell up and get off my titty some." I picked up my phone and called him.

"Y'all left the mall yet?" I rolled my eyes in my head.

"Not yet we just chilling."

"There ain't that much to do at the mall, you been gone for two hours already."

"OMGEEEE! It took us almost 45 minutes to get here. We ain't even hit a lot of stores yet. All these men you got following us around, I'm sure they're reporting back to you."

"Watch your fucking mouth, Brayla."

"I didn't call you for this, I was calling to tell you that ya boys gone be at the Oak Room on Saturday."

"How the fuck you know that? You been talking to that nigga?"

"Okay you're paranoid as fuck, no they posted it on social media."

"Yeah, I don't believe you."

"You don't have to; I just thought you would like to know. I'm gone though, I ain't about to deal with this shit right now." I hung up the phone and he called me back ten times before I finally turned off my phone.

This was my first time at Hanes Mall in Winston Salem. This shit was big and nice as hell and I intended to explore my ass off.

"Ortiz wants you home?"

"That ain't my fucking home, nigga want me up his ass all the time and I ain't with that."

One of the niggas that he had with us tapped me on the

shoulder and handed me his phone. I know good and damn well he didn't call somebody else because I wouldn't answer. I swear this shit was getting out of hand.

"Hello?"

"Don't you ever hang up on me again."

"Are you fucking serious?"

"Yeah I am, now I need you and Jernisha at that party. I'm about to make some noise." He said like that wasn't already in my plans, but I let him have that. He could think that he gave me permission all he wanted, if it made him feel better.

"Anything else, Ortiz?" I had an attitude and I wasn't feeling him right now. This happened with us a lot. He thought I was the other bitch he was with, but I was far from that and I wasn't trying to fill her spot. I just wanted to be me and get money.

"Your fucking mouth."

"Hey, I'm me." I shrugged like he could see me.

"We'll talk when you get here." This time he hung up the phone and I it handed back. I was over this shit.

"We going to the party bitch!" I tried to get my mind off the shit that had just happened.

It was the night of the party and I was ready to let my hair down and get shit popping. Ortiz had some shit set up, he didn't tell me what, and I didn't care as long as I didn't have to do nothing but go out and chill.

When we got back from the mall he told me that he just needed me to go and call him when I see Kayson and the rest of those Barnes brothers. He told me what he needed me to do and then after I did that to get back and stay out of his way. He didn't have to tell me twice, I just wanted to party anyway. I had no intentions on going to his house tonight either. I was about to find me another nigga to kick it with. Fuck Ortiz!

"It's thick in here already." Jernisha said in my ear. I had to damn near beg her ass to come. Talking about she wanted to chill with her man. I had to tell her dumb ass that her man was gonna be working according to Ortiz. She was so fucking stupid.

"Hell yeah, you know Kendrick performing."

"Oh shit, I love his ass."

"Right!"

We bopped our heads to the music and headed straight to the bar. I ordered two long island ice teas and guzzled them down. I wanted to get drunk as shit tonight and I was well on my way.

"Girl, slow down."

"Nah, I ain't wanting to slow down."

"I'm not babysitting yo' ass, Brayla." She yelled over the music.

"Bitch I ain't asking you to. You are blowing my fucking high."

I turned on the stool so that I was facing away from her, but I could still see the door. I noticed immediately when

Omari walked in with his bitch. It was like they had a spotlight on them or something. All eyes were on them and I could feel the envy radiating off Jernisha.

"You aight, bitch?" I laughed because she swore she was sooooo in love with Cello but here she was drooling over Omari. "He don't want you." I laughed again.

"Just like Kayson don't want you." Now it was her turn to laugh. I didn't even bother with a response because she was right. I would give just about anything to be on the arm of Kayson tonight.

We watched as he kissed all over her and they walked over to their VIP section. They flirted, and I couldn't help but be jealous, the Barnes brothers were fine as fuck and their status was through the roof, to be associated with them was something. It pissed me off that Kayson didn't pick me, but all that shit was about to be out the window anyway when Ortiz get a hold of that nigga.

Jaako and his girl walked in next and a little while later in walked Kayson. I drooled when he stepped in the light. He was dressed plain in some black jeans and a black button up that clung neatly to his chest. His dreads were twisted back into a very masculine man bun and you could see the fullness of his lips, while his light brown eyes danced under the light. That man was a fucking God, don't debate me on that.

I tore my eyes away from him and landed on that bitch he was with. My eyes zoomed in on her little pregnancy bump. I had created a fake page on Instagram, so I knew she was pregnant, but to see it hurt my feelings. She was still cute in a little black dress matching Kayson's fly. Whatever Ortiz had planned, I hoped it included her ass. Kayson's eyes met mine and the hate in them caused me to shiver, it was like he was silently warning me to stay away.

I rolled my eyes and pulled out my phone to let Ortiz know that they were here. He told me to do what we talked about and that he had the rest. He said that he would call me when it was time for me to leave.

"I need another drink."

I turned back around to the bar and ordered a shot and another Long Island. I took that and drank my drink. The music started turning up and so did I, the drinks had me feeling good as hell.

"I hate them all." Jernisha said. I had almost forgotten that she was here. The drinks had me in my own little world.

When she said that, I looked in their direction. Kayson was grinding all over that bitch; his dick was hard I could tell. It wasn't like you could miss that print. Ortiz told me to just go and tell security that they all had weapons to get them thrown out of the club and then go sit my ass down but something took over me when I saw how happy they were. I just had to go say something, I had to.

I started in their direction, "Brayla, don't." Jernisha tried to stop me and I jerked away and walked right over there clapping my hands to get their attention. The look on Kayson's face let me know that I had just made a big ass mistake.

Chapter Sixty-Three
KAYSON

With all the shit that had been going on with Unc getting killed and the shit with Chelley being sick, a nigga just needed a minute to breathe. We got Chelley set up with nurses that were there around the clock. After that day she seemed to get worse and Kaylin wasn't taking it well. I wanted to make sure that she knew that this all wasn't on her.

She had been spending a lot of time with Jenacia, and that seemed to be the only thing that made her feel better. Tonight she wanted to go home and stay with her mother, so we were gonna go out and have some fun. I needed that, hell we all did.

It was Omari's birthday weekend, he wanted to hit the club scene, and I wasn't against it. Shit just felt weird as fuck knowing that Unc wouldn't be there. The fact that he was my biological father didn't make things right either. I knew the man my whole life, but I didn't know that side of him and for that reason he would always be Unc to me. I missed his ass something serious, but I kept those thoughts to myself or when I was alone with my woman because I needed to be the strong one. They looked to me for that and I planned on being that for them.

Business was picking back up and things were moving along quite nicely under the circumstances. Unc had shit all planned out as if he knew some shit was gone go down, but his ass always told me to always be prepared for anything. Thanks to him things just kept moving like his ass was still here and I was thankful for that shit. We had to get everything moved and changed around, but shit was back right, and we were good.

"You 'bout ready, Jen?" I asked Jenacia who had just changed for the fifth time. It didn't matter how many times I tell her that she was beautiful and looked great she found something wrong with what she was wearing. She kept trying to find shit that would hide her little bump and I hated that shit. She was pregnant and carrying twins, my twins and I wasn't no little ass nigga, her best bet was to get over the shit.

"I can't find anything to wear." She whined.

"What the hell was wrong with the dress you just had on, Jenacia?"

"My belly was sticking out."

"And?"

"Ugh you don't understand." She rolled her eyes.

"Jenacia you do understand yo' ass is pregnant right? I mean I'm just asking, 'cause you keep on saying that dumb shit."

"I know I'm pregnant Kayson, that don't mean I want to parade my belly around."

"Oh, so you trying to pick up a nigga then?"

"Wait what? How in the hell did you come to that conclusion?" She gave me a confused look.

"I'm saying, I'm ya man, and you carrying my kids. Why in the fuck you worrying about what the fuck you look like and shit?"

"You just don't get it, I don't want to be standing by your side looking all big and shit while all ya little bitches salivate over you." She crossed her arms in front of her chest.

"My baby jealous." I walked over closer to her and kissed her jaw.

"Shut the fuck up, Kayson."

"You know good and got damn well I ain't checking for nobody but you, so you can kill that shit and quick. Pregnant or not, you killing the scene and any bitch on it." I kissed her lips. "Now put that sexy ass black dress back on, so you can show off my babies." She blushed. "That shit had my dick hard as hell."

She pushed me and went to put on the dress that I was talking about. I wasn't lying though. The twins had spread her hips a little bit more and her ass had started to plump up, Jenacia was always beautiful to me, but that glow made her even prettier. She finished getting dressed and then we were out the door. I was ready to sit back and chill with my brothers and celebrate O's birthday because after tonight shit was about to get real.

That nigga Ortiz and that nigga Roger been breathing too got damn long for me and I needed to take care of that. I felt like less of a man, with them niggas still walking around living life like shit was good and Unc was gone. Don't get me wrong, we looked for him but getting the business back up and running was more important at the time. We had people watching out for all of us just in case he tried some more bullshit. I needed to get eyes on that nigga Roger too. I know his pussy ass was just following orders, but he fucked with the wrong people, so I would make sure that he paid for it. I owed him anyway for fucking with my woman. Their time was coming but tonight. We partied and hard as hell.

The whole ride to the club I prayed that Denari didn't start no shit tonight. I knew how he could be when he was high off that shit and drunk at the same time. I just hoped he held his shit together, so we could enjoy at least one night. The last time we all got together the shit with Zemia went down and fucked the whole night up. I hated that happened to her though, bro said she trying to get through it, but how in the hell do you get over something like that? I was almost positive that my brother was gonna kill her pops, the only question was when?

The parking lot to the Oak Room was packed as hell, Kendrick Lamar was due to make an appearance and every fucking body and they mama was here to see it.

"Damn, it's packed in this bitch." I said out loud.

"It really is, thank goodness we got VIP." Jenacia said looking around the parking lot.

I didn't trust my truck out there with everybody else shit. So I rolled up to the guy doing valet and gave him strict instructions on what to do with my car and made sure that he was aware that his life depended on how he handled my shit. Muthafuckas could be ruthless when they wanted to and do dumb shit out of spite and I ain't with that shit. So I made sure that he knew if he was one of them niggas that my shit would be the last one that he fucked up.

I grabbed Jenacia's hand and we walked inside, and I immediately got pissed the fuck off. Brayla's dumb ass was there and you best believe she noticed when we walked in. Jenacia didn't see her and I was glad about that, I wanted to have a good ass night. Butknowing that this bitch was here, wouldn't guarantee that.

We pushed our way through the crowd to our designated VIP section where Jaako, Yameka, Zemia, and Omari was already there. I wasn't expecting Denari to be on time so that was no surprise.

"Shit jumping in this bitch." O said bobbing his head to *Mask Off* by Future.

"Happy birthday, nigga." I threw him a head nod.

"'Preciate that bruh, I'm ready to turn the fuck up."

I agreed and called the bottle girl over so we could get the drinks flowing. Kendrick Lamar was known to put on one hell of a show, so I knew the night was going to be epic. The drinks came, and I ordered Jenacia orange juice and water. We sat back and enjoyed the music just sitting there fucking around with each other.

"Aye the party's here." We all turned to see Denari walking in with his girl. I must say, even though that nigga had her strung the hell out, she is the only woman he been with. I ain't seen him with another bitch since Krista. So she must be doing something right. I was gonna try my best not to get in his ass tonight; we were there to have fun so long as he kept his act together.

The vibe in the club was cool as shit and for once I was chill and not on edge. I looked over at Jenacia and she was swaying her hips in the seat. I grabbed her hand and pulled her up to stand in front of me. I wrapped one hand around her waist and one hand automatically went to her stomach.

She started twerking her ass when *Pop it, Shake it* by YG came on. She threw her hair over her shoulder and started going the fuck off. I smiled and let my baby do her thing. Hell, for a second, I forgot that we weren't the only ones in the club. I almost ran my hands up her got damn dress but Denari yelling aye brought me back to reality.

"Yo, you starting shit, so don't play that I'm tired shit when we get home either." I whispered in her ear.

"I got this, don't worry about me."

"Keep talking that hot shit and we gonna have to take a trip to the bathroom." She laughed, but my ass was dead ass serious. She had my dick on brick and it was about to get her in a world of trouble. Right as I was about to say something else my song came on and I forgot about everything else.

"If one more label try and stop me it's gone be some dread head niggas in yo' lobby hu hu," we all sang along with Chance The Rapper's new song *No Problems*. That was our shit and we turned the fuck up whenever it came on. We were hype as shit and feeling damn good by now. The drinks were flowing, and we were feeling good.

"Turn the fuck up!" Omari yelled over the music, Zemia was dancing in front of him. I looked up and we had the attention of everyone that was around us. I noticed a few of the females had sour looks on their faces and the most of them I'm sure we smashed, but it is what it is. They were where they were for a reason.

Even Jaako was dancing and that nigga didn't dance for shit, he was the sit back and sway kinda nigga. Yameka was taking him out of his element because she was getting down, I didn't think her Ivy League ass had it in her.

It felt good to see everybody dancing and having a good time. This is what I wanted; I wanted us to do what we did and get to enjoy life, not have to worry about what nigga wanna act fucking stupid. I was ready to get all the drama out of my life and just be fucking happy. Was that too much to ask?"

"Well, look what the fuck we have here." I heard Brayla's voice before I could even look in her direction. I closed my eyes in hopes that when I opened them her ignorant ass would just go on about her business. "Hello Kayson."

"Bitch you can leave." Jenacia said and I grabbed her because there was no way that I was about to have her out here fighting and she pregnant with my seeds. She should have already known that shit wasn't about to go down.

"Get the fuck on somewhere Brayla, we chilling minding our got damn business I suggest you do the same before you piss me off."

"Well, if you didn't want anyone to know where you were then why did you advertise it on social media?" She smirked, and I frowned because I don't do bitch shit like that.

"The fuck you talking about?"

"Denari put up on his social media that y'all were partying for Omari's birthday and we wouldn't want to miss that." I wanted to slap that smirk off her face. I don't know what the fuck Denari was thinking, he just made us sitting ducks and our women were with us.

"The fuck, D?"

"What the fuck I do now, got damn." He yelled over the music.

"You put where we were gonna be on social media?"

"Yeah, so."

"Nigga!" Omari said pushing his ass. "Yo, get them out of here." Omari said to the dudes that were standing in the next section. You would have thought that they were just partying and shit, but they were with us and them niggas were deep. We were ready, but I don't do dirt with my lady and Denari just fucked up everything.

"Baby go with them, you'll be okay." I looked Jenacia in the eyes.

"I'm not leaving you, Kayson."

"Aww ain't that cute, you a rider." Before I could stop her Jenacia had punched Brayla dead in her got damn mouth and was trying to go back for more. Her little friend Jernisha that Omari used to fuck with stepped up like she was gonna do something and I pushed Jenacia behind me.

"Bitch, didn't I tell yo' ass to mind your fucking business? This is my man you ain't got shit to do with this. Don't let the belly fool you, I'll fuck you up."

"No the fuck you ain't Jenacia, your little ass better chill." I looked back at her and she rolled her eyes. "You know I don't play that shit."

"But I ain't pregnant." Out of nowhere Zemia came through swinging her ass off. She was fucking both them bitches up and you would think that they would have had the upper hand but Zemia ass was too fucking quick. The whole time Jenacia was trying to get away from me and into the action but I had a hold on her. "I'm sick of you dumb ass bitches. You need to learn ya got damn place." She yelled while she was stomping Jernisha. Brayla got up and was gonna try and sneak her but Omari got in between them and pushed Brayla down and snatched Zemia up.

"Chill man." He said to a still swinging Zemia.

"Nah fuck that, let me go. I owe that bitch for the shit she tried in the hospital."

"Z, calm yo ass down." Omari raised his voice and she

chilled a little. "Yo, get them out of here." O yelled at the security we had with us.

Four of them came and each grabbed a girl, as they were headed out Brayla opened her mouth again and said something slick to Yameka and before I knew it she dropped her. Like you could hear the lick over the music and all. I had to grab my jaw after that shit. Got damn! The dude ushered them out the back where the cars where.

I looked down and there was a phone by my feet and I notice that a call was coming in. I had to look twice thought because I thought I was tripping when I saw Ortiz name pop on the screen. I bent down and picked it up, I noticed the phone was Brayla's because she conned me into buying it for her a while ago. I walked toward her and she backed up.

"Bitch, you gotta be shitting me." I yelled. I was so pissed I didn't know what to do. I wanted to strangle that bitch right there in the club, but I knew there were too many people watching. But her ass was damn sure going with me. "Yo, snatch that bitch." I pointed to Brayla. "Both of 'em." The Jernisha girl took off running but ran right into the chest of Omari.

"Yo, you going somewhere?" He smiled, and we headed to the back to make sure that the girls got out okay. When we got out back the truck was gone. I should have just kept my got damn keys. I told security to park back here just in case something went down so we had a ride. I just didn't want to leave my shit here all fucking night, that was a choice I made though.

"So, you been up to no good, huh?" I said as I pushed Brayla into the back of one of the Suburbans.

"I don't know what you're talking about," she cried.

"I bet you don't, but we about to find the fuck out." I had her phone in my back pocket and I could feel it vibrating. "Yo, take us to the warehouse."

"Please don't do this, Kayson."

"What the fuck you got going on with Ortiz?"

"He's my boyfriend, what does it matter to you? You didn't want me, remember?" She cried.

"You know I got beef with that nigga? He sent you here to set me up?"

"What? No Kayson I would never do that, just let me go and you won't have to ever worry about me again."

I laughed. "I ain't gonna have to worry about you no more anyway." She sobbed.

"Damn y'all just fucking up all the way around." Omari pinched Jernisha's titty to be a smart ass and she pushed his hand away.

"Don't touch me." She growled.

"Oh, I can't touch you now? You were hell bent on telling my mama that you were my girl, now I can't touch you." He laughed. "Ain't nobody want yo saggy ass titties anyway." We all laughed.

"I hope Ortiz kill all them bitches." Jernisha said and got all our attention.

"What the fuck did you just say?" Omari asked with his

hand around her throat. She was struggling to breathe so she couldn't really answer him.

"What the fuck is she talking about, Brayla?"

"Nothing, she just talking out of her head. Don't listen to her."

Omari was still choking her, and she was scratching at his hands. I could tell that his ass was mad because he couldn't hear shit that we were saying. Jaako was trying to get him to chill but he wasn't having it until that bitch was dead.

"Chill O, got damn!"

"Nah fuck that." He lifted up and climbed on top of her and tightened his grip until we all saw her take her last breath.

"Noooooooo!" Brayla screamed. "Jernisha!" She cried.

"You next if yo' ass don't tell me what the fuck I need to know." Her phone vibrated again, and I reached for it and it was Ortiz, so I decided to answer the phone.

"Brayla? You better not have fucked me over." Ortiz yelled into the phone.

"Brayla is a little busy right now." I laughed.

"Ahhh which Barnes bitch do I have the pleasure of speaking with today?

"The one that's gonna cut yo' ass up and feed you to the fucking fishes, nigga."

"Not before I get a hold of these pretty little women." He laughed, and my blood boiled. "They look mighty cozy in this SUV but not for long. Tell Brayla her services are no longer needed anyway."

"Ortiz help me! Help me!" Brayla yelled and I slapped her across the face to shut her up.

"If you touch my wife, I promise you I will kill everything you love."

"Your uncle tried that, and you see where that got him." He laughed and then hung up the phone.

"We got to get to the girls, Ortiz following them." I said frantically and Jaako busted an illegal ass U-turn in the middle of the fucking road. I said a silent prayer that they would all be okay.

"Call them niggas." O said, and I did. I needed to let them know to be on the lookout.

Chapter Sixty-Four
JENACIA

We jumped in the car and only two guys got in with us. I heard the other two say that they would follow. We pulled off.

"Leave it to bum ass bitches to fuck up a night." I fussed to no one in particular.

"Right, but that bitch got her ass beat." Zemia said rubbing her knuckles.

"Both of them." Heaven said and we both laughed.

"I didn't think you had it in you, Yameka." I teased.

"I'm usually quite reserved because of my job but damn it looked like y'all were having fun." She said. "Nah, but seriously she was talking a lot to not even have the label of side chick."

"That bitch been giving me issues since me and Kayson

decided to make things official. She deserves everything she gets plus some. I'm over her shit right about now."

It was the truth; I don't know what Kayson did to this girl and why she didn't get the point that she was no longer needed. He used her to pass the time, I'm back in his life and I don't plan on going anywhere so I didn't get what she didn't understand.

"Girl I know how you feel, I thought I was gone have to defend myself in a murder trial if that bitch Krista came at me one more time." Yameka rolled her eyes. "I got a lot to lose, but I don't do well with disrespect. After she got her ass whooped at the funeral," she looked over at Zemia and she shrugged. "She's been quiet."

"So, you the beat a bitch ass sister, huh?" Heaven asked. This was the most I have ever heard her talk. I guess the drinks got her opening up because normally she would just sit there and look at us and laugh.

"Shit, I'll take that." Zemia cheesed. "I just hate a shit talking bitch and my attitude and temper won't allow me to be around it. So, when I get mad, I put my hands on folks."

"Well if you ever need representation, I got you sis." Yameka added and we laughed.

"Y'all are so cool; I used to be scared to talk to y'all." Heaven shed light on the reason she doesn't talk much.

"Why?" We all said in unison.

"Well you know Denari's situation with his brothers and I didn't know if I would be seen the same way. You know I'm not like y'all, you all have careers and are successful." She dropped her head. "I let a man take all that from me and I never got it back. I just thought that you would think I wasn't worthy, if that makes sense."

"One thing about me is I don't judge people, we all make stupid decisions and I was where you are before, but I just made a decision to put me first and here I am." I looked back on the things I went through with Kayson back in the day and the stuff I went through with Roger.

"Exactly, it's never too late to make shit about you."

"Thanks ladies." She smiled.

"Hello." The guy that was driving answered the phone. He started looking all in the rearview mirror and shit like he was looking for something, he had me checking too. I noticed a few cars that were behind us but nothing out of the ordinary.

All a sudden, the driver slammed on brakes and we were hit from behind. I jerked forward and we all screamed.

"Get down." He yelled and we all listened and jumped in the floor. Only thing that could be heard was screams and gun shots. I prayed that either Kayson would come or the guys that were supposed to be following us would show up. I didn't know what was going on, but I knew it wasn't good.

Once the gun shots, ceased I stuck my head up to only be pulled back down by Zemia. I looked at her and she shook her head. I looked around to make sure that everyone was okay, and it seems as though everyone was. Heaven was in tears, I think she knew more than we did.

"Get them out and let's go before someone sees us."

"Oh God, no!" Heaven whimpered.

"Who is that?" I whispered.

"Ortiz."

My heart sank to my chest because I already knew it was about to be some shit. I didn't know him, but Kayson made sure to tell me about any beef he had with anybody just in case I was ever caught off guard. I prayed that someone got here soon.

The car door opened, and two guys climbed in with guns pointed. I just knew this was the end for me.

"Get the fuck up." They said, and we slowly got up off the floor. "Give me all ya shit." We handed over our purses and phones. Zemia was hesitant, I could look at her and tell that she was about to flip out, but I touched her shoulder to remind her that these niggas had guns and shit and we didn't. Once they had our stuff, they got out of the car and hopped into the front.

"Heaven baby, did you miss me?" The guy looked through the rearview mirror. He wasn't a bad looking guy, but I could tell that he wasn't a nice guy either.

"Just let them go and take me; I'm the one you want anyway." She tried to reason with him.

"Sorry, I can't do that love."

"Why not Ortiz, please." She begged.

"Because I said so!" he yelled and caused us to jump.

"It's gonna be okay." I whispered to her.

"Will it?" Ortiz and his partner laughed from the front seat. I sat back and rubbed my belly. I knew my man would be there to save me in no time. It felt like we were driving forever and then we stopped at a house in the woods. I was trying to follow my surroundings just in case I needed to make my way back here with Kayson.

They removed us from the truck and took us into the house. When they opened the door, I got so pissed I didn't know what to do. There stood Roger and his bitch. Why the fuck was they here? Why in the fuck was I here?

"Sit the fuck down and don't say shit." Me, Zemia and Yameka all sat down on the same couch and slid in close together.

"Well, well, well, what do we have here?" Roger walked over and stood in front of me. I was sitting in the middle and he moved my hair out of my face. "Where yo' man at now?" He laughed.

"I can't wait for him to put a bullet through your skull." I hawked and spit in his face. He cocked his hand back and hit me in the face and Zemia punched him in his.

"Get the fuck back Roger, why the fuck you worried about her and you got my sister over there." Ortiz grilled him, and Roger walked over to sit down with his bitch. I smirked and shook my head because she was definitely a downgrade from what he had.

"So, you're the bitch he was cheating on me with." The dumbass sitting across from me tried to say. Roger whispered something in her ear that made her roll her eyes and I laughed; there is no telling what he told this girl.

"I'm sorry, but you are mistaken."

"Excuse me."

"I mean not that it matters because finding about you and your babies was the best thing to ever happened to me. Me and Roger were together for over a year and we were living together, so I was not the side chick, you were." I shed some light on her little situation and she was not happy about that.

"Shut the fuck up, Jenacia." Roger gritted.

"No, keep talking Jenacia." The bitch said but she was looking right at Roger.

"I don't even care anymore; I just want to go home."

"Well that's not happening any time soon." Ortiz said walking over to Heaven who had yet to sit down. "I thought I told yo' ass to sit the fuck down." He said through gritted teeth.

"No Ortiz, just let them go and you can do whatever you want to me."

"Oh, so these are your little friends, what are y'all some type of sister wives or some shit?" He laughed but he sounded stupid because the sister wives fuck the same man and we don't do that. "I said sit the fuck down." He yelled a little louder while pointing to the chair that she was beside, but she shook her head no. He walked over and pulled out a gun and put it to Zemia's head.

"Nooooo," I yelled and pulled her closer to me.

"Sit the fuck down or I blow her head off."

She sat down in the chair and just stared at him. It was like no one else was there but them two. I could see the hatred she had for him and the feeling was definitely mutual. I don't know what he had planned but I was ready to get the fuck out of there. I looked down at my belly and let the tears that I was holding go. When I looked up again Roger was staring at me and I flipped his ass off, closed my eyes and said another prayer. I didn't want my life to end like this, and if I knew my man, it wouldn't.

Chapter Sixty-Five
JAAKO

To hear some muthafucka may have their hands on my woman had me on fucking ten. I knew I needed to call Tate, but that's the last thing I needed right now was for him to say I told you so. With all the shit he had been saying, it was all coming to light and I felt fucking sick.

I busted that fucking U-turn so fucking fast, I was ready for fucking war. We headed in the direction we told the men to go. As we were riding, we saw some shit in the road that was alarming. We pulled up and jumped out, it was the men we sent with the girls.

"What the fuck!" Kayson yelled.

"Where the fuck is the truck?" I looked around. I headed back to the car and pulled that bitch Brayla out of the car and forced her on her knees. She was crying and pleading and shit, but I didn't hear none of that shit. Until I had Yameka back in my arms every fucking body was expendable. "Where the fuck he at?" I had her by the hair.

"I don't know." She screamed. I jammed my gun in her mouth and asked her again and she started mumbling something.

"Say what?" I pulled the gun out.

"I know where he lives, but I don't know if that's where he went." She cried.

"Take us there." I yelled and pulled her up by the hair. I was pissed, and I wanted to kill a muthafucka with my bare hands.

"Aye, throw that other bitch out." Kayson yelled, and I threw Brayla's bitch ass in and pulled the other girl out on to the road and Brayla cried as she watched me.

"If something happens to my woman, I swear I'll make you watch me kill your whole fucking family." I gritted.

"77 North," was her answer. I thought the bitch would see shit my way.

Security had followed us there and we told them to follow us. We didn't know what the fuck we were walking into, so we needed as much backup as we could get. We hit the highway with Brayla giving us directions. She didn't know it but after she showed us where he lived, I was deading her ass.

Once we got off the exit she told us to take a left. I looked at her like she was crazy because all you could see was woods. She told us that his house was in the country. We went down a few winding roads before she told us to turn and the house was at the end of a dirt road. I wondered how in the hell he found this shit. It was way the fuck out there. We parked at the top of the road, off in the woods. We didn't need anyone knowing that we were coming.

"Aye, here go the address right here!" Kayson said pulling out her phone.

"She lie?" He did something on the phone.

"Nope, shit is showing at the end of this fucking street." He looked back and smirked.

"See y'all can let me go now." We all laughed.

"Nah bitch, you're a liability." I said before I put my hands around her throat and squeezed with everything in me, I was so mad that I blacked out and started beating the shit out of her. It wasn't until she started screaming that I realized where I was, and I put my hands back around her throat until she stopped moving. "Dumb bitch."

"How yo' ass know I didn't wanna do that shit." Kayson laughed. "I'm convinced yo' ass is fucking crazy." He shook his head and I shrugged.

"Let's go." I said and we all got out. Kayson went back to holla at the two cars that were with us. About ten of us headed for the fucking house. We sat in the woods for a minute, I knew they were in there because the truck was in the driveway and you could see muthafuckas walking back and forth in front of the window.

We surrounded the house with the four of us in the front;

I raised my foot and broke the door down. I heard screams and a whole bunch of fucking movement. When everything calmed down that nigga Ortiz had Heaven in a head lock with a gun to her head.

"Let her go, muthafucka." Denari yelled with his gun trained on Ortiz.

"Fuck you bitch, make me." Ortiz laughed. I noticed movement to my right and I turned my gun that way but one of the guys that was with us already had that handled. It was that nigga Roger that killed my uncle, I was going to make sure I killed him with my bare hands, he didn't deserve anything less.

"You okay, baby?" Kayson asked Jenacia with his gun trained on the man that was beside Ortiz.

"Damn, y'all didn't waste any time." Ortiz taunted.

"You had to know we were coming, nigga. I mean you came back to where you lay yo' fucking head." Kayson said.

"Hell, I thought you would kill the bitch."

"Oh, I did." I growled.

Click click! Guns were at the back of Ortiz and his little friends' heads and the guys were waiting on our go ahead.

"Shoot me and I shoot her, I gotta hair trigger on this bitch."

"Let her the fuck go, Ortiz." Denari sounded like he was on the brink of tears.

"Or what?" He laughed.

"Fuck it." Denari ass took a shot and it landed in the

middle of Ortiz skull and his body slumped but as he was hitting the ground his gun went off and hit Heaven and she went down. Kayson slumped the other nigga that was standing beside him.

"Nooooo my brother!" The bitch that was sitting beside Roger started screaming. I noticed that she was pregnant, and I knew that I wasn't gonna be able to do that.

"Heavvvveeennnnnn!" Denari ran to her and cradled her in his arms. He rocked back and forth and even released a few tears. "Baby, wake up. Baby, talk to me baby." He didn't get a response. "Noooo, baby I love you, wake up."

I had never heard my brother confess his love to anyone, or even pretend to care about anyone but himself, so to see this was something. I felt so bad for him. I couldn't imagine if that was Yameka laying on that ground bleeding from her head. I didn't even know how that shit could happen but it did, and I hated it.

"O, get them out of here." I yelled to my brother to get the girls out of here. They didn't need to see that shit. He ushered them out the door and they were all in tears, looking back at Heaven.

"You killed my brother." The pregnant bitch yelled in Denari face once she made her way.

"Fuck you, bitch." Denari raised his gun and shot her in the head and she slumped beside her brother. I was stuck for a minute, I didn't know what to do or where to turn, so much shit was going on right now.

"Muthafucka you wanna put yo' hands on females, huh?" When I heard that it snapped me out of my trance. I looked over and Kayson was beating the shit out of Roger. "You hit my wife while she pregnant with my seeds, huh bitch?"

He hit him over and over until he was no longer breathing but that wasn't good enough for him, he grabbed his gun and shot him repeatedly in the face until you couldn't recognize him.

"Bitch ass nigga." He looked around and then at the men that were with us. "We gotta torch this bitch." They nodded and went to get what they needed out of their cars. These were men that worked with Unc, so they knew to always be prepared.

"Denari," Kayson approached him covered in blood.

"Naw bruh, I can't leave her like this, what if she wakes up." He looked up at Kayson and I could see his heart break because mine did.

"She gone, baby bruh." Denari just dropped his head and sobbed. What I wouldn't do to take this pain away.

"Nah man, nah." He cried.

"I'm so sorry." Kayson grabbed him up in a hug for a few minutes until he calmed down. "Damn baby, I love you." He said and then grabbed the necklace that was around her neck. He slowly slid her out of his lap and just looked down at her before he slid the necklace into his pocket. "I'm sorry, baby." He said and then we walked out and let the men do what they did.

When we got back to the car Denari broke down, and the

girls comforted him the whole ride home. Tonight was something that was gonna change a lot of stuff for all of us. I hated that shit for my brother. We were all going to Mama's house; we needed to be together at a time like this. This family has taken enough hits, hopefully this shit was over.

Chapter Sixty-Six
KAYSON

6 MONTHS LATER

Shit was finally starting to look up for us, after getting rid of Ortiz, shit just started falling into place. Only thing that wasn't right was Denari. Watching Heaven die did something to him, he wasn't himself. He was quiet and reserved, he didn't crack jokes, he just kind of existed. I hated to see him like this, I couldn't imagine if that was Jenacia and because of that we just let him be.

The funeral was something; I had never seen Denari that emotional about anything. He was a cold hearted, selfish son of a bitch and to see him crying out for someone else broke my heart. For a good two months he wouldn't talk to anyone but Mama. I guess she finally got him to open up, after that he started coming around again, but it was just different. His drinking had picked up, he wasn't getting high anymore, I knew that much.

"Yo, how Chelley doing?" Omari asked.

We were sitting in the warehouse getting shit prepared to distribute. Chelley and I had really gotten to know each other over the course of the last few months. She was really a different person than what Mama told me about. We were connecting in ways that I didn't think were possible. She would never hold the spot in my heart that Mama did, but I loved her. Even she and Mama had started to build a relationship and I was grateful for that because I didn't want to feel like I had to choose between the two. Her condition had not improved, and the doctors said there wasn't much they could do for her but keep her comfortable so we all just surrounded her with as much love as possible.

"Shit don't look good, but she is living her last few days to the best of her ability, you know?"

"Yeah, shit gotta be hard for Kaylin, little sis holding up like a champ though."

"Her ass is in heaven having four big brothers she can mooch off." We laughed because ever since I introduced them to Kaylin, she been eating they asses up even more than she did with me. Jaako was the worst, he couldn't tell her ass no for shit. She got in trouble at school and I told all of them not to give her ass shit and found out that he was still sneaking her ass money. We loved her little ass, so it was understandable. "But yeah, she trying to stay strong, but it hurts more than she says."

"How she liking the house?"

"Her ass is in love with that got damn pool." I laughed again.

Jenacia and I bought a six-bedroom, seven-bathroom house to accommodate the twins and Kaylin. I promised Chelley that when the time came that I would keep Kaylin with me, and I wanted to make sure that she was comfortable. In the back there was a big ass three-bedroom mother in law suite that her and Mama moved into. Mama didn't want to stay in that big ass house she shared with Unc, so we moved her in and she was in heaven. I knew she wanted to be near when the twins came, so it was perfect.

"I'm glad everything is working out my nigga." Omari dapped me up. "Now we just waiting on my little niggas."

"Any day now, bruh." I smiled. We went to the doctor today and they said that her cervix she was thinning out and had already started to dilate. So we were just waiting on them to want to come out. "I'm ready."

"I bet yo' ass is," he paused and looked at me. "Zemia's ass is pregnant, she doesn't think I know but I'ma give her time to tell me herself before I confront her ass about it."

I grabbed him in brotherly hug. "Good shit, nigga."

"'Preciate that, bruh." He smiled, and I knew that he was happy because he really loved that girl and I was happy for them. "What time that nigga Perry supposed to fucking be here?" He looked at his watch. "I'm tired of waiting on his ass."

Omari still didn't like Perry worth a shit, even after he proved himself to be legit. He just kept saying it was something about him that he didn't like. About a month ago, we had a meeting and we decided to finally bring him in on that. Perry was pushing numbers like it was no tomorrow. His ass was working, we hadn't seen that kind of money since Unc died.

"Why you don't like that nigga?"

"I just fucking don't, something about that nigga rubs me the wrong way." He had a mug on his face.

"He doing his thing though."

"You right he is, but I still don't like his bitch ass." I laughed and then we heard the warehouse door open.

"What's good my niggas?" Perry walked in with a duffle bag.

"My nigga." I dapped him up. To me the nigga was cool as fuck. He kept it 100, we kept tabs on the nigga for a good three months and we didn't see shit out of the ordinary. He kept his word, if he said he was gonna do something or be somewhere he was there. I had no reason not to trust the nigga. Omari's ass just didn't like no one. I laughed to myself.

"What's up, O?" Perry smirked. He knew Omari didn't like his ass and they even came to blows a time or two. I warned Perry not to fuck with O, he was a silly muthafucka, but his hands were a beast.

O hit him with a head nod and went back to what he was

doing on his computer. He had since got the smoke shop off the ground and was thinking of opening a few more so that we could clean our money that way. Jaako's ass had been talking about opening a restaurant, but I heard that shit was too time consuming. I was gonna think of some shit to do, because I wasn't trying to be doing this shit all my life. At least not on the forefront, if you catch my drift, I would rather be behind the scenes just cashing in on a check.

"Alright, I need to double up." Perry smiled, and I returned it.

"Got damn we are doing it like that out in South Carolina?"

"Hell yeah I told y'all I don't play no fucking games. Niggas coming from Georgia to get served, what you mean?"

"Fuck yeah, keep doing what you doing and you get a spot on the fucking team." I said, and I heard O stop typing. I turned to look at him and he had a yeah fucking right look on his face. I laughed and so did Perry.

We collected his money and told him to be looking out for the next drop. We didn't give shit from the warehouse, hell our shit wasn't even here. We learned from the last time; never keep yo' shit where you do business. When Unc's car blew up we could've got in a shit load of trouble if the police got there before the clean up crew. So, we had two places. One, where we conducted business and one where we kept our shit.

"Hello! Jen you good?" I yelled into the phone on the first

ring. I was always on edge when I see her name pop up on the screen.

"Son it's time, we're headed to CMC hospital, get here and quick." Mama said and hung up the phone.

"Fuck yeah!" I yelled and took off running.

"Bruh." Omari yelled out.

"Jenacia is in labor." I smiled. Most muthafuckas would be scared but I was happy as hell.

"Shit, I'll call Zemia and we on the way."

I didn't bother responding, I hit my truck and was one way to meet my twins.

"Push baby push." I coached Jenacia. By the time I got here she was fully dilated and they didn't have a chance to give her any medicine. She said that she took a bath and she guess her water broke while she was in the tub, she didn't even know she was in labor until a contraction hit her so hard it knocked her down.

"Shut the fuck up, Kayson," she gave me the evilest look. "I'm never fucking you again." She cried.

"Alright I see baby number one's head I need one good push." She lifted up and pushed as hard as she could, and I looked down and all I saw was a head full of hair. "One more time and we'll be half way done."

"I fucking hate you, Kayson." She screamed as she pushed one more good time and Kayson Jr. lit the room up with vocals. I smiled as the doctor told me to come and cut the cord. "Oh shit." Jenacia yelled as I was cutting the cord.

"Okay, they not trying to give you a break." The doctor laughed.

"And fuck you too." Jenacia said to the doctor. I swear I had never heard her curse that much.

"Okay, big push." The doctor coached because I was scared to say anything else. Every chance she got she gave me the look of death. "Here we go again, Jenacia you're doing great."

"Come on, baby." I kissed her forehead. My baby looked exhausted. I felt so bad for her, but this is making me love her that much more and it's making the surprise I had for her that much better. I had been thinking about this for a while and this just solidified it all.

Jenacia pushed a few more times and Kyndon Barnes came into the world three minutes after his brother. I kissed her all over her face until she pushed me away. The doctor said she had to birth the after birth and he needed to clean her up so while he did that I went to check on my boys. I knew the moment she told me that she was pregnant that she was gonna be giving me a junior; I was even more blessed to find out that she was giving me two boys.

Kayson Jr. was a little bigger than his brother at 7lbs 4oz and Kyndon was 6lbs 10oz but they both were healthy, and they looked just like me, down to the eye color.

CMC did this thing called parent bonding, so it was just me, Jenacia and the twins. We both took turns holding the boys on our bare skin. It was funny seeing Kayson Jr. trying to get to Jenacia nipple during his bonding time with her. His little ass was gonna be greedy. I could already tell. This was the best feeling that I think I ever felt, and now was the best time to do what I should have done years ago.

I had Kyndon and I laid him down in his bassinet and I picked KJ up off Jenacia and she looked like she wanted to protest until I held up my hand to tell her to chill for a minute. I placed him in the bassinet with his brother. It was almost time for them to let visitors in and I wanted to do this before they all came in.

"I need to talk to you." I went and sat down on the chair that was right beside her. "From the moment I saw you all those years ago, I knew that you were gonna be the one for me, I just wasn't ready and when I got another chance I knew it was fate. I had to do what I needed to do to make sure that you were in my life forever." I looked in her eyes and they were glossy. "I can't imagine living this life without you, you make me better. So, with that being said, will you do me the honor of being my wife?"

She put her hands over her mouth and nodded her head and I looked at her like she was crazy, I had said all that and all I got was a head nod.

"You gonna leave a nigga hanging?"

"Yes baby, yes." She barely got out between cries. I pulled the ring out of my pocket and opened the box and she cried harder. I gave her a 3.5 carat princess cut diamond, her favorite according to Zemia.

We kissed, and I went back and got the boys, so they could join in on our family celebration. Not that they knew what was going on but just having them there made the situation complete.

"Aye, aye, cut that out and give me one of my babies." Mama said wheeling Chelley in with her.

"And give me the other one." Chelley said and we laughed. I picked KJ up and gave him to Mama and Kyndon to Chelley and they oohed and aahed over them. We were gonna have trouble out of them two, I already knew it.

"Congrats bruh, I can't wait to teach them a bunch of bad shit." Omari said standing over Mama looking at KJ. Mama reached back and slapped him in the face.

"You will do no such a thing." We all laughed. The door came open and it was Denari, I wasn't expecting him to come but he did, and I was happy about that. He walked over to Chelley to check out Kyndon and he turned to look at me and for the first time in six months he smiled.

"Why they look like yo' ugly ass though?" He joked, and I saw a glimpse of my baby brother coming back.

Jaako and Yameka were the last ones to come and we all just sat around, and they lapped the twins. The girls pined over Jenacia's ring and my brothers gave me shit about it because they knew that sooner or later they were gonna have to step up too. We all chilled until visiting hours were over. Once everyone was gone and it was just us again, I looked at Jenacia who was half asleep laying in my arms in this little ass hospital bed.

"I love you so much, Mr. Barnes," she mumbled.

"I love you more, Mrs. Barnes." I pulled her close and we both closed our eyes to get some much needed rest, well until the boys woke up for their two-hour feeding.

This was my life and I was in love with it already. I really needed to find a way out of the game because this was way more important, and I'd be damned if I lost it to anybody.

Chapter Sixty-Seven
PERRY

I was chilling at the house counting up, just thinking about how bad shit was. A nigga was starting to feel bad as fuck about all this. Come to find out them niggas was cool as fuck. I wished shit was different because we could have been good ass partners. I mean them niggas was talking about bringing a nigga in. I would have been a rich son of a bitch fucking with them. I hate I fucked all that up all behind a bitch like Krista. I needed to get out of this house before I ran myself fucking crazy.

As soon as I backed out of the driveway the phone rang through the speakers of my car, I looked, and it was Special Agent Milgram.

"How'd it go?"

"I'm sure you heard how it went, Milgram." I was getting pissed because they had me wearing a fucking wire. That shit was dangerous as hell when it came to them. When the shit first started they tried to say that I wasn't moving fast enough, and they thought that I was trying to run, so they made me start wearing a wire.

Once I got in good with them and showed them what I could do, they started to trust me a little more and invited me into their warehouse. I attended meetings and shit, which were all caught on tape. I felt like a snake ass nigga, if they ever found out what I did they were going to do some damage, that's why after this, I was leaving and ain't nobody hearing from me again.

"You right we did, we got enough from the tapes and pictures from the drop off with Denari. Next drop, this will all be over."

"Good, I'm over this shit. They don't even deserve this." I didn't mean to say that out loud, but I did.

"Are we having second thoughts again?"

"Nah I'm good, so after I do this I'm good right?"

"Yeah after you testify against them you will be fine."

"TESTIFY!"

"Yeah we got all of this evidence and we have to have a way to prove how we got it."

"I can't testify, you don't know them and the reach they got, my whole family would be in danger if I testify."

"You don't have a choice. We will protect you."

"What about my family you asshole, this wasn't part of the fucking deal."

"Yes it was, and you will testify or go to jail. I need you and Krista to testify."

"What the fuck does she know?"

"She was in a relationship with one of them before, so we will bring her on as a character witness. You don't worry about that, just get ready."

With that he hung up the phone and I needed to talk to Krista to see if she knew about this shit. I wasn't gonna call her; I needed to be face to face with the bitch. This shit wasn't looking good at all. I sped to her house.

When I pulled up, she was ushering a nigga out of her house, I had never seen him before. He was square ass nigga and I don't know why it pissed me off, because I didn't fuck with her since she dimed a nigga out and got me in all this bullshit. I had feelings for this bitch, from the minute I saw her, but now look. I parked my car down the street so she couldn't see me, and no one would see my car in her driveway. I was taking a risk coming here, but I needed to holla at her about all this shit.

"So, this is what you do while I'm out here trying to make sure yo' hoe ass doesn't go to jail?" I said as soon as I walked up.

"What in the hell are you doing here, Perry?" She said looking around. "I thought you said it wasn't a good idea for you to be here?"

"That ain't what the fuck I'm talking about, you talking all this shit everyday about me not getting at that nigga Denari because he killed my baby. Was that even my fucking baby, I mean you were fucking a few of us." I glared at her and I didn't even know why all this was coming up all a sudden but seeing that nigga coming out of her house had me pissed and I forgot everything that I came here for.

"So, what you want me to sit around, and wait on you to get your head out your ass. You stopped talking to me on that level remember. Shit a girl got needs."

"No, a hoe got needs, you know what, I don't even need this shit. I'm gone; I don't even give a fuck about you going to jail. Handle that shit on your own. I done put my whole got damn family in jeopardy for you and this is what the fuck I get."

"Whoa calm down okay, what you mean you gone? You running?" Her eyes got big and she smirked.

"Yeah, they telling me that we gotta testify."

"Duh Perry, what did you think, they were just gonna get all this evidence and then let you go on your merry little way? It doesn't work that way."

"Do you know what they will do to us if we do that?"

"They going to jail," she laughed. "Probably for life, so they ain't doing shit but trying not to drop the fucking soap."

"You just don't get it, they don't have to be out to touch us, you fucking idiot. They got reach." I ran my hands down my face. "Why in the fuck did I even get involved with you?"

"Because my pussy got a hold on yo' ass." She smiled, and my dick got hard instantly. "See." She pointed at the bulge in my pants.

"That don't mean nothing, that's just a reaction. My dick

doesn't think, that's how I got in the situation that I'm in right now."

"Standing out here in the open ain't smart, come in." She said looking around.

I thought about it for a minute and the smart thing to do would have been to get the fuck away from there, but my dumb ass just had to follow her inside. Once we were inside she turned on her persuasion.

"Listen, you can't run." She slowly walked over to the sofa where I had sat down. I had a gun in my waistband that I took off and sat beside me in the seat. "I need you, because I can't go to jail."

"I don't want to go to jail either, but you don't understand that if we testify we're dead and all our family is too."

"They are not everything people talk them up to be. I know for a fact they don't go after families because they don't believe in that. So, all that is just hype. Just man up, let's do this, and then we can live happily ever after."

I licked my lips and grabbed her hips, then I thought about the nigga that just left, I pushed her back and she put her hands on her hips.

"I did not fuck him, we were just talking."

Right as I was about to say something the door busted open and my fucking mouth dropped. "Don't believe that shit homey."

Chapter Sixty-Eight
DENARI

A nigga ain't been right since I saw Heaven hit that ground and never get up. What I wouldn't do to just hold her in my arms again. I need to feel her just one more time. I never got to tell her I loved her, I always had this thing about never saying that, and now I hate I never did.

Heaven was the only person that knew me and loved me for who I was, whether I was being the ultimate fuck up or if I was just being the carefree, silly ass me. She loved every part of me, and to know that I won't ever have that again hurt my heart to the core. All I wanted was to lay on her stomach and feel her hands through my dreads.

I hadn't touched coke since that night because that was something that I associated with her. That was something that we did together. I guess that's one good thing that came out of this but where I didn't do coke, I damn sure drank in its place. I had my good days and my bad days, like today was a bad day for me. My brother just proposed to his girl and they just brought two handsome and healthy boys into the world. I never thought that was something that I wanted until I no longer had the option. Now I would give anything to have that in my life. You never miss ya water until your well runs dry; I used to think that was bullshit, but boy was I wrong.

My brothers had been hella supportive through all this shit. For two months straight, I didn't leave the house, better yet my room. I didn't want to see anybody or talk to anybody. Mama would come every day and bring me food and make me eat. When she couldn't make it, she would order food and threaten my life if I didn't get it. If it wasn't for her, I probably would have killed myself.

I still see her every now and then, especially when I'm sleep. I see her beautiful smile. Which is why I don't get much sleep, knowing that it was all a dream was too much for me to bear. Today, I needed to get the hell out of the house, so I was headed to the warehouse to see my brother. Omari reached out every day and I just didn't have the energy to talk to him, but that didn't stop him from trying. The girls were supportive as shit too, they came down with Mama sometimes too.

I pulled up to the warehouse and noticed that Omari was there and Jaako too. He reached out a little, but our relationship was strained and it was my fault. After all the shit went down I had a little time to think and I reflected on all the bullshit I started, and I was sick to my stomach. I put my brothers through a lot of shit and I see why they cut me off. Instead of being there with the family after Unc died, I went off on my own doing dumb shit. I wish I could take back everything I ever put them through, but I couldn't, so my thing now was to do whatever I could to be the best brother I could be to them. Even if I didn't like the shit they had to say.

"Aye, what's going on?" I greeted as I walked through the door.

"What up, D." Jaako greeted seemingly happy to see me. If I were him I would never speak to me again, but I was grateful that he loved me enough to not think about that.

"Not shit, a nigga needed to get out of the house. What y'all up to?"

"Not shit, just trying to make sure shit is good on this end."

"I feel that, y'all need me to do anything?" They both had shocked looked on their faces and I laughed because I knew what they were thinking, but I was trying to introduce them to the new and improved Denari. "Fuck y'all man, look I know I been on some shit but I'm trying to do better from this point on, if you let me."

"Look at this nigga." Jaako smirked.

"Well the first thing you need to do is go get yo' shit lined up nigga, you look like a fucking homeless person." Omari joked, and he was probably right because I wasn't keeping myself up like I normally would. Ever since Heaven died I didn't have a reason to. I guess if I was gonna be representing the family business, I couldn't look like a bum.

"Shit has been rough, man."

"I know, and I can't even imagine." Omari said shaking his head.

"I'm getting better though. I need to go by her grave today. I ain't been in over a month and that shit been bothering me."

They nodded, which was the norm during conversations like this. They just let me talk and get it all out, I get the occasional head nod or a "bruh it's gonna be alright" here and there. Mama was the only one who went in depth with me, these niggas were too hard to get in their feelings 'bout shit like that.

"Well shit we done here, I just needed to crunch some numbers to see if we were good to open up another smoke shop."

"Yo, them shits doing hella good." I gave him props because that's all people were talking about, Barnes Smoke House. Hell, this nigga was inspiring me to want to do my own shit. "Got a nigga wanting to get his grown man on."

"Nigga you should, we all should. I ain't trying to do this forever."

"Exactly, that's why I got Yameka looking into me opening a little soul food diner. I want something to fall back on when this shit gets old."

"I want a car wash, something that I ain't got to do much with but collect." I rubbed my hands together. "I ain't trying to make a bunch a money then be so tied up in the business I can't enjoy it. Restaurant shit is time consuming."

"Yo' ass sound like Jaako. The shit can run itself if you hire the right people."

"Yeah, whatever." I waved him off.

"Y'all got all this shit going, y'all trying to put my woman to work. Making sure I don't get no pussy." Jaako flipped us off and we laughed. Yameka was our lawyer and she not only handled our criminal stuff, she handled other shit like contracts too. So, if we were all doing shit she was the one to handle it.

"Sorry, bruh." Omari shrugged his shoulders and looked at his watch. "Shit, I forgot Zemia's parents and brother was coming over and shit. I gotta go."

"Yeah, I told Yameka I was gonna spend time with her today." Jaako's words kinda dragged off and then they both looked at me apologetically. I held my hands up to stop any apologies that were sure to come.

"Y'all good, I want y'all to be nothing but happy. I'm good I promise. I'm 'bout to go chill at Heaven's grave and talk to her a little bit then go see the twins and Mama 'cause you know her ass is right over there."

"Hell yeah." Omari chimed in and we laughed. Ever since them babies were born if you were looking for Mama and she wasn't at work she was somewhere with Chelley and the twins.

I said goodbye to my brothers and headed back out to my car. I got in and I just sat there for a minute. I looked at the passenger seat and remembered all the good times I shared with Heaven. She was the definition of a rider.

"I'm on my way to see you, baby." I patted the seat then let the engine on my Camaro roar and for good measure, I spent my tires and burnt out of the parking lot.

I turned on that old school Biggie which was Heaven's favorite and let the sounds pump through my system. I was at peace, if just for a moment. I had to smile as I thought about her sitting beside me trying to rap the lyrics. I was so into my memories that I had to do a double take as I rode by and noticed Krista walking into the house with Perry or his fucking lookalike.

I rolled slowly down the road and tried to tell myself that I didn't just see that shit. As I was rolling, I rolled up on a car that looked just like Perry's car. I turned around and parked right behind it. The cemetery where Heaven was buried was right down the road from where Krista and Jaako used to live. I never really paid attention to it until right now and I'm glad I fucking did.

I grabbed my gun and got out of the car. Maybe this was just a coincidence and he just met her. I mean we all know Krista will fuck the devil for the right amount of money so that very well could have been it, but I needed to see because if his ass was fucking us over, I needed to handle his ass and quick. I brought his ass in and I would never want to see my brothers take the fall for that.

I walked up on the porch and the door was still cracked

and I listened to what they were saying, I wanted to make sure that it was something before I reacted.

"Listen you can't run. I need you, because I can't go to jail." I heard Krista say.

"I don't want to go to jail either, but you don't understand that if we testify we're dead and all our family is too." Testify? Against whom I thought to myself.

"They are not everything people talk them up to be. I know for a fact they don't go after families because they don't believe in that. So, all of that is just hype. Just man up and let's do this then we can live happily ever after." This bitch.

"I did not fuck him, we were just talking."

I walked in the house without them noticing me. "Don't believe that shit homey." They both turned to me with their mouths hanging open. "Who the fuck you testifying against?"

"Man, I don't know what you talking about. I—I'm just here with my lady trying to chill. What you doing here?"

"Oh, Krista didn't tell you we used to fuck. She was supposed to be pregnant with my baby, but I beat it out of her." I smirked.

"Fuck you, Denari," She yelled with tears in her eyes. "He's lying Perry."

"Again, who the fuck you testifying against, because if you on some bullshit, which it sounds like you are, I'ma just dead both you bitches right now and be done with it." I shrugged my shoulders and pointed my gun at Perry and before I could get a round off I felt the bullet pierce my chest.

"Fuck!" I heard Perry yell.

"You got 'em, baby!" Krista hoe ass said. I couldn't go out like this. I grabbed my phone out of my pocket and pushed a button that I was hoping was dial so I could call the last person I called which was O. "Muthafucka deserves to die." She leaned over me and spit.

"We got to get out of here." Perry yelled, and I could hear them moving around the house. I was gasping for air, it was becoming harder and harder to breath. Next thing I know I heard the door shut as soon as did I grabbed my phone out of my pocket and hit dial because I didn't before. It rang and rang and then went to voicemail.

"Perry is a—" was all I got out before everything faded to black.

Chapter Sixty-Nine
OMARI

Zemia's brother, Lyndon, turned out to be cool as fuck. We hung out a lot after we met that first time. He moved in with me and Zemia for a while until we put him to work and he was able to get his own place. At first, Zemia was against him being in the game, but like I told her if I don't put him on he's gonna go somewhere else and get put on and that's where he would get into trouble. Once I broke it down for her, she agreed.

Lyndon was a fucking natural; I didn't have to teach him much. He mostly did the THC vape juice with me, he damn near ran the fucking smoke shop by himself which was why I wanted to open another one.

We were currently chilling at the house playing the Xbox. Zemia was in the kitchen with her mother trying to learn to cook. My baby was not domesticated at all, but seeing as though her ass is pregnant she needed to learn. She still hadn't told me that she was pregnant and I was giving her 'til the end of the week to do it or we were gonna have some got damn problems.

"How Kayson doing with them twins?" Her stepdad asked.

"They doing real good, that nigga love being a daddy. I don't know how they are doing it with two babies, but they are."

"Two kids are a lot." Her step dad laughed. "I couldn't have kids of my own, so when I got to raise these two it was a blessing, but I didn't have to do the baby stage."

"I want that." I said loud enough for them to hear in the kitchen. A glass was dropped, and I knew Zemia was the one that dropped it and I smirked. Sneaky heffa.

"You do?" Lyndon asked.

"Yeah, why not?" He shrugged, and we went back to playing the game.

A little while later, we were told that dinner was done. We all washed up and got ready to eat. We cut the game off and I turned the news on. I liked watching the news while I ate. Mama got me into that old person shit and it never left me. We all sat down and Zemia said grace. She took one bite of food and then took off down the hall to the bathroom.

I smiled and wiped my mouth with my napkin and went to follow her. I got to the back and she was tossing her cookies in the bathroom. I leaned up against the counter and waited for her to finish.

"Ugh, I thought it was supposed to be morning sickness not all day sickness."

"So, when were you going to tell me?" She didn't say anything. "Zemia!"

"I wanted to go to the doctor first, and my appointment is tomorrow."

"Why wouldn't you tell me when you found out?"

"Because I didn't know how you would take it."

"What the fuck do you mean how I would take it? I love you and I want this." I pointed between the two of us and then placed my hand on her stomach. "Have I ever given you any indication that I didn't want this?"

"No, but we never talked about it."

"Because it never came up." I shrugged. "But that don't mean shit."

"You're right; I guess I was scared that's all. But then I saw you with the twins and I knew it was okay, so I planned to tell you."

"I can't believe you." I narrowed my eyes at her.

Thinking that I wouldn't want to take care of my responsibilities was like saying that I wasn't a fucking man. I wasn't raised like that at all. Even if I wasn't ready, I would get ready. But seeing how happy my brother was made me want that, and I couldn't be happier.

"Don't do that baby, I just didn't know."

"I forgive you this time but don't hide shit like that from me." She nodded. "Let's go eat, a nigga starving."

"I don't want to tell anyone until after we go to the doctor, is that cool?"

"Ya mama gonna ask questions about you getting sick, but it's whatever you want to do."

"Food poisoning." She smiled, and I chuckled.

We went back in and sat at the table to finish eating and just like I suspected her mom asked her a bunch of fucking questions about what was wrong with her and she went with the she think she ate something bad. I could tell that her mom didn't buy it and her brother or stepdad damn sure didn't buy it because they both looked at me and I shrugged my shoulders and tried to hide the smile that was threatening to show.

"So, you know they arrested Fin." Lyndon said out of nowhere.

"Huh?" Zemia asked with a mouth full of food. She seemed to be fine now.

"His girlfriend did some research after that night and found out that he had been with all three of her little girls, so a few months ago she filed charges. Well apparently, the girlfriend before her found out about it and asked her two daughters and he molested them as well. So, they all filed charges and his ass is gone for a long time." Lyndon said looking straight at Zemia. I couldn't read the expression on her face. "He called me from jail to tell me that it was all a lie, but if they took it to trial he would probably be gone for the rest of his life, so he took a deal, 15 years."

"He deserved life for what he did to those babies." Zemia said.

"And to you." Her mom reached for her hands and she let a few tears fall. "I wish you would have told me, I would have killed the son of a bitch."

"It's okay, I'm okay. I'm just glad the son of a bitch is getting what he deserved."

After that night at Strike City, Zemia asked me to go with her to talk to her mom about everything. She told her what happened and why she didn't tell her. They talked about the fact that she still loved her dad despite everything and her mom told her that it was normal. Zemia was a lot better after that, I was glad.

"I was gonna kill em." Lyndon said, and his mom laughed.

"And I was gonna help him." She stopped laughing and looked at the both of us. I don't think she understood how serious we were. She rubbed Zemia's hand.

"You are in good hands." She smiled.

We all finished eating and talked about life and planning family vacations and shit. I loved all of this and I couldn't wait to start doing this with my own little family. Things were really starting to look up, and I was happy about that.

Chapter Seventy
JAAKO

"Fuck, baby." Yameka moaned as I was digging her back out. I had her bent over and her ass arched up just right while I was grinding into her wet pussy.

"Throw that ass back." I said through clenched teeth. I was trying not to moan out, but the shit was feeling hella good, especially when she started matching my thrusts. "Fuck yeah baby, do that." I threw my head back and enjoyed every moment of it. I slapped her across the ass and watched that muthafucka jiggle.

I could feel her walls choking my dick and I knew she was 'bout to explode. I grabbed her hips and pulled out and jammed my shit back in going as deep as I could go. She cried out in pleasure, I did that a few more times until I felt her juices rolling down my balls. I bit my lip and rolled my hips making sure I was hitting everything. I got to the point where

I was about to cum and I threw my leg up on the bed for leverage and put my hand in the center of her arch and started working her pussy like I had a point to prove.

"Yes, yes, yes."

"Give it to me baby." I taunted as I grabbed two handfuls of her ass and nutted all in her. I knew that she came with me because the bed was soaked, and it was all from her.

"Shit, Jaako." She panted.

"That was some good ass shit." I collapsed on the side of her.

"We need to start using rubbers." She said lying next to me with her head on my chest.

"You just made my dick sad, look, he just went all the way down when you said that shit." I pointed to my dick. "We don't like the word rubbers."

"Well, we don't need no kids right now." She pouted.

"Why not? I'm good, you good, and ain't either one of us going nowhere. So what's the problem?"

"I want you to be out of this profession before we start building families and shit." She said looking up at me. "And I'm 32 years old, so my clock is ticking."

"That ain't got shit to do with it, hush."

"It does Jaako, I ain't trying to be wobbling around here at 45 just having my first baby. No."

"Halle Berry did it." She rolled her eyes. "Jennifer Lopez too."

"And they got money, they hire nannies and shit."

"We got money; we can hire nannies and shit." I laughed.

"And then I will go to jail for killing you for trying to sleep with 'em."

I rolled on top of her and looked her in the eye. "You ain't ever got to worry about no shit like that, you hear me?" She nodded. "Ain't nobody getting this dick but you." She smiled.

"I still ain't having no baby that late in life, so you better be looking into a career change and soon if you want a family with me."

"I already been thinking about it, I want a restaurant." I laid back down beside her.

"Really?"

"Yeah I have been thinking about that for a while now. When Omari started talking about his smoke shop, I knew right then and there I wanted something of my own on top of this drug shit."

"I like the sound of that; we need to start looking into that, baby." She smiled.

"We can do that," I ran my hand down the side of her face. "I don't want to do this forever, I just want to be stable when I do jump out." She nodded in agreement.

"I get that. Just don't wait too late, you know?"

That has been on my mind a lot lately, so far, we had been lucky as shit to have been in the game this long with no major issues. Partially because of how we ran our shit, it was hard to penetrate that unless you were on the inside. The other part was having Tate on our side, keeping an eye out. We just needed it to stay like this until we were ready to get out the game.

"You gotta marry me first before you try and jack me for seeds." She slapped my chest.

"I don't have a problem with that."

"Good, because I love you and I don't know if I could live without you. When all that shit happened and Ortiz grabbed y'all, I thought I was gonna lose my got damn mind."

"I don't want to talk about that."

Yameka hated talking about that situation, we almost broke up after that shit happened and I had to work my ass off to assure her that I would forever keep her safe. She was over it, she had never seen someone killed up front and personal like that. It's something that she will never forget, but she didn't wanna talk about it and I get it.

"I can't wait to spend my life with you." I whispered in her ear.

"I can't wait to spend my life with you." She giggled. "I wanna go see the twins." She said out of the blue. I swear she wanted to be around them more than me, little niggas had everybody wrapped around they little ass fingers already.

"Umhm." I turned my head.

"How can you be jealous of something so damn cute?"

"'Cause them niggas get more attention than I do."

"Whatever!" She laughed, and her phone rang. She grabbed it and looked at it funny. "Hello?"

"Meka, they locking me up." Tate said and then you heard a bunch of commotion and somebody throwing out orders.

"I'm coming, Daddy," she yelled before the line went dead.

She jumped up and started to get dressed. "I gotta go, you need to call your brothers."

I got up grabbed my phone and called them, I talked to Omari, but Kayson didn't answer. I would just have to go over there. I don't know what the fuck was going on, but we needed to find out and quick.

Chapter Seventy-One
KAYSON

Being a dad was the best fucking thing in the world. There was not a minute that I didn't want to be near my sons and I got pissed when I had to leave them. Jenacia thought the shit was funny, but I didn't. I wanted to be a part of everything from bathing them to feeding them to putting them down for bed. That's how dedicated I was to them.

Mama's ass made sure that she was a part of their care too, between her, Chelley and Kaylin, I damn near had to fight just to get my time in, but I made sure I did. I was thankful that there were two of them. I swear I wanted to put a few more in Jenacia but she wasn't having it right now. She said after that labor I had to give her a few years and then she was only giving me one. I wasn't hearing that shit at all. She didn't have no say so in what I did with my pussy and I plan to knock her ass up again as soon as Kayson and Kyndon turned one.

"Kayson, will you get out of here before you wake them up." Jenacia poked her head in the nursery where I was just standing and looking over them. When I say that I'm obsessed with fatherhood I meant that shit.

"You shut up. Is our six weeks up yet? I need some pussy."

"No nigga, it ain't even been a solid month yet." She laughed.

"I think that's long enough."

"Hell no, you ain't slick. Doctor said my womb is wide open and I ain't trying to fill it up no time soon, so you can forget it homey."

"You don't tell me what to do." I smirked and walked toward her.

"No Kayson, I'm not playing with you, get the hell back." She laughed.

"Make me."

"Stooooppppppppppp," she whined. I was breaking her ass down and I knew it. She wanted me just as bad as I wanted her.

"Shut up and stop whining. I need to get in them guts." I said looking in her eyes. "A nigga got blue balls and shit."

"You a got damn lie, I just gave yo' ass head this morning." She rolled her eyes.

"And it was good, but it's not the same. I need to feel them walls." She shook her head. "I'll wear a rubber." She paused and looked at me like she was debating it and then she smiled.

"You got about 30 minutes before they wake up."

"My boys got my back, they ain't waking up until Daddy finish." She took off to the room and I was right behind her, happier than a kid in a fucking toy store.

She dropped her robe and stood there ass naked. For her to have carried twins less than four weeks ago, her body was right back the way it was. I was more turned on now than I think I had ever been. I don't know if it was because she carried my kids or if I just loved her that much more.

I walked over to her and laid her down on the bed, I wasn't with all the foreplay today I just want to feel the inside of her. I walked over to the drawer where the condoms were that I bought a couple days ago for just in case a moment like this one.

"Where the hell them come from?"

"Well, I bought them the other day in hopes that you would agree to this." I looked down at my hard dick praying she didn't start acting crazy.

"So, you were just sure of yourself, huh?"

"Nah, I would just like to think that I know my woman." I winked and that did it because she spread her legs and I placed my dick at her opening and proceeded to try and push my way in. She was like a got damn virgin all over again and I didn't understand that shit. I was right there when her shit stretched damn near the size of a basketball. So how that shit was possible, I didn't know.

"Sssss," she hissed as I finally worked my way into her center. "Ummmm."

"Damn it, how in the fuck are you this tight?" I threw my head back and enjoyed the feeling I was feeling. I wasn't no minute man, but I swear this wasn't gonna be my usual, and I hoped like hell she understood that. I would be sure to redeem myself tonight.

"Is that your phone?" Jenacia sat up a little and I looked at her like she was crazy, I didn't hear shit, but I was in a whole other world. "Kayson, your phone has been ringing off the hook." She sounded like she was aggravated.

"Fuck that phone," I pushed her shoulder so that she was lying flat on her back again. I placed my thumb on her clit so she could reach her peak with me, 'cause mine was on its way.

"Ohhh baby." She clinched the covers and I knew what that meant. I could feel her walls tightening against me dick and I was about to lose it at any minute.

"Fuck baby I don't know if I can hold on, cum with me."

"Ummm I'm cumin, shit." She bit down on her lip and her legs started shaking. I sped up a little and before I knew it I was filling up the condom and Jenacia was screaming like I was hurting her ass. "Oh, oh my God! I needed that." She panted.

I couldn't say anything I just stood there with my bottom lip tucked between my teeth, popping my toes. I was so fucking sensitive I couldn't even pull out. Jenacia was trying to wiggle herself free.

"Jen, stay the fuck still, man."

"The babies crying, Kayson." She said and slid me out of her. She jumped up and ran to the bathroom to wash off so she could go and tend to the babies. I was still standing in the same place trying to get my shit together. I didn't know what the fuck was going on, but my ass was stuck right now. My phone started ringing again right as Jenacia ran out the room. I leaned down to pick it up and saw that I had like ten missed calls from Jaako and about two from Omari.

"Yo, what the fuck?" I said as I answered the call as it started ringing again. I hate for a muthafucka to blow me up, and they knew that shit, so it better be fucking important.

"Nigga, why the fuck you ain't answering your got damn phone?" Jaako barked.

"'Cause I was fucking my wife, that's why."

"Nigga, get yo' fucking mind right. Tate ass just got locked the fuck up."

It was like time stopped for a minute. My breath got caught in my throat and my head went for a spin.

"Did you hear what the fuck I said?"

"How in the hell did that happen?" I snapped back into it.

"Yameka went to check on his charges, but right now it's not looking good."

"Shit y'all get here, now!"

"We already on the way." Jaako said and then hung up.

I hurried and went to the bathroom and got cleaned up, something was giving me a really bad feeling. I had this same feeling when Unc died and I didn't like it. I needed to find out what the fuck was going on. All a sudden, this nigga getting locked up?

Shit I forgot about the meeting we had with Perry's bitch ass tonight. I needed to hit him up and tell him that shit wasn't going down; we had some family shit to handle. I picked up my phone and dialed him up.

"Yo, what's good?"

"No go for the party tonight, family shit came up."

"Damn man, where you at? I can come to you." He sounded desperate.

"Nah nigga, you know I don't do shit where I sleep."

"This putting me in a bad place, my nigga."

"I don't give a fuck; my fucking family comes first." I yelled and then hung up. I didn't have time for this shit, I needed to figure out what the fuck was going on with my peoples. He legit just pissed me the fuck off and the next time I see his ass I was gonna let him know to never question me. When I make a decision, it was final. I wasn't Denari, and I could show him better than I could tell him.

Once I had myself together I went downstairs and Jaako and Omari was already there. Denari wasn't downstairs and to think about it, I hadn't heard from that nigga today, I know Jaako said he was gonna stop by and see the twins after he left Heaven's grave, but he never showed up.

"Where Denari?"

"Shit we thought he was already here. I keep calling him and he won't answer." Omari said looking at his phone. "Oh shit, he called me a while ago and left a message and I didn't even see it." He put the phone on speaker, so we could all see what the hell he was talking about.

"Perry is a—" was all that was said before we heard before it sounded like someone took their last breath. That couldn't be Denari, somebody was playing a cruel fucking trick, and I wasn't feeling it.

"What the fuck?" Omari said and threw his phone. "I need to find Denari."

"Let's go." I went to grab my keys as Jenacia was on the way down the stairs with the boys, one in each arm.

"Everything okay?"

"It will be," I kissed her and both my boys. "I'll be right back." She nodded.

"Zemia is on her way here."

"Okay."

"Yameka is too, once she leaves the court house."

"Y'all are freaking me the fuck out." She said with glossy eyes.

"It's gonna be cool, just chill and take care of my babies." I kissed her again and left out the door.

"They ain't giving her no information on Tate, they ain't even giving that nigga a fucking phone call. I don't know what the fuck is going on but it's bad, my nigga." Jaako announced.

"What the fuck man!" I yelled and hit the dashboard.

"Yameka said to lay low until she finds out more."

"Aight," I said feeling defeated that we couldn't find Denari and overwhelmed with all that was going on. We weren't gonna stop looking for bruh, just right now wasn't a good time to be out, with all this shit going on. I just needed to find somebody that could trace his cell phone and we would know right where he was.

"Something ain't right." Omari said.

"I feel that shit too." I admitted. "That Perry nigga was pushy as fuck when I told them that wasn't shit cracking." I thought about how pissed off he had me. "Nigga almost made me pull him through the phone."

"I told y'all it was something about that nigga that wasn't right. If I find out he did something to my brother, I am going on a fucking war path."

"Nigga, we all are." Jaako said looking at Omari through the rearview mirror.

We pulled up to the house and it was lit up. So I knew everybody was here. We walked in and all the girls ran up and hugged us like they were afraid we weren't gonna come back.

"What's going on, Kayson tell me something." Jenacia cried.

"Baby, I just need you to be strong." A part of me wanted to tell her what was up, and then another part wanted to keep her shielded from all this mess.

"Stop doing that!" She yelled and pushed me away when I tried to kiss her. "I'm not a fucking baby, and if we're in trouble I need you to tell me and tell me now!"

I looked at my brothers and we all made a silent agreement to be real with them. We sat them down and told them what the fuck was up. Mama, Chelley, and Kaylin were there too. We weren't exactly sure that shit was gonna go down, but we needed them to be prepared in case it did.

"But, Yameka can take care of this right?"

"Yameka is good at what she does, she the best, so we have faith in her."

"You didn't answer my fucking question." Jenacia was losing patience and that's the one thing that I didn't want. I needed her head to be focused, just in case I needed her to ride for me.

We talked for about another hour or so until Yameka pulled in. When she walked in the house I could tell that she had been crying. That alone had my ass shook.

"It ain't looking good, I got to talk to him. They are trying to trump up some racketeering charges, but I don't think they will be able to make them stick." She wiped her eyes and I sighed a sigh of relief. "But they are holding that shit over his head in hopes that he will turn on y'all." The last part had my heart beating out of my chest.

"What the fuck you mean?" Jaako asked.

"Somebody turned state, well in this case FED! They know a lot about y'all and what you've been doing. My dad isn't saying shit because like I said those racketeering will never stick, and they know it. Worst thing they can do to him is fire him and take his pension and he's okay with that."

"So, what do we need to do?"

"All we can do right now is wait and see how bad shit

really is."

"Perry!" I said and picked up my phone to try and call him, but I got the voicemail. "He won't answer."

"I promise on everything I love." Omari said. "I can't just sit here."

He jumped and before he could take one step the door was being broken down. We all jumped, and I went to reach for my gun but the semi auto's that were being pointed in my face let me know that I needed to cool it and fast.

"They're all here." One officer spoke into his wrist.

"Kayson Barnes, you are under arrest." The officer said putting me in handcuffs. I looked over at Jenacia and I never wanted to see her like this. I hated it. "You have the right to remain silent anything you say can and will be held against you in a court of law, you have a right to an attorney and if you can't afford one—"

I didn't hear shit else that was coming out of his mouth, the only thing that I could concentrate on was the fact that my woman was sitting there crying her eyes out. My sister was screaming, and my mama was clearly heartbroken and there was nothing that I could do about it. I was happy as hell my babies were too small to really understand what the fuck was going on.

They drug us out of the house one by one. Right before I was pushed in the car I could hear Jenacia crying her heart out, I knew this was killing her. I mouthed the words I love you and ducked into the police car. Shit was all fucked up, I just hoped like hell we can get out of this shit.

EPILOGUE

"Kayson Barnes, I hereby sentence you to serve no less than 15 years, and no more than 25 years. This court it adjourned."

When the judge sentenced me, I could have fell out in the fucking floor. By the time I get out of jail my boys will be grown. How in the hell did I expect Jenacia to wait around on me for 15 years?

Jaako and Omari got 10 years each, but they charged me as a kingpin. Perry had tapes of us for months and even pictures of his drop offs with Denari, who we found out was killed in Krista's house. No one had said anything about why he died and who did it, but I could bet my life I knew who it was.

"Oh no, not my baby." I heard Mama cry.

"Baby, no." Jenacia cried right along with her.

"Don't worry I have already filed an appeal, this will not stick I promise. This judge was just trying to make an example out of you, but I got this." Yameka was sure of herself but until I saw something different in her eyes and I was accepting my fate.

"Listen baby, I made this choice so I gotta live with the shit. I won't make you ride this out with me. Just know that I love you and my boys with everything in my heart and I promise that I will do what I can from in here."

"You shut up, I will never leave your side." She pointed in my face. "You will beat this."

I smiled because she was so sure. I took one look at my boys and I smiled because they were getting so big. I hadn't been able to touch them since they were a month old and they were pushing seven months now.

"I love y'all." I said as they drug me out of the court room. I wanted to see my brothers, but I couldn't, they held our trials separate and that shit pissed me off.

When I got back to my new home, I just sat there and stared at the pictures that Jenacia sent me of the boys crawling. I smiled and let one lone tear fall down my face. My family was my pride and joy and I loved them more than I could ever explain to anyone. I prayed that God kept them safe, just in case this was my destiny.

I felt bad for Omari, Zemia ended up losing the baby from the stress of the trial. Jaako wrote me and told me that he didn't take it too well, that they had to put his crazy ass in solitary confinement. How in the hell did we get here? Shit was going good for all of us; even Denari had gotten his shit together and now this. His funeral was sad, that was the last time I got to see my brothers, when we were burying one of us. All this was breaking Mama down, I just hoped she knew we didn't mean for any of this to happen. I gotta take all of this and put it in God's hands, well and Yameka's.

Krista and Perry testified against us and I hoped like hell I got the chance to handle them. I was going to make it my business that if I couldn't get to them, that they wouldn't be breathing long.

I promise though if I get out of this I ain't touching another muthafucking drug, fuck that. My family is way more important. Can't blame anyone but ourselves. The drug scene is amazing when you coming up in it and making all kinds of money and shit, but in all honesty it's never worth it especially when you end up in here. When you break it all down it's all just a Beautiful Mistake!

The End...... Maybe!

"Muthafuckas think it's a game, I'm back and it's time for some Beautiful Revenge." I said out loud as I rubbed my hands together. I don't know why muthafuckas thought shit was good. Time to fuck some shit up and wasn't no one making it out breathing. Fuck with my family and it will cost you your life.

-Unknown

CPSIA information can be obtained
at www.ICGtesting.com
Printed in the USA
LVHW082211231221
707101LV00022B/270